IT HAD TO BE YOU

BETH MORAN

First published in Great Britain in 2024 by Boldwood Books Ltd.

Cover Design by Alice Moore Design

Cover Photography: Shutterstock and iStock

A CIP catalogue record for this book is available from the British Library.

Paperback ISBN 978-1-80483-370-4

Large Print ISBN 978-1-80483-369-8

Hardback ISBN 978-1-80483-371-1

Ebook ISBN 978-1-80483-368-1

Kindle ISBN 978-1-80483-367-4

Audio CD ISBN 978-1-80483-375-9

MP3 CD ISBN 978-1-80483-376-6

Digital audio download ISBN 978-1-80483-373-5

Boldwood Books Ltd
23 Bowerdean Street
London SW6 3TN
www.boldwoodbooks.com

For the brave and beautiful Bella
Daughter of my heart – forever

For the brave and beautiful Bella
Daughter of my heart – forever

1

I was more used to sudden puddles appearing on my kitchen floor than most. However, despite it being the third time it had happened this year, it still gave me tingles.

'Libby, I think I just wet myself.' Daisy looked at me in horror. Despite celebrating her eighteenth birthday a week ago, she still embraced teenage theatrics. 'Nobody look!'

The only other person in the room was Tari, her best friend, and she didn't seem to be able to stop looking. Her saucer eyes framed with electric-blue lashes were transfixed on the trickle of liquid running down Daisy's bare leg.

'This is a nightmare!' Daisy wailed, pressing both hands over her face. 'Why did nobody tell me about this until it was too late? If I ever see that twazzock Raz again I'm going to kill him.'

As she continued lamenting about how her life had become a disaster, I put down the tray of cakes I'd been preparing to take outside and gently placed my hands on her shoulders until she opened her fingers wide enough to peek at me through the gap.

'Take a deep breath. It's fine. That isn't wee, it's amniotic fluid.'

'What? What the fudge is that?'

'Your waters have broken. Remember, we talked about it a couple of weeks ago?'

Daisy was thirty-seven weeks pregnant, just inside the time-frame for full-term, so I wasn't worried.

'Tari, fetch a couple of towels from the cabin, please.'

Tari was still staring, her mouth hanging open in fascinated revulsion.

'Tari!' Daisy shouted. 'Get me a fudgin' towel!'

Having slightly misinterpreted a discussion that morning about how her unborn baby could recognise her voice, Daisy had decided to cut out swearing.

'Pee off! My boy ain't going to have a foul mouth like mine,' she'd pronounced during our Preparation for Parenting session, in response to the other expectant mums' teasing. 'One of the only things I remember my mum saying to me was to shut the eff up. I'm not going to be like her.'

'So, you'll tell your baby to shut the fudge up instead?' Kaylee, who was pregnant with twins, asked.

'No.' Daisy patted her bump. 'I'll tell them to talk to Mummy about whatever they fudging well like.'

At that, the group started laughing so hard I wouldn't have been surprised if it had contributed to the current puddle. But a few of the others had decided to think more carefully about their choice of language as well, and I didn't hate that the chatter now buzzing around my garden was slightly less blue, given that my own eight-year-old son had a habit of repeating any expletives he overheard to his schoolteacher.

Tari jolted out of her trance and glanced quickly at me before scuttling through the open patio doors and across the garden to the outbuilding where I held antenatal and parenting classes for clients ranging from uber-rich couples to today's group of teenagers and their female birth partners.

'I'm starting to think I should have listened to you, Libby, and asked Lisa to be my new birth partner.' Daisy groaned as she waddled towards the table and leant on it with both hands.

'Wild horses won't stop Lisa from being there,' I replied. Lisa was Daisy's foster carer. Usually, around half the teenage mums who came to my Monday sessions were 'looked after' or 'care experienced' children, most of them with specific mother and baby foster placements. Others – like Daisy – had been in the same foster family for years. Currently, three of the group lived in hostels, a couple had already been set up in a council flat and I occasionally accepted mums who lived with family but still faced particularly challenging circumstances. I'd started the Monday sessions three years ago, when my sister and I established our charity, Baby Bloomers. It had been challenging and heart-breaking in equal measure. Every one of the young people I welcomed to the cabin had faced troubles or trauma, often in the form of grooming or abuse. Some had deliberately got pregnant because, after a life of rejection, they simply wanted someone to love them unconditionally. The youngest group member had been thirteen.

Daisy had been engaged to Raz, the father of her baby, until a few weeks ago when she found out he'd slept with her arch-enemy from school. After a break-up that could be heard across Sherwood Forest, and while quite possibly not in a sound state of mind, Daisy had chosen her best friend to be her new birth partner. Earlier that morning, Tari had confessed that she found the whole idea of pregnancy and childbirth 'freaky and gross'.

To give her credit, she wasted no time in hurtling back into the kitchen with a bundle of towels. I handed one to Daisy and spread another over the puddle. Daisy's head was lowered, eyes closed, and she was no longer talking, igniting a prickle of alarm that had me scanning the room for my phone.

'She's not going to have the baby, like, any time soon though, is she?' Tari asked, now hovering by the patio door. 'You said first babies take ages. Like, a day. And just because her waters have broken doesn't mean she's even in labour yet.'

'I did say that.' I nodded, more than a little impressed that she'd listened in the first place, let alone remembered. 'But occasionally once the waters have gone, a baby can come pretty quickly.'

Daisy reached out her hand, grabbed onto mine and squeezed, tucking her chin into her chest. This baby was not going to be taking all day.

'I'm getting my nails done at three.' Tari shot a worried frown in her friend's direction.

'Yeah,' I said, my voice tight as Daisy squeezed again while emitting a groan that made Tari's eyebrows shoot halfway up her forehead. 'I wouldn't cancel just yet. You might still make it. In the meantime, come and hold her hand.'

I placed Daisy's hand firmly in Tari's, then hurried to the door and scanned the garden for my sister, who also happened to be a part-time GP.

'Anyone seen Nicky?'

There were around twenty people sitting on garden chairs or helping themselves to a lunch of sausage pasta and sides from the trestle tables (my oven had been broken for a few weeks now, so options were limited). I couldn't see my older sister's violet pixie-cut amongst them.

'She's in the cabin setting up a craft,' Ingrid said. Ingrid was a foster carer who'd been accompanying pregnant teenagers to my Monday sessions since the first class. Once the babies were born they'd swap to my Wednesday postnatal group for a few months, usually until the mum moved on to independence, and then Ingrid would soon be back on Mondays with someone new.

'Can you let her know I need help in the kitchen? Immediately?' I asked Ingrid, trying to convey the gravity of the situation without alerting the young mums.

'Is everything okay?' she asked, failing to pick up on my silent message due to being distracted by the choice of salads.

'Daisy's had a spillage.'

Ingrid looked up, her forehead creased in confusion.

'A *leak*. Which I think is about to be followed by another... something... ending up on the kitchen floor if we don't act fast,' I said, as quickly as possible.

There was a sudden groan from behind me, and Ingrid snapped to attention. She'd heard that sound all too many times before. Unfortunately, some of the other occupants of the garden heard it too.

A second after I'd shot back across the kitchen to where Daisy was still standing, bent over with her head resting on the table, a clamour of eager voices appeared at the patio doors.

Tari had at some point in the past minute flipped into birth-partner mode, not only locked into Daisy's death-grip but also rubbing her back. I gave her a reassuring smile as she slid my phone along the table towards me.

At that point my arteries were swamped with adrenaline. But for the sake of Daisy, Tari and the wide-eyed faces ogling us through the now closed – thank you, Ingrid – patio door, I was a vision of competent serenity.

I'd have asked someone else to call the nearest labour suite, which was at King's Mill Hospital in Mansfield, but had learned from experience that a panicked teenager screeching down the phone might not be taken as seriously.

'It's Libby, from Baby Bloomers. I have a young woman here whose waters have just broken and is now in rapid-onset labour.'

'Hey, Libby! How's it going?' Lillian was so used to calls from half-hysterical fathers-to-be that at some point over her thirty-something years on labour suite reception, she'd lost any sense of urgency. Even when, as in this case, things were urgent. 'We had one of your mums in here a few days ago. An older one, not a Bloomer. Had a right time of it, as it turned out...'

'*Shittlecocks!*' Daisy groaned through a clenched jaw. 'It's coming!'

'Okay, forget that.' I hung up on Lillian before she could breach patient confidentiality and dialled 999, just as Nicky calmly slid through the patio doors.

'Ah. Okay. I'd assumed Kaylee was exaggerating.' She took one look at Daisy before removing her cardigan and starting to wash her hands. 'The last time she summoned me to a desperate emergency, Harley had ripped off a false nail.'

Nicky glanced over at the cluster by the door, before making a firm shooing motion. 'You really need to get blinds.'

Living down a single-track country lane, my garden overlooking a quiet corner of Bigley Country Park, an offshoot of Sherwood Forest consisting of over a thousand acres of woodland and wildflower clearings, I really didn't need blinds. That was until now.

As Nicky began a deft examination of the labouring mother, Ingrid and I herded the gaggle of eager spectators into the cabin. After handing Tari the giant cushions I brought back with me so she could help Daisy get comfortable, I ducked into the living room and left a message with Daisy's foster carer, her social worker and the community midwife, stepping back into the kitchen just in time to see the miracle of a whole new person taking his first breath.

'Fudging fudge, Libby. You said this would take ages.' Daisy gasped, her head collapsing onto Tari's shoulder. 'It wasn't that bad!'

'Well, let's hope the rest of motherhood turns out to be as easy.'

I very much doubted it, as Nicky did her thing and I held the baby until Daisy was ready for him, at which point Tari made everyone the standard post-labour tea and fetched some bread and other bits from the lunch table. While the birth had been brilliant, and her little boy was as close to perfect as it got, Daisy had a long, hard road ahead of her. Statistically speaking, the odds weren't great. But, of course, the whole point of Bloomers was to empower women like Daisy to defy the odds, smash the stereotypes and conquer that long, hard road together.

'What?' A sudden screech from the new mother interrupted my musings. 'That bleeping b-word Sienna has only gone and shared a photo of my bare bits! Someone take my baby and someone else help me up. I'm going to fudging kill her!'

2

Usually, Nicky left once the Bloomers session ended, but after the drama of the day, she invited herself for dinner. Nicky was thirty-one, two years older than me, and had married Theo – the loveliest man I'd ever met – five years ago. She'd gone on to set up Baby Bloomers with me while simultaneously qualifying as a GP and competing in brutal triathlon-type competitions involving mud, sweat and tears.

I could have found all this success a bit irritating, except that the reason she filled her life with other things was because she couldn't have the thing she wanted most, which was a baby. And in addition to her time spent helping pregnant young women, she also found time to provide love, cuddles and stories to her niece and nephew, for which I would be forever grateful.

'Auntie Nicky!' My children, Finn and Isla, came bursting through the front door, down the hall and into my living room, having seen their aunt's electric car in the driveway.

'It's Finn McCool and the Isle of Wight!' Nicky yelled, jumping up off the sofa and scooping them up in a hug.

'Shoes!' I pointed pointlessly at the door back into the hallway. 'School bags on the rack and lunchboxes by the—'

'Yeah, yeah, lunchboxes by the sink. We kno-o-ow-w-w-w,' Finn replied, rolling eyes the exact same blue as mine from where he was pressed up against Nicky's ribcage.

'Well, if you know, then why do you make me say it every single day?'

'*Well*, perhaps we need more incentive. Lorcan gets five pounds pocket money *every week* if he tidies his room and cleans out his rabbits,' he said, flicking an overgrown strand of thick, dark-blond hair off his face.

'We don't have any rabbits,' Isla said, slipping out of the embrace and coming over to hug me. She had her father's grey-green eyes, but her hair was the same mass of mahogany curls that I'd had when I was five.

'Shoes!' I repeated, spinning her around to show her the fresh trail of mud across my sage-green rug.

'But I needed to give you a hug!' Isla's lip wobbled precariously.

'That's lovely.' My daughter would spend hours entwined around me if possible. 'But it takes five seconds to take off your shoes, then hug me. It will take a lot longer to clean up the dirty footprints.'

'Hello-o-o!' My dad appeared in the doorway, wearing shorts, socks pulled halfway up his shins and no shoes. His hair was a white cloud enfolding his head, his beard bushier than ever. 'Oh, dear. Did you scallywags forget to take your shoes off again?'

'They did. As I've mentioned, it would really help if you reminded them. Especially when you decide to walk home from school through the fields.' I hated the irritability in my voice, but I was beyond tired after yet another sleepless night followed by the drama of a baby being born in my kitchen, and adding cleaning the floor to the billion well-overdue tasks on my mental list made me want to roll myself up in that muddy rug and scream.

'My apologies. I was checking your tyres. Could do with a bit more air in the rear two. I'll run it over to the garage, if you like.'

'Thanks, Dad.' I got up and kissed his cheek, an unspoken apology for snapping. My dad had been a lifesaver in recent years. After retiring from fostering six years ago, when he was fifty-five, he'd tried a few part-time jobs but failed to stick at any of them. After Isla was born he'd downsized from our family home to a tiny cottage and now survived on his share of the profits and a modest pension. He refused to accept any money for picking up his grandchildren from school three times a week, but I paid him in food, craft ales and the occasional gift voucher.

'Did you check my tyres, too?' Nicky asked, gesturing at Finn to take off his mud-encrusted shoes.

Dad winked. 'What do you think?' Then he disappeared into the kitchen, no doubt looking for any leftover cake from the Bloomers.

Nicky flopped back into a chair as soon as the kids had followed him. 'Once upon a time you would have resented Dad insinuating you couldn't take care of your own car.'

'True. But that was the old Libby who had a point to prove. The new, improved, utterly knackered Libby is happy to admit that she needs help whenever it's offered.'

She shrugged. 'As I keep saying, you need to give yourself a break.'

I glanced at my dilapidated living room – the scribbles on the wall from Isla's 'creative phase', the tatty old sofa, myriad stains and scuffmarks and pile of random toys and clutter. Mentally compared my sister's tailored sleeveless dress showing off toned arms with my faded dungarees and roll of leftover baby bump.

The List of a Billion Things to Do flashed into my mind, and I wondered if there'd ever be a day I could find time to even think about a break, let alone give myself one.

'Looking after two amazing but sometimes excruciatingly exasperating children. Working four days a week and two evenings. Spending your days off dropping round meals to new mums or holding their newborns so they can nap.' Nicky snorted. 'If you don't start taking care of yourself, all that is going to start falling apart.'

I didn't dare tell Nicky that I suspected it already was. Starting with me.

'You need to get the dropout to help more. His amount of so-called support is pathetic.'

I cringed at the very thought.

'I'm not sure Brayden would be especially helpful.' I refused to call him 'the dropout' out loud, even if he had chosen to drop out of our family. He was still the father of my children, despite spending half our marriage sleeping with a woman he met at the gym. I'd discovered his affair when Isla was five months old, and coping with a divorce while raising a baby and toddler and trying to kickstart my business had nearly broken me. A couple of months ago he'd made a passing reference to his new baby, due in early autumn, which he'd assumed I'd known about because he'd announced it on his social media. When I'd replied that I hadn't looked at his social media since our divorce came through, he'd seemed genuinely stunned. I would have questioned whether letting the mother of his current children find this out on an Instagram post was okay, but I was too busy trying not to burst into tears in front of him.

So, while happy to accept help from my dad, especially knowing that he was as lonely as me, I couldn't imagine how bad things would have to get before I asked for anything from my ex-husband.

* * *

Once Dad had pootled off with my car, the kids played on the trampoline while Nicky and I reheated us all the leftover spaghetti from lunch, prepping a huge bowl of fresh salad because Nicky generally ran on about ten portions of fruit and veg a day.

'Mummy, why is there a giant and tiny pair of pants under the table?' Isla asked, her mouth full of pasta.

Before I could react, Finn had dived underneath and sprung up again with the underwear dangling off the end of his fork. 'Giant and tiny,' was an apt description for Daisy's deep-red maternity thong. I leant over to grab the fork, but before I could reach it Finn flicked the knickers across the table, and they landed perfectly draped across his sister's face.

'Mu-u-u-u-u-ummy!' Isla screamed, frozen in horror with both hands in the air. 'They smell like Finn when he needs a bath! Get them off me!'

Despite Nicky's super-quick reflexes as she plucked the thong off Isla's face and stuffed it into a plastic bag she conveniently had tucked in her satchel, it was too late. My anxious daughter had descended into floods of tears, while her brother channelled his guilt into defiance. By the time I had bundled Isla into the bath, dissuaded Finn from kicking a hole in his bedroom wall and tried to walk the fragile path between loving my children and overindulging them, the meal I was desperate to eat after missing out on lunch had congealed on the plates, and my sister had left with an apologetic hug.

She messaged hours later, after I'd cuddled Isla to sleep, read to Finn until he stopped feeling the need to punch himself for being a bad brother, and had resorted to cold spaghetti and pyjamas in front of the television.

Sorry I had to bail!

No worries. I'd have bailed too if I had the option

Theo's clan were here to plan the camping trip. It's not too late for you to join us – see if the dropout will have his own children overnight for once?

My stomach clenched. In marrying the lovely Theo, Nicky had also gained two new parents to replace the one she lost soon after, as well as three siblings, all of whom loved each other fiercely and weren't afraid to show it. They regularly went off on adventures including activities like white water rafting or bouldering, and, while I was pleased for Nicky, the contrast with our family was stark.

She often invited me to join them, but with two small children, the List of a Billion Things to Do and no money, let alone the energy for running up mountains, even if I'd wanted to be the hanger-on at their family outings, it would have been impossible.

Too tired for another debate about the sorry state of my social life, I sent her a vague reply and moved on to chatting about the exciting events of the afternoon. Daisy had decided to name her boy Bolt, as he'd arrived so quickly. No one was trying to talk her out of it, given that her and her ex-fiancé Raz's previous choice had been Cobra. We also needed to discuss the fallout from Sienna taking pictures of Daisy in labour. She'd only posted them on the Bloomers WhatsApp group, and they were blurry enough to show not a lot, but it was a serious safeguarding issue, and we'd had to contact her social worker as well as making sure that none of the other eighteen people in the group had kept or shared the images.

Just as Nicky was suggesting again that I invested in blinds, my phone rang with an unknown number.

'Hi, is this the Baby Bloomers?' a man asked. That grabbed my attention. Usually the only men who called to ask about the sessions were social workers, and they wouldn't be on the phone this late in the evening.

'Yes. Can I help you?'

'I'm wondering if you have any space in your antenatal classes?'

'We had a baby born today, actually, so will have room for one more in our Monday sessions. But they aren't strictly speaking antenatal classes. They're weekly four-hour support sessions for pregnant mums who fit specific criteria. If you wanted a standard course, I offer a range of those, too. There's a link on the Bloomers website.'

'It's for my sister. And she needs the Bloomers.'

'Right. Perhaps it would be best if you told me a bit about her?'

'She's nineteen.'

I grabbed a scrap of paper and a pencil from the pile of junk on the kids' craft table. 'Okay.'

'She went into foster care age six. Lived in a few different homes before ending up in a residential unit at thirteen. Moved out at seventeen and has lived with various men since.'

Oh boy. I'd heard different versions of this story far too often, but my heart broke every time. Behind this man's dispassionate, factual telling of it, I detected a devastated big brother.

I also detected a hint of something familiar in his voice, but I dismissed that as I clearly didn't know this person.

'After she got pregnant, I persuaded her to move in with me.

She's six months now, and her midwife said she could qualify for your group.'

'Is there any involvement from the father?'

A brief, grim silence.

'No.'

'Any boyfriend, or partner?'

'Not that I know of.'

'Okay. I'll email over a form for her to complete before I can confirm, but it sounds like she'd benefit from joining us. Does she have a birth partner?'

Plenty of times our young mums had no one to fulfil this role for them until they became a Bloomer. Nicky and I had held the hands and wiped the brows of twenty-three mothers between us. There were a few baby girls in Sherwood Forest with the middle names Elizabeth or Nicola.

Another pause. 'That will be me.'

'Right, okay. The Monday sessions are female only, but you're welcome to come along to our Thursday evening group. Like the Mondays, it's a rolling session rather than a fixed-length course, so you can pop along and give us a try whenever.'

'Thank you. We'll be there this week.'

I finished my cold pasta while emailing all the details and forms to his sister. While he was the one to make the call, it was important that she started to take responsibility for her role as a mother, where she could. The completed forms came back so quickly she must have been sitting waiting for them.

I paused briefly as I read her name: Ellis.

I'd known an Ellis who'd been in foster care, once. She must be about the same age as this one.

More significantly, I'd known her big brother.

I scanned straight to the box where people could add the

details of their birth partner, my heart sinking – in either relief or disappointment, I wasn't sure – at the unfamiliar name.

The truth was, I'd not simply known him. He'd been my first kiss. The love of my life.

Loving him had nearly destroyed our family.

Losing him had almost destroyed me.

3

THEN

Growing up in a family who fostered, you got used to waking up to strange children sitting at the breakfast table. And alongside my nice, geeky, middle-class friends who enjoyed swimming lessons, Girl Guides and youth group, I learned to love all different kinds of strange.

To keep things simple, our foster siblings were mostly girls. The few boys that we did welcome were always several years younger than me. My parents specialised in emergency or bridging placements. That was, children who needed somewhere to stay for anything from a few nights up to a year until the court made a decision about their long-term care.

Mum and Dad had been fostering for nearly twenty years, although they'd taken a year off when each of their daughters was born. To date, they'd seen thirty-nine children come and go, either alone or with a sibling. And now, on my sixteenth birthday, I'd mooched into the kitchen in my ratty old pyjama shorts and vest top to be confronted with the fortieth. Who also happened to go to my school. Oh, and did I mention that this was a *he*?

'Libby, this is Jonah,' Mum said in her chirpy, let's-act-like-this-is-all-totally-normal voice, placing a stack of pancakes in front of him.

'Hi.'

I already knew that this was Jonah King. Every one of the eight hundred pupils at my school knew.

I had an uncomfortable flashback to the one and only time that we'd acknowledged each other's existence.

I was waiting in Reception at the local primary school. Mum had nipped to the head's office to discuss the girl we were fostering, and as usual she'd ended up taking forever. On the other end of the row of four chairs sat Jonah, head buried in a fantasy novel. We ignored each other until he turned a page and a clump of other pages fell out, drifting onto the floor in front of him.

'You must really love that book,' I said, handing him the few that had ended up closest to me.

He shrugged, face intent on reassembling the pages. 'It's my only one.'

'Right.' I waited until the book was back in order and he'd started reading again before I replied. I mean, offering advice to the notorious new boy was not on my to-do list for today, but I couldn't bear to think of someone being limited to one book. 'You could try the library.'

He didn't take his eyes off the page. 'You need a form signed and stuff.'

I didn't question why his parent couldn't sign a form for him. I'd met enough kids in similar situations.

'Here.' It was automatic, digging out my purse and finding my library card. 'You can have mine.'

'No. I couldn't.' He frowned, turning away slightly, but not before I'd seen the hunger glowing in his eyes. They were a dark amber. A wolf's eyes. A sudden question burst into my head – what would it be like to have that hunger turned on me? Swallowing away that mortifying thought, I stretched over and poked him with the card.

'It literally pains me to see a book falling apart like that. Please, take it for my sake.'

'Thank you. I can give it back to you on Monday.' He reluctantly took the card, holding it for a few seconds before slipping it into the pocket of his battered leather jacket.

'Keep it. I can use my sister's. She never goes to the library, so she won't care.'

A couple of days later I saw him at the back of class reading the next book in the series. A few weeks after that I got an email from the library informing me that *The Twinkletown Fairies Save Christmas* was a week overdue.

Now, on my birthday morning, Mum pulled me back into the present with a full-body scan before her eyes fixed on mine with a look that said, 'That is not appropriate clothing, which you know full well.'

No lounging about in strappy nightwear in a foster fam, even if it was ridiculously warm for early March. I surreptitiously glanced at Jonah, his tall frame hunched over the table. No surprise to see him in his black leather jacket, the hood from a dark-grey sweatshirt covering chin-length, light-brown hair. It looked as though he'd slept in his clothes. I guessed he probably hadn't slept at all.

The scowl I threw back at Mum said, 'It's my *birthday*. One of the rare days you never say yes to someone new staying, meaning I don't have to do a risk assessment on whether my favourite pyjamas are *appropriate*.'

What we actually said out loud was, 'Happy birthday, darling!

Would you like to pop back upstairs and get ready for school while I make you a birthday breakfast?' and 'I'm not hungry.'

Part of me wanted to stay and damn well eat my birthday pancakes – Jonah King could deal with having to keep his eyes to himself. The other, loserish part of me was painfully aware that I'd not brushed my mass of dark-brown hair, and the new spot by the side of my nose felt the size of a marble.

I sloshed out a glass of orange juice and stomped out.

Mum caught me up at the top of the first staircase, on my way up to the attic bedroom opposite Nicky's.

'We'll do your presents and cards after you've been out with your friends,' she whispered. 'You still look half asleep. It'll be nicer to open them when you're awake enough to enjoy it. Come and have some pancakes, though, once you're dressed. Or there's cereal?'

'Whatever.' I'd arranged to walk with my friends to an ice-cream parlour on a local farm after school, which was the part of my birthday I was looking forward to, but I wasn't about to let her off the hook for breaking the promise about new kids on special days.

'Oh, darling. Please don't be like that.'

I climbed a few steps before turning to look back down, challenging her to provide a credible excuse for the apparition in my kitchen.

She pursed her lips. 'They'd tried everywhere. It was three in the morning when the call came, and he'd been at the police station since midnight.'

'Not our problem, though. Not today.'

'Libby, it was us or a residential unit a hundred miles from his siblings. His school. His friends.'

I scoffed. 'He doesn't have any friends.'

She went very still. 'You know him?'

'He goes to Bigley.'

'No. On the form it said somewhere in Mansfield.'

'And, what? These forms are never wrong? He transferred after Christmas. Got kicked out of his last school for assaulting a teacher, according to the rumours.'

Mum shook her head, as if dismissing that highly relevant piece of information. 'It's only one night. He'll have moved on by the time you come home.'

'*Only one night.* How many times have we heard that before?'

Nicky found me attacking my frizz with a hairbrush a short while later. She perched on the edge of my dressing table, her sixth-form outfit of denim shorts, black tights and a stretchy T-shirt in sharp contrast to the grey skirt, navy blazer and stripy tie that made up my Bigley Academy school uniform.

'Happy birthday, sis.' She held out a small package perfectly wrapped in lavender tissue paper finished off with a silver ribbon, the edges expertly curled.

'Mum said we're doing presents after school.' I took the gift anyway.

'Because it would be weird for a vampire to have to sit through our family celebration.' She pulled a face. 'I want to say I can't believe they said yes. But that's not true. I can totally believe it. I just think it sucks. We always open presents before school, so you can open this one now.'

I unwrapped the paper to find a journal, the cover decorated with trees, in the midst of which was a tiny, enchanting cottage.

'I know your dream is to live all by yourself in the middle of a forest. Now you can write out your dreams inside one. I know it's not quite the same, but, well...'

'I love it.' I abandoned my hair to give Nicky a hug. I supposed most families knitted together through their unique challenges and adventures. But sharing our parents and our home with so many other children over the years, having said hello to foster siblings who became like genuine sisters and waved goodbye to some we couldn't wait to leave, Nicky and I had bonded in a way that few could understand. When my friends grumbled about their brothers winding them up or sisters nicking their stuff, I wished I could make them appreciate the consistency of a person who's been there for all the in-jokes and the tough memories and the quirks that make your family yours.

Don't get me wrong, I loved that my parents did this amazing work. I'd cared about every child who'd spent time in the two little bedrooms below mine. But all too often, amidst the chaos and the meltdowns, the revolving door of social workers and what felt like every precious conversation with my mum being interrupted or overshadowed by children who had *real* problems, I longed for a cottage in the woods, just for me. A place where I could stroll about in my underwear if I felt like it. Where my thoughts and feelings mattered. This journal would become my hideout that year. My metaphorical cottage in the woods, home to my deepest feelings and what became my biggest, wildest secret.

4

NOW

Weekday mornings generally followed the same routine. After yet another night of torturous tossing and turning, I heaved myself out of bed at seven and attempted a supersonic shower with a broken showerhead that needed one hand holding it in position before being interrupted by Isla banging on the bathroom door needing a wee. Then began the chaos of getting two kids ready for school. Every morning I made the same promise to myself as I slurped a mouthful of scalding then somehow, seconds later, cold coffee, packed and then repacked lunch boxes due to Isla suddenly deciding she hated whatever she'd loved the day before, cajoled her into eating breakfast while preventing Finn from eating everything, located lost shoes, brushed teeth, settled arguments and wiped Isla's ever-ready tears: tomorrow, it would be different. I'd get organised the night before, go to sleep at a decent time, get up earlier. Then I'd have time to eat more than Isla's toast crusts, and maybe even dry my hair properly so it didn't explode into frizz.

But without fail, by the time evening arrived it was all I could do to get the kids into bed before I either taught another class, caught up with messages and other admin or collapsed onto the sofa with a bar of chocolate.

My personal life, like my house and my hair, was a mess. The problem was, I didn't have the time, energy or brains to figure out what to do about it.

We finally set off on the twenty-minute walk through trees and fields that was yet another reason why I was so grateful to live on the edge of a country park.

'Can I take this in for the nature table?' Finn asked, stopping to pick up a large snail shell.

I hesitated, knowing what would come next.

'Please, Mum. It's perfect, see?'

It was exquisite. That wasn't the problem.

'Go on, then.'

'Can I take this?' Isla asked, bending down and grabbing something for herself.

'No!' Finn smacked his forehead with one hand. 'The nature table is for interesting finds. What's interesting about half a leaf?'

'Well, what about this?' She immediately dropped the leaf and picked up a twig.

'It's a broken stick! That's rubbish.'

Isla stopped dead on the footpath, the corners of her mouth turning down in an expression I'd grown to dread in recent weeks. 'Mummy, Finn said my interesting find was rubbish! It's not fair because he always finds the good things and now I don't have anything for the nature table.'

'That's stupid!' Finn exclaimed, while I was still taking a breath in preparation for defusing the situation before it exploded into a full-on tantrum. 'The nature table isn't even in your classroom so no one cares if you bring anything in or not.'

'I'm not stupid!' Isla wailed, her voice rising to a shriek. 'And it's not fair! I never have an interesting find.'

'Woah!' I knelt on the sandy path so that my eyes could meet hers, taking two tiny flapping hands in mine and gently stilling them. I hadn't expected my training as an antenatal educator to come in quite so handy as a mum, but my skills in calming people down had been invaluable with Isla recently. 'We've got a whole stretch of path before we get to school. Let's keep the stick for now but see if we can find something even better.'

I held my breath as her lip began to wobble, but a few more reassurances, a hug and a mumbled half-apology from Finn and we were ready to keep going. As I would have predicted, by the time we reached the school gates and she spotted her best friends in the playground, Isla shoved the dandelion, rough pebble and mangled feather she'd collected at me and, after a long hug, hurried to join them, the drama already forgotten.

'She's getting worse.' Finn shot me a glance that suggested if I was a half-decent mum, I'd be able to fix it. I held back the bone-deep sigh that would confirm I agreed with both his words and the look.

'Today was only a wobble, and she's fine now.'

'She doesn't even care about the nature table. No one from the other classes brings stuff in. I don't get why she's started kicking off all the time.'

Neither do I, I thought, once we'd fist-bumped goodbye – our compromise since he'd decided he was too old for a hug. Even worse, I fretted as I hurried home, this was yet one more problem I had no idea how to handle.

I tried to put my worries to one side once I got back and started preparing for work. Dwelling on my failures as a mother wasn't helpful when I was about to teach other people the fundamentals of parenting.

Tuesdays were the flip side to the Bloomer sessions. Like Mondays, we spent time in the morning looking at childbirth, with topics ranging from hypnobirthing techniques to caesarean sections. After lunch we moved on to life with a baby, including the basics like feeding and what to do when your newborn is screaming so loudly you can't think. There were some fundamental differences between the Bloomers and my other clients – for example, the tendency to use TikTok as their primary information source. The private classes also didn't include what my Monday mums called 'fun time', the couple of hours when they could simply enjoy being teenagers with mini spa sessions, crafting or music. However, I'd learned over the years that pregnancy is the great leveller. No matter their age or circumstances, what just about every new mum needs most is a confidence boost, a comfy bra and, above all, other women to hand them a hot drink and cuddle their fractious baby while providing some much-needed perspective.

I enjoyed both types of session for different reasons, but the main motivation for carrying on with the private clients was that, after a couple of fluke referrals, I'd got a reputation for being the go-to antenatal educator amongst the region's wealthier circles, and this meant people were now prepared to pay a serious amount of money for what Nicky and I branded 'bespoke and discreet sessions'. These could be one-on-one, or in small groups of 'similar minded' people – i.e. similarly rich – usually in person – I had one couple arrive by helicopter – or occasionally online. Men were welcome, although they often dropped out or had to leave due to 'more important' commitments. I did draw the line at nannies or other professionals attending, after a bizarre session where a baby psychic tagged along.

Today I had four couples booked in for the first of five group sessions. It was a reasonably priced course, with clients more likely to arrive in an Audi than be chauffeur-driven. I spent an hour setting up the cabin, accepted a lunch delivery from a local caterer and checked that everything else was ready. Unfortunately, due to the delay with Isla, I didn't have as much time as usual to then go and tidy myself up. I wore my standard uniform of cotton dungarees over a pretty T-shirt, but only noticed as the first car was pulling up that I had a smear of chocolate spread across my chest, and I'd also had no time to tame my curls or apply the light make-up that I saved for my fancier clients to avoid appearing like the exhausted wreck I felt.

I settled in Jemima, a thirty-something, and Chris, her husband, who assured me, while offering a knuckle-crunching handshake, that having four older children meant he was here for moral support only. Another couple and a single mum who'd brought her friend as a birth partner also arrived. That left only one more, and I did wonder if I might find a chance to sneak into the bathroom to straighten myself out, but while I was still sorting drinks and listening to Chris's blow-by-blow account of his second wife's forty-three-hour labour, the final mum appeared at the cabin door.

'Is this the bespoke, exclusive antenatal class?' she asked, frowning while cradling the pert bump exposed beneath her cropped tank top.

'It is the antenatal class, yes.' I smiled, hoping to offer some reassurance, but her scowl deepened as she marched in and took a seat on one of the sofas. I couldn't help thinking that she looked vaguely familiar, but it was only when Jemima introduced herself, causing this new attendee to force a smile, that it hit me who she was.

I'd not seen this woman for years, and had hoped never to see her again.

When her birth partner strolled in, it only added to the tidal wave of horror surging through my guts.

'Liz,' Brayden, my ex-husband, said with the smile that I'd

once found charming, his grey-green eyes scanning the rest of the room.

For the best part of a minute my brain froze. Thankfully, no one seemed to notice as Brayden sat down beside his partner and gave her hand a reassuring squeeze as if this were the most natural, normal thing in the world.

It was only when Claudia, the single mother, asked where the bathroom was that I snapped back into action. Just in time to hear Brayden telling Chris about how he was also a veteran dad, having been through this 'malarkey' twice before.

Once before, a bitter voice inside my head countered. Brayden had missed Isla's birth due to being at what he'd claimed to be a conference. That had been my fault, of course, for having the audacity to go into labour nine days early. As an expert, I should have foreseen this and warned him not to book himself into a hotel with another woman and a pot of edible body paint, his phone switched to silent.

'Would you both like a drink before we get started?' I asked Brayden, leading him over to the refreshments table while doing a sterling job of keeping my smouldering shock in check.

'What on earth are you doing here?' I snapped, smile intact, as I faced the table.

He shrugged, choosing a coffee pod and sticking it into the machine. 'We wanted the best classes for our baby. You should be flattered that, after detailed research, we chose this one.'

'Why didn't you warn me?'

He waited until his mug was full before offering a puzzled glance. 'You must have seen the enrolment forms.'

I quickly ran through my mental list of the class members, all of whom had enrolled via my website. Brayden and Sarah had definitely not been on there.

'Liz, please tell me this isn't going to be a problem. We're both professionals here.'

Before I could query the professional link between him getting lucky with a niche cycling app and my antenatal classes, Sarah suddenly appeared by the table, arms snaking around Brayden's neck as she rested her head on his shoulder. The scowl was now replaced by a smirk, but there was a definite hint of fear behind her eyes. After all, who knew what the deranged ex might do when confronted by her upgrade?

'I don't mean to be rude, but you might want to sort that stain on your breast,' she whispered, pulling an 'oopsie' face as if we were pals.

'Green tea.' I handed her the drink she'd requested, did my best to stuff my stunned outrage behind a smile and got on with providing the group with a brief introduction to the course.

'Right, in a moment you'll have a chance to have a think about what you hope to get from these sessions – after all, it is a *bespoke* course.' I nodded at Sarah, still mentally trying to remember the names she must have used on the form. 'But before then, I'd love it if you could introduce yourselves.'

Jemima and Chris went first, Chris again using it as an opportunity to showcase his expertise in gruesome childbirth ordeals that not one of my hundreds of previous clients had had the misfortune to experience. Claudia happily filled us in on how she'd deliberately got pregnant via a one-night stand with a neurosurgeon. 'I mean, I'd already tried a maths professor and a lawyer. If you're choosing your baby-daddy on a dating app, might as well pick someone smart as well as hot, am I right?'

The other couple seemed remarkably unfazed by all this, but then revealed themselves to be who Nicky and I referred privately to as the 'naturals' of the group. There was usually one couple. While I would fully endorse a birth free from medical intervention where safe to do so, and in fact had Isla in a birthing pool in my living room, this couple informed us that, alongside refusing any involvement from a qualified health professional, they were also rejecting registering the birth, structured education or food that they hadn't grown or foraged themselves.

'Are you also rejecting Child Benefit and paid maternity leave?' Chris asked.

'We won't be accepting a financial sedative designed to lull us into overlooking institutional corruption, no,' Gordon, the dad, declared.

'Well.' His partner, Astrid, shifted position on the beanbag they were sharing. 'We'll maybe see how much the benefits are, first. We're self-sustaining so maternity leave isn't an issue.'

Brayden and Sarah went last.

Or, should I say, Brayve and Silva, as Silva kindly spelled out when inviting us to follow her on social media?

'They're unusual names.' Claudia looked impressed. 'Were your parents free spirits like Gordon and Astrid?'

I looked at Brayden, daring him to go along with this farce.

'We actually took the initiative during a personal rebrand,' Silva said, while Brayden inspected the plain white ceiling. 'Sometimes the only way forward is to dissociate from the past and embrace our true selves.'

'Wow, that's awesome.' Gordon offered Brayden – *Brayve* – a high-five, which, after a moment's hesitation, he reciprocated.

'And how did your children react to your new identity?' I asked with a brittle smile, before I could stop myself. Brayden's true self currently saw his children one day a fortnight for fast food and a play at the park.

'Ooh, do your kids have really cool names, too?' Claudia said.

'Unfortunately not,' Brayden said, as if he hadn't chosen the name Finn himself. 'They were conceived prior to the rebrand.'

Okay, I thought, while trying not to gag at the reminder that this man and I had ever slept together. *He's not going to share that we were married. That's useful to know.*

'Anyway,' Silva snapped, as if equally revolted by her partner's choice of words, 'I'm thirty-two weeks and four days pregnant with our darling daughter, and we'll be keeping our followers up to date, so please let Brayve know if you aren't happy with images or quotes being shared on Insta.'

'Um, no,' I interrupted. 'These classes are confidential, as stated in the terms and conditions on the form. You can't take images or mention other clients online.'

'I don't mind,' Claudia said, smoothing out her slick ponytail. 'As long as I can check the images first.'

'It's in the terms and conditions,' I repeated, increasingly aware of the migraine now throbbing at the back of my head.

'But selfies are okay?' Silva asked. 'And general comments? I mean, this is all publicity for your little business, Liz. I can't see why you'd object.'

I didn't bother stating that I didn't need publicity, or explaining the importance of client privacy. I took the kind of deep breath that got labouring women through contractions, wiped pointlessly at my chocolate-stained dungarees and got on with educating some people about the realities of birth and parenting, while trying to pretend the next four hours weren't one of my actual nightmares come true.

To be fair, the group seemed to bond okay with each other, which always made things easier, and Chris mostly listened when Claudia's birth partner asked him to 'leave the horrible stories in the past where they belong'. It would have been a reasonably enjoyable class, if it weren't for 'Brayve's' subtle references to his own experiences, all of which included digs at his ex-wife.

'Are we going to be discussing when to go into hospital? My ex insisted upon going after the first couple of twinges. We had to traipse all the way home again and come back later, which I'm sure contributed to her failure to progress.'

'We tend not to use that term these days. It's not especially helpful,' I said, quietly, while resisting the urge to remind Brayden that he was the one panicking the second my contractions started, so I let him drive us in just to stop him freaking out.

'Failure to progress?' Brayden looked surprised. 'That's what the doctors wrote on the notes. No point sugar-coating it, unless you're claiming a quick, easy birth is somehow down to how strong or capable the mother is.'

5

I sent Nicky a barrage of messages venting my frustration during the lunchbreak, but she was at the surgery on Tuesdays so I knew she wouldn't see them until later. Instead, I spent the hour after the session had finally finished pacing up and down having imaginary arguments with Brayden – I just couldn't call him Brayve – until Dad drove the kids home from school in my now fully serviced car.

'Long day?' he asked, when he found me in the kitchen.

'A surreal day,' I said, handing both the kids an ice pop and sending them into the garden. 'Brayden turned up at my class.'

'What?' Dad paused for a moment in surprise, before instinctively flicking the kettle on. 'He gatecrashed your workplace? What on earth did he want?'

I grimaced. 'Antenatal classes.'

Ignoring the kettle, Dad instead went to the fridge and pulled out two beers.

'He hadn't told you he'd booked on?'

I shook my head, taking a delicious ice-cold sip. I didn't normally drink while the kids were around, but a few mouthfuls of beer wouldn't hurt. 'He never tells me anything,' I mused. 'Expects me to check his social media for updates.'

'The children haven't mentioned the baby. Do they know yet?'

'Not that I know of. Sarah – *Silva* – is never there, so they wouldn't have noticed her designer bump.'

Dad shuffled closer and put his arm around me. 'I'm sorry. It beggars belief that he had the audacity to turn up to your classes, let alone without telling you. Did you kick him straight back out again?'

'I wanted to.' I leant my head on his shoulder. 'But he was being all cool about it – said we were both professionals and there was no reason not to behave civilly – and he didn't let on to the others that he knew me, so I just sort of went into automatic mode and carried on as normal.'

'Well, it means he's actually paying you some decent money for once.'

'Ex-husbands are the worst.'

Dad squinted out of the window. 'Well. I suppose the pro of your ex-wife running off to sea is that she won't turn up when you least expect it.'

'Doesn't quite balance out the cons, though, does it?'

Dad seldom spoke about Mum since she'd upped and left a year after they'd stopped fostering. It was the first time he'd referred to her as an 'ex'.

'Speaking of which, there was a postcard on the doormat.'

'Ugh, are you joking?' I made to leave the room, but Dad pulled it from his shorts pocket, having already picked it up.

'The usual nonsense?'

He looked affronted. 'I was hiding it from Finn and Isla. I didn't read it.'

I took another gulp of beer and took a brief look at the picture of a dolphin before handing it back. 'She's still legally your wife.

Feel free to read it if you want. Preferably out loud, so we can share the pain. Although I understand completely if you'd rather use it as a dartboard.'

Dad took a moment to read the card before replying. '"Having the best time exploring Madeira, but just found a restaurant serving Yorkshire pudding that had me yearning for England. Am wondering if my journey might be drawing to an end." Three exclamation marks. "I could be seeing you very soon." Four exclamation marks and a smiley face. "Love, Mum."'

'*What*?'

Almost the moment Mum said goodbye to her last foster child, the remnant of mental health that she'd been clinging onto had disintegrated. She'd then spent almost a year recovering from what she'd described as a 'compassion-fatigue-induced breakdown'. This had increasingly included references to how she'd no identity outside her caring role and needed to 'find out who Helen is'. When Dad had pointed out that he'd frequently encouraged her to take time off for herself, it had only led to arguments.

The longer she'd spent talking to her online support group for 'Invisible Women', the more she'd fixated on how she'd sacrificed her best decades to other people.

Six months after her eldest daughter's wedding, two months before her youngest's marriage had fallen apart, my mother had decided that the only way to make a full recovery was to take some proper time out for herself. Without breathing a word to any of us, she'd sold her car and raided their savings account to buy a ticket on a year-long world cruise.

When challenged about what this meant for her marriage, she'd replied that she wasn't equipped to make that decision while still living with her 'enabler', and the least we all owed her was some space to decide if the 'new Helen includes being Tony's wife'.

Months after the cruise had finished, she'd been lingering in Spain when the Covid pandemic hit. This had become the perfect excuse to avoid deciding whether this break was a break-up. Dad, still holding out hope that the woman he'd been with for almost forty years would eventually come to her senses, had refused to push her for an answer.

Since the borders had reopened, she'd set sail again, getting random jobs on other cruises, according to the postcards sporadically arriving from all around the world. These were posted to me and Nicky, never her husband. She usually sent something on our birthdays, but 'hope you have a lovely day!' scrawled on the back of a photo of a Greek island means little when the sender doesn't bother finding out whether your day was, in fact, lovely, or whether it included a cry mid morning about how much you missed your mother or how upset you were at the way she treated your father. She refused to have a phone and was a ghost online. We'd had a couple of calls a year that were more static than words, where the most we'd been able to share was that everyone was alive and well. Isla couldn't remember meeting her grandma, and Mum's insistence that she needed a total break from bearing her family's burdens meant I'd not told her about my marriage ending. We assumed she stalked the public Facebook account Nicky and I set up, because a few months after I'd posted a picture of my new cottage on there, a place Mum would have known well, a postcard arrived at that address. On our angrier days, we had to talk each other out of deleting the account because she didn't deserve to know anything about us or her grandchildren.

It had taken a long time to stop waiting for her to come home. Because Dad never spoke about it, we had no idea whether he was still waiting. Eventually, Nicky and I had decided that all we could do was try to be such wonderful sisters, as well as brilliant daughters to our dad, we'd barely notice Mum had vanished.

We did notice.

Like a splinter stuck under a fingernail, the pain of which sometimes dulled thanks to the busyness of everything else but at other times was impossible to ignore. After sharing our mum for so many years, we didn't find it easy to forgive her for abandoning us now.

'What does she mean, she could be seeing us very soon? Does that include you?'

The ulcer-like ball of anger that made itself present every time I wanted to phone her started to throb.

'It's been nearly four months since she's called. For all she knows, I've moved away. You could have found a new partner. Or died!'

'She'd have seen that on Facebook.' Dad gave my hand a gentle squeeze.

'If she's bothered to go online and check the account since she last stepped on shore.' My voice trembled with painful rage. 'How are you not fuming about this? She left you and didn't even have the guts to admit it. She never shows any interest, ever, in how her children are or what we're doing, so why would she want to come back?'

'I suppose one upside of her paying a visit is that we can finally ask some of these difficult questions.' Dad rubbed his forehead. 'I have been angry. But I'm also worried about the woman I've been married to for most of my life. I'm scared about the "new Helen", while unable to stop hoping she might have found the old Helen I fell in love with. At least if she comes home, I can know for sure.'

'I think I'd rather not know,' I whispered. I couldn't comprehend upping and leaving my loving husband and children without any way of keeping in touch.

Which always drew me back to one thought, slithering about in the deep, dark depths of me.

What if, no matter what Mum said, or how much Nicky insisted I was wrong, she still blamed me for what happened? In the lowest moments of her illness, when she'd complained about how we'd all sided against her, I'd known exactly what she referred to. What I'd done at sixteen had not only wrecked the future family she'd longed for, ending three children's hopes of a family in the process, it had been the fatal wound that eventually destroyed our family, too.

And now she was threatening to come back?

This, on top of having spent a day watching my ex-husband lovingly stroking his new partner's baby bump while she took photos, felt like way too much.

6

THEN

'You really don't have to do this,' I muttered to Jonah, having found him sitting in the living room in front of a coffee table covered in presents, balloons bobbing around his legs. To no one's surprise, a longer-term foster carer hadn't suddenly become available in the last few hours, and Jonah would be staying with us for another night. Foster carers were in short enough supply as it was. Foster carers with space for an older teenage boy were on the endangered-species list.

He shrugged, giving me a rueful glance from under the scraggly fringe that had escaped his hood. 'It's less awkward than hiding upstairs. But I can go if you want. Let you do your family thing.'

I tried to hide my surprise at this response. When Nicky referred to Jonah as a vampire, she didn't mean the pleasant, *Twilight* kind. We were in the same class for only two subjects, history and science, and since joining our school he'd been slinking in late to a seat at the back and spending most lessons staring out of the window with his earphones in, reading books that only I knew he'd taken out on my library card or with his head on his desk, asleep. Anyone else would have been the recipient of our history teacher's caustic tongue-lashing at the very least, if not kicked out. My best friend, Alicia, decided Mr Matthews was scared to confront such a blatant rebel.

'That's ridiculous. He isn't scared of a student. He probably weighs twice as much as Jonah,' my other friend in the class, Katie, said as we walked to our English lesson a couple of weeks ago.

'Not even one who got kicked out his old school for shivving a teacher?' Alicia shot back.

'If he'd shivved someone, he'd be in youth detention, not at Bigley,' I said, before pushing through the classroom door. 'Those rumours are a load of rubbish.'

'There must be some reason teachers pretend not to notice him being weird,' Alicia said, trailing after me to our seats. 'Don't you think he's creepy?'

Katie dumped her folder out on the table. 'Kind of. But in a hot way, if you know what I mean?'

'Hot creepy?' Alicia, who had the biggest crush on Luke Hughes, the nicest boy in Year 11, screwed up her face. 'That's rank. Libby, back me up here.'

At that exact second I glanced out of the window and saw the person we were discussing trudging across the car park towards the exit. He had on the same jacket, sweatshirt and faded school trousers that he always wore, a rucksack on his shoulders. Head down, scrappy hair partially obscuring his blank face.

I knew all too well why teachers left certain kids with unwashed clothes and a defensive posture alone.

'He's probably got reasons for being how he is.'

'What, hot or creepy?'

'I don't think he's creepy! Just... finding it hard to fit in at a new school when everyone's already decided he's a serial killer.'

We turned to face the front of the room as our English teacher called for everyone's attention.

'I notice you didn't deny finding him hot,' Katie whispered, earning a glare from the teacher as she and Alicia burst into giggles.

Did I find Jonah King hot, now he was sitting hunched up on my sofa, while my parents fussed about in the kitchen?

Honestly? I found him... more intriguing than I was comfortable with. Mum had given us all a lift to and from school, rather than making Jonah walk as Nicky and I normally did. As always, Mum let the foster kid have the front passenger seat, inviting him to choose a radio station or a CD from the pile of random genres crammed into the glove box. I'd spent a lot of car journeys listening to kiddie pop or heavy metal, and braced myself for whatever depressing emo dirge Jonah might normally be blasting through his headphones.

Instead, he twisted around in the seat to where I huddled in the back, feeling guilty about how grumpy I felt.

The curve of brow above his amber eyes still made me think of a wolf.

I could feel my face turning red for no other reason than I was a socially awkward sixteen-year-old with a not-unattractive, broodingly mysterious boy looking right at me.

'It's your birthday. What do you want to listen to?'

If anything, that made me blush even harder. What did I want to listen to, or what did I want Jonah King to *think* I wanted to listen to?

'It's fine,' I mumbled, shifting my gaze to a field of sheep outside the window. 'You choose.'

A few seconds later the opening bars to an obscure local band filled the car. I glanced across in surprise, catching the tiniest hint of a smile from Jonah in the wing mirror. I wasn't one to advertise my tastes on branded clothes or fan merch, but Katie, Alicia and I had been to their concert in Nottingham a few months ago. The bag I'd bought was my favourite shade of bright blue, so I'd starting using it for school. Quickly averting my gaze back to the sheep, I reminded myself for the millionth time that I really needed to stop letting wild rumours influence my opinion of people. Especially this person.

Now, in response to his question about hanging around while I opened my presents and did other birthday things, I found I not only didn't mind him staying downstairs – after all, how awful would I have to be to banish him upstairs on his first proper evening here? – I sort-of wanted him to.

'If you stay, it might help everyone try not to embarrass me quite so much.'

'Okay.' He attempted a smile, but mostly just looked tense.

'My parents have been fostering since before Nicky was born. You being here honestly isn't a big deal.'

He raised one eyebrow at me from under his hair.

'Okay, I know for you it's a huge deal. I just mean we're used to different people being around. Birthdays, Christmas, whatever. It's cool.'

'The more the merrier?'

'Are you describing yourself as merry?'

He laughed then. A deep rumble that, for a split second, produced the urge to put my hand against his chest to feel the vibrations. Fortunately, before I could feel any more embarrassed, Nicky walked in.

'They're fussing about the cake,' she announced, flopping onto the other end of my sofa. 'Neither of them remembered to buy more matches after the fire-starter kid moved on, and Dad's trying to light fifteen candles using the stove.'

'You mean sixteen.'

'Nope.' She grinned at me. 'They could only find fifteen.'

I slumped back into the cushion, body in full post-sundae sugar crash. 'Please tell them I don't want any candles.'

'Come on, Libby. *They* want candles, and that's what matters here. Them proving what attentive, loving parents they are, despite having had no sleep last night.' She looked at Jonah. 'No offence.'

Before he could respond, the door flew open and Mum walked in carrying a cake topped with fifteen unlit candles and a wax crayon. Dad was right behind her, singing 'Happy Birthday' at full volume.

After a slightly cringey present opening, we ate Mum's home-made chocolate cake followed by takeaway pizza, and, sticking to family tradition, Dad set up the karaoke machine.

'You really don't have to stay for this,' I reminded Jonah, who threw me an amused look conveying that he wanted nothing more than to hear four weird people sing cheesy pop songs.

It wasn't unusual for the teenagers we fostered to start off by spending a lot of time downstairs, rather than in their bedrooms. Being dropped off in a house with strangers meant there were countless unwritten rules that were often a world away from anything they were used to. Even a small thing like having a drink posed numerous questions: *Can I help myself to a drink, or do I have to ask? Can I have the juice, or is that only for certain times? Do I have to drink it at the table, or can I take it into another room? What do I do with the glass when I'm finished?*

Generally speaking, they figured this out by watching how we did it. Or at least doing it when one of us was there so we could tell them. They weren't hanging out with us primarily because they liked us, but because they were working out whether they could begin to trust us, even the tiniest bit. For many of them, they'd already moved on before the answer to that question could become yes.

But, seriously, karaoke?

'Maybe we should play a board game instead?' I suggested.

The rest of the family looked at me askance.

'But we always do karaoke on our birthdays!' Nicky said, a wicked glint in her eyes.

'We don't usually make someone endure that torture on their first night with us.' I didn't add that this was because my parents never welcomed a new child around a birthday but hoped that my tone implied it.

'Torture?' Mum said, pretending to be offended before grinning idiotically at Jonah. 'Speak for yourself.'

'What do you reckon, Jonah?' Dad asked, microphone in hand. 'We've got a cupboard full of board games ranging from tiddlywinks to Risk.'

'I reckon we should start with Bon Jovi,' he replied, with a face so straight I knew he must be laughing on the inside.

'Fine!' I snapped, hating how huffy I sounded. 'Fine.'

I grabbed the other microphone, stood to my feet and decided that if Jonah King wanted to hear me crucify 'Livin' on a Prayer', then who was I to deny him that pleasure? It wasn't as though he had a high opinion – make that *any* opinion – about a girl like me, anyway.

If we were going to do this, then I might as well enjoy myself.

At ten, Mum insisted we called it a night, sending us all up to bed while she and Dad cleared up the wrapping paper and left-over pizza.

'I'm guessing that after tonight you might be relieved to move on to a long-term placement,' Nicky said, pausing at the top of the stairs to grin at Jonah. 'Maybe that was my parents' plan all along. They are expert at this stuff by now.'

'Nah.' Jonah gave a small shake of his head. He'd taken off his hoodie at some point, and his hair, sweaty after his eventually being unable to resist joining in with our medley of rock classics, was pushed back, showing a smooth forehead and the full impact of his amber eyes. 'Watching Tony impersonate Beyoncé was a perfect distraction from the craphole that is my life right now. I'm kind of hoping I have to stay a bit longer.'

Was it my imagination, or did his eyes flicker to where I was waiting behind Nicky on the stairs?

'It'll be September before we karaoke again.' Nicky laughed. 'That's my nineteenth, by the way, in case you are still here and want to start planning my present early.'

'Duly noted.'

It was a definite glance my way, that time. A ghost of a nod before he disappeared into his bedroom.

Nicky said nothing, but I knew her well enough to decipher the look on her face as we reached the tiny attic landing.

'Seems like the vampire has a heart after all. Be interesting to see what happens if he does stay.'

I slipped through my door before she could interpret the look on mine.

7

NOW

On Wednesday we managed to make it to school reasonably incident free. Finn hit Isla over the head, as usual, but with a stuffed sheep rather than his lightsabre, so the ensuing tears were minimal. This was a relief, as not only was I a complete emotional wreck after Brayden and a postcard in quick succession, but today Nicky and I were hosting twenty ex-Bloomers and their babies. Another ten or so dads and partners were joining us in the afternoon. During the last hour, they would brush up on some baby skills and dad-talk while the mums enjoyed their 'fun time'. For those with no one to hand the baby over to at this point, each week three volunteers who loved nothing better than cuddling tiny ones came over to ensure every mum had a break.

Today Nicky was going to lead a baby massage class before I facilitated a discussion on routines. I was setting up the mats, towels and other equipment when a car pulled up that was far too noisy to be Nicky's Tesla.

'Hello?' I called, placing the last towel on its mat and walking over to the cabin door – almost always propped open this time of year.

'Hi.'

One of the mums, Courtney, was hovering in the driveway, her boyfriend, Toby, holding their two-month-old girl, Hazel, in a car seat. I caught a whiff of exhaust fumes as the car skidded away.

'Hey, Libby,' Toby said, shifting the car seat from one arm to the other. 'Mum didn't have time to drop me off later. I thought I could sort out those broken benches while I'm waiting for the lads' bit. Give them a fresh coat of paint, if you let me know what colour you want. I've brought my tools and stuff.' He turned around to show a rucksack.

'You're asking if I mind you mending my broken benches?'

'Um. Yes. I know what I'm doing, like.'

'Toby, I know you know exactly what you're doing. I've seen the table and chairs you made for your mum, remember?' Seventeen-year-old Courtney and baby Hazel were living with Toby, his mum – also Hazel – and four younger siblings in their three-bedroom terrace on the other side of the village. I'd called in for a visit the week after Hazel was born. The house was absolute carnage, but the garden furniture was beautiful. Toby was studying joinery at college, and loving it.

'That would be brilliant. How much will I owe you?'

Toby looked horrified. 'A load of free parenting classes? The meal you brought round for us? Lunch every Wednesday?'

'I get paid for that, Toby. Just not by you.'

'Not the point.' He shook his head, determined.

Courtney, on the other hand, nudged his arm. 'If Libby wants to pay you, let her,' she said, scowling. 'If you're going to make a go of the business, you have to charge people properly. It's not like we don't need the money.'

'I'm honestly very happy to pay you.'

Toby took his girlfriend's hand. 'I'll take some before and after pics, and you can write me a review. How about that?'

'It's a deal.'

I'd also slip a gift voucher for the local supermarket inside a thank-you card, but he didn't need to know that now.

'Why don't you help yourselves to a drink while I finish setting up?' I checked the time on my phone. 'The others should be here in about twenty minutes.'

Toby found a spot in the shade for Hazel, then fetched two glasses of juice. He disappeared off to the Bigley hardware shop for some blue paint while Courtney slumped in a garden chair several metres away from her baby, furiously tapping on her phone.

I glanced out the cabin window a few times while waiting for Nicky. It wasn't unusual for one of our mums to appear more interested in her phone than her baby. But most of them would have at least chosen a seat beside them, or looked over occasionally. When Hazel started squawking, Courtney just sighed and shifted away in her seat.

Again, this wasn't so unusual. But for the vulnerable mums I worked with, postnatal depression wasn't that unusual, either, and I was constantly on the alert for any signs that someone might be struggling. Courtney had been on my radar since switching from Bloomers to the postnatal group. She'd been full of enthusiasm when pregnant, thrilled that Toby's mum had invited her to move in, meaning she could stop living with her own parents, who drank too much. Full of TikTok ideas about life with a new baby, she'd not been interested in hearing about the tougher reality of motherhood. Courtney had also assumed Toby's mum would be on hand to cook, clean and babysit. Being a working single mum with five kids, Hazel wasn't about to start treating Courtney and her baby like two more.

So far, it had been Toby who had stepped up. I was very much hoping that, like a few other young mums we'd helped, Courtney simply needed more time to adjust to the huge leap in responsibility. As I watched her bury deeper into the sun-lounger, my hope did droop a little.

'Hi, Courtney!' Nicky arrived and scooped up Hazel just as I'd been about to give in and go to her myself. 'Hey, little lady! What are all these tears for, then?'

When Courtney ignored her, Nicky carried Hazel over.

'Hazel's crying, Courtney.'

It took another couple of tries before Nicky patted Courtney on the shoulder, causing her to switch the music off on her phone and pull out an earbud. 'What?'

Nicky smiled as if she wasn't resisting the urge to knock Courtney's phone out of her hand and stomp on it.

'Your baby needs you.'

'Oh, don't worry about it. She's always crying for no reason.'

'Okay, so how about we check whether there's a reason this time?' Nicky asked, in a voice that left no room for arguments. 'Can you remember the crying checklist?'

With a vigorous eye-roll, Courtney ticked off on her fingers. 'She was fed an hour ago. Nappy changed. Not tired. Not ill or too hot or cold...'

'What's the last one?'

'Being a needy pain in the arse?'

Nicky visibly flinched. I could practically see her safeguarding antenna spinning. However, before things deteriorated any further, Courtney got up and took her baby back. 'Chill out, I'm only messing!'

She started walking up and down the lawn, cooing into her daughter's ear, and after a few moments Nicky felt reassured enough to join me in the cabin.

'Worth a quick chat with Hazel?' she asked, automatically

straightening a towel that was out of line by one millimetre, before moving on to scrutinise the rest of the set-up.

'I'm not sure she'll be able to understand us just yet.'

Nicky gave me a pointed look.

'You don't have to check every bottle. I've made sure they're the baby-safe oils. And yes, if I can't have a discreet word when she comes to pick them up, I'll pop over to see Grandma Hazel in the salon. I'm sure she'd notice if there was anything to worry about.'

At that point, the first group of mums appeared, having walked together through the village, and by the time we'd caught up on hellos and how their little ones were doing, the others were arriving thick and fast. To my surprise, Daisy and baby Bolt also turned up.

'Are you sure you're feeling up to this?' I asked, taking a delighted peek at Bolt's tuft of black hair. 'You must be exhausted.'

'Nah.' Daisy shrugged. 'I feel better than I did when carrying this lump around inside me twenty-four seven. You told us to make the most of them early days when baby sleeps all the time, so I am.'

I raised my eyebrows at her foster carer, Lisa, who waited until Daisy was distracted showing off Bolt to the other mums before saying, 'She was up and dressed at seven-thirty, asking if she could come. I think the shock of how it all happened is starting to hit her, and she needs the reassurance of being with the other mums, and you and Nicky. She's missing Raz, too, of course.'

'Okay. We'll make sure she takes it easy, and Nicky will keep a close eye on her.'

'You're a pair of angels,' Lisa breathed, disappearing before I could change my mind.

Bolt was too young for a massage, but he enjoyed a cuddle with his Auntie Libby while Daisy reclined on a beanbag, answering dozens of questions about her dramatic labour.

'You lucky cow' was the general consensus by the time we broke for drinks and cake. 'Less than an hour, no being jabbed with needles or stitches? We'd have loads of babies if it was that easy.'

'I dunno.' Daisy grimaced. 'If Dr Nicky had offered me a shot of painkiller, she could have jabbed it wherever she fudging liked.'

* * *

I went to admire my partially restored benches at lunchtime, while Nicky handed out soup and sandwiches.

'These are going to be gorgeous, Toby.'

He beamed at me, eyes glowing with pride.

'I think you might need to paint the rest of the wooden chairs another time. The benches will show them up.'

'Of course! I saw a couple of holes in your fence, too.'

There were more than a couple. I had even less motivation to maintain the outside of my property than I did the inside, and let's just say the inside was all shabby and no chic.

'On one condition.'

He ran a hand through the curly mop of honey-coloured hair on top of his head, before giving the shaved sides a good scratch. 'It kind of has to be on a Wednesday. I can't really get here with all my stuff any other day. And I've college three days a week.'

'Wednesday morning is fine. But I'm going to pay you,' I carried on, before he could protest. 'No. I mean it. None of the other parents feel the need to provide free labour in return for the sessions. That's the deal.'

I told him how much I would pay him for two hours' work, and after spluttering for a few seconds, he made a counteroffer.

'You know, Courtney's right. You won't make much of a living if you don't value your services.'

He looked sheepish. 'Mates rates or nothing.'

I made a final offer, and we shook on it. I liked Toby. In contrast to his own father, he was determined to be a good dad. Being an older brother to four siblings probably helped. He'd clearly done his fair share of nappy-changing and bottle-feeding over the years. I only hoped his positive attitude would help Courtney get through her bumpy start. Her lack of engagement with the morning session hadn't eased my concerns.

'How's Courtney doing?' I asked, while we were out of earshot of everyone.

His face instantly dropped. 'I dunno. She's still dead tired. I thought now I was doing the night feeds it would help, but she wakes up anyway because I don't get up fast enough.'

'You're doing all the night feeds?' *And going to college?*

'Yeah. Hazel's sleeping better, though. It's only once or twice, now.'

'What about during the day? How is Courtney coping then?'

'It's tough, isn't it? Every new mum finds it hard, like you told us. Marnie loves being an auntie, she'll cuddle the baby and change her nappy, give her a bottle when she gets home from school. Mum watches her on Monday mornings, and I'm around at weekends so Courtney can see her friends or go out or whatever.'

'It sounds like she's got some fantastic support.'

'Yeah.' He sighed, glancing back at where she was sitting with a plate of food, once again scrolling on her phone. 'I guess so. It doesn't seem to make any difference, though.' His voice dropped lower. 'I know she's not going to love every second of being a mum. But sometimes I wonder if she likes any of it. If she even likes Hazel.'

I waited for him to pull his eyes off the ground and look at me. 'You remember when we did the postnatal-depression session?'

A bleak nod.

'Do you still have the leaflets we gave out?'

'They're in the folder.'

'Have a read, show them to Courtney, see if she thinks any of it might relate to her. It can affect some mums' ability to bond with their baby, so is worth considering.'

It broke my heart to see this hulking great lad blinking back tears. 'Thanks, Libby. For everything.'

'No problem. It's what I'm here for. Now, let's get some lunch. You don't want an empty stomach for Nicky's discussion on sex and relationships after childbirth.'

8

On Thursday my private class wasn't until eleven, so I took the long way home after dropping the kids at school and called in at Bigley's hair salon, Snips. Shanice, the manager, was flipping the sign to 'open' as I arrived.

'Hey, Libby!' Shanice had been one of my first Bloomers. She'd been living in a children's residential unit in Manchester when a drug dealer got her pregnant. After being relocated to a farm called the Green House, not far from Bigley, where two couples provided a home for older teens, Shanice had started an apprenticeship at Snips, completing it once her twin boys were born.

Shanice had thrived as a mother and a hairdresser, and I was beyond proud when she was promoted to manager a few months ago. She always looked immaculate, and today was no exception. Her thick braids were twisted neatly around her head, the ends a vibrant pink to match her shift dress, heels and bejewelled nails.

'Are you looking for an appointment?' After giving me an enormous hug, she ushered me inside. 'We're pretty busy today, but you know I can always find space for the woman who got me through the worst day of my life.'

Shanice's labour had been beset with complications. I'd been there from start to finish, and she'd not let me pay for a haircut since – I had, however, been exceedingly generous with my tips.

She took a closer look at my hair, eyes narrowing. 'Yep. I can definitely fit you in. Hazel, can you take my nine o'clock with Sue? I've had an emergency walk-in and it might take a while.'

'Thank you, but I'm not here for a haircut.'

'Are you sure?' Shanice wrinkled her nose. 'Because, and I think I can speak freely given that you've seen me naked from the waist down, you really need one.'

'Okay, I'll book myself in soon, I promise.' I ran a self-conscious hand through my mass of tangles. 'You know it always goes mad in the heat. But for now, I was hoping for a quick chat with Hazel?'

'Oh?' Shanice tried not to look offended.

'Once you've brought me up to date with your gorgeous boys, of course...'

After hearing all about how brilliantly they were doing, in between trying to wrestle each other to death, I found Hazel fiddling with the coffee machine in the back. In contrast to Shanice's simple elegance, Hazel looked as though she'd slept in her shapeless grey tunic, and the bags under her eyes and wan complexion suggested she'd barely slept at all. The only exception was the lustrous blonde hair, curling to her shoulders.

'Did you want something?' She sighed. 'No offence, Libby, but I'm really busy.'

'I won't be long. I just wondered if Courtney was okay. She seems to be struggling a bit with Hazel.'

'Yeah, struggling with all those lie-ins and nights out.' Hazel shook her head, jaw set. 'She's barely lifting a finger. Has decided giving birth is enough work for one lifetime. Everyone else manages to have a kid *and* cook, clean and do whatever else needs doing. When Dex was a baby I had four other kids to look after, my own house to run and this job.'

I opened my mouth to ask whether there was any possibility Courtney was struggling with her mental health, but Hazel wasn't finished.

'And that lad doesn't help, either. Pandering to her every whim, letting her get away with being a lazy cow. He's cut his rent without even discussing it with me, says he needs money for the baby, while madam spends the Child Benefit on Smirnoff Ice and false nails. What he's giving me barely covers their food, let alone everything else. So now I'm basically paying to have three extra people sleep in what used to be my dining room. Mess everywhere, and yet more work for me. I'm sorry, Libby, but I'm rapidly running out of sympathy for either of them. I need to think about the others, and I'm not interested in being mum to another kid, even if she is supposedly my granddaughter.'

Supposedly? Baby Hazel looked so like her dad that if she wasn't Toby's I'd be suspecting his younger brother, Harry. Things were worse than I'd thought, and I couldn't imagine how they'd begin to improve without Hazel's support.

'It sounds really tough, for all of you, but I was wondering if you could just look at a leaflet...'

'Sorry, Libby, my client's here. Talk to Toby if you're worried about his girlfriend. I don't have time to sort her life out because she's not in the mood to grow up.'

She pushed past me into the main salon, conversation over.

* * *

I spent two hours in a one-on-one class with a couple who split their time between London and Monaco and so didn't want to attend a traditional antenatal course. That was probably just as well, because their constant references to the ultra-exclusive private hospital, 'mummy concierge' and ludicrously expensive high-tech equipment – thousands of pounds on a handcrafted mattress? Really? – would have jarred with our normal discussions about NHS maternity services and life with a newborn. They were a perfectly pleasant couple, whose faces lit up every time they mentioned becoming parents; they simply led a very different life from my other clients, and I was grateful they'd opted for private sessions.

Finn and Isla stayed on for the school football club on Thursdays, so I ignored the List of a Billion Things to Do and took the opportunity to pop over to the Green House, where Shanice had lived before moving into her own flat.

The farm was nestled at the other end of Bigley Country Park, tucked in a hollow with fields on one side and the forest on the other. As well as the main house, painted a cheerful apple green, there were outbuildings including a gym, stabling for two horses and an actual greenhouse for nurturing plants not people. I'd been visiting here for as long as I could remember. The Green House was infamous amongst local fostering families, and we relished their regular fire-pit nights, film and pizza evenings and whatever other excuse they came up with for a gathering.

The two brothers who lived there, Bob and Benny, vibrated with boundless energy despite how old they appeared thanks to Bob's shock of white hair and Benny's freckled bald head. They spent hours around the farm with their foster teens, chopping wood, digging vegetable patches and mucking out the stables, their laughter echoing behind them. Their wives, Mary and Maria, were the calm to their husbands' zeal. I'd witnessed them being screamed and sworn at, breaking up brawls and discovering the shed had been deliberately set on fire, and the only time I'd seen either of them the slightest bit ruffled was when a dog went missing – he was fine; one of the kids had run away and taken the dog with her, but as soon as it had started raining, she'd slunk home.

In recent years I'd been invited back in a professional capacity, visiting whenever they had a pregnant young person living with them, or a new mum – which was most of the time. Today I was meeting Petra, who had moved in a couple of weeks ago. She claimed not to have realised she was expecting, but it took Mary and Maria about ten minutes to figure it out. Around six months along, thankfully she and baby were both doing well. Physically, at least. Petra was not at all happy about the recent discovery.

'She's still in bed,' Mary said, with a gentle smile. It was two o'clock in the afternoon. 'I'll let her know you're here. Maria's in the kitchen if you want a drink.'

A few minutes later Mary reappeared. 'Sorry, she's not getting up.'

'Is she awake?'

This wasn't at all uncommon. For many of the children who arrived at the Green House, healthy routines had descended into chaos before things reached breaking point and they had to move, and it wasn't uncommon to find them in bed no matter what time I arrived. And while some of the young women loved the attention from yet another professional, others regarded me as a highly unwelcome intrusion.

'She's in the blue bedroom,' Maria said. 'Good luck! Oh, and here's your tea and a hot chocolate for Petra. She can't resist squirty cream.'

I had to knock three times before receiving a grunt in return, but the first step in earning this girl's trust was respecting her personal space.

'Hi, Petra, it's Libby from the Bloomers group. Maria's made you a hot chocolate. Is it okay if I bring it in?'

'Whatever.'

The first thing that struck me about Petra, as I placed her mug on the bedside table, was how young she looked. I knew she was fifteen, but – oh, bless her – there was no way she could be mistaken for anything except a child. She shuffled up the bed into a sitting position, huge blue eyes fixed on the pretty duvet covered in forget-me-nots, her thin, badly bleached hair stuffed in a yellow scrunchie and her vest top revealing scrawny shoulders.

My heart cracked, as it did for every young person who found themselves in a similar position. But I wasn't about to show Petra any pity.

'I like what you've done with your room.'

Every room in the Green House was beautifully designed to be a place of peace and security. The kids often did their best to change this, finding mess and mayhem more their comfort zone, but Petra's room was immaculate. She'd covered one wall with photos, hung a huge brightly coloured scarf on another, and the bookcase was full of battered stuffed toys, grouped together in similar colours.

Petra scowled, picking at her nail as if she couldn't wait for me to leave.

'I love this picture!' I walked over to a framed sketch hanging on the wall. It hadn't been here last time I'd visited the blue bedroom, so I was taking a chance that it was Petra's. 'What a gorgeous cat. She looks like a queen.' I paused, glancing back at the bed. 'Is it a she?'

A quick nod.

'Stunning. This is so lifelike I wouldn't be surprised if she sat up and stretched,' I said, with a well-practised blend of casual and impressed.

The scowl almost disappeared this time.

'What's her name?'

'Cleo. Short for Cleopatra.'

'The Egyptian queen?'

Petra flicked up one corner of her mouth in a smile, and I breathed a secret sigh of relief. She'd been expecting me to bombard her with questions and information, to pretend I knew how she felt or tell her what she should do next. That was the last thing she needed.

'Cats were considered sacred in ancient Egypt. When they died, their owners shaved off their eyebrows and mourned until the eyebrows grew back.'

'Wow. I heard that sometimes people mummified their cats back then.'

'Yes. They even had cat cemeteries.'

We chatted for a few more minutes before I handed her the drink.

'Is your bump big enough to rest a mug on yet?' I asked.

Petra furrowed her eyebrows, pushing back the duvet and giving it a go, but the moment she rested the mug on her rounded belly, a sudden movement beneath the skin sent it wobbling dangerously, causing her to burst out laughing in surprise.

'That'll be a no, then.' I smiled, taking a sip of my own drink.

'Will I get much bigger?' she asked, her smile disappearing.

'It'll feel big, but some of the mums who come along to Bloomers have much rounder bumps at this stage. And it'll be September by the time you're due, so hopefully it won't be so hot, and you'll be a bit more comfortable.'

I left a moment of quiet before adding, softly, 'I had my first baby before any of my friends, and one thing that helped most was when I found some other people to hang out with who were dealing with the same stuff. That's really what Bloomers is about.'

I went on to explain how the Mondays and Thursday evenings worked. That there was no pressure, she could come along once and see how it went.

'Can Mary stay with me?'

'If you've chosen her to be your birth partner, then she can stay.'

She went pale, clutching her mug more tightly. I ignored the urge to wipe off her hot-chocolate moustache and give her a hug. 'I haven't even thought about that.'

'That's fine. There's plenty of time. If you're nervous, you can always hang about with me, but I promise that everyone remembers how awkward they felt their first week, so they're all extra kind to new faces. How about you come along this evening? It's only an hour and a half.'

I knew if I left her to think about it until Monday, that would give Petra far too much time to worry herself into deciding not to come.

She gave a hesitant nod. 'Okay. If I'm not too knackered.'

I smiled as I left. 'Given that you're still in bed and it's past two o'clock, I think you'll manage it. I can't wait to see you there.'

As I dropped off my mug in the kitchen, it happened.

Back when I was sixteen and heartbroken, it had happened all the time. Far less so once I'd started going out with Brayden, though from time to time I still stopped in my tracks, the sudden bolt of adrenaline sending me dizzy, the sense of surrealism lingering long after I realised that of course it wasn't him. He was miles away.

Beyond the kitchen window, on the far side of the huge lawn, beneath a horse chestnut tree, I saw the silhouette of the boy who was my first heartbreak.

Standing with Bob, clearly deep in conversation. It was the tilt of the head, how he crossed his arms.

And then he shifted, gripping Bob's shoulder in a friendly gesture, and I realised that this was no boy, but a man, his back several inches broader than Jonah's, a relaxed confidence to his stance instead of Jonah's wary posture. I shook my head, annoyed and embarrassed at my pounding heart. Then again, I supposed it wasn't too surprising I'd had a false sighting, after the person called Ellis had booked onto my class, dredging up old memories.

It was only later, when I was on my way to pick up the kids, that I realised Jonah King was the same age as me. He was no boy any more. I tried to imagine how Jonah would appear at thirty, but it was impossible. His future had rested on a knife's edge at the point I'd last seen him.

Literally, on his darker days.

I'd occasionally given in to the temptation to search for him online in the aftermath of Brayden leaving us, but brief searches had yielded nothing, and so I'd always given up before it became anything more than a fleeting curiosity.

But now, as I parked the car and hurried over to the school field, it burned in me with the fire of a teenager's first love.

What had happened to Jonah? Had he coped with moving to a strange town, from a family to an institution? Had he ended up a statistic, or a success story?

The last thing I wondered, before Isla ran into my arms, bursting into tears because she'd scored her first goal, was whether he'd ever wondered about me.

9

THEN

Over the next few days our family adjusted as usual to having a new person living in the house. Mum continued driving us to school, and once home I was either finishing off my GCSE coursework in my bedroom or Jonah was out with my mum or dad, replacing all the things he'd left behind, or never had – clothes, toiletries and a phone.

At mealtimes he was polite enough with my parents, although he mostly remained quiet unless asked a direct question, and he occasionally chatted with Nicky about their similar music taste. For me, it still felt strange. Jonah King was an enigma at school. Silent, friendless, slightly terrifying because no one knew what lay behind that blank face and badass attitude. Far too cool to notice someone like me. At home, we shared the same bathroom, drank the same juice, and when I opened a carrier bag, thinking it was the Topshop jeans I'd bought with my birthday money, I found a pack of Topman boxer shorts.

I nodded when I passed him in the hallway at home. Did the same at school. But when it came to more than that, I couldn't seem to get the friendly, welcoming words bumbling about inside my head out of my mouth.

Honestly? Every time he looked at me – and this boy was bizarrely good at making direct eye contact – my breath caught. I didn't trust myself to speak to him because I didn't know what this was or how to handle it.

After five nights of my ducking my head and being even quieter than usual at mealtimes, my parents called Nicky and me into the dining room while Jonah was visiting his younger brother and sister, who were now living with a foster carer in a nearby town.

'So, Jonah is still with us,' Mum said, using her Serious Voice.

'What, he's still here?' Nicky asked, her face a picture of innocence. 'Oh! So that explains why the bathroom stinks of Lynx and the snack cupboard empties within moments of you restocking it. I was wondering who the giant trainers in the hallway belonged to.'

'Social services are having a really tough time finding him a longer-term placement.'

'Well, duh!' Nicky rolled her eyes. 'A teenage boy with a violent criminal record? I can't imagine why.'

'He's not got a criminal record!' Dad retorted. 'Where did you hear that?'

She shrugged. 'Rosie's brother said he beat the crap out of someone. And he's been done for stealing.'

Dad took a deep breath. 'When his mother's boyfriend hurt Jonah's sister, there was a minor physical altercation. And yes, he has stolen food. Again, for his siblings. And you two know never to repeat this information outside this house.'

'Is he staying longer, then? Is that what this is about?' I asked, not wanting to think too hard about Jonah's six-year-old sister, Ellis, being hurt.

'We've been thinking about it. We really like Jonah, and we can't bear the idea of him being moved so far away from Ellis and Billy after everything they've been through. He's basically raised them himself. But obviously we all need to be happy with the decision. So, please be honest. What do you think about us offering Jonah a home here for a while longer?'

'How much longer?' Nicky asked. 'Until they can find a long-term placement nearby?'

'No. We'll be the long-term placement.'

'Until he's eighteen?'

'At least until then,' Dad replied.

'Fine.' Nicky shrugged, playing with the end of her artificially orange plait. 'I'll be gone in September, anyway.'

Nicky had an offer to study medicine at Cardiff University. I was proud and miserable about her moving away in equal measure.

'Libby?' Mum asked. 'I know this might be strange for you, with him being at the same school. But it's only another few months, and in September he'll be starting college. How would you feel about him staying with us?'

Honestly, if my parents had an inkling of how I was starting to feel about Jonah King, he'd be out of here first thing in the morning. But when I thought about how much his siblings would miss having him nearby, I resolved to not allow a tiny, weird, sure-to-be-unrequited crush cause these children yet more suffering. He'd become like a brother soon enough, and any trace of feelings would fizzle out until even the idea of liking him that way felt disgusting.

'If there's nowhere else, then I think he should stay here,' I said, keeping my voice as level as possible. 'For Ellis and Billy's sake.'

Nicky gave me a swift, sidelong glance before focussing her attention back on her plait.

'Are you sure?' Dad asked. 'There's nothing you want to discuss first? More rumours you've heard about, or other issues?'

'Maybe rather than the girls speculating, we should fill them in before we make a final decision?' Mum suggested. 'You know we can't tell you everything, but it might be helpful to share the bare bones, so you're aware of how it might impact us as a family.'

And so, I got to hear the short version of Jonah King's story. The kind of information that half my year would gorge on like a dessert buffet. That, when it is a young person living in your house rather than the misfit kid at school, pierces you right between the ribs, making it almost impossible not to want to give them the kind of home they never had.

Jonah's story was similar to ones we'd heard many times before. A mother with mental health issues, scraping by on benefits, an uninterested dad and an extended family who didn't care. She'd muddled through until Jonah was nine, when she'd become embroiled with a violent man who got her pregnant. Another man soon replaced him, and a year after Ellis was born, she was pregnant again. Over the next few years Jonah and his siblings endured a nightmare roller coaster of abuse and neglect as various other men came and went, none of whom were interested in three children.

A week ago, instead of aiming at Jonah or his mother, her latest boyfriend left the imprint of an army boot on her daughter's semi-emaciated back.

When their mother ran in the kitchen and found Jonah wrestling with her lover on the filthy linoleum, she called the police.

Jonah was not the one carted off in handcuffs that day, despite his mother's protests.

And now, here we were, a random, ordinary little family in Bigley Bottom, having been offered the potential to change his whole life.

Mum blotted her eyes, gave each of us a grateful hug and called the social worker.

10

NOW

On Thursday evenings we expected around twelve Bloomers and their birth partners for an antenatal class. Numbers were fewer than Mondays because some didn't want to come if there were males present and others weren't interested if there was no food or 'fun time'.

The birth partners were about an even split between family or foster carers and the babies' dads. It was my most challenging session of the week but, when it went well, by far my most rewarding. I got my kids into bed, set up the intercom in case they needed me, and was reading a message from Mary at the Green House letting me know she'd be dropping off Petra when the first couple arrived.

'Hi, you must be Ellis!' I heard Nicky greet them, offering the usual introductory spiel as she showed them to a seat.

I glanced up to see a tall young woman wearing a sleeveless top and oversized jogging bottoms. Apart from her tiny, football bump she was painfully thin, with jutting cheekbones and mousy hair, worn in a shaggy chop, brushing her shoulders. She had multiple piercings on her face and badly drawn reptiles tattooed across her arms and chest. Her expression was sullen, dull eyes wary, and her body language that of an animal torn between whether to play dead or run.

Which was how most of our Bloomers looked on their first session, so I was confident she'd fit right in.

But then she moved to the side, and everything inside me stuttered to a stop.

I hadn't recognised the nineteen-year-old version of the little waif who'd visited our house to play board games and draw pictures with her big brother.

But I'd never mistake the man who stood beside her.

Jonah.

The form had been filled in with the name Joe Green. It went without saying that I'd checked.

His amber eyes scanned the room before quickly swivelling back to rest on me.

It was fair to say that the shock was mutual.

For an endless moment everything else – Nicky, Ellis, the other people now arriving, the rest of the room – faded into nothing.

My heart must have resumed beating because I could hear it pounding like an industrial engine.

We stood there, for who knew how long, staring at each other.

I wished that I'd had time to wash my hair that morning, rather than twisting it into a messy bun. My outfit was a pair of wide-legged jeans and a navy T-shirt.

I'd pressured myself into wearing make-up for the fancy class that morning, and suspected that, after an afternoon rushing about, I now had mascara smeared under my eyes.

Would he notice? Did it matter?

I noticed that he had a few days' worth of stubble where, before, his skin had been smooth beneath my feverish fingers.

As I'd seen that afternoon at the Green House – because now I knew it had been him – he'd broadened out, added a new confidence to his posture, but his eyes were creased with exhaustion and there was a tiny hole in the side of his grey T-shirt.

In an abstract way, I registered that Jonah King – Joe Green? – had transformed into a startlingly beautiful man.

All I could think was that he was here, in my cabin, staring at me as if I were a lost treasure, and in ten minutes I was going to be talking to him about maternity pads.

'Where is she?' A sudden bellow snapped me back to the room.

Daisy's ex-fiancé, Raz, had burst through the cabin door with all the vigour of a rampaging rhino.

'I know she's here. Where is she? Where's she hiding my baby?'

My stomach lurched as though I'd tossed it out of an aeroplane window.

Up until he'd broken up with Daisy, Raz had been to the class every week. He'd always come across as so timid, I'd been surprised he'd had the confidence to sleep with someone else. This barbarian would be unrecognisable from that mousy boy if it weren't for his bright ginger mullet.

'Raz, calm down.' Nicky strode over and took an assertive stance in front of him. 'There are pregnant women here.'

'No, I won't calm down! She's got my baby and I demand to see him!'

'Raz, this is the antenatal class, for people who haven't had their babies yet. You know this. Now, let's take a couple of deep breaths...'

By the time I and one of the other dads, who happened to know Raz, had manhandled him into my kitchen, where we'd forced him to drink a cup of tea until his mum arrived – she'd been to visit baby Bolt that afternoon but had the good sense not to tell Raz that – Nicky had my session on what to pack in your hospital bag well under way. When I slipped back into the cabin, Ellis and her brother were sitting on a sofa on the far side of the room from the door. Ellis had her head down, apprehensive eyes on the carpet, while Jonah studied the handout. I froze for a long moment, wondering what on earth to do and where to sit, but then spotted Petra in one corner, looking utterly lost.

'Hey,' I whispered, sliding in next to her. 'Great to see you!'

She glanced at me, chewing on her lip.

'How's it going?'

Petra nodded at the handout gripped in her hand. 'I don't have any of these things,' she whispered back. 'I'm not ready.'

'That's okay.' I smiled. 'You've got weeks to go yet. Mary knows all about this stuff. She'll make sure you have everything you need in time.'

'No.' She shook her head vigorously, eyes pleading. 'I'm not ready!'

Then she burst into tears, crumpling over her bump in anguished, noisy sobs.

No one batted an eyelid as I gently led her into the back room of the cabin, the place where we stored all the equipment alongside a tiny kitchenette and office space. She was by no means the only mum to start crying in a Bloomers session. She probably wouldn't be the only one crying that night.

I sat her down and made another cup of tea.

There were two minutes left in the refreshment break by the time I persuaded Petra to give the session another try.

'Do you want me to keep going?' Nicky asked, when I joined her by the biscuits.

'No, I'm fine to do the next bit. You can handle any other emotional outbursts, thanks,' I said, picking up the weighted doll we used to help people practise holding a newborn as I walked to the chair at the front of the group and called for everyone to find their seats again.

'Right, for those of you who haven't met me yet, I'm Libby. For the next part of the class, we're going to be thinking about how to soothe a crying baby.'

'Will we also be learning how to soothe a crying missus?' one of the young men piped up, nudging his partner. 'Because this one won't stop. Found her bawlin' yesterday because her cracker broke when she tried to spread butter on it.'

'Dude!' another lad called across the room once the mix of laughter and angry retorts had died down. 'You'll be the one crying when you get home tonight. If you had half a brain inside that lumpy skull, you might have figured out that what she's really crying about is having a kid with an ugly dumbass like you...'

And so it went on. Like I said, the Thursday classes could be hilarious. They could also make me wish I did something easier, like breed scorpions for a living, instead.

The ongoing banter was, however, an excuse not to look too often at the far side of the room, where Ellis was alternating between pretending to be asleep and huffing about our no-phone-in-class rule. Her brother was making such copious notes, I suspected it might be his excuse not to look too hard at me.

We always ended the sessions with a simple relaxation technique, and the second Nicky announced this was over, Ellis sprang off her seat and pushed past the cluster of sofas and chairs to the door. Jonah-slash-Joe, on the other hand, stood up but remained where he was as everyone else slowly filed out, chatting and laughing while exchanging more insults and fist-bumps. I had a strict no-hanging-about-afterwards-for-no-good-reason rule, otherwise some would end up loitering well past my bedtime, but I would make an exception in this case.

Before I headed over, I waited for Nicky to finish answering a mum's question about her Braxton-Hicks contractions, then stood with my back to Jonah while I faced her.

'Did you recognise him?' I asked, sounding embarrassingly breathless enough to make her suddenly alert, peering at me.

'Who? Raz?'

'No. Ellis's brother.'

'Who?' Nicky was tired, having spent several hours at the surgery seeing patients before heading straight over, no doubt nibbling on a few slices of apple or a handful of nuts for her evening meal.

'The new mum who looked even more detached than usual, Ellis. Her birth partner is her brother. Joe.'

'I thought he looked pervily old to be with a vulnerable teenager. My safeguarding siren was wailing.'

'It's Jonah King.'

'Jonah who?' She suddenly clicked, her jaw dropping.

'Oh,' she said, softly, eyes darting over my shoulder to where I guessed he still stood. 'Yes. Of course. Oh, Libby.'

Oh, Libby indeed.

'Have you spoken to him?'

I shook my head. Her reaction had made my throat clog up with thirteen years' worth of tears.

'He's waiting for you.'

I nodded frantically.

'Okay. Take a deep breath. Let it out slowly,' she said, in her childbirth-coach voice. 'You're going to turn around, take six steps over to him. Stop. Smile, then say, "Hi, Jonah, what a huge surprise."'

'What then?' I whispered.

'I don't know. Improvise?' She patted my arm. 'You aren't sixteen any more, Libby, you'll figure it out.'

Maybe I wasn't, but right then I felt like a clueless teenager.

Realising my sister was about to spin me around and strong-arm me over there, I saved her the trouble and me the humiliation and walked over to Jonah myself.

What did she tell me to do now? my garbled thoughts demanded. *Oh yes, smile and say hi.*

'Hi.'

As I'd approached him, Jonah's eyes had been on the rug, but once I'd spoken, he slowly slid his gaze up until they once again met mine.

'Hi.'

A jolt of electricity zapped through my nervous system. 'I'm... what... I didn't realise it was you when you called.'

He opened his mouth and closed it again as if lost for words.

'Joe Green was on the form.'

'That's my name now. I mean, only Ellis and Billy call me Joe, but she filled the form in. Joe King didn't really work, and, well, I changed my surname a while back. You know, a fresh start.'

'Did you know it was me?'

He shook his head, a hint of a smile at the corners of his mouth as he seemed to release his breath for the first time since I'd approached. 'Of course. I mean, you look exactly the same.'

'No, did you know before you got here?'

'Oh. No.' He shook his head. 'Your name has changed, too.'

I'd kept my married name, Donahue, because I wanted the same name as my children. The Bloomers website also had me down as Liz, which Brayden used to call me and I'd still been using in a professional capacity until a couple of years ago.

'I'm glad, though.' His gaze was so intent, shivers skittered across my skin. 'I might have thought twice about coming if I'd known. But this is exactly what Ellis needs. And, well.' He paused, blew out a slow sigh. 'It's good to see you, Libby.'

'Yes,' was all I could manage. *What the hell does that mean?* I screeched inside my head. *You're agreeing that it's good for him to see me?*

It had been thirteen years since a male rendered me a gibbering wreck. No surprise that it was the same man.

'Is it okay?' he asked, understandably, given that I was now standing there, melting with embarrassment while still staring straight into his eyes. 'I mean, us coming along?'

'Yes,' I repeated, managing to add, 'Of course, it's not a problem,' to clarify that I wasn't just a Libby android stuck on my yes function. 'It's really great to see you both. Although, I'm sorry Ellis has had such a rough time of it. But you, you're...'

He grinned, breaking eye contact for the first time as he rubbed a hand self-consciously through neatly cropped hair. 'Still alive.'

'I guess they still need you.' In his darkest moments, Jonah had repeatedly said he was only staying alive because his brother and sister needed him.

He pulled a wry face. 'More than ever, as it happens.'

'Well, Ellis is waiting. I won't keep you.' I turned to wave feebly at where she was standing in the doorway, simmering like a kettle about to boil.

'I'll drop her off on Monday, then?'

'Yes.'

'See you then.'

'Yes.' *Oh, for goodness' sake!*

Before I could think of anything more intelligent to say, he'd gone.

* * *

There was no way that Nicky was rushing off now. She thrummed with impatience while we packed up, and after checking that the kids were both asleep, I found her on the sofa, two glasses of wine poured, despite it being nearly ten o'clock.

'Jonah!' She gasped. I couldn't remember the last time I'd seen her so skittish. Her violet hair was sticking up in clumps as if she'd been tugging at it. 'I can't believe I didn't recognise him.'

'It has been a while. Shorter hair, different context and all that.'

'*You* knew straight away.'

'I actually saw him earlier, standing on the other side of the Green House garden, and, after thinking it might be him, dismissed it. So maybe my brain was more prepared.'

That, and the fact that he'd been hovering on the edge of my consciousness for aeons.

'How do you feel?' She took a sip of wine, watching me carefully.

I took a long, slow breath while I tried to wade through all the churning emotions, figure out which were worth acknowledging.

'I'm not sure yet. I feel... relieved that he's doing okay. I've been carrying the guilt about what happened for so long now.' I stopped, swallowing back the ache in my throat, shocked by how powerfully that confession still affected me.

'It was a rough time for you, though. Your first heartbreak. All the knock-on effects with Mum and Dad, your exams. It must be hard, having those memories ambush you like that.'

I gave up trying to keep my feelings in check and found a tissue, blotting my eyes as I replied. 'At the time, it was devastating. You know what it did to us all. And teenage heartbreak feels like the worst, doesn't it? But we mended. I moved on. And you can't compare it to what happened with Brayden, especially given that my children were involved.

'I'll probably dream about being sixteen tonight. I can't promise I won't be going over it in my head a few times.' I took hold of her hand. 'But I'll be fine. I *am* fine. Jonah was a good guy, underneath the issues. I honestly did love him.' I gave a weak laugh. 'It'll be nice to catch up, see how the vampire turned out.'

'And you never know...' Nicky arched a sly eyebrow, before catching the look on my face. 'Too soon to tease you about that?'

'Yes, too soon! It'll *always* be too soon to in any way whatsoever imply that there might be the possibility of *anything at all* between me and him! Ever! Anything!'

'Wow.' She laughed. 'Just to clarify, am I right in picking up that you'd rather I didn't raise the topic of *anything* possibly ever happening between you and Jonah? Ever! Or did I read that wrong?'

I rolled my eyes in exasperation but couldn't help the smile tugging at my mouth.

'We were kids. Completely different people. Us being together has some horrible memories associated with it. And you know I'm not in the right place to even think about stuff like that at the moment.'

'At *any* moment in the five years since your marriage ended,' she interrupted.

'While Isla's going through her thing, and Mum's threatening to come home...'

'Wait, what the hell do you mean, she's coming home?'

'Didn't you get a postcard?' Usually, they were sent in pairs.

'If I had, don't you think I'd have mentioned it?' Nicky looked shell-shocked. 'Why the hell didn't *you* mention it?'

'I don't know, it felt like an in-person conversation, and you had to rush off straight after the session yesterday. It only arrived on Tuesday...'

Subject successfully changed, we went on to discuss this traumatic family scenario until our glasses were empty and Theo messaged Nicky to check she'd not been in a car crash because it was nearly midnight and she had a wild swim arranged for five-thirty the following morning.

Which was, it turned out, about the time my brain finally ran out of steam, stopped unpicking every Jonah memory for the squillionth time and let me get a pitiful ninety minutes of sleep.

11

THEN

The first time that I dared to wonder whether my awkward, mixed-up feelings for Jonah might not be completely one-sided was the first Saturday of the Easter holidays, nearly two weeks after it had been agreed that he was staying at least until the court made a decision about his long-term care in the autumn.

We had a family outing to the cinema to watch some bland film that Mum had deemed suitable for traumatised teenagers, stopping off first at a cheapo chain restaurant because some of the kids we looked after had never eaten out before and found fancier places more overwhelming.

My parents pretended not to get antsy when Jonah slouched back in the diner's bench seat, not even opening the menu. However, when the waiter came, he ordered an obscure burger with no hesitation.

'Have you been here before?' Mum asked, once the waiter had left.

'Sometimes.' He shrugged. 'When Warren wasn't around.'

Warren was his mum's boyfriend.

'Ah. I'm sorry.' She screwed up her nose in apology. 'I should have checked.'

'It's fine. It was another one, near where we lived.'

'Still. We can always leave. There's a Nando's across the road.'

He gave a short, sharp shake of his head and the table descended into uncomfortable silence. Unable to bear the awkwardness, I did an uncharacteristic thing and blurted the first thought that came into my head.

'I like your hat.'

Everyone turned to look at me. Everyone except for Jonah, who was already sitting opposite and so simply flicked his hooded eyes up to meet mine.

'Do you really?' Dad asked, sounding confused. 'I wouldn't have thought that was your style.'

No. I really didn't. Jonah's hat looked as though he'd found it in a puddle. The brown wool was so matted it looked stiff as cardboard. The logo on the front might have been a wolf, once.

I shrugged, mumbling something about how I liked wolves. Not entirely untrue, since I'd been looking into those amber eyes.

'It's a jackal,' Jonah said, meeting my glance with that blank expression that gave nothing away.

'Oh, okay! Cool.' I pulled the pot of sauce sachets towards me and started examining them as if suddenly fascinated by the ingredients of tomato ketchup. 'I mean, jackals are awesome, too.'

'Do you remember that book you had about the wolf, Libby?' Mum said, grabbing the topic with both hands. 'You were scared stiff of it! We always had to read *Winnie the Pooh* afterwards or you'd be too afraid to sleep. Then, when that boy in your class – the one who said you were smelly – brought a toy wolf in…'

And off she went with another attempt to make Jonah feel less crap about himself by showing how embarrassingly imperfect we were – or, more to the point, *I* was.

I looked at the floor, the table, my sister rolling her eyes in sympathy. Every time my gaze darted back to Jonah, his eyes remained unwaveringly on mine.

I somehow ended up sitting next to Jonah in the cinema. He was at the end of the row, and Nicky was on the other side of me, my parents next to her.

That was fine, of course. Yes, he made me nervous and I had no idea what he was thinking – especially when it came to me – but all I had to do was sit and stare at a screen for two hours.

Except that wasn't all I had to do. There was popcorn to eat – suddenly the noisiest, most undignified snack on the planet. Nicky put her giant slushie in the shared armrest holder on my side, so I had an agonising wait to see which side Jonah used for his and whether or not I'd have to hold my freezing-cold cup. I tried to keep innocuously still, right in the centre of the seat, but pins and needles meant I was forced to wiggle my leg, every movement magnified. Even breathing felt heightened around Jonah.

Then, about forty-five minutes into the film...

Something warm brushed against my arm.

Every nerve alert, body frozen still, I slid my eyes through the darkness to find him slouched low in his chair, his elbow jutting so far across the armrest that it now stuck out onto my seat, hence it bumping into me.

While I held my breath in the darkness, he gave a subtle stretch, his head moving closer until it reached the tiny gap between our seats, a significant portion of his forearm coming to rest against mine.

He'd taken his jacket and sweatshirt off, for quite possibly the first time ever, so the skin now touching mine was bare.

Could he feel every hair on my arm standing up through my thin cardigan?

For the next few minutes of the film, it was all I could do to keep my lungs moving.

Slowly, slowly, his arm relaxed into mine.

Needless to say, not a single muscle in my body was relaxed.

At some point, in a moment of madness, I sat forwards, took off my cardigan and then slid down to Jonah's level in the seat, trying to feign innocence as I angled my body towards his and carefully positioned my now equally bare arm on the armrest.

Immediately, not even bothering to be subtle, he moved his arm next to it.

Our little fingers were touching.

Our heads were about two inches apart.

It was the most thrilling, intimate moment of my life so far.

I could only pray that no one asked me anything about the film, because I didn't take in a single second of it from that point on.

When the credits rolled and the lights came up, Jonah sat up, tugged his hoodie on, collected his rubbish and walked out without a second glance. He offered to ride in the back row of the car on the way home – we had three rows of seats for the times we fostered two children at once – and disappeared into his bedroom as soon as we got there.

12

NOW

Fridays were my official day off. Nicky's comments about taking care of myself still lingering in my head, I'd had every intention of trying a run once I'd dropped the kids at school, but after falling asleep at five-thirty, I'd then snoozed the alarm one too many times and had an even more hectic morning than usual. Instead, I forced myself to walk a longer way home, adding maybe another kilometre to my journey.

It was a start, I tried to kid myself as I trudged along the footpath. I'd try running next week, when hopefully I'd had more sleep.

While my body might have been slow, my head flew along thought pathways and sped through worries as if it were competing in the Olympics.

I briefly considered the postcard, before dismissing it as far too vague and insubstantial to bother about yet. I fretted for maybe half a kilometre about Isla. She'd seemed slightly more settled this morning, until Finn had mentioned their fortnightly outing with Brayden the next day and she'd had a full-blown meltdown on the pavement outside school. I had no idea what to do about her reaction to seeing her dad, which seemed to grow increasingly fraught the older she got. Isla was struggling to relate to this man who took her to the park but showed no further interest in her life. A couple of weeks ago she'd asked Theo if he could be her daddy, and when he'd gently explained all the benefits of being an uncle, she'd settled on Finn taking on the role when he was older.

How obligated was I to force a relationship if it seemed to be more harmful than helpful? Was this a blip to work through, or a slippery slope? Wouldn't a daughter benefit from having a father around if he was, underneath all the nonsense, a half-decent guy?

But then that thought, as I skirted the edge of a sweetcorn field, segued into Brayden having the audacity to turn up to my antenatal class without checking with me first and how on earth I was going to handle the next four weeks of him plus a post-birth reunion party. With gritted teeth, was about all I could come up with. After all, his baby deserved parents who were well equipped for the role as much as anyone. I decided I'd do it for Finn and Isla's half-sibling, if not for my own sense of pride and proving to Brayden and Silva that I was totally cool about however my ex-husband treated this child compared to his others.

I spent a brief minute, while following a bridle path back towards the cottage, thinking about the Bloomers. I made a note to visit Daisy and check she wasn't being bothered by Raz as well as following up with Courtney and Toby after Hazel's unhelpful input, then moved on to the topic taking up by far the biggest space in my head.

Jonah.

And Ellis, of course.

I hoped the promise of a manicure would be enough to bring her back on Monday.

I wondered if Jonah would drop her off, which led to questions like when had he passed his driving test? Who'd paid for lessons? Where had he been living at the time? Did he work? Doing what?

Why was he here, and what on earth would that mean?

Would I ever sleep properly again, unless I found out everything?

The last two questions, the biggest ones, jostling about behind the others, only managed to worm their way to the front of my mind once I reached my back gate.

Had I ever stopped loving Jonah?

How did he feel about me?

* * *

A shower, late breakfast and two hours of strenuous cooking later, I still couldn't stop thinking about it, so decided to distract myself with some real problems.

Firstly, I walked over to Daisy's house and dropped off a pot of chilli. As well as caring for Daisy and Bolt, Lisa was currently fostering sisters aged two and three. When Daisy handed the dish to Lisa, she had to blink hard a few times before offering me a cup of tea.

I made Lisa and Daisy a much-needed lunch, then sat on their living-room rug playing one-handed with the girls while cuddling Bolt so both mums could rest for an hour.

After that, I whizzed over to Courtney and Toby's house. It was two-thirty, Hazel was still at the hair salon and Toby's brothers and sisters would be at school, so I was hoping to catch Courtney and baby Hazel alone.

It took several knocks before she answered the door. I would have given up if the television weren't blaring.

'Oh. It's you.'

Courtney wore pink jogging bottoms and a grey sports bra, revealing an almost flat stomach. Her hair was perfectly straightened and she had on a full face of make-up.

'Is it okay if I come in for a few minutes? I brought you some chilli.'

'I'm going out soon. But the others can eat it.'

'I'll put it in the fridge.' I nudged my way in, not waiting to be invited, and waded through the cluttered living room to find the kitchen in an even worse state.

The fridge was practically bare, so I left the dish on an empty shelf and turned on the kettle.

'You've got time for a drink before you go? It feels like a while since we've had a proper catch-up.'

Courtney glanced at her phone, face pinched. 'Sure.'

'Where's Hazel?' I asked, rinsing out two mugs after failing to find any clean ones in the cupboards. I wasn't normally so bossy and interfering, but I was genuinely worried about Courtney and could see that she wasn't going to reveal anything easily.

'At work.'

'I meant baby Hazel,' I said, my concern twitching. 'Is she okay?'

'Yeah, fine,' Courtney said, with zero enthusiasm.

I waited until the drinks were ready and we'd cleared enough debris off the sofas to sit down before resuming my interrogation.

'And how are you?' I asked, attempting a careful balance between warm and casual.

'You know. Knackered. Bored. I was meant to be going to this thing at my mate's house. Like, it was really important to me, everyone was going, and I've not been round to theirs in ages. But Toby refused to skive his college assessment, and Hazel wouldn't let me leave the baby in the salon. I mean, it's hardly a big deal if she sleeps in the corner for a few hours.'

Courtney was scrolling down her phone as she talked, sending off a couple of quick-fire messages. 'She's always on at me. Why haven't I done this, gone shopping, waited on them hand and foot? She just wants a slave.' Courtney screwed up her face, continuing to scroll as her voice grew increasingly bitter. 'Always interfering with me and Toby. I reckon she's jealous because I've got a man and she tried three and they were all losers.'

'Wow. I hope you didn't tell her that.'

Courtney narrowed her eyes, still on the screen. 'Why not? It's true.'

She suddenly sat up, face brightening. 'Oh, wow. My mate went and got the sickest tattoo. Check this out.'

And so the next half an hour went on. When cries started drifting down the stairs, Courtney swore, ignored it for three more TikTok videos she *had* to show me, then stomped upstairs to fetch her daughter.

'You want a cuddle?'

I most certainly did.

'Oh, bless you,' I cooed, after patting her bottom. 'She's sopping wet, Courtney.'

Normally I wouldn't hesitate to change a baby's nappy while visiting a mum, but I wanted to see whether Courtney showed any emotion towards her daughter while caring for her.

It was worse. She glanced up, saying, 'Marnie will be back in a few minutes. She'll change her. I told you, I'm going out as soon as they're back.'

'When the kids are back?' Marnie was fourteen. It wasn't illegal for her to be left responsible for a baby, but I'd met Marnie and I wasn't sure it was advisable. 'You aren't waiting for Toby, or his mum?'

She rolled her eyes. 'Nah, they'll be gone ages. We're meeting at four for predrinks.'

After finding a pack of nappies behind an armchair, I got on with it.

I had to leave well before baby Hazel's uncles and aunties finished school, but my visit had done nothing to ease my worries about Courtney. She didn't seem especially depressed – she'd been positively enthusiastic when talking about her new outfit or a friend's new boyfriend. But she'd not referred to her daughter by name the whole time I'd been there. Generally speaking, new mothers talked about their babies all the time. Especially with their antenatal and parenting group leader, who wouldn't get bored as her peers might.

Courtney's example of motherhood up until now hadn't been great. But she had Grandma Hazel, and Toby, and numerous friends at Bloomers, and while pregnant had directed a fair amount of her enthusiasm towards her baby, rather than her social life.

I was very concerned that Courtney was deliberately dissociating herself from Hazel. I'd seen this type of behaviour before, and it rarely ended well.

* * *

The Friday night before the kids saw their dad, I always tried to keep things calm and cosy. On the way home from school we stocked up on ingredients, and, due to the main oven being broken, made a sort of pizza toast we'd invented, Isla and Finn going to town with a multitude of random toppings – carrot and pea pizza, anyone? No? They took turns in the bath, then we grilled the cheesy toast before eating in front of a favourite film. Once Isla hit that sweet spot between snuggly and overtired, I tucked her into bed. Finn was allowed a secret extra half-hour downstairs on a Friday, and this evening he asked if I could read to him for the first time since he'd learned to process the words faster than I could say them.

'Are you feeling all right about seeing Dad tomorrow?' I asked, once we'd finished two chapters and despite his eyes growing soft and heavy he'd asked for another one.

Finn shrugged. 'Yeah.'

'You don't sound too sure.' I tried to keep my voice casual, but my mum antenna was on full alert.

'No. I am sure. I like seeing Dad, mostly.'

'Why only mostly?'

I followed him up the stairs, but he did the classic move of waiting until he'd brushed his teeth, been tucked in and my hand was on the light switch before answering the question.

'It's just if Isla starts screaming in Café Fried Chicken like last time.'

'*What?*'

A ripple of panic skittered up my back.

'Dad forgot to get her a straw, so she started crying, and that got on my nerves, so I sort of accidentally hit her over the head with mine, and, well, you know.'

I did know.

'What did Dad do?' I scooched up beside him on the bed.

'He made me sit on a different chair and then just kept telling her it was okay. But it didn't work.'

'Did he get cross?' Brayden didn't have much of a temper, but I couldn't imagine him keeping calm in that situation.

'No.' Finn's narrow shoulders shrugged underneath his football-covered duvet. 'But his eyes went big and his hand was shaking. He kept looking about as if someone else would come and help while Isla got louder and louder, screaming for you.'

'Oh, honey. That must have been stressful.'

His solemn nod made my throat tighten. There was no point berating him for hitting Isla with a paper straw. The look on his face showed how bad he felt. I hated the thought of Isla being in so much distress when I wasn't there. Screaming for me but instead getting Brayden flailing around, clueless. I couldn't bear to think of my precious boy having to sit there feeling terrible as he watched his father unable to cope.

My anger at Brayden buzzed like a bees' nest kicked by a cow.

'Well, it was at first, but then I told Dad he should try that game on his phone, the pony one. We took our food to the car, and he drove around for a bit while I held the phone and pressed the buttons for her, and in the end she stopped.'

'Sounds like you saved the day. Why didn't you tell me about it?'

He yawned. 'Dad bought us an ice cream and said he was really sorry, it was his fault for forgetting the straw and he was the dad so he shouldn't have got stressed, then I said sorry too, so he said we could forget it happened. Then he made a joke, so Isla started laughing and it was okay. It's not that big a deal, Mum.'

No big deal?

Sitting downstairs, thinking about Isla screaming for me in the café, Brayden pointlessly pleading with her to be quiet, Finn feeling terrible, I grew increasingly irate. Why didn't he call me? Why didn't he *tell* me? If he'd been a proper dad, the kind who showed up for meetings about their daughter's emotional health, who was around enough to know what she was going through and how to help her manage it...

I had to settle for a torrent of one-sided, imaginary arguments with my ex-husband that evening because he didn't answer or return my calls. When he pulled into the drive the next morning as if he'd not even bothered to listen to the brusque message on his voicemail, I stepped outside to talk.

'Is there a problem?' He folded his arms across his chest. 'If it's about the antenatal classes, then—'

'I'm not going to start a professional discussion when you're here to pick up your children, Brayden.'

'It's Brayve.'

'You really want me to call you that?'

He glanced to the side before looking back at me, shoulders drooping. 'No. Brayden's fine.' He paused. 'As long as Silva's not around.'

'Right. Anyway, Finn told me what happened at Café Fried Chicken.'

'What?' He had the audacity to look momentarily baffled before realisation suddenly dawned on his face. 'You mean Isla getting upset?'

'Yes,' I ground out, making every effort to keep my voice down.

'It was nothing. I forgot her straw. We sorted it.'

'And by *we*, you mean my eight-year-old son?'

'*Our* son. Who initially didn't help before he showed me the game she likes. The place was heaving, so the sensory overload didn't help, but once we'd moved to the car she soon settled. No harm done.'

'*No harm done?*' I retorted. 'You don't think they found it upsetting, Isla screaming for me? Finn seeing you clueless?'

'I wasn't clueless!'

I narrowed my eyes.

'Okay. So I did panic a bit. I've not seen her like that before. But we handled it.'

'And what, I'm supposed to just merrily wave the three of you on your way today, knowing you've no idea how to prevent something like that happening?'

Brayden tipped up his chin. 'From what Finn told me, it's been happening for months. Yet this was the first time she lost it with me.'

'Your point being?'

He shrugged. 'Maybe I'm not the problem, here.'

I was too stunned to speak.

'Maybe,' he went on, 'if you'd bothered talking to me about it, I'd have been able to deal with it better.'

'Maybe if you'd turned up to the meeting, you'd know.'

'I was in Amsterdam with work! You messaged saying there was a school meeting, with no explanation. I assumed it was parents evening.'

'You didn't bother to check.'

'No. Which is my bad. Next time I'll be sure to check. But you also didn't tell me.' He put his hands on his hips. 'Almost as if you were setting me up to fail.'

Again, speechless.

'If you'd put aside your grudge against me long enough to prioritise your daughter, you could have made a simple phone call warning me that she might flip out and that the pony game sorts her out. Perhaps then our son wouldn't have to act as go-between.'

He did his best to stare me down. I resisted the urge to say what I really thought, knowing I'd regret it later.

'If Isla gets upset again, please let me know. And if you can't sort it quickly, call me.' I wrangled my rage back under control, for my children's sake. 'I'll send you the links to some helpful websites.'

I stepped back inside and called for the kids to come and get their shoes on. To my irritation, Brayden followed me in.

'Have you considered that some changes in your parenting strategy might resolve the issue?' he asked as the children thumped about upstairs.

'What the hell do you mean by that?' I whispered.

'If you instigated some healthy routines and, I don't know, a less chaotic environment, it might help your children to feel less anxious. I mean, for goodness' sake, Liz. Look at this place. It's a shambles. You're not twenty any more. Surely it's time to take responsibility for yourself before you hit a full-on nervous breakdown and drag our kids down with you.'

Mercifully, at that point Finn and Isla appeared, preventing me from dragging Brayden down onto my scraggy hall carpet and throttling him.

I gave both kids a reassuring hug, despite my urge to bundle them back inside the house and lock the door, and went to make my shambles of a house slightly less shambolic.

13

After an hour of rage-fuelled cleaning, I decided to walk over to Dad's for lunch. I'd been worrying about him ever since he'd read the postcard. Next time, I'd look at it after he'd gone. On top of that, I was stressing about what he'd do if he found out about Jonah and Ellis turning up at Bloomers.

'Ah. Libby, I wasn't expecting you,' he exclaimed, when I let myself into the garden via the back gate, calling hello as I rounded the corner of the house.

Well, that quickly became clear.

The patio table was set for two. And, by 'set', I mean with enough cutlery for three courses, cloth napkins and a vase of daisies. A second later a woman appeared at the open kitchen door, carrying two glasses containing what looked to be prawn cocktails.

It took me a moment of taking in her ash-blonde bob, immaculate cream trousers and white blouse to realise it was the headmistress at Finn and Isla's school, Miss Marsden. Or Janet, as Dad now introduced her.

'Libby, hello. Fancy seeing you here,' she said, as if I didn't spend more Saturday lunchtimes here than at my own house. 'Don't tell me Tony has to be on family duties at the weekends as well as most of the week. Let the man have a day off to enjoy his own life!'

That stopped me in my tracks. Was that how Dad saw looking after his grandchildren, as a duty? Did he tolerate me calling over at weekends out of pity? I was here to check that he was okay!

'I'm joking.' Janet laughed as she placed the glasses on the table, but there was a distinct chill behind her smile. 'I know how much he loves you. He talks about you and the kids all the time.'

There was an alarming moment where it felt as if the world had tilted slightly, just enough to send my insides lurching. My dad, who'd needed me as much as I'd relied on him for the past few years, had a *date*. Or was this more than a date? Janet had certainly made herself at home, I noticed as she poured out two glasses of wine.

I'd only ever seen Dad drink beer.

He'd had a haircut and was wearing a proper shirt and full-length trousers.

Did he have a whole other life – his *own life* – that I knew nothing about? Was I *that* child, the one who thought they were company for their lonely parent when actually he couldn't wait for them to grow up and stop bothering him?

For a dreadful few seconds I had to fight back tears.

Then Dad pulled up another chair and started splitting his prawn cocktail into two glasses, giving me no polite way to avoid gatecrashing whatever this was, and I had to pull myself together and act as if everything were normal.

'I didn't realise you two knew each other,' I said, once we'd covered the basic how-are-yous.

'Well, I do pick the kids up three afternoons a week,' Dad replied.

'I don't normally see you around the playground at home time,' I said to Janet, trying not to sound as though I was interrogating her.

'Well, you aren't a single man with a decent pension and a striking head of hair.' Janet winked at Dad, and I almost choked on a prawn.

'Another joke!' Dad chuckled. 'My pension is abysmal. We simply got chatting about how I could help at the summer fete, and found out we have a lot in common. Of course, we're just friends.'

Are you? I wondered, noticing the frozen smile on Janet's face as Dad started talking about the fete. He'd said nothing about Janet referring to him as single. It was weird, seeing him having a nice time with someone other than Mum, but I realised with a sinking heart that it shouldn't be. Mum had been gallivanting across the world for years. Should the thought of him and Janet being more than friends feel so terrible?

I stayed for a bowl of home-made pasta, but by the time Janet nipped inside to assemble the meringues she'd brought for dessert, her not-so-subtle glances made it clear I'd been playing gooseberry long enough.

'I'm going to leave you to it,' I said, standing up.

'Why?' Dad appeared genuinely baffled. 'You love meringue. I wanted to hear what you thought about Janet's plan to create a school eco-garden.'

I sat down again, checking the back door was clear before leaning closer and taking hold of Dad's hand. 'I think Janet would prefer it if I left.'

'What are you talking about?' He shook his head, offended on her behalf. 'Janet likes you. She told me.'

'Yes, but that doesn't mean she wants me gatecrashing. This is a date, Dad, whether you knew it or not.'

Dad's mouth dropped open at the very thought. 'But I'm a married man. I stated very clearly that we're simply friends. Why on earth would she think that?'

'I don't know – a three-course lunch with a bottle of wine?'

Before he could reply, Janet reappeared, causing him to swiftly cover up his rattled demeanour by pouring her another glass of wine, tipping half of it all over the pretty tablecloth.

I left them to clear it up.

* * *

The instant Brayden's car pulled into the drive the rear door flew open and Isla tumbled out, streaking across the drive, her orange sundress flapping behind her.

As I opened the front door, she shot through, ignoring my wide-stretched arms and hurtling up the stairs. I caught a glimpse of her tear-streaked face as she passed me. I would have followed her, but Finn was now outside the car, and Brayden wasn't the only person standing with him.

'Hi,' I said, making the split-second decision to find out what had happened before heading upstairs.

'Mum!' Finn said, turning to face me. To my surprise, he was smiling. 'Silva and Dad are having a baby!'

'Wow. That's... massive news!' I vaguely registered my stomach shrivelling into a hard, angry ball. 'Is that why your sister's crying?'

He shrugged. 'Either that or because one of her chips was wonky or today had a letter Y in it.' He glanced at Brayden and Silva, waggling his eyebrows to share the joke.

'Okay. But I don't think Isla crying is something to joke about.'

'Yeah, but she's—'

'Go inside, please, while I talk to your dad for a minute.'

'What? I haven't said goodbye yet.'

'Quickly, then.'

Finn fist-bumped his dad, and then disconcertingly gave Silva a hug before disappearing into the house.

'What the hell, Brayden?' Added to the drama that had been bombarding me over the past couple of days, this had me about ready to blow. 'You sprang this on them without discussing it with me first?'

His jaw set firm. 'What, are you vetting the conversations I have with my kids now?'

'If it's something this serious then you could at least warn me. I could have helped prepare them.'

'Brayve wanted to share the happy news with his own children without you twisting it into something negative first,' Silva said.

'Stay out of this. It's none of your business.' I swung my body around to face my ex-husband, daring him to let that comment from his girlfriend go.

'Maybe let us talk this one out, babe.' Brayden grabbed Silva's hand and kissed it, gazing into her eyes for a nauseating few seconds before turning back to me.

'Finn wanted to play football, so Silva very kindly brought my ball to the park. The kids wanted her to stay, and when she got out of the car they noticed her bump.'

My eyes flashed over to Silva's skintight strapless dress.

'They needed to find out anyway. It's not a big deal. You saw Finn; he's fine with it,' Brayden went on.

'And while we're discussing it,' Silva interrupted, 'it's vital that we cultivate a positive relationship between all of Brayden's children, so we'll be spending a lot more time together as a family from now on.' She then caught the look on my face and quickly clamped her mouth shut.

'It's not Finn I'm worried about.' My voice was trembling with emotion. 'I can't believe we spoke about Isla only this morning, and then you did this to her. There's not a chance in hell of you spending more time together when, every time she sees you, she ends up upset. Right now, I'm seriously considering whether it's a good idea for you to see them at all.'

'Keep your voice down,' Brayden snapped, nodding behind me. I turned and saw Finn standing in the doorway holding his favourite stuffed elephant while trying to put his trainers on. Mercifully, he didn't appear to have heard me.

Before I could respond, Isla pushed past him, racing over and pressing one of her own cloth dolls into Silva's hand.

'Sorry, sorry. It took me ages to find it. I wanted my new baby sister to have my best one. Mummy!' She spun around, eyes shining. 'Did you know Silva and Daddy are having a baby? I'm going to be a big sister and have a little sister! I was so happy and excited when they told me, I couldn't stop crying all the way home.'

Then she flung her arms around Silva's midriff and pressed one cheek against her bump. 'Hello, baby sister. I love you!'

Brayden said nothing while he kissed both his children goodbye and gently helped his partner get into their low-slung sports car, carrying the elephant and the doll. After the years we'd shared a life together, he didn't have to. The raised eyebrow and defiant puff to his chest said it all.

* * *

Nicky messaged me that evening.

What are you up to?

I had a quick debate with myself about whether to be honest: *throwing a full-on pity party for one.*

In the end I stuck to the facts.

Watching TV with a jumbo bag of tortilla chips

She replied instantly.

Perfect! My open-water swim club is going to the new comedy club in Newark and Miranda's got a migraine

Did you forget the minor detail of me having two small children?

Can't you ask Dad to watch them?

I remembered Dad pouring the lovely, slightly formidable Janet a glass of wine and shuddered.

He's on a date

WHAT?

She sent me two more messages.

Ok, you absolutely have to come now

Hang on

I turned the volume up on the tedious game show I was pretending to watch and stuffed in another mouthful of crisps.

Miranda's babysitter's more than happy to do it. Roisin used to be a TA in Finn's class so you probably know her. I'll pick her up and see you in twenty.

Don't worry about the ticket or babysitter, my treat

No, being forced out after what was one of the most unsettling, emotional weeks I'd had all year was not a treat.

Sorry but I'm going to have to pass. B's girlfriend turned up at the park and told the kids she was pregnant. I'm not leaving them with a stranger this evening.

A split second later Nicky called me.

'What the hell?' she said, outraged on Finn and Isla's behalf. 'He hadn't warned you first?'

'Of course not. Apparently, I'm far too crap a mum to have a say. They're his kids and he'll tell them what he likes.'

'Ugh. Just when I think he can't get any worse. I'm so sorry. Are they really upset?'

I closed my eyes. 'Still processing.'

They'd spent the rest of the afternoon and early evening chattering excitedly, wondering what the baby would be like and all the things they'd do together, so this wasn't technically a lie. What I probably should have said was that *I* was really upset. About Dad's date, the postcard, Brayden deciding to become father of the year. Jonah and Ellis. Courtney and Hazel... The realisation that I had zero life outside work, my kids and gatecrashing my dad's dates.

As I said, majorly self-indulgent wallowing was in full swing.

For a fleeting moment I wondered about accepting the spare ticket and going out for the first time in longer than I cared to think about. The truth was, my kids were great sleepers who wouldn't make a peep until morning. I'd met Roisin a few times. She was absolutely lovely, and Isla and Finn both knew her.

But then I thought about me going out with Nicky's friends, who got up at the crack of dawn and jumped into lakes together, no doubt spending the rest of the week doing equally wholesome activities.

What did twenty-nine-year-old women even wear to a comedy club on a Saturday night? Probably not dungarees and a saggy T-shirt. Definitely not the pyjamas I was currently in.

Spending an evening with intimidatingly awesome women felt like something that would not help me feel any better right then.

'Best if I give it a miss this time. I don't know how long it'll be before Isla's settled. But thanks for asking. I hope you have a great night. Call me tomorrow and I'll fill you in on Dad's "friendly" lunch.'

For the first time in a very long time – thirteen years, in fact – I flat out lied to my sister.

14

THEN

I couldn't sleep.

It was early April, the summer term had started and all anyone in Year 11 was supposed to be thinking about was our GCSE exams, beginning in five weeks and six days, according to Katie, who was counting down.

I'd made the obligatory revision timetable, stuck it up on the noticeboard above my desk and spent an hour sitting with my chemistry textbook open, staring at the same diagram of covalent bonds until the time was up.

I usually had no trouble finding the motivation to study. I was planning on doing A levels in science and maths next year, so I could apply for a midwifery degree. Katie and Alicia were mildly jealous that I'd known for years what I wanted to do, and, if I put in a reasonable amount of effort, would be able to do it.

These past few days, my concentration had been slipping.

Since the cinema, Jonah's nods had progressed to that full-on-eye-contact hidden smile he did when passing me at school or in the kitchen. Speaking of which, we seemed to end up in the kitchen together a lot more often than we used to. Maybe the thud of his trainers going downstairs did occasionally prompt me to notice I was thirsty. But equally often – yes, I was keeping a rough tally – he would appear after I'd been the one to head down for a snack. One day I found my library card in my jacket pocket, with a scrawled note: 'thanks'.

We rarely exchanged a word. Maybe 'Is your dad around?' or 'Mum's made cookies if you want any.'

But the atmosphere crackled with unspoken thoughts. It was as though the air were thin, empty, until he was there, when it became hot and heavy, ripe with anticipation. Anticipating what, I daren't consider. I drank in every glance, each time he brushed past me to reach for a glass or when he sat at the opposite corner to me at the dinner table. And while I could barely eat in his presence – thank goodness I had the excuse of exam stress, or Mum would have panicked about me developing food issues – I *hungered* for more of him, while at the same time feeling scared witless at the very thought.

He was my foster sibling. It went without saying that there were very firm boundaries that must never be crossed. So I dealt with my growing obsession by convincing myself that it would forever remain in my head, where it was safe. A silly teenage thing that no one, least of all Jonah, would ever suspect, and if he did, he'd be as disgusted and horrified as everyone else, so I didn't have to stress about the consequences.

It didn't stop me from dreaming about him, though.

Or keep me out of the kitchen.

So, on that April night, when the air was muggy, charged with a potential storm brewing, after spending hours twisting up in my duvet, stressing about my appalling lack of revision, pointlessly berating myself with all the reasons not to like Jonah, I eventually gave up and went downstairs to fetch a drink and some painkillers for the headache compressing my skull.

It was two in the morning. I could argue that it never crossed my mind that anyone would be up and about, so there was no need to pull a hoodie on over my vest top and pyjama shorts, or bother with a bra. But if that was true, there was also no need for me to brush my hair or check the mirror for new spots.

I slipped down the two flights of stairs and into the dining room, where we kept the medication locked in a filing cabinet as per fostering rules, the key hidden behind Dad's favourite Robert Ludlum novel on the bookcase.

Two paracetamols in hand, I padded into the kitchen and navigated filling a glass of water in the dark, resisting the twinge of disappointment that the rest of the house was silent. Not ready to return to bed, I decided to step outside to finish my drink, hoping that the night air might help clear my head and cool my fevered heart.

I wandered along the side of the house to the wooden chairs on the far side of the patio, the slabs ice-cold against the soles of my feet. The only light source was a scattering of stars and sliver of moon above the roofline. I was about to sit down, when a slight movement made me jerk around to find a darker patch of shadows filling one of the other chairs.

I pressed a hand against my thumping heart, eyes adapting to the darkness as Jonah shifted again, the cigarette he drew to his mouth illuminating an apologetic smile. He was lounging back in one chair, his feet propped up on another.

'I scared you. Sorry.' A stream of smoke accompanied his words.

I was the type of girl who considered smoking to be a disgusting waste of money, scorning those who might consider it to be cool, let alone sexy.

But standing there, shivering in the darkness, a few paces away from this wild-looking boy, all angles, shadows and unknown dangers, who lived by his own rulebook – one that I hadn't read, and couldn't hope to understand – I felt bewitched. Consumed. Like if I took one step closer, it would change everything.

'I didn't expect anyone else to be out here.'

He glanced at the watch that my parents had bought him. 'Understandable.'

'I couldn't sleep. Thought fresh air might help.'

'Here.' He removed his feet from the chair, pushing it a foot or so closer to me in the same movement.

'Thanks.' I gingerly sat down, pulling my knees up and wrapping my arms around them as I cursed myself for not putting on something warmer – something *sturdier* than the flimsy, faded cotton that hung loosely around my modest chest.

Jonah took another puff and then stubbed out the butt on a chipped plate that my parents had designated a makeshift ashtray, despite the strict rule that there was no smoking in the house.

'Exams?' he asked, eyes golden as they reflected the moonlight. I looked for any hint of disdain for the girl losing sleep over something so trivial but couldn't spot it.

'Partly.' I grimaced. 'Revision isn't exactly going well.'

'Does that explain all the snacks? Stress eating.'

My brain scrambled at the confirmation that he'd noticed my frequent trips to the kitchen. *Of course he had. Jonah noticed everything.*

I wished again for my sweatshirt.

'Getting up and walking about for a couple of minutes helps get your brain working.' I shrugged, relieved that my voice sounded impossibly calm. 'What's your excuse for being up? Are you worried about how your exams will go?'

He flashed a grin that disappeared so quickly I could have imagined it, if my bones hadn't instantly disintegrated into mush.

'I know full well how my exams are going to go. The only question is quite how spectacularly I'll fail them. I'm wasting no time stressing about that.'

I didn't offer any platitudes about how there was still time, or you never knew what might happen if you tried. I'd learned not to underestimate the impact of years of trauma followed by the monumental upheaval of being plonked in a strange house, the future a gaping black hole over which you had virtually no control. I found a stupid crush distracting. How anyone was supposed to care about physics or history while facing genuine problems like whether the court would send them home or if their mum was back on hard drugs was beyond me.

'I guess exams aren't really a priority right now.'

'Right now—' he stretched out his long legs until his feet almost reached mine '—the priority is to survive until Ellis and Billy don't need me any more.'

'What then?' I asked, expecting him to share a wild plan about travel or a job.

He picked up the dead cigarette and rolled it between his fingers before slowly grinding it into the plate.

'Then my work here on earth is done.'

I wasn't shocked by his admission. Only that he'd shared it so willingly.

'Maybe things will have got better by then.'

'*Things* probably will get better. I won't.'

His voice was flat, matter-of-fact.

'You don't know that,' I whispered. 'There's always hope.'

He glanced at me, eyes glinting. 'Why is it that you're the first person to say that who could make me want to believe it?'

I shrugged, completely lost for words.

'I've never met someone so relentlessly hopeful.'

'What?' That was news to me.

'You chose "Wuthering Heights" for karaoke, despite not being able to sing for shit. You then belted it out as if ten-thousand people were loving every note.'

'It sounds worse if you don't go for it.'

'You keep watering that plant on the kitchen windowsill. It was already long dead when I moved here.'

I shook my head. 'Someone's got to keep believing in the underdogs. You never know what a bit of love and attention might do.'

Jonah gave me a sidelong glance. Neither of us missed the double meaning in that comment.

'Okay, so you've just given me a new life mission.'

He raised an eyebrow in question, mouth creasing in the beginnings of a smile.

'Somehow, I'm going to find a way to infect you with my relentless hope. By the time Ellis and Billy don't need you any more – which, by the way, is probably never; I can't imagine not needing Nicky, and you've been through far too much together already – I'll have given you a whole load of other reasons to stick around on planet Earth.'

'Such as?'

I shrugged. 'There are a lot of karaoke songs we didn't get round to on my birthday.'

Before he could answer, the patio was suddenly flooded with light. Someone had turned the conservatory light on. I was still blinking away the dazzle when this was followed up by two gentle thuds on the window behind us.

Turning around, I saw Nicky, wearing her favourite llama onesie, peering at us with a huge 'What the hell?' expression on her face.

Before she could come outside and humiliate me, Jonah casually got up and walked back to the kitchen. As soon as he'd disappeared inside, Nicky slid open the conservatory door.

'It's two-thirty, Libby. What are you doing?' she rasped, face still incredulous as I got up and pushed past her to get inside, flopping onto a wicker armchair.

'I had a headache and couldn't sleep, so needed painkillers.' Although, for some reason, I'd totally forgotten about the hammer causing havoc inside my skull. 'I decided fresh air might help, and Jonah was already out there, smoking.' I shrugged my shoulders, as if trying way too hard to act innocent.

'So, what, you thought you'd join him?'

I raised my eyebrows. Nicky had smoked more than a couple of illicit late-night cigarettes with girls who'd lived here previously.

She rolled her eyes in full-on big-sister mode. 'I'm not talking about whether you shared a drag or not. Although, don't. Smoking is totally grim and not your vibe. You were sitting alone together in the dark...' She spluttered. 'Half naked. Alone. Together. In the dark.'

'Actually, Jonah was in jeans and his jacket,' I said, fake cheerfully.

'You are so not funny.' I wasn't often on the receiving end of Nicky's glare. It would have been intimidating if I weren't still oozing with giddy warmth from the conversation with Jonah.

'You are so not my mother,' I bit back.

'Thank goodness! If Mum or Dad found out, they'd go ballistic.'

'Why?' I snapped. 'I was having a drink of water.' I held up the glass as evidence. 'In the garden. We weren't in my bedroom.' No foster child, whatever their age, was allowed in there. 'If I'd known he was up, I'd have put a jumper on. But I don't think me in my ratty old pyjamas is that tempting. We were just chatting. We weren't even sat near each other.'

Not near enough, anyway.

'About what?' she huffed.

'Exams. What else? A token gesture of awkward conversation. Honestly, it was nothing.'

It was everything.

'If I'm up and about at night again, I'll wear my old dressing gown. Okay?' I gave her ankle a playful nudge with my toe, hoping to defuse the tension. 'Seriously, Nicky. Do you honestly think I'm sneaking around with Jonah King in the middle of the night? Right underneath Mum and Dad's window?'

She chewed on her plait, eyes assessing me.

'Even if he wasn't our foster brother, just no! The very thought is completely rank. Give me some credit.'

'Yeah.' She squeezed in next to me on the chair, resting her head on my shoulder. 'I'm sorry. It *is* rank. I'm ashamed for thinking it. I was just surprised to see you. And you actually look extremely cute in those pyjamas with your hair all mussed.'

I took a steady breath, deliberately relaxing my shoulder. 'How often did we chat in the garden with Sabine, or Rani? You know they liked us to keep them company when they were up half the night, stressing. That's honestly all this was. One minute of exam small talk with our new, long-term foster brother.'

'Bronah.'

'What?' That made me burst out laughing.

'That's what I'm calling him, in my head. Is it too soon to try it to his face?'

'Not at all. It's perfect.' I giggled, unable to think of a less suitable nickname. 'Just make sure I'm in the room when you do.'

I got up. Without the distraction of Jonah, my headache was

making itself known again. 'Anyway, what were *you* doing up at this scandalous time of night? Looking to mooch a cigarette?'

Nicky closed her eyes, settling into the chair as if planning to stay there a while. 'You aren't the only one stressing about exams.'

I left her to it, a tentacle of guilt wrapping itself around me as I climbed the attic stairs. As far as I could remember, that was the first time I'd outright lied to my sister. Over the next few months, it wouldn't be the last. Unable to share the truth with anyone, instead I pulled out my journal and poured it out between the pages of my dream house.

15

NOW

It was somewhere around three in the morning when it hit me. I'd been dozing fretfully, in between floundering about in a puddle of pathetic self-loathing, when I suddenly jerked awake, eyes springing open, head startlingly clear.

I'd founded a charity to help empower people to make positive changes that often cut through years – if not generations – of destructive choices. Day after day I told the Baby Bloomers that, while they couldn't change the past or even a lot of what was happening to them in the present – these babies were coming out one way or another! – they had so much more control than they realised. They could decide who they wanted to become. Although it wouldn't be easy to become her. It might take lots of practice, and mistakes, and dusting themselves down and trying again. Focussing on what we called small yet significant choices. It would mean building emotional – and sometimes physical – boundaries to protect them from some people. It would include being uncomfortably honest about their own limitations and struggles and need for support. It would mean facing down the foe we all instinctively fight – fear of change.

And yet, here I was, wondering what on earth to do about my own miserable mess of a life.

Small, significant choices.

I'd start first thing tomorrow.

Or the next day, when I'd had some more sleep and a bit more time to think about what those changes would be.

By the middle of the week, I'd replaced the impossible List of a Billion Things to Do with something far better. Half a dozen small yet significant changes I wanted to make. This included finding a handful of friends beyond my dad and sister, deciding what to do if my mum made proper contact. I'd find time every week to spend on sorting out my house, and, once I'd proven I could keep it clean, I'd move on to proper renovations. Starting with an oven that worked, and a shower curtain that wasn't held up with duct tape.

I'd go for an actual run. Overall, the plan was to make changes that resulted in me having some energy instead of dragging myself through life like a crab with four broken legs.

For three days I didn't add anything about romance or dating to my list. Then I wrote, in tiny letters:

Maybe one day think about something to do with romance or dating.

There. Let the future begin.

By the end of the week, the actual changes I'd made were... putting three loads of washing away, rather than leaving them to pile up on the landing.

Oh, and I'd booked a hair appointment with Shanice for Saturday afternoon, when Brayden and Silva were taking the kids *to their house* in Newark, twelve miles away, so Silva could provide them with, as she'd assured me after Tuesday's antenatal class, 'a nutritional meal for once'.

'For once, as in it's the one time Brayden has cooked his children a meal?' I asked, congratulating myself for graduating to passive-aggressive rather than plain old aggressive. Brayden had been angling for more time with the kids. I couldn't agree to a whole weekend, so we'd settled on every Saturday for now.

'I mean, compared to that chicken place!' She grimaced. 'You're a parenting expert, Liz, you know children can't reach their potential on cheap, hormone-riddled meat, fried in carcinogens.'

I thought my snipe had gone over her head, but then she went on. 'And he'd have cooked them plenty of meals if you'd trusted him to take them home before now.'

I made a non-committal, indecipherable noise then turned away to prevent myself from launching the imitation pelvis I was holding at her head. Maybe the crap food I made them thanks to a broken oven and broken life explained Isla's issues. After Brayden moved out, feeding my kids a baking tray of cheap, carcinogen-soaked meat was about all I could manage most days. Somehow, five years later, I was still resorting to the same rubbish.

I added 'start cooking nutritional meals' to my new list, then went to find the leftover fishfingers I'd not had time to eat earlier.

* * *

I did have another reason for finally getting my hair cut. At the postnatal Bloomers session on Wednesday, Courtney had blanked Toby for most of the day. While the mums decorated cupcakes, the dads had a refreshingly banter-free discussion about mental health. When they joined their partners to taste-test the cupcakes, Toby mentioned the topic to his girlfriend.

'I can't believe you're going on about that again. Are you deliberately getting on my nerves now?' she asked, turning her back.

'I'm worried about you, that's all. You're sad and angry most of the time, and a doctor might be able to help.'

Courtney spun back around, eyes flashing. 'Do you want to blurt it out a bit louder? Because I'm not sure everyone heard you say I'm a nutcase.'

Hardly anyone had heard Toby, as he'd been speaking discreetly. But Courtney had caught the attention of the whole cabin, and everyone immediately fell silent so they could listen to what came next.

'Happy?' she shouted, gesturing at the onlookers. 'Now everyone knows you think I'm the problem, not my selfish, nagging boyfriend, his bitch of a mother or being stuck all bloody day and night with a baby who won't stop screaming.'

'I wonder who the baby takes after?' someone muttered, causing a faint ripple of awkward laughter.

Courtney barged past Toby, ignoring Hazel in her car seat, and went to stand on the drive, despite there being another fifteen minutes until the end of the session.

Nicky followed straight out, so I stayed to talk to Toby.

'Hazel's teething,' he mumbled, face red as he frantically rubbed a hand through his curls. 'I try to get home as early as I can, but sometimes we need to stay and finish off a project, or the bus is late.'

'Is Courtney still going out a lot?' I asked, handing him a mug of tea.

Toby nodded. 'We had a big fight on Sunday, after she got drunk Saturday night and Mum went mad. One of her friends picked her up and she didn't come home until yesterday morning. Blocked me on everything, so I only found out where she was when some girl put a photo of her on Insta.'

'Oh, I'm sorry. That's really tough.'

'It was actually the most peaceful few days I've had since Hazel was born, just the two of us. Except I had to skip two days of college, so now I'll need to stay late to catch up for the rest of the week. And Mum was fuming, of course. She was mouthing off about not letting Courtney back in the house. At first I thought she didn't mean it, but...' He shrugged, shoving in a cupcake in one huge bite and swallowing it. 'I didn't want to say anything in the session, but I'm dead stressed, to be honest with you, Libby.' He looked down at me. 'It can't be good for Hazel, can it? Being around all that fighting.'

'What will you do, if things reach breaking point and your mum does ask you to find somewhere else to live? Will you stay at home, or go with Courtney and Hazel?'

'Mum's as mad at me as she is with Courtney. If they go, I go.' He clenched his jaw. 'I'll figure something out. That's my job now, isn't it? Providing for my girls.'

'Well, you know where I am if you need any help.'

I made a mental note to contact Courtney's social worker, and then called Shanice.

* * *

But before Saturday's small yet significant haircut transformation, I had a Thursday evening antenatal class, and that meant another ninety minutes trying to act as though seeing Jonah hadn't tipped my world on its axis. He'd dropped his sister off for the Monday Bloomers, and Nicky had paired her up with Petra, the fifteen-year-old from the Green House. It turned out Ellis used to have Petra's current social worker, who was an interesting character, to say the least, with no time for new-fangled things like risk assessments or paperwork. This resulted in Ellis uttering several sentences, as well as a sarcastic joke, which was progress.

I had so many questions about her and her little brother, Billy. I had even more about Jonah. But while mentioning that I'd briefly known her as a child might be a positive way for us to connect, Baby Bloomers was a place of fresh starts. I wasn't about to bring up her past, let alone say that I was part of it. I knew my questions would have to wait.

I thought I'd be ready to see him. Every time the door opened, I made sure I focussed on whoever I was chatting to, or making a drink for, rather than swivelling my eyes over to see if it was him. But that old feeling had started creeping in – the one where the room felt duller, more dismal without him in it. Every nerve was braced to see him. Hear him. Smell him – because although the whiff of cigarettes had gone, he smelled as if he still wore the same brand of toiletries my parents had given him.

When he did arrive, I felt my whole face go stiff, mid smile, as one dad was showing me the lullaby playlist he'd made.

'Hi, Jonah, Ellis!' Nicky called, loud enough to ensure I heard. 'You've just got time to grab a drink before we get started.'

I was by the refreshments table, and if I bent my head any lower over this guy's phone, I'd knock it out of his hand with my nose. I didn't know what I was doing, except behaving as irrationally as an infatuated teenager.

This wasn't good.

About the same time Jonah added one sugar to his black coffee – three less than he used to dump in – I managed to straighten up. Turning around with my oh-so-casual, how-perfectly-pleasant-to-see-you smile at the exact same time he was moving towards me, either he, I or both of us – but probably just me – misjudged the distance and my arm knocked straight into his mug, splashing scalding hot coffee over both our hands.

I yelped, he swore, and as we both jumped back our eyes locked. For a precarious second we were teenagers again. I don't know how long we stood there for, frozen in time, but it was long enough for my heart to collapse in on itself like a dying star, for my head to remember everything it had spent thirteen years trying to forget.

'Here.' A cold, damp cloth pressed onto my hand jerked me back into reality, and I caught Nicky's knowing glance as she lifted the cloth off, quickly checked me for damage then gently pressed it back down again.

'Stick it in cold water for twenty minutes,' she said, before glancing over at Jonah, who was now mopping his hand with a tissue. 'Both of you. I'll do the icebreaker.'

I led Jonah into the back room, where I found two plastic tubs and started filling them with water.

'I'm so sorry,' I managed to mumble over the sound of the squeaky tap. 'I've had a busy week and I'm all over the place.'

'No, I'm sorry. It was my fault for practically sneaking up behind you. You couldn't have known I was there.'

Oh, I'd have known if I'd been blindfolded and wearing ear-defenders.

'Both our faults?' I asked, offering him a tub.

We stood there, each of us holding onto the tub while he kept his eyes firmly on the water slopping about, but it was there, the hint of a smile I'd fallen in love with.

'If that makes you feel better.'

I let go, picking up the other container and submerging my red-raw hand with a wince.

'How's yours looking?' I asked.

'It was only a quick splash. It'll be fine. Are you okay?'

'I think so.'

I was somehow both very okay and definitely not okay all at once. Time would tell which one won out.

I spent the rest of the evening trying to co-lead an antenatal class while avoiding looking at one member of the group the entire time, while also making sure that my sister didn't spot me avoiding him. It was exhausting.

'You need to invite him out for a drink,' Nicky murmured into my ear while the parents-to-be were brainstorming different ways they coped with pain.

'Who?' I asked.

She simply raised one eyebrow.

'What? We spoke about that already,' I whispered, shaking my head vigorously. 'I'm not interested!'

'Maybe not romantically, but it's clear there's enough interest there to make it impossible for you to look in his third of the room. It's hardly helping Ellis feel welcome. Invite him for a catch-up over a coffee, don't tip it all over yourselves, ask a few questions, say what needs to be said and then you can finally move on. Or not.'

'What do you mean, "finally"?' It was hard to convey the extent of my pretend outrage when speaking so quietly. '"Or not"?'

'Libby.' My sister's voice was so soft I had to strain to hear it. 'I haven't seen that look on your face since you were sixteen. Just... talk to him. Find out who he is now. If who he is still fits so perfectly with you.'

Fits so perfectly?

In the end, he left before I had a chance to say anything, let alone decide whether I wanted to ask him for a catch-up coffee.

Was there going to be a single damn night this century that I got some proper sleep?

16

THEN

The next time I was alone with Jonah – and I mean properly alone, with no one else in the house – was a Saturday afternoon, around a week after our conversation in the garden. Unsurprisingly, we once again ended up in the kitchen. Mum had asked me to make a curry, so I had every excuse to be there. Jonah appeared, then took a knife, came to stand beside me and started chopping peppers as if prepping dinner together like an old married couple.

'So. How about rockhopper penguins?' I asked, breaking the silence.

He glanced up from dicing the second pepper to ascertain whether I was being serious. I hoped the casually amused expression I was trying to adopt worked, because I was feeling anything but casual.

'Have I missed something?'

'Yes!' I exclaimed. 'You've missed the wonder of witnessing rockhopper penguins in the wild.'

He continued staring at me blankly, so I pressed on. 'Or if penguins aren't your thing, which I find very hard to believe –

what kind of aberration doesn't love penguins? – how about whales? Or marmosets. Oh – jackals! Like your hat.'

'What?'

'Wouldn't it be cool to see actual penguins in the wild? Isn't that something worth seeing?' I chopped up a couple more mushrooms with a faux-blasé shrug.

He put the knife down and turned to face me. 'Okay. Is this your attempt to give me a reason not to kill myself?'

'Um... maybe?' My skin was growing so warm I could probably brown the chicken on it. 'I've come up with quite a few. This is just an initial testing the waters. I mean, Ellis and Billy would probably love to see penguins, too.'

'Good idea. I'll be sure to buy three tickets to Antarctica as soon as I've finished here.'

'Um, shouldn't that be four tickets, given that it was my idea?' I attempted an eye-roll but was unable to smother my smile. 'Rude.'

He shook his head but smiled back, and for a second we stood there, grinning at each other, before he resumed chopping, still smiling. His whole face transformed when he smiled. Like a cliff face opening up to reveal a secret garden hiding behind it.

Jonah had a surprising amount of cooking advice for a teenage boy. After he'd inspected the row of spices I'd got ready, he swapped two of them out and added a potato.

'When did you become a curry expert?'

He flicked an eyebrow at me. 'I've been cooking since I was old enough to reach the hob. When you're scratching meals together from whatever leftover crap you can find, you learn how spices can make things edible.'

He shook some cumin over the meat and vegetables, smelled it, then added some more.

'I'll teach you sometime if you like.'

My breath caught behind my ribcage.

'Okay.'

'Or, even better, once exams are over, I'll cook for you.' He gave the pot a stir. 'For all of us, I mean.'

'I'll look forward to it. Now, pass me the coriander.'

Ice now broken, we started chatting as we chopped, and by the time there was a pot of jalfrezi simmering on the stove, I'd told him all about my plans to be a midwife, how I thought helping a new life into the world must be the best job ever. I learned that he'd sat his GCSEs last year – he was already seventeen – but having failed them all was now resitting four and had no plans beyond earning enough money to take care of Ellis and Billy.

'You must miss them,' I said, stating the obvious.

His face seemed to fold in on itself. All he could do was nod.

I started washing up, and that must have given Jonah enough time to compose himself, because he grabbed a tea towel and started talking as he dried.

'Ellis has this thing we do before going to sleep. We never had books at home, until we started going to the library.' He paused in acknowledgement of the library card. 'But there's a tiny one that some social worker gave her once. It's far too babyish now. Falling apart at the spine and covered in scribbles. She keeps it under her pillow. But it's our thing. No matter what's gone on in the day, or the state of Mum and Warren, we wait for Billy to fall asleep – he crashes the second his head hits the pillow – and then read the book together, out loud, doing the same silly voices. Then we say a prayer.' He hunched his shoulders. 'I mean, I stopped believing God answered our prayers years ago, but she wouldn't go to sleep without saying it.'

'What did she pray for?' I asked, after a brief silence.

'That someone would rescue us. Take us away to a beautiful

house where Warren can't find us. With food, toys, a bath and a puppy.' He stopped, screwed his eyes shut. 'And someone to kiss me goodnight, because I kissed her and Billy and I didn't have anyone to kiss me.'

There was nothing to say, nothing I could do except wipe my soapy hand on my jeans and then wrap it around his. We stood there, him gently resting his side against mine, until the front door banged open.

I spun over to the kettle and flicked it on, grabbing two mugs as Mum walked in laden with carrier bags.

'Oh, hello, you two.'

'Hi.' To my relief, she looked more pleased than suspicious at finding us together. Obviously. There was nothing suspicious about two people living in the same house both being in the kitchen.

'Something smells delicious!'

'Yeah.' I took a teaspoon from the drawer and carried on making two mugs of coffee. I didn't even really like coffee. 'Jonah helped.'

'Ooh, that's lovely. Thanks, Jonah.' She beamed as he relieved her of the bags and put them on the table. 'Is this a revision aid?' She nodded at where I was now sploshing in milk.

'We thought we'd do some history together, seeing as we're in the same class,' Jonah said, with the practised ease of someone for whom lying was a survival skill. He then turned and reached behind me to take the sugar pot from its shelf, his arm brushing the back of my head.

'Perfect!' Mum couldn't have been happier. 'You can use the conservatory or the dining room. Oh, and there's chocolate fingers in one of these bags. If you can find them, they're yours.'

I watched as Jonah carefully scooped four heaped teaspoons of sugar into his mug, holding my breath as he stretched behind me again, his sweatshirt riding up to reveal a strip of olive skin.

Beyond flustered, I picked up my mug and turned around at the same time he must have turned towards me with his. Our mugs collided, sloshing boiling hot liquid over both of our hands.

I yelped, he swore, and Mum rushed over as we hurriedly dumped the mugs back on the worktop. She dragged us over to the sink where she stuck our hands under the cold tap and ordered us not to move while she put the shopping away.

We'd ended up with Jonah half behind me, pressed up to my back. Standing there, water cascading over our hands, I could feel his heart pounding against my shoulder. Slowly, carefully, his free hand moved up and rested just below the waistband of my jeans, out of sight of Mum bustling about on the other side of the breakfast bar.

I could barely breathe. Every nerve alert as I stood there, frozen. When Mum finally left the room, I dared to close my eyes, almost imperceptibly leaning back into his solid chest.

I don't know what it was about this boy that made me so bold. I guess it must have been that relentless hope again.

'Do you think that's long enough?' I asked, in a whisper.

I knew it was long enough. My hand was numb.

'Another minute.' His words were a low rasp, the breath tickling the top of my head.

We stood there, our lungs rising and falling in sync, watching the stream of water, until Mum returned. Jonah swiftly moved his body away in one fluid motion.

'Here, let's have a look.' Mum inspected first my hand and then Jonah's. 'I think we caught it in time, nothing serious. If it's sore, then let me know and I'll get you some painkillers. Okay?'

I nodded, drying my hand on the towel Jonah had used for the pots.

'Okay, Jonah? You will let me know if it starts to bother you?'

Jonah must have nodded. I daren't look at him.

She carried on chattering on about nothing while I cleared up the spilt coffee and made fresh drinks, since the first ones were now lukewarm. We fetched our revision books, sat side by side at the dining-room table and, after a hesitant start, spent the next two hours alternating between quizzing each other on history facts – Jonah knew far more than I expected considering how little attention he paid in lessons – and chatting about music and films, school and stupid things we'd seen on the Internet. Nothing serious, nothing to do with his family or life prior to this one. It was the longest conversation I'd ever had with a boy my own age. The intense atmosphere of the kitchen had been replaced with playfulness, what felt like friendship. But a few times, our eyes caught as we laughed about something, and I'd blush and he'd maybe nudge my knee with his or poke my arm with his pen. I didn't know what this was, yet. But it was the best thing ever and, by the time Dad came in to ask us to pack up our things as dinner was ready, I was yearning for more.

17

NOW

It was my second Friday off since deciding that I had to do something about my pitiful life, rather than avoiding it by trying to fix everyone else's on my days off. I pondered my new list, wondering whether to go for a run, do some cleaning or try searching online shops for clothes that didn't make me look as if I were auditioning for *Farmer Wants a Wife*. Instead, my exhausted body decided for me, as, while still mid ponder, I ended up falling asleep.

It was almost lunchtime when I jolted awake. I tumbled off the edge of the sagging sofa onto a pile of Lego, wrestled the ringing phone from my pinafore pocket and saw with a mix of dismay and resignation that it was school. Isla had been struggling all week. Most days had been punctuated with tears, screams and even a few slaps, so this wasn't a complete surprise.

'Libby, are you free for a brief chat?'

It was Janet, the head teacher who'd been at Dad's house for lunch. She'd never called me before. This couldn't be good.

'Is Isla okay?' I pressed a hand against my fluttering heart. 'I mean, I know she's not okay. It's been a difficult week. Her dad sprang the news about a baby on her, and—'

'She's fine.' Janet cut me off with the assertiveness of a professional woman with no time for waffling parents. 'Relatively speaking. She's told us all about her new baby sister, and seems very excited. What I wanted to talk about, if you don't mind, is you.'

'Um. Excuse me?'

'Isla's class have been looking at a topic called "My World and Me". This included talking about their world, what they like about it and what they might like to change.'

'Yes, she told me about it.' A rock of dread began sinking to the bottom of my stomach.

'Isla wrote a very imaginative story about how she'd like her mummy to meet a handsome prince who can take care of you all so, hang on, let me find the quote, "Mummy can stop being tired and sad and lonely because we can move into the prince's palace." She described wanting a bathroom that isn't mouldy, and being able to eat proper pizza because the oven isn't broken. Lights that work, so she doesn't have to use a torch because she gets scared when it's dark.' Janet paused, as if waiting for me to reply, but I couldn't speak.

'Libby, is everything all right at home?'

'Um.' I lay back on the pile of Lego, the bricks digging into my back like a bed of nails. 'The house needs a few repairs. Most of the lights work, actually. But I'm working on it. I've just been busy, with work and... everything.'

And *nothing*. Because I did *nothing* apart from work and apparently do an abysmal job of looking after my kids.

'What I mean to say is, are *you* all right?'

'Yes! I'm fine. Of course I get tired, I'm a single mum running a charity and a business. But why wouldn't I be fine?'

Then I burst into tears. Years of held-back, stuffed-down-so-I-could-pretend-to-still-be-a-relentless-optimist tears.

It was not the brief chat Janet had intended. Twenty minutes later I was still sobbing. I suspected she'd stuck me on speaker-phone and got on with some paperwork, but once I'd started, I couldn't stop. I barely even said anything, just bawled.

Eventually, I managed to wrangle something of myself back together enough to apologise, weakly assure the head teacher that I was having a bad day but was honestly okay and if she asked my dad, he'd confirm that, generally speaking, I was coping fine. Isla had been reading a fairy tale about a girl living in a tumbledown shack who marries a prince, and we'd joked about someone fixing our broken oven. That was all. I was fine, really.

It would be fine.

The truth was, I realised once I'd hung up and buried my head in the sofa in mortification, it was a very long time since anyone apart from my sister or Dad had asked me how I was. It had been even longer since I'd given an honest answer.

So, what are you going to do now? Keep writing things on the new list until it's as long as the old one, or finally do some of them?

The voice inside my head sounded disconcertingly like my mother's. The thought of her turning up on my doorstep and finding all of this was enough to propel me into action.

I clambered up off the floor and found the new list, then wrote beneath it:

Stop ignoring your own parenting advice
Stop being a damn hypocrite
Be a good example to your kids for once

I added one more thing, that only made me cry again:

LEARN HOW TO LOVE LIBBY DONAHUE, AND THEN START ACTING LIKE IT

* * *

I arrived fifteen minutes early to my hair appointment the next day. Shanice, Hazel and the other staff were all busy with clients, so I took a seat near to Hazel's workstation and kept my ears open.

'How are you, anyway?' the middle-aged woman having her roots touched up asked, after a protracted conversation about her recent diabetes diagnosis.

'Oh, you know. Run off my feet trying to keep the four musketeers under control.'

'I thought you had five kids?'

Hazel dabbed a bit more vigorously with the brush she was using to cover the woman's grey. 'Yeah, but Toby's a dad now. As far as I'm concerned, if he's old enough to have a kid, it's up to him to stop acting like one.'

'I always liked your Toby,' the woman mused. 'Even in his delinquent phase, when he smashed up the park gazebo, he did a lovely job putting it right.'

Hazel huffed but said nothing.

'And you're a granny now!' her client went on. 'That's lovely! I can't wait for one of mine to give me a grandbaby, though I can't see it happening any time soon. You must be over the moon. All the loveliness of a baby and none of the responsibility.'

'I wish!' Hazel snapped, adding so much dye to the woman's thinning hair her scalp was now glowing Raspberry Rebel. 'They're living at mine, so I've got the sleepless nights, baby junk everywhere and a hungover teenage girl snoring in my dining room. The only time she gets out of bed is to go out, use up all my hot water or empty my fridge.'

'Ah. Perhaps you need to have a family conference, set some ground rules.'

'I'm past talking and way past ground rules,' Hazel practically growled as she stepped back to frown at her handiwork. 'I'm too old for this crap, Pauline. I've laid down my ultimatum and now it's their choice. Either I come home this evening to a spotless house, settled baby and a hot dinner or they can find someone else to sponge off. It's not too much to ask them to clean up their own mess and cook dinner once in a while, is it?'

'It certainly isn't!' Pauline said, cowering slightly. 'Anyway, have you been watching that new crime drama with the actress from Nottingham? I can never remember her name, but she's got a lovely way about her...'

'Libby!' Shanice strode over and grabbed a lock of my wayward hair. 'I've been itching to get started on this for days. Why anyone who gets free haircuts would allow things to end up in this state is a mystery. Get in that chair and let's sort it out.'

An hour later, my hair was sorted. When Shanice had asked for my thoughts about the cut, I'd ummed, aahed and mumbled about a new start and not wanting to look like a farmer's wife until she'd burst out laughing and told me to sit back, relax, and let her do her thing.

It had to be said, her thing was fabulous.

The wild mahogany frizz had become shoulder-length, glossy curls that somehow made me look more mature and yet years younger at the same time. Shanice stuck some products in a bag, gave me a brief lecture on what to do with them and when to come back to the salon and then made everyone else give me a round of applause before I left.

'Eh, Libby, I hope you've got somewhere fancy to show that

off!' Jade, who had also been one of the Bloomers and now worked in Snips as a beautician, called.

'Even better, *someone*!' The young woman getting her nails done laughed.

As the rest of the salon joined in, adding a couple of whoops and a wolf whistle, only one person flashed into my head.

If last night's continuation of what seemed to be a slow-motion emotional breakdown had proven anything, it was that I was in no fit state to be dating anyone. But a drink and a catch-up with Jonah? Somewhere with a working oven in case we wanted some cake?

Now that I might be ready to handle.

In a fit of amazing-hair madness, as soon as I got home I opened my emails to find where Ellis had added his number as an emergency contact on the application form. Then, in a blatant breach of data protection, I messaged to ask if he and Ellis wanted a coffee sometime. I didn't even read it through myself, let alone check with Nicky whether it was appropriate. Although, yes, I did then spend the rest of the day checking my phone while faking my interest and enjoyment in hearing the kids describe, on a seemingly never-ending loop, how amazing Brayden and Silva's house was and how they had a soda stream, a hot tub and a giant television. Once they'd gone to bed, I got to spend my Saturday night waiting for the non-existent reply while agonising about what the hell I was thinking.

I only checked my phone for half the night, because the other half was taken up with something else entirely. It was nearly one in the morning when I heard a car slowing down outside. This was a quiet road, and any traffic was noticeable, but when the lights swung around to shine through my bedroom window, I sat up and paid attention.

I held my breath, hand clutching my phone as, after a brief silence, two doors slammed and then the car reversed off. Had someone got out? Who? Why? At what point should I call the police? Or at least Nicky?

The knock on the door sent my heart scrabbling up my throat.

Not a burglar, then. Or a murderer.

Then again, I thought as I shrugged into a big cardigan and gingerly opened my bedroom door, it could be a murderer pretending to have a flat tyre, or be lost, or some other pretext to get a vulnerable woman to let them into their house...

Another knock, slightly louder this time. I'd have to answer it, or Isla would wake up, and if she thought people were sneaking about in the middle of the night, she'd never sleep again. After tiptoeing down the stairs, I grabbed Finn's plastic sword from the mound of junk at the bottom.

'Hello?' I called, aiming for assertive but ending up sounding very much like a woman scared witless. I inched along the dark hallway in the feeble glow of my phone torch, clicking the outside light switch before remembering that the bulb had gone months ago.

Was that a large shadow looming through the tiny window in the door, or was it my rattled imagination?

When they knocked for the third time, my instincts decided to be more afraid of Isla waking up than of whoever it was, and I flung the door open before my rational brain could overrule it.

18

'Libby!'

I raised the torch beam until it hit the blinking, squinting face in front of me.

'Toby?'

'Yeah.'

'And Hazel?'

He nodded, lifting up the car seat he was holding as confirmation.

'What are you doing here?' After the conversation I'd earwigged in the salon, I could have a good guess why Toby wasn't at home. Why he was standing at my front door with a rucksack on his back was another matter.

'Courtney came home stinking of weed and Mum went ballistic. She'd left this list of stuff we needed to do, but Hazel's teething again so it was impossible to get done by myself. I asked the others to help and they grassed me up, so she was already mad about that.'

'Courtney didn't help?' I stood back to let him in. Whatever the situation, I wasn't about to leave a tiny baby on my doorstep.

'She'd been out since yesterday morning. I tried to message but she's blocked me again.' He followed me into the living room. 'To be honest, Libby, I don't think it would have made any difference. She only came home to pack a bag.'

'She's moved out?'

'Moved before she was pushed.'

'Where's she gone?'

He collapsed onto my sofa, his large frame causing the cushions to sag so low the mess I'd stuffed underneath was probably jabbing into his backside. 'I dunno. Someone sent me a Snap of her with some bloke. I don't think it's in Bigley, though. She's been getting the train up to Sheffield to hang with her cousin and their mates.'

Sheffield was nearly an hour's drive away.

'What did she say about Hazel?'

Toby ran a weary hand over his face. 'She said she couldn't deal with it right now. Why should she get landed with her, just because she's the woman?'

'Oh, Toby. I'm so sorry.'

Hazel began to grizzle, so I gently lifted her out of the car seat and cradled her against my shoulder, adopting the universal bounce-and-sway motion to settle her again.

'Don't be. I wouldn't have let her take Hazel if she'd tried.'

'Well, I'm sorry that she didn't want to stick with you both and work something out. I'm sorry she found being a mum so hard, and you've been left to figure parenting out on your own.'

He sat up. 'Yeah, but I'm not on my own, am I? I've got my sleeping bag so will be fine on the sofa, and Hazel can go in the travel cot from the cabin. We'll be no trouble.'

'You want to stay here?'

He wanted to stay *here*?

'You said if I needed any help to just come over.'

I wracked my brain, trying to dig out the conversation we'd had earlier in the week. I'd said I'd help, but couldn't remember saying anything about my sofa. Everything in me wanted to call them another taxi, or at least ask his mum to take them back for one more night so we could find an alternative option tomorrow. I couldn't manage my own family's problems, let alone take on this one.

Then I caught a glimpse behind Toby's determined expression – the raw fear of finding himself homeless with a baby when in so many ways still a child himself. I felt the warmth of Hazel's head as she nestled into my neck.

'You can stay here tonight,' I conceded. 'The key to the cabin is hanging on a hook by the noticeboard in the kitchen. I'll fetch some bedding.'

It wasn't much later before we had the travel cot set up beside the sofa, Hazel gently snoring inside it, and Toby huddled under a duvet sipping a hot chocolate in between stuffing down slices of toast.

'Have you let your mum know where you are?' I asked.

He dropped his head. 'She's blocked me, too.'

Wow.

I was almost as worried about Hazel, acting so callously towards her son and granddaughter, as I was about them. I decided to wait and message her myself at a more reasonable hour. If she wanted to know whether Toby was safe in the meantime, she could unblock him.

He talked for a while longer about Courtney, the building tension in the house, how his college grades had suffered as a result. I handed him a tissue when he eventually crumpled into tears, and then tossed propriety aside and gave him what he really needed – a proper hug.

It was nearly three by the time I gently insisted he tried to get some sleep. An hour later Hazel started wailing for another feed.

Thank goodness it's Sunday, was my last comprehensible thought before I finally drifted off to the dawn chorus starting up in the trees outside my window. *I can sleep in a little.*

It was eight minutes past six precisely when Isla ran squealing into my bedroom, having discovered a strange man peeing in the bathroom.

'I'm so sorry, Libby!' Toby gabbled, his cheeks scarlet. 'The lock on the bathroom door's broken. I didn't think anyone was up yet, so it wouldn't matter.'

Tucking Isla in bed with me, I snatched a desperate few more minutes of sleep before Hazel demonstrated just how loud a teething baby can be.

* * *

I was whipping up pancake batter, thanks to Toby demolishing the rest of the bread before we'd got up, nursing my headache with a super-strong coffee and keeping one eye on Finn and Isla, happily amusing Hazel with funny faces, when my phone beeped with a text.

After glancing at it, I immediately put down the whisk and took another gulp of coffee.

Jonah.

> I'd love that. It's not easy pinning down Ellis at the moment, but she said she'd come over to Bigley before the class on Thursday, if you wanted to have dinner somewhere? Otherwise, might have to wait a couple of weeks.

I did some mental calculations then messaged Dad:

Any chance you could babysit around teatime on Thursday? I'll treat you all to fish and chips x

We were sitting at the table, Finn squirting the last of the syrup on his fifth pancake, when Toby sauntered in.

'Right, the lock on the bathroom's sorted. I noticed the showerhead holder was loose, can't figure out how you shower without having to hold it in position.'

Yep, that sounded about right.

'Anyway, I've tightened it up so it should be steady for now.'

'Would you like a pancake?' I asked, blinking in a blend of shock and gratitude. The thought of standing in a shower with two free hands to shampoo my hair felt too good to be true.

'Just the one?' Toby winked, going over to pick up Hazel and plant a kiss on her wispy head.

'Mum said there's only enough batter left for one more,' Finn announced, smearing at the chocolate spread on his face with the back of his hand.

I handed him a paper towel. 'There was only one more for boys who've already eaten a plateful. Toby can have as many as he likes.'

* * *

I'd just flipped the final pancake when Dad replied:

Sorry, Libby. I'm spending the evening with Janet. I hope it's nothing urgent.

Ugh. It hurt when Dad said no, because this confirmed all my fears about depending on him too much, although it did mean I could delay telling him why I'd asked. I usually only asked for extra help when I had a meeting or important appointment.

For a second I debated asking Brayden. But I was still processing how I felt about Brayden and Silva wanting to involve the children more in their lives, and, alongside feeling anxious about where this was heading, I still didn't trust him not to cancel at the last minute.

Nicky was at the surgery until six-thirty on a Thursday.

But, oh, the thought of having a proper conversation with Jonah, having some of my questions answered.

Those words, shining at me from my phone screen:

I'd love that

It was hard to contain how much I'd love it, too.

Could I bring the kids to dinner? Glancing up to see Finn brandishing the metal balloon whisk an inch from his sister's face, declaring he was a mad scientist about to scoop her eye out, Isla already hitching her little lungs in distress, I ditched that idea.

Toby, pacing up and down the kitchen with his daughter on his hip, picked up a pancake and stuffed it in his mouth, grabbed the whisk and tossed it over to the sink, where it landed perfectly in the washing-up bowl, and then plonked Hazel in Isla's lap, showing Isla how to hold her safely and instantly distracting her from the fear of losing an eye.

'The shower curtain needs more fittings, but the hardware store should have the right ones.' He glanced up at me, keeping a steady hand on Hazel. 'I'll grab some of the mould killer Mum uses when I'm there, too. Best to sort it before it gets into the plaster. An hour or two scrubbing should do the trick. I'm in college tomorrow, but could sort it once I'm back?'

I stood for a moment and tried to catch my breath. Here was this man-child, his baby and countless associated problems in my house, inserting himself into my life. My life, like my house, had more than enough problems already. I couldn't take this on. I simply *couldn't*.

But then I thought about the shower I'd had that morning, dropping the giant shampoo bottle Shanice had given me onto my toe because I was trying to open it one-handed while holding the stupid shower head upright. When I'd bent to pick it up, water had squirted all over the bathroom. Isla had slipped in it when she'd rushed in five minutes later desperate for a wee, yanking the shower curtain off the wall as she'd fallen, and then in the ensuing drama she'd wet herself.

I knew how impossible it would be to find somewhere for a teenage dad and his baby to live. The refuges I worked with only took women. There was no way I was about to send Toby and his daughter to a homeless hostel or the kind of temporary housing the council might scrabble to find at urgent notice.

I liked Toby. I loved Hazel. It wasn't her fault her gums were sore.

When I'd decided I needed some new people in my life, this wasn't quite what I'd had in mind, but that didn't mean it wasn't the right thing to do.

Actually, it felt like one of the foolhardiest things I'd ever done, but I did it anyway. Perhaps there was an optimist still lurking inside me after all.

'Toby, how would you feel about staying a bit longer? I mean, just until we found somewhere more suitable?'

Toby winked at me, six feet three of eighteen-year-old charm. 'I thought you'd never ask.'

'I don't suppose you happen to be free on Thursday...'

* * *

Nicky messaged me mid morning. Probably in between swimming a few miles down the river Trent and cycling back home, drying off in the slipstream.

BBQ is ready to go, see you all at 1

I could have objected to the assumption we were free, but I didn't have the energy for comedy that morning. I took a nosy at Nicky's social media to confirm she'd been out with Theo's family on another adventure – sunrise kayaking, this time – which meant that they'd be at the barbecue, usually an automatic no for me.

I had a decent excuse to say no, for once. I had to buy more food – an extraordinary amount, if Toby carried on like this – and sort a more suitable spare bed than my woeful sofa.

On the other hand, Finn and Isla would love to see their auntie and uncle, and mass of extended family. They might even stop squabbling. If Isla got upset, we could always come home...

I sent a message back.

Can I bring a baby?

Nicky replied with a string of shocked and happy emojis.

Have you got me a baby as a present? Perfect gift but I'm not sure it's legal...

* * *

Toby was fine with us taking baby Hazel off his hands for a few hours. I spoke to his mum, and she agreed that if he walked round to pack up the rest of his and Hazel's things, then she'd drop them back in her car. There was still nothing from Courtney, and when Toby tried her friends, they ignored him.

'Probably all still asleep,' he said, trying not to sound as disheartened as he must have felt. 'I mean, she can't ignore me forever.' He tugged at his curls. 'Well. She can. But she can't ignore her daughter. Can she?'

I patted his shoulder. It wouldn't be the first time I'd seen a teenage mother run away, leaving her baby behind. Far more often, they took the baby with them, but Courtney had been dissociating herself for a while.

'I'll speak to her social worker tomorrow. They'll do what they can to find her.'

'They won't try to take Hazel off me, will they?' Toby asked, his face turning ashen.

'Are you on the birth certificate?'

'Of course!' he said, sticking out his chest.

'Then you have parental responsibility. Hazel's social worker will want to make sure she's safe, and being cared for, but that should be obvious.'

'I'm living with a parenting teacher. They can't ask for more than that.' He let out a nervous laugh.

'Have you thought about childcare for Hazel when you're at college?' I asked.

'They've got a nursery. I could see if they have space. We break up in two weeks, anyway.'

'Perfect.' I nearly added something about how I could look after her for the next two Fridays. A week ago I'd have offered without even thinking about it. But a week ago I'd not been making plans with my new housemate while prepping a salad to take to a busy family gathering, wondering whether the playsuit I'd found in a forgotten heap at the back of the wardrobe would work for my dinner with Jonah – *Jonah!* – in a few days' time. So, I kept quiet for now. If there was no space at the nursery, then maybe I'd think about offering. The key being the thinking part. I was done with knee-jerk reactions. Time for some proactive positive choices. Small yet significant.

* * *

The barbecue was okay. More than okay. Maybe even nice. I spent most of it too tense to eat, nervous that no one would speak to me, equally anxious that they would and I'd have to think of a reply that didn't make me sound as much of a lost, lonely loser as I felt.

It made my throat clench to see Finn and Isla running about with Theo's younger brother, chattering to his mum and playing peekaboo with his sister's toddler. Isla cried, once, when a fly landed on her sausage, but, before I could swoop in, the people nearest to her gently laughed it off in a way that defused the situation perfectly.

Nicky was gobsmacked when I told her that Toby and Hazel were staying at the cottage.

'How long for?' she demanded to know, along with a heap of other questions like where would they sleep, would I charge them any keep, did I trust Toby and what if he also did a runner and left me with Hazel?

I smiled, shrugged, said not to worry, I was a grown woman and we'd figure it out.

'Who are you and what have you done with my baby sister?' She laughed, eyes round with amazement.

The only stumble in the afternoon was when I noticed the postcard, tucked under a pile of letters on the hall table. I wouldn't have thought much of it, except that I'd had that same postcard a couple of weeks ago. I resisted the urge to flip it over, instead going to find Nicky, Hazel on her lap.

'You got a postcard?'

She stopped, her grimace confirming who it was from before she answered. 'She's having a fabulous time in wherever she is now, but even the longest roads must come to an end. Home and hearth calls, or some BS like that.'

'Do you think she's serious?' Despite the June sunshine, my bare arms had broken out in goosebumps. 'And what does she mean by home? Is she expecting Dad to welcome her back?'

Nicky shrugged. 'It's a horrible stunt to pull if she doesn't turn up. But then, since when did our feelings come into it?'

She screwed up her eyes, cuddling Hazel closer. 'Part of me really wants her not to come, to just be making throwaway comments that never become a reality. But if she is, then what? We never see her again? Never get to explain how awful it was for Dad to have no proper closure? How hard it can be waiting for her to contact us, or how we created a stupid Facebook account just so she'd know we were still alive?'

'And then we get a call one day to say she's sunk in the middle of the ocean?' I shook my head. 'I hate myself for feeling so angry about how she controlled all contact, even if I can sort of understand why. The only way to deal with her not being around is to get on without her. But she owes us the chance to forgive her. Or at least to ask why she needed to leave us as well as Dad.'

'You've always been so much kinder than me, Libby. I want the chance to shout in her face. To show her what she's missing and then decide whether she gets to not miss it any more.'

I wrapped my arm around her, grateful to be able to share this pain with someone else who understood. 'Either way, then, we're sort of hoping she shows up at some point.'

'Ugh. It would seem so.' She buried her nose in Hazel's fluff of hair. 'Would be nice if she had the courtesy to let us know when.'

'Another couple of postcards, first?'

She narrowed her eyes. 'My guess is three.'

My sister always was the smart one.

19

THEN

'Is Bronah sending you messages?'

It was nearly a week after my study session with Jonah. There'd been more secretive smiles, the odd stilted sentences at dinner – or rather, I was stilted; Jonah just sounded uninterested. I'd skulked downstairs and into the garden late one evening, but it had been empty. I'd barely seen him at school. I'd not even told Alicia and Katie that he was living with us, because we were meant to keep these things confidential, and I didn't want to discuss Jonah King with people who had pronounced him to be either creepy-hot or just plain creepy. Only my journal knew the truth about how I felt about him.

I'd tried to convince myself that it was better – vital – that we maintained a safe distance, giving my crush the time to fizzle out before I did something awful. But then I'd remember leaning back against him as we stood by the kitchen sink, the flash of something deeper in his eyes when we'd laughed together. It was terrible and thrilling all twisted up together. Indulging in forbidden fantasies about Jonah might have seemed harmless when I was certain that was all they'd ever be. It had become dangerous the second his hand rested on my hip.

And today Nicky had followed me into my bedroom as soon as we'd got home from school.

'He doesn't even have my number,' I said, frowning.

'Not texts. The songs in the car.'

I flopped onto the bed, resting back on my elbows. 'What are you talking about?'

I knew exactly what she was talking about. Since Easter, Nicky's school year had been allowed to stay at home on study leave. Today she'd gone in for a revision session, the first time she'd been in the car with us in ages. It was also, coincidentally, the first time Jonah had played the new CD he'd made by burning tracks from the family computer.

'Firstly, it's all your favourite music. No one who's ever met Jonah would believe he's a fan of Bruno Mars.'

'So? Maybe he's being nice. The last couple of songs were bands I'd never heard of.'

'That was my secondly!' Nicky sat down on my desk chair, arms folded, eyes animated. 'Did you listen to the lyrics?'

'Not really.' I shrugged as if bored by the whole conversation. The truth was, I'd listened to every word, and any second now Nicky was going to spot my heart thumping against my school shirt.

'That emo song about secretly falling for the girl the guy was living with, pretending he didn't care, or long to touch *her dark hair*.'

'What?' I lay back on the bed so she couldn't see my expression. 'That doesn't mean anything. He's probably never even listened to the words himself.'

'"I made her a mix tape to tell her I love her, 'cos I'll never be able to tell her that I love her"? And that other song was literally about waiting in the garden in the middle of the night for the girl you can't stop thinking about. You have to admit it'd be a weird coincidence.'

The day before, Jonah had put on a song about a messed-up boy being in love with a 'nice girl'. The chorus was all about how he needed to stay away because he was 'too broken to not break her heart'.

I'd wondered, obviously. When I'd glanced in the wing mirror from my position in the back seat and caught his eyes on mine, my breath had frozen in my chest. I had no idea where he'd found these songs, but if even Nicky thought they might be about me, then surely they might be about me?

This was bad.

If only my heart agreed.

'Ew, no, Nicky!' I sat up, deciding to go for incredulous. 'That song was about a garden *party*. And did you hear the last verse of the other one – the man set the house on fire! You're taking random lines and twisting them into something... sick.' I shook my head. 'Do you honestly believe our new foster brother – *Bronah* – would be sending *me* – the girl he barely acknowledges exists, unless forced into uncomfortable conversation by Mum and Dad – secret messages via CD? Jonah would never be interested in me. We have nothing in common outside of randomly ending up living in the same house. If he did like me, do you really think he'd jeopardise his placement here by doing something about it? Even if he was that reckless, sending secret song-lyric messages happens in high-school romcoms about nerdy girls taking their glasses off and suddenly becoming gorgeous. It's not real life.'

Nicky pursed her lips, considering all this.

'Okay. Fair points. I just needed to ask in case there was something going on. I get that you and Jonah would be world's most unlikely couple. But, I dunno, he seems different sometimes, when you're around.'

I actually scoffed. 'Different? How?'

'I don't know.' She chewed on her plait. 'Less withdrawn? As if he relaxes a bit more when you're there.'

It took everything I had to screw up my nose rather than float away on a cloud of happiness. 'That feels a bit... Milo.'

Milo lived with us for five weeks when he was six. I'd been eleven, and initially flattered when he chose me as the target of his hero-worship. It had been less fun when he'd started trailing after me everywhere, including creeping into my bedroom in the middle of the night to check I was still alive – his older sister had died from a heart condition, triggering the chain of events that had led to him being taken into care.

'Jonah is definitely not a Milo,' Nicky said.

That was true.

'I'm a very non-threatening person,' I mused. 'And a year younger than him. He's bound to feel comfortable with me compared to the intimidating soon-to-be med-student who's also edgy and popular.'

'You think he finds me intimidating?' She stood up, stretching her lithe arms towards the ceiling. I dared to hope the interrogation was almost over.

'Most people do.'

'Okay, time to start calling him "Bronah" to his face. He needs to know I'm as geeky as the rest of you.'

'Nicky?' I asked, although she was already halfway out of the door.

'What?'

'Promise me you'll drop this? It's enough having the school vampire being my foster brother. You implying there's something else is grim and makes it even harder to try being friendly.'

'Message received and understood.' She gave a mock salute then disappeared.

After an evening meal where I managed to avoid even looking at Jonah, I spent the rest of the evening doodling song lyrics in my journal. The following day, I left a note in his blazer pocket:

> *When there's a storm outside but you get to stay in all day reading a brilliant book under a blanket, with a hot chocolate and a massive piece of cranberry tiffin, a dog asleep on your feet.*

A couple of days later, Jonah's car playlist had a new song, by Bob Dylan. It was called 'Shelter from the Storm'.

20

NOW

I came back from the barbecue in the early evening and found my living room empty of both Toby, and all Toby and Hazel's things. He wasn't in the kitchen, or anywhere else in the house.

Leaving a sleepy Finn and Isla watching a film in their pyjamas, I carried Hazel over to the cabin to fetch the baby bath we used to practise bathing with dolls. Opening the door into the back room, I discovered what had happened to Toby.

'Wow.'

'Not bad, is it?' He grinned, placing a stuffed toy on the wooden cot now positioned in one corner of the room.

I took in the fold-out bed, all made up with Spider-Man bedding. Shelving units that had previously been a chaotic, jumbled mess were now organised rows of equipment, books and handouts. The new order had left a whole shelf now full of clothes for Toby and Hazel. A desk that was supposed to be for Nicky but in reality had been a dumping ground for yet more mess was now a changing station. Toby pulled open the drawers to reveal neat stacks of nappies and wipes. Underneath it was more baby stuff, including a plastic bath.

It looked crowded, but I had to admit it was cosy.

'Toby, this is an amazing job, but you can't live in my office.'

'Yeah. Not for long, anyway. But I was wondering about this?'

He led me to the old walk-in storeroom next to the bathroom.

'What if we cleaned this out, tidied it and I put in some shelving here.' He pointed to one wall. 'And then a desk here. Get one of those proper racks for the gym balls. My mate Baz could easily fit a sink in this corner, with a little unit for your kettle, fridge here, shelves up there. A new blind, lamp, coat of paint. It'd be a nice space with a bit of time and effort.'

'While I have to agree this could be a good space, you and Hazel can't live in the cabin.'

'Why not?' His brow wrinkled up; he looked genuinely confused.

'How's it going to work when I'm teaching? I'll be working through the summer when there's no college.'

'Then me and Hazel can help out with Finn and Isla in the cottage, can't we?' He winked. 'It'll probably take me the best part of the summer to get all the jobs sorted. I thought I could decorate while I'm at it. Sort of instead of paying rent.'

'If you work on my house as speedily as you've done this, it'll be showroom ready by the time school breaks up.'

'Then I'll start on the garden.' Toby's smile disappeared. 'Seriously, Libby. We're that grateful you've said Hazel and I can move in. I can't keep sleeping on your sofa, can I?'

Um, wasn't the agreement that you'd stay until we found somewhere more suitable?

We agreed that he could stay for the summer, providing it had no impact on my classes. Rent would be in the form of DIY, gardening and childcare.

'Your pregnant mums and dads won't know we're here. Especially the posh ones. We're not only going to be no trouble, before long you'll be wondering how you managed without us.'

I had to admit that I already sort of was.

* * *

Monday morning, Isla was not happy. That deadly combination of tired and wired after a weekend visiting her dad's house for the first time, adjusting to fun new housemates and a full-on day with family – she was more fretful and grouchy than usual. We were so late I'd given up on checking the clock by the time I finally wrestled her into shoes that 'felt wrong' and grabbed the lunchbox of food that she of course now hated, despite having demanded it in the supermarket a few days earlier.

Finn was a coiled spring of frustration. 'It's PE this morning!' he whined, standing in the doorway, kicking the doorframe while Isla and I underwent the pantomime of me putting on her second shoe while she took off the first one. 'I'm missing my favourite lesson because of my stupid sister! It's not fair! You should make her go to school with no shoes on, then she'll learn.'

'You know I can't do that.' I gasped, finally doing up a buckle.

'Then I should get to walk by myself!' he yelled, spinning around and marching down the path. 'I'm sick of her ruining my life!'

'I'll walk with him,' Toby said, appearing from the kitchen as he crammed in a corner of toast, Hazel in a sling across his chest. 'We oldest kids have to stick together.'

Isla stopped crying, mouth dropping open as she twisted her head to watch Toby hurrying off down the path after her brother. Without another word, she stuffed her foot into the other shoe, grabbed her bag and lunchbox and started running.

'Wait for me, Toby!'

'Come on, then.' Toby held out his hand and she grabbed it gleefully. 'I think Mum could do with a few minutes' peace before work starts, so I'll take you to school today.'

The second they'd disappeared around the overgrown hedge, I sat on the doorstep and cried.

* * *

By the time Toby returned I was reclining on my restored bench, cradling a mug of tea and trying to summon the energy to start getting ready for the Bloomers arriving in an hour.

'That was some morning,' he said, coming to sit beside me.

It was all I could do to nod, scared to speak in case I started crying again.

'Is it always like that?'

'No.' I shook my head. 'Well. It's often *like* that, but rarely that bad.'

'I thought a baby was hard work.' He blew out a comical sigh.

'Thank you for taking them to school. This has been... forty minutes of bliss.'

We sat for a minute, watching the butterflies dancing around a patch of purple thistles poking through the broken fence.

'Can I make a suggestion?' Toby asked.

I bristled slightly at the thought of an eighteen-year-old having a suggestion to make about my parenting challenges, but on the off chance it was about DIY, I nodded for him to go ahead.

'Maybe you should find time for this more often.'

You think?

'That's a great suggestion. I don't suppose you have an extra couple of hours in the day I could borrow, do you? Because I can't seem to find any. And by the evening, when I finally have some time to catch up on useful things like cleaning or reading a book, I'm knackered. Some days I barely have the energy to eat.'

'You might find if you took a bit of time out for yourself at the start of the day, the rest of it seems easier.'

'Maybe.'

'Also...'

'Also, what?' I huffed. 'Might as well tell me what you think!'

'Have you thought about being more... organised?'

I had to laugh. 'Am I seriously being told to sort my life out by a technically homeless, teenage dad?'

'Okay, so technically I'm not homeless. First job of the day, once I've spoken to college, is to transfer everything official to this address. Secondly, it's like those boiling frogs Nicky was telling us about. I didn't realise how bad things had got with Courtney, it happened so slowly. I needed you to give me some hard truths. This is me returning the favour. How much better do you feel having had a bit of time to sit and soak up the sunshine this morning?'

I had to admit, I felt like a whole new person.

'You've seen how it is, Toby. I know it makes sense. But I've got a lot of stuff going on.'

'Well, like I said, it's a good job you've got me, then, isn't it? How about I cook dinner a couple of times a week, play with the kids while you use the extra time to do whatever else needs doing?'

'What do you get out of this?' I asked.

'A home. A big sister.' He rolled his shoulders. 'Someone to show me how the hell to be a dad.'

* * *

'Hey, Libby, is it true you're bunking up with Toby Smithson nowadays?' Sienna asked, interrupting the point I was making about water birth with a flutter of her fake eyelashes.

'Ooh, cougar!' someone else crowed. 'Love it, Libby. You deserve a bit of fun!'

'He's more than a bit!' a girl everyone called Tiny cackled. 'Me and Tobes had a load of fun before Courtney came along, if you get me.'

'Yes, we all get you, thanks, Tiny,' Nicky called over the hoots and catcalls. She glanced at me, and to my disbelief there was a glint of amusement in her eyes.

'This is not funny!' I hissed at her.

'This is not funny!' she said to the group, trying not to laugh. 'Libby is most definitely not bunking up with Toby, or anyone else. Toby is temporarily renting—'

'Permanently!' Toby, supposedly making himself scarce, popped up at the window, brandishing a pair of pruning shears.

'This class is confidential!' Nicky called back.

'Heard my name, didn't I?' He winked, leaning against the windowsill.

'Ooh, Toby, are you back on the market?' Tiny asked, sticking out her three-days-overdue bump.

'Nah. Only one girl got my heart,' he said, nodding to where Hazel was snoozing in her pushchair under a tree. 'Sorry, ladies. Call me in about eighteen years.'

'Well, I hope that clears things up,' Nicky went on. 'Toby is renting a room from Libby. I'm sure she'd have done the same for any of you, had you needed a place to stay.'

'Aw, she would have done as well, wouldn't you, Libby?' The room buzzed with assent about how lovely and helpful I was, and how I'd do anything for anyone, including giving up my own bed if necessary.

Maybe I *was* too nice.

* * *

'Am I too nice?' I asked Dad, when he dropped the kids off after school.

'I'm not sure that's the word I'd use,' he said, gently.

'What word would you use?'

'A helpaholic,' he said, without hesitation.

'Wow. You've thought about this.'

He handed me a glass of juice. It was twenty-eight degrees outside and proving impossible to stay cool.

'Have you ever considered whether you spend so much time doing things for other people because it provides an excuse not to tackle your own problems?'

'I'm doing everything I can to help Isla,' I said, a lump of humiliation in my throat. 'What problems am I avoiding?'

He shrugged. 'You tell me. All I know is that my daughter rarely smiles, pretty much never laughs. I can't remember the last time she expressed being truly content, or happy.'

I almost choked on my juice. 'I was happy and content this morning!'

I remembered that moment, sitting on the bench with a mug of tea, watching nature do its thing.

'That's good to hear. I hope you can find more of those moments.'

I pulled out my phone and set my alarm for six-thirty. An hour earlier than usual. That evening, while Toby cooked a pan of chilli, I scooped up the kids' uniforms, washed what was dirty and set out what could be worn another day. I checked their school planners and made sure they had everything they needed in their bags. While I washed up, Toby helped them make lunches for tomorrow.

I then used the momentum to choose my outfit for Tuesday's antenatal class. My nicest jeans and a silky blouse, because Brayden would be there and, while I no longer cared whether he found me attractive or not, I wanted him to think I wasn't a disaster.

Feeling strangely energised rather than even more tired than usual, instead of slumping in front of the television, I poured myself a modest glass of wine and went into the garden with a book and a blanket. The kids' windows were open, I would hear if they needed me. Toby and Hazel were nowhere to be seen, and for a long hour, I didn't even need the book. I sipped my wine, watched the sunset over the treetops and, for the first time in what felt like forever, I simply breathed.

21

When my alarm went off an hour earlier than usual, it took everything I'd got to avoid the snooze button, instead pushing back the covers and slowly hauling myself up. I crept downstairs like a teenager sneaking off to a party, tiptoeing about the kitchen as I made a mug of tea before slipping outside into the crisp morning air.

Oh, it was a tiny slice of heaven. I spent half an hour alternating between thinking and not thinking, and another fifteen minutes reading my book. I was upstairs, out of the shower and half-dressed when Isla burst into my bedroom. Rather than bracing myself as usual, I was ready for her.

'Hey, lovely. How did you sleep?'

'Okay.' She narrowed her eyes suspiciously. 'I had a dream about a hedgehog pricking me with its prickles.'

'Ouch! Did you feel the prickles in your dream?'

'No.' She folded her arms. 'Why are you so woken up already?'

'I got up a bit earlier than usual. Shall we see if Finn's up or get some breakfast just the two of us, first?'

'Breakfast just two of us!' Suspicion evaporating, she thundered down the stairs loud enough to wake her brother up. Thankfully, by the time she had a plate of toast with a banana milkshake, she was happy enough to share her mummy with Finn.

The rest of the morning went, if not like clockwork, not like a clock that is dysfunctional and broken. We were ready on time. Isla had cried only once. She'd laughed her head off when Hazel had thrown up down Toby's shirt.

'This was good, wasn't it?' Finn asked as we walked to school, spotting a rabbit in one of the fields alongside the path. 'Shall we do our lunch the night before every day? Maybe then Isla will stop crying all the time.'

I knew it would take more than an organised morning, or a mum who'd had an hour to gather herself before the onslaught of the day. But we would be doing our lunch the night before, that much I did know.

My buoyant mood carried on into the first half of the antenatal class with Brayden and Silva, up until the lunchbreak, when Brayden cornered me by the coffee mugs.

'Liz, as you'll have noticed, I'm struggling to interact with you today.'

'Oh?' No, actually, I hadn't. It had been a practical session so far, looking at comfortable positions to support labour, which mostly involved the couples working together while I wandered about making the odd helpful suggestion and answering any questions.

'To be honest, I nearly didn't come. I wasn't sure I could trust myself to keep my cool and put our private lives to one side. You know what I'm referring to.'

'Sorry, I really don't.' My mind started flicking through possible reasons for Brayden to lose his cool with me. He'd seemed in a great mood when he'd dropped Finn and Isla off on Saturday. I couldn't imagine what had happened since.

'It's only fair that I tell you Silva and I are discussing whether we need to apply for custody. The plan was to start some weekend sleepovers, a few days away in the school holidays. But we are gravely concerned.'

'Um, what? What plan?'

'I knew you were struggling. But at this point, the question needs to be asked whether you're simply clueless and desperate, or have genuinely lost your mind.'

'Excuse me? How dare you speak to me like that?' I still had no idea what was going on, but my hands had started trembling with rage.

'How dare *you*? This must breach all professional standards. If it was the other way around, and a male in a position of authority had acted like this with a teenage mother, people would be contacting the police. Maybe they already have. You'd be fired if you weren't your own boss. What the hell does Nicky say about it?'

To my horror, the rest of the class had at some point tuned in to Brayden's increasingly loud rant.

'Are you accusing me of something, Brayden? Because I think you'd probably best say what the hell it is I'm meant to have done rather than throw cryptic statements around.'

He turned up his nose in a sneer. 'Are you denying that you've shacked up with a teenager from one of your classes? Moved him into the house with my children, and got him playing daddy?'

There was a collective intake of breath from everyone in the room, including me. I waited a moment, forced myself to take a couple of slow, deep breaths and counted backwards from ten.

'Yes, I'm denying it. Where on earth did you hear that?'

'A concerned parent at Bigley Primary told me that this *boy* walked the children to school. Isla was very happy to tell everyone that he'd moved in, and was going to be her new daddy.'

'And you believed it?' I pulled back my shoulders, ignoring the very real urge to vomit in horror, and tipped up my chin, looking my ex-husband right in the eye. 'Last week Isla told her teacher that she had a flying bed and I'd flown her to fairy land. You were married to me for years. Which one of those stories do you think is more likely?'

'I have zero evidence for a flying bed. A lot of people saw this boy with my children.'

'Do they also think I'm two-timing him with Theo, my brother-in-law? It wasn't so long ago that Isla asked if he could be her daddy.'

'Well, no.' For the first time, Brayden started to look discomfited. Everyone else in the room was frozen still. It was the first time most of them had discovered that Brayden and I knew each other outside the course, let alone had children together.

'Are you seeing the theme, here, Brayden? I wonder why Isla is so desperate for a new daddy. Maybe because, up until two weeks ago, the father who deserted us when she was five months old spent less time with her than he did making TikToks.'

'That's not fair,' Silva interjected. 'Cultivating our online presence is part of our business.'

'Brayden has no business!' I snapped. 'He sold an app for a preposterous amount of money and now farts about while you take photos. You have less followers than Baby Bloomers!'

She opened her mouth to argue, but now we were here, talking about this, I wasn't about to let Silva sidetrack the conversation.

'The point is, you can't suddenly decide you want to play daddy and expect me to hand over the children I've raised single-handedly for sleepovers and weeks away. You have no right to make snap judgements about me based on playground gossip and the testimony of a child you barely know. You are *completely out of order—*' my whole body was fizzing with fury now '—bringing up my personal life, my children, *any of this* here. Now, is anyone still eating lunch, or shall we move on to talking about sleeping patterns?'

'Wait,' Claudia, the single mother, said. 'Brayve is your baby-daddy? And he's brought his new woman to your classes?'

'He's my ex-husband,' I mumbled, having started to run out of steam.

'Talk about rubbing it in your face!'

'Who left who?' Claudia's birth partner asked.

'That's none of your business,' Silva barked. 'We've heard more than enough for one day.'

'Actually, now that Brayden's started sharing, I think it's best to let people know the situation. They'll only be wondering, otherwise, which will make it harder to concentrate and detrimental to their learning.'

'See!' Claudia said, crunching on the last of her pickled onion Monster Munch.

'Brayden and I married when I was twenty. We had our son a year later, then a girl nearly three years after that. He...'

Oh, how I itched to complete the story. He left me for Silva, the woman he'd started sleeping with before I got pregnant with Isla, leaving me with two tiny children.

'We...'

Brayden looked as though his internal organs were shrivelling up. Silva blinked defiantly, but the knuckles clasping her falafel wrap were white.

'It didn't work out, for all sorts of reasons. We were young, these things happen. But what matters now is that we're committed to parenting our children as best we can. Just like for all of you. Whoever makes up your baby's family, what counts is that you share the same goal, to provide them with the best childhood they can have. Full of love and security. So, that brings us on to an activity that might be relevant now, thinking about your support networks...'

'She's wrong.'

Brayden's voice was a rough croak.

'Excuse me?' I asked, wondering how much more of an arse this man could be in one lunchbreak.

'Now's not the time, dude.' Gordon winced.

'It didn't work out because I failed as a husband and a father. Liz was amazing. Even when I was cheating on her throughout a risky pregnancy, she was strong and brave and kept on being the best mother to Finn. When she was fighting for our marriage, at the same time I was actively destroying it, she always put our children first. Silva and I aren't here to rub it in Liz's face, to gloat or show off or any of that. We're here because she's the best parent I know. And goodness knows, I've got a lot to learn about parenting, so we wanted to learn from the best. For what it's worth, Liz, I'm sorry.'

You could have heard one of those unborn babies burp, the room was so still.

'I'm sorry for failing you. I'm sorry for all the extra sacrifices you've had to make because you married an immature waster. I'm sorry for everything Finn and Isla have missed out on. I can't put that right. But I can start being there for them now. I'd like to try.'

Silva was staring at the floor, face stricken.

'Oh, and I'm sorry for accusing you of living with your teenage childminder in front of your clients.'

'Oh no, I am living with him,' I said, when I'd managed to get my brain back working.

Another audible gasp.

'He's renting that back room off me. I could use the extra help, since you've been promising to pay me child support in the form of shares in your still-non-existent new business. But I appreciate the apology. Shall we get on with the session now?'

I might be a wreck in all sorts of ways. I was lonely, and more than a little lost. But, boy, Brayden was right about one thing. Building my brilliant business while raising two small children had made me tough and brave and, below the stress and the mess, understand what really mattered. I was so grateful that I was finally putting that into action.

'He left you for Silva? When you had two littlies?' Claudia's birth partner suddenly asked. 'That's not cool.'

'And whatever the excuse, it's a bit much bringing her to the classes.' Chris, the dad with four kids, turned to his partner. 'See? You think I was bad!'

'You were bad,' Jemima replied. 'You told your not-yet-ex-wife that I was your niece. On balance, that's probably worse.'

* * *

I powered through a one-off private antenatal class on Tuesday evening, and the Bloomers postnatal session on Wednesday. Doing my best to keep on top of things while adding more items to the new to-do list, the one with an achievable number of things to do, rather than a billion. When I found myself wide awake at one o'clock on Thursday morning, I dug out an old notebook and tried journaling again for the first time since I was a teenager, the process reminding me of how cathartic putting my feelings onto paper could be. I scrawled pages about Brayden and his unexpected apology, the wonderful weirdness of adjusting to Toby and Hazel being around, and – of course – my hopes and fears about the upcoming dinner with Jonah and Ellis.

My fears? That Ellis still resented me for what happened. That it would be stilted and awkward and we'd have nothing to talk about. Jonah would hear how my life had turned out and conclude I was a loser. Then he'd throw into the conversation some anecdote about his incredible girlfriend, or wife, and, even though I couldn't and didn't want to be either of those things, I'd choke on a piece of chicken and the grumpy waiter with sweaty hands would perform the Heimlich manoeuvre in front of everyone.

My hopes? I tried to hope for an enjoyable evening with people I once cared deeply about. I wanted to hope that I'd connect with Ellis well enough to become a supportive friend, or at least enough to keep her coming along to Bloomers.

But the events of the past few days, seeing Jonah again, the very fact that we were meeting up, had stirred up that old naïve optimist inside me. The things *she* hoped for, I wouldn't even admit to my journal.

* * *

The evening was overcast, so in a last-minute panic I threw on a newish pair of jeans – two years old counted as new compared to the rest of my wardrobe, anyway – a thin-knit jumper with a flattering neckline that made me feel more curvy than dumpy, and a pair of sandals that were so old I had a feeling they were back in fashion again. I dug out my old hair tongs and played about with my new hairstyle, then dabbed on a smattering of make-up.

Jonah or Ellis wouldn't care, but it had been far too long since I'd cultivated some personal pride, so it meant a lot to me.

'Looking good, Libby!' Toby winked when I nipped into the kitchen to check the kids were eating their fishfingers without causing any trouble.

'I'll be back for bedtime,' I promised them. 'You can skip a bath tonight, but if you're good for Toby and get everything on the new chart ready for school tomorrow, I'll read you an extra story.'

'I *love* the new chart!' Isla sighed, dreamily.

'Especially if we get a special treat at the end of the week!' Finn added.

'Me, too.' I gave them both a kiss on the forehead, taking care to avoid ketchupy fingers.

'What's your special treat, Mummy?' Isla asked. 'There's nothing on the list for you.'

'Seeing you two happy is enough for me,' I said, checking, for the third time, I'd got everything I needed in my bag.

Toby folded his arms and blocked my exit from the kitchen. 'What's your treat, Libby?' he asked. 'How are you showing these guys that mums deserve to be happy, too?'

I paused, glancing at the clock on the microwave, which, thanks to Toby, was now correct for the first time in forever.

'I don't have time to think one up now. I'll add something to the chart later.'

Toby slowly pulled the pencil from behind his ear and handed it to me. 'I think we can all agree you've put it off long enough.'

'Fine!' I grabbed the pencil and scribbled 'bar of chocolate' on the treat list.

'A bar of chocolate?' Toby said, making no effort to hide his contempt.

'That's rubbish, Mum.' Finn shook his head mournfully. 'Ours are way better. You've worked almost as hard as us at the chart.'

Almost?

I was tempted to write down 'a child-free weekend in a luxury spa hotel' but was scared Toby would somehow force me to go through with it.

'I'm really late!' I handed the pencil back to Toby, not wanting to admit how stumped I was when it came to thinking up something nice for myself. 'You pick one.'

'Fair enough.'

'Make sure it's sensible,' I called from the hallway as I slipped my shoes on. 'And cheap!'

'One sensible, cheap treat coming right up,' he called back, laughing.

'You do have to complete your list of things on the chart first,' Isla shouted as I grabbed my keys and opened the front door.

I didn't stop to reply, because I was about to complete an important item from another list – attempt to make a new friend.

22

THEN

I was torn between feeling besotted and envious. Jonah's younger brother and sister had come over and it was revealing a whole different side to the vampire.

After playfighting with four-year-old Billy for a while, he was now sitting at the coffee table with Ellis, helping her make a bracelet. Mum was reading Billy a story, although she kept stopping and glancing over at Jonah and Ellis as though seeing them together was mashing her heart into a squidgy mess. I knew how she felt. Ellis was chattering to her big brother the whole time she was picking out each bead and threading it onto elastic. He was watching and listening with the tender focus of someone trying to absorb every millisecond, knowing that all too soon he'd have to revert to relying on memories.

After a few minutes, Ellis rested her head against Jonah's shoulder, and he instinctively wrapped his arm around her, moving across to tuck her against his chest as she carried on building the bracelet.

'Did you miss me?' she asked, scanning the beads.

I was pretending to read, curled up in a chair in the corner of the room, but it was impossible not to listen in.

'Every second.'

'As much as last time?'

He squeezed his eyes closed. 'More.'

'I wish I could come and live here with you.'

'Here?' Jonah asked gently. 'Not back home with Mum?'

Ellis froze. 'I don't know,' she said, hesitantly.

Her brother gently took the bead gripped between her fingers and slipped it onto the bracelet. 'That's okay. It's a big decision.'

'Do you think Mummy misses us?'

He took a deep breath. 'Yes. But that doesn't mean we should go back.'

'Clare said she's poorly and that's why she didn't take care of us very well.'

'That's one way of putting it,' Jonah muttered, before picking up a flower bead. 'Here. How about this one?'

'I think Mummy will like that one. Do you think she will? I'm giving her the bracelet when it's all finished so she can wear it and won't miss me so much. Clare said we're going to see her after playing here. Are you coming? Billy is, but he isn't making her a bracelet because he's not big enough.'

Jonah's features had set like stone. 'No. I'm not coming.'

He turned to my mum, eyes like lasers. 'They're going to see her?'

Mum screwed up her face in sympathy. 'Clare didn't tell you?'

Clare was the children's social worker. She'd spoken to Jonah in his bedroom while Mum and I played with the younger kids.

'No. She asked if I wanted any contact, and I said no. Obviously. How can they let the kids see her?'

The doorbell rang.

'Libby, that'll be Clare. Can you answer it, please?'

I missed whatever conversation happened while I was letting Clare in, waiting for her to take her shoes off and faff about with a raincoat, but by the time she walked into the living room, Jonah was a ball of furious protest, sitting on the floor with both the kids pressed tightly against him.

'They aren't going.'

'Jonah,' Clare said calmly. 'Believe me, I understand your concerns, but they'll be closely supervised at our family centre. Warren won't be there.'

'You think that'll make any difference? Isn't the whole point of being taken into care so she can't ruin our lives even more?'

'You're welcome to come along and see for yourself.'

'She tried to have me arrested for protecting my sister from that mutant she pretends is our dad. What part of that don't you people get? If I see that witch the day I kill myself, it'll be too soon.'

Ellis started to cry. Billy was like a baby ghost, peeping over the top of his brother's elbow.

'That's your choice. But I'm sorry, you don't get to choose whether Billy and Ellis spend time with their mother. Like I said, it's in a supervised—'

'You can shove your supervised family centre—'

'Jonah,' Mum said, gently. 'Why don't we go into the kitchen and talk about this properly?'

'So she can sneak them out the door the second I'm out the room? I'm not going anywhere.'

His eyes were wild, his breathing heavy. I was used to seeing young people dysregulated, but this was clearly upsetting his siblings.

I walked up to them, crouching low enough to put a hand on Jonah's shoulder. 'You're scaring Ellis and Billy,' I whispered, my eyes flicking to where they were clutching onto him, then back to meet his again.

He glanced down, frowning when he realised how tightly he was gripping onto them.

Slowly, he dropped his arms, but the children still knelt there, pressed up against his waist until Mum came and took hold of their hands.

'Let's find a snack while Clare talks to your brother.'

But before Clare could say anything, Jonah had barged past her, thundering up the stairs and slamming his bedroom door.

'I'll talk to him once he's calm enough to listen.' Mum smiled as though this was all in a day's work, which it often was.

While Ellis and Billy were putting on their shoes, she knocked on Jonah's door and tried to persuade him to come and say goodbye, but he simply turned up the volume of his thrashy, angry music.

I waited ten minutes, until a softer, more depressing song came on, then made two mugs of coffee, placing them on the floor outside his door then tentatively tapping on it.

When he didn't reply, I decided to be brave.

'It's Libby. I brought you a drink.'

The door opened while I was still bending down to retrieve the mugs.

'I thought you might want some company.'

He stared at me, his expression impossible to interpret.

I nodded at my shorts. 'There's a Wagon Wheel in each pocket.'

'You aren't allowed in my room.'

'Mum's gone to pick up Nicky from her friend's in Middle-beck, so no one will know. But…' I shocked myself by giving him a sidelong glance from beneath my lashes '…if you're that much of a stickler for the rules we could sit on the landing.'

His mouth twitched as he stepped back to let me in.

'Ooh, I like what you've done with the place.' I waded into the absolute pit of mess while trying not to breathe in the stench of teenage boy and dried-up food.

'Yeah, well. I wasn't expecting *company*.' He shrugged, kicking a pair of boxers under his bed while appearing disarmingly sheepish.

'To be honest, mine isn't much better.'

'I'll keep things tidier in future.'

I smirked as I handed over one coffee. 'Four sugars. Does that mean you're expecting me to come back?'

He quirked his eyebrow in a way that made my heart flip over. Stubbornly ignoring my brain's frantic questions about what the hell I was doing in Jonah's bedroom, I instead took a sip of my drink and perched on the corner of his bed.

'The court makes kids keep seeing their parent until the final decision's made about where they'll live, in case they end up going back home.'

Jonah was leaning against the desk. He paused with the mug a few inches away from his mouth. 'They aren't going back. That isn't our home any more. The witch has made it clear she's choosing Warren over her kids.'

'Yeah, but it's the judge who ultimately decides.'

He ran a hand over his face. 'I know exactly what Mum will be saying to Ellis and Billy. How she'll twist things, mess with their heads so they want to go back.'

'The contact worker will intervene if she does. These professionals can tell which parents genuinely want to change and who'll pretend to agree to anything to get their kids back. They won't be fooled if your mum is lying.'

He shook his head. 'She's fooled them enough times before.'

'Yeah, but this time you aren't protecting her.'

He sank down onto the bed next to me. 'The judge can't make them go back, can they?' he asked, in barely a whisper.

I slipped my hand into his, and he gripped it tightly. I'd seen this scenario enough times not to lie to him about it.

After a brief silence, he nudged me with his elbow.

'Thanks, by the way. For snapping me out of it, before. I know I can be scary when I lose it. The kids are used to me. But, I don't know. It's different, here.'

'I'm not scared of you.'

I'd tried to sound light-hearted but instead the words hung in the room like a cloud.

'Really?' He let out a trembling laugh. 'I'm terrified of you.'

I was trying to pluck up the courage to ask him about the songs he'd been playing in the car, when the front door banged shut.

As Mum called hello up the stairs I dropped Jonah's hand and sprang towards the door.

'Here.' He pressed the empty mugs into my hand, bending down to meet my panicked eyes. 'You were bringing me a coffee. It's fine. No big deal.'

In one smooth motion he opened the door, bundled me out and closed it again.

It cracked open an inch while I was still standing there, collecting myself.

'My door's always open. I mean, metaphorically. Even if it isn't, like, literally open,' he said, his face hidden from sight.

'Maybe try opening a window, too,' I whispered over my shoulder, before skidding down the stairs.

'There you are,' Mum said, appearing at the kitchen door. 'Are you okay?'

I worked hard to keep my smile subdued, my tone indifferent. 'I'm fine.'

'Phew. Just checking.'

Nothing about this was okay. Least of all me.

I wrote it all down in my journal that night…

I'm upside down and inside out and have no idea who I am any more.

I don't know what's going to happen or how this will end.

I know that I can't stop. And even if I could, I don't want to.

If this is falling in love, I want to keep on falling forever.

23

NOW

Despite my being almost ten minutes late, Jonah wasn't at the Ruddy Duck, the family pub in the centre of the village with a decent menu and nice bustle, where we'd arranged to meet. When he pushed through the heavy door a short while later, my growing prickle of nerves only intensified at the sharp creases between his eyebrows. I knew from experience these meant he was tense, or annoyed. For a second I wondered whether he'd heard the rumours about my teenage lover, but if he believed that, then he'd surely have cancelled.

'Libby, hi.' The furrow eased slightly as he sat down, shrugging out of a brown jacket, the scent of leather sending ripples of nostalgia over my skin.

'Hi.'

'Sorry I'm late. I was waiting for Ellis.' He pulled his phone out of his jeans pocket and frowned at the screen. 'She's ignoring my messages.'

'Is that usual?' I asked.

He shook his head. 'Not recently. At least, not until last Saturday.'

'Did something happen?'

'It did. But I'd really like a drink in my hand before I talk about it.'

'Oh... I mean... you don't have to tell me. It's none of my business...' I began scrutinising the menu, despite having already chosen what to order while waiting for him to get here.

'I'd love to hear your expert opinion on what's going on with my pregnant baby sister. If that's not too much like unpaid overtime.'

We ordered drinks using the table QR code and then decided to go ahead and add some food while we were at it, seeing as Jonah had little faith that Ellis would get herself to the pub. We made meaningless small talk until his beer and my lime and soda arrived, then after a long sip he sat back with a sigh.

'Ellis's ex showed up on my doorstep, late Saturday night.'

'The baby's father?'

'No. Damon's been around since she moved into her last residential unit, when she was sixteen. He shows up, wreaks havoc for a few months then disappears again. He was in prison when she got pregnant.'

'That's awful. He doesn't mind that she's expecting someone else's baby?'

Jonah looked grim. 'He doesn't care because he knows he'll be gone by the time the baby is born. I think it makes him feel powerful, like he's superior to the father.'

'What does wreaking havoc look like?'

'When he's here, nothing else matters. She'd skive school, miss curfew and visits with me and Billy. He feeds her enough weed and alcohol to keep her compliant, then cuts her off from everything else. One time, her social worker had managed to find her a place to live away from the latest loser, we'd persuaded her to enrol in college and then Damon showed up. Two weeks later she was living with him in a hole in Mansfield Woodhouse. Three months after that she turned up on my doorstep with a broken arm and a half-empty bin bag.

'I can't tell you how relieved Billy and I were when he finally went to prison. We hoped she was free of one scumbag, at least. I thought that, with enough time, having moved to a tiny village in the middle of nowhere, he might not bother looking for her. If it was just her, that's one thing, but there's a baby now...' He stopped, his voice catching. 'I don't know what to do, Libby. I thought the Bloomers might help.'

I clutched my glass with both hands. I'd heard so many stories like this one, but it hit harder when I'd known them as a little girl, let alone when I felt partly to blame.

'The Bloomers might well help. I know a couple of the current group who she'd probably find it useful to talk to. And remember, Ellis knows it's different this time, too. Having a baby can sometimes be the catalyst women need to make a break from harmful relationships.'

Sometimes. Not nearly often enough, in my professional experience.

We spoke more about Ellis and her challenges over the past few years, and how Jonah had tried – and in his opinion failed – to help her, until our food arrived. I couldn't help noting the absence of any mention of a wife or girlfriend.

'Anyway, I hope there's no one who's going to mind this ending up being the two of us,' I said, after the waiter had moved away.

'What?' Jonah squinted at me, confused.

'Well. If you've got a partner, or something. She might not appreciate you having a meal with your old... not that I was ever your girlfriend or anything. A meal with a girl who used to like you?'

To love you. With everything she had.

He sat back, that rare and precious grin all over his face.

'No partner. Or something.'

'Okay. That's good, then.'

'Is it?'

Jonah's grin faded. He looked at me, and his eyes were like rings of gold encircling vast, dark pools. I'd once told Jonah I wasn't scared of him. That look sent shivers up my spine.

'Well. Um. I'm not saying it's good you're single. I mean, not that there's anything wrong with it. Plenty of people are happily single. But, well. I wouldn't want to have put you in an awkward situation, that's all. You being in a relationship or not makes no difference to me, obviously.'

He raised one eyebrow. 'That wasn't obvious, no. But thank you for clarifying.'

Oh my goodness.

Jonah sounded as if he genuinely hoped him being single would make a difference to *us*.

I prattled on.

'I mean, I've actually been single for years now. Happily. On purpose. So, no judgement here either way...'

Jonah mercifully switched his focus to his meal, eating a mouthful of steak and ale pie before replying.

'Yeah. At the risk of creeping you out, I need to confess something.'

'Oh?' The pasta in my stomach formed a solid lump of apprehension.

'I know you're mum to Finn and Isla, who both love football. I know you all spent a long weekend in Dorset at Easter, and last weekend had a barbecue with Nicky and her in-laws.'

'Um, what?'

'I sometimes, on a lonely, sentimental day, when trying to

remember a brief chapter in my life when I felt safe, and cared for, look at your family Facebook page.'

'Oh, thank goodness for that. I was seriously starting to freak out for a moment. Phew!' I let out a jerky laugh.

'You don't think it's creepy?'

'To occasionally look at the social media of someone you once shared a home with? Your first love?'

My cheeks were on fire, but I'd always found it impossible not to be honest with Jonah. I tried to lighten my words with a smiley eye-roll. 'If it is, then there's a heck of a lot of creeps out there. I'd be a creep, too, if you were considerate enough to be online.'

'I'm surprised you don't keep your account private, given your business.'

'Well, that's partly why I use my married name for work. But the Facebook profile has a specific purpose.'

I was halfway through explaining about the situation with Mum, Jonah expressing reassuring levels of astonishment and sympathy, when his phone pinged several times in rapid succession.

'Ellis,' he said, scanning the messages. 'She fainted outside the chemist, so Damon—' here, Jonah's mouth twisted up in distaste as he continued reading '—took her to the antenatal clinic at King's Mill and she had to wait ages to get checked out. She's okay, baby's okay. Just anaemic, and she'd not eaten. While she was waiting her phone died. Damon dropped her home, but she's knackered and is going to bed.'

Jonah sat back with his eyes closed for a moment, blowing out a long sigh.

'Do you need to go?' I asked. We'd almost finished eating, anyway.

He shook his head, sitting up again as he started to type a reply.

'No. She's either going to bed by herself, in order to sleep, or with Damon. Either way, there's no point me being there.' He put down his phone. 'I'll still come along to the class, if that's okay? I need all the information I can get, especially while Ellis's attention is elsewhere.'

I screwed up my face in apology. 'Sorry. We really can't have a male attending alone, especially if he's not the baby's father. It's hard enough for some of the mums to relax around men as it is.'

'Of course. I should have thought. Okay. I guess I can find some videos online... buy a book, if you can recommend anything?'

I replied without even thinking about it. The thought of Jonah missing the classes, of potentially not seeing him every week, felt far worse than it should have done. I still had so much to ask, apologies to make, stories to share.

'I do plenty of private, one-to-one classes, if that would be helpful? I mean, the only time I've done them without a mum present was for a gay couple who adopted, but it's different when it's an old...'

I trailed off, unable to call Jonah my foster brother after everything that had happened. He'd never been Bronah to me.

'Old love?' he filled in, using my word from before, with a lopsided smile that sent my heart thumping.

'Old friend?' I said, ducking my head.

'When can you fit me in?'

'Tuesday? You can come over about half seven, once the kids are in bed.'

'Sounds perfect.'

'Oh, and just come to the house. I've got a lad and his daughter living in the cabin.'

Jonah clicked his phone on the QR code to pay, then stood up, ready to leave. 'So I heard.'

24

The plan was that on Friday morning I was going to wake up ready for a day carefully divided into house-care, self-care and childcare, resisting the urge to message, call or visit any of the Bloomers or other women I worked with. I did need to spend some time on business admin, but that was a carefully scheduled hour in between a power walk in the forest and lunch in the garden with a book.

Things started off awry when my alarm didn't go off. I woke up to Isla squeezing my cheeks and asking in a high-pitched wail if I was dead. After a horrified check of the time, I decided a shower could wait until after the school run, along with breakfast and a second's peace to myself.

Shooing Isla off to get dressed on my way to badger Finn out of bed, I consoled myself with the knowledge that the lunches were made, bags packed and uniforms ready.

'Mummy, my trousers are yucky!' Isla screeched down the stairs as I fruitlessly rummaged in the fridge for butter and jam, which didn't take long due to the shelves being virtually bare.

'Where did you put your lunches?' I asked Finn, as he

slouched into the kitchen with his eyes half closed, hair sticking up in every direction, before tripping over a robot dinosaur and crashing into a table leg.

The second I'd helped him clamber onto a chair, Isla hurtled into the kitchen in her school polo-shirt and knickers.

'I said I've got no trousers!'

'We didn't have time to make lunch because we had a water fight and then Hazel started crying really loud and didn't stop and then we were really late for bed,' Finn mumbled, his head buried in his arms, which were folded on the table.

After dragging myself away from Jonah the night before, I'd raced straight to the Bloomers class. A quick call to Toby on the way had assured me that everything was fine and under control.

'Where's your summer dress?' I asked Isla, scraping the dregs of an ancient jar of peanut butter onto her toast.

'It got wet in the water fight,' she said, taking one look at the breakfast I placed in front of her and making a gagging sound.

'And it hasn't dried overnight?'

'Well not really but anyway it smells because Finn ran out of water so he threwed some milkshake on it instead.'

'Did you get the food for Roman Day?' Finn asked, suddenly springing upright.

'The what?' I asked, handing him a plate of toast. He immediately stuffed in half a slice, so I had to wait for him to answer.

'It's Friday. We need to bring in Roman food for the Roman Day picnic.'

'Why are you only telling me this now?'

'It was on the letter!'

I swapped Isla's plate for a bowl of cereal. She dipped her spoon in and let the contents dribble back into the bowl, face contorted as if I'd handed her a bowl of maggots. 'What letter?'

'I gave it to Grandad on Wednesday.'

'Well, he never passed it on to me.'

'But I need some Roman food! I'll get a negative point for Rabbit table if I don't bring any!'

'I don't want this, it's disgusting,' Isla said. 'I want Roman food! Why does Finn get Roman food and not me?'

'You don't even know what Roman food is,' Finn retorted.

'Please, enlighten us, because I don't have a clue,' I added, searching the cupboards frantically for something to put in packed lunches.

'Well, I don't know, do I? That was part of the homework,' my son scoffed. 'You're the adult. You should know.'

At that point, the patio door slid open and Toby stepped in, a screaming, red-faced Hazel with him.

'Any coffee on the go?' he asked, slumping into a chair, which, as per the law of babies, only made Hazel scream louder. 'We've had a bummer of a night. I think the fridge might have conked out. It was squeaking and rattling and then an hour ago sort of just stopped.'

Isla dived under the table, hands over her ears and knickered-bottom poking out, which Finn of course found irresistible not to boot with his foot.

There were now two small children crying in my kitchen and I felt more than a little tempted to join them.

'No, there's no coffee,' I snapped, while scooping Hazel out of Toby's arms and bouncing her on my hip. 'There's no milk, unless you want the run-off from Isla's rejected cereal, which she's been forced to eat due to there also being no butter or jam. I'll be sure to brew you a fresh pot as soon as I've found Isla a non-existent summer dress that isn't covered in sour milkshake, rustled up a couple of packed lunches from fresh air and an old packet of rice cakes and created some Roman-themed food for Finn despite none of us knowing what Romans ate. Would you like me to feed and change your baby while I'm at it, or is *everything under control*?'

'Um...' Toby's eyes darted everywhere but at me. 'I'll see if there's any milk in the cabin fridge that made it through the night.'

I was still standing there, steam tooting out of my ears, when Toby popped his head back through the patio door. 'Finn could take in some grapes. Or olives,' he said, before swiftly disappearing again.

Finn ran to the fridge and yanked the door open. There, at the back of the top shelf, was a jar of olives.

Best before date, seven months ago. I grabbed a plastic pot and dumped them in. None of the eight-year-olds were going to eat olives anyway. Especially if Lena's mum had made one of her over-the-top cakes. Probably in the shape of Julius Caesar, or the Colosseum.

We made it to school a solid twenty minutes late. A week ago, that wouldn't have felt so bad, but after three days of the new, super-smooth schedule, it felt like a stressful slide back off the wagon. Had mornings really been this draining? As soon as I got home I climbed straight in my clanky old car and headed to the nearest big supermarket. Loaded up with replacement food I couldn't really afford, including a bottle of wine and a slab of fancy chocolate, because this was supposed to be a self-care day, I chuntered my way home.

I was now two hours, breakfast, a shower, chapter of my book and at least two mugs of coffee behind schedule. The temptation to ditch the tasks on my to-do list and blob on the sofa instead was strong, but that felt like self-pity rather than self-care. I'd start with breakfast and then decide how to salvage the precious few hours until school finished.

I was unloading the shopping when our postwoman strolled

down the drive, handing me the single postcard with a sympathetic nod.

On one side, a picture of a Portuguese castle.

On the other, words that sent my stomach plummeting into the bottom of my scruffy trainers:

Having a blast while winding my way back home!

I was still staring at the postcard when the front door opened.

'I'll get those,' Toby said, striding out and grabbing all six bulging carrier bags. 'You, follow me.'

Feeling too defeated to put up any resistance, I traipsed after him into the kitchen.

'Here.' He handed me a large mug of coffee. Not my instant sludge, but a caramel cappuccino from the café in the village. 'Upstairs next.'

'Excuse me?'

Assuming Toby must have something DIY related to show me, I followed him to the bathroom. My assumption was incorrect.

'What's this?'

He shrugged one shoulder. 'An apology for last night. And a disastrous morning. I daren't admit on the phone that I'd lost control about the same time we finished dinner, in case you got mad and kicked me out. My plan was to get up early and sort everything, but then Hazel, and the fridge... and I get that not telling you was worse. Sorry, Libby.'

'You ran me a bath?'

'It always helps my mum when she's having a bad day.'

He moved past me to light the candles dotted around the sink and on the windowsill. The flames were barely discernible in the June sunshine, but alongside the basket containing a face scrub, hand cream and hair mask, the tiny box of chocolates and pile of clean towels, it was like standing in someone else's bathroom. Someone else's life.

He dipped one hand in the bubbles. 'Still hot. Should be good for a decent half-hour.'

'Half an hour?' I considered a full five minutes in the shower a luxury. 'What am I supposed to do in there for that long?'

'Drink your coffee. Listen to this.' He clicked on his phone and music started playing from a speaker he'd stuck to the wall. 'Or read one of those.' He nodded to a small stack of magazines balanced on the laundry basket. 'Do whatever you do with the potions and lotions. If Hazel keeps napping, brunch will be served in forty-five minutes.'

'I can't believe I'm crying over a bath.'

'Tissues are beside the books.'

He gave me a wink and left me to it.

* * *

By the time I'd eaten a plate of eggs Florentine in the sunniest spot in the garden, Hazel cooing happily beside me while her daddy mowed the lawn, I felt sufficiently re-energised to tackle the business admin with a smile on my face, clicking send on one last email before it was time to fetch Finn and Isla from school.

In the meantime, Toby had taken my gas oven apart, cleaned it until it sparkled and put it back together again.

'Dirty ignitor,' he said, turning the oven on and gesturing his thumb proudly at the flames. 'Common enough problem. I got some dough bases and toppings and stuff, so the kids can have proper pizzas tonight.'

'Is it weird that I want you to stay forever?'

'In a big sisterly or cool auntie kind of way?'

'Well, I'm not sure about the cool, but yes.'

'Not only is it not weird, Auntie Libby, it's pretty much inevitable.'

'A week ago you were a homeless, single dad, and now look at you. Irrepressibly hopeful.'

He turned the oven off and closed the door.

'Best way to be, I reckon.'

Yeah. I used to reckon that, too.

* * *

Friday evening was pretty much perfect. We ate our pizzas in the garden, then played board games, none of which ended up with Finn hitting his sister over the head with a Jenga block or Isla throwing herself onto the floor because she wasn't winning.

It wasn't until Isla's head started drooping that I realised, instead of me counting down the minutes until bedtime, we'd somehow slipped straight past it.

'Are we seeing Daddy and Silva tomorrow?' Isla asked as she snuggled into bed.

'Yes. They're taking you to the farm park, remember?' I felt a twinge of apprehension. Farm animals provided Isla with countless opportunities to get scared or upset.

'Silva said we could feed the ducks but only using the special food. Bread makes them poorly.'

'That's right. Do you think you'd like to do that?'

She smiled, eyes closing as she curled around her stuffed unicorn. 'Yes.'

Wow. No anxious questions. No protests when I'd told her it was bedtime. When a chunk of pepperoni had fallen off her pizza and slid an orangey trail down her favourite T-shirt, she'd laughed and called it a sausage slug.

What was the difference? I mused as I wandered back downstairs where Finn was watching a wildlife show with Toby for his Friday night extra half-hour.

And then my mind flashed back to something Toby had said when we were making the pizza and Finn had dumped all his toppings in a big mound in the middle of his base.

'We're not like you girls. Trying to arrange everything all perfectly. You girls are so stressy about everything. It wouldn't hurt you to try being a bit more like Finn once in a while. Chill out a bit!'

He'd laughed, but the comment had hit home.

I thought about Brayden, a couple of weeks ago, suggesting that Isla's anxiety was linked to my shambolic parenting.

I'd been happy when I picked them up from school today. More *chill* than I'd been in ages.

Was Isla not stressing about seeing her dad tomorrow because *I* hadn't been stressing about it? It seemed too obvious, far too simple to be true. But it was something.

25

Resisting the urge to rely on Dad, instead I called Nicky at seven-thirty on Saturday morning. If she were a different sister, I might have waited until a more decent hour on her day off, but if I waited any later, she'd already be busy.

'What's happened?' she answered, in a breathless rush.

'Nothing! Well. Nothing to worry about. Brayden's picking the kids up at ten. I don't suppose you're free for a coffee or some lunch?'

'Okay, now I'm definitely worried and therefore I'm also free. I'll be at yours for ten past ten.'

We decided to walk through Bigley Country Park to the visitor centre, just over a mile away. Partly a concession to Nicky having to cut short her run, and also because it meant I could tick both 'do some exercise' and 'actually spend time outdoors in the woods you chose to live next door to' off my list for that day.

'So, why the random meet-up?' Nicky asked, the second we left the back gate. 'I'm trying very hard not to panic.'

'Is it really that unnerving for me to ask if you wanted a coffee?'

'Beside the fact that I don't drink caffeine? Yes, sister dear. It is. The last time you did that was probably... oh, crap. You're not pregnant, are you?'

'It hasn't been that long since I invited you out!'

It had probably been that long.

'Not that you being pregnant would be so terrible,' Nicky back-pedalled, the leaf shadows dancing across her face masking her expression. 'Just... well... you're swamped as it is... Oh my goodness. Please tell me those rumours about Toby aren't true.'

'Stop!' I came to a standstill right in the middle of the path, ducking to the side a moment later to allow a couple of cyclists past. 'Of course I'm not pregnant. Do you really think I'd have another baby without being in a solid relationship, given how *swamped* I am? And *Toby*? What the hell, Nicky?'

'I know! I know! I didn't mean it. I just... you haven't got the best track record when it comes to this stuff, okay? You were halfway through your midwifery degree when you got pregnant with Finn. And can you honestly say you'd have married Brayden if you'd waited a year or two longer?'

'Wow. You forgot to mention how me falling in love with Jonah also ruined everything. I mean, shall we compare my past screw-ups to some of the questionable choices you made pre-Theo?'

'I'm sorry, I'm just worried...'

'Maybe you want to go into more detail about how my children are a mistake?' I started up along the path again, anger powering me through the trees. 'Jealously is not a good look. And you wonder why I don't invite you out for coffee more often?'

'Wait!' Nicky called after me. At three inches taller and about a zillion miles of running fitter, she caught up in six strides, pulling me off the path and into a patch of sun-baked grass surrounded by wild blackberry bushes. 'Wait. I'm sorry. I don't know why my brain even went there, except maybe I am paranoid and jealous because our third receptionist this year has just gone on maternity leave. But me being worried about you is real. You still seeming so lost has me worried. Brayden and Silva suddenly showing up, *pregnant*. Jonah, the postcards. I got another one a couple of days ago, by the way. And yes, you moving a random teenager and his baby into your already overloaded, exhausting life has me worried. I've been waiting five years for you to either admit you need help or figure out how to rescue yourself. Honestly? It's hard enough trying not to miss Mum. It kills me to still be missing my sister too.'

'We see each other twice a week, at least. I came to your barbecue last weekend. I'm not lost.'

Yet another lie, but this conversation felt like a knife being jammed between my ribs because she was right but hadn't noticed that I was finally doing something about it.

'Okay. But you're so stressed and sad and, I don't know... defeated. Like your life is just crap now, forever, because the dropout ran off with a silly, wannabe influencer.'

I sank onto a log at the edge of the clearing. 'Do you think Isla's issues are my fault?'

'What?' She baulked at the sudden change of topic, but not quickly enough to hide the confirmation flash across her face first. 'What makes you think that?'

'I don't think that. At least, I didn't. But Brayden thinks that having a mess of a mother is making Isla anxious. Like, she doesn't feel safe because our lifestyle is so chaotic.'

'Ah.'

'I'm starting to wonder if he's right. If it's all my fault. But if it is because of me, then isn't that his fault, too? He left me to cope as a single mother, and honestly, Nicky, it's so damn hard.'

We sat for a long moment in the stillness of the forest. The only sound was a bee, industriously buzzing between the blackberry blossoms.

'Do you really want to know?'

I shook my head. 'Not if it's anything like the rest of this conversation. But I think I need to.'

'You've been using the single-mother excuse ever since Brayden left. I accept that I can't imagine how hard it is to carry the weight of not only the day-to-day parenting but the big stuff, too. I saw you in those first few months, when Isla was still a baby. It was brutal. But they aren't babies any more. And running a charity doesn't mean you have to expend every ounce of energy on the people we help. Honestly? I think you busy yourself with work so you can avoid fixing your own life. The run-down cottage that was supposed to be your dream come true. You're afraid to confront who you've allowed yourself to become, or face the pain and struggle of becoming who you want to be. But what do we tell the Bloomers? It is far easier to be a good mum if first and foremost you're a good woman. We spend so much time drumming into these girls the need to care for themselves, trust themselves. I wish you would listen to your own advice for once.'

'I have been trying.' I sniffed. 'It's why I phoned you. It hurts that you assumed it was an emergency. Knowing that's my fault hurts even more.'

'It kind of is an emergency,' she said, gently linking her arm through mine. 'Just a very long, slow one. For one thing, Jonah is back; we need to get you back on track just in case. For another, that postcard terrified me. I will not have Mum turn up to find you wallowing in a dilapidated deathtrap.'

'Okay, so Toby is fixing the cottage instead of paying rent. And I've made a to-do list to DIY myself.' I showed her the current list on my phone. The latest item was 'be kind to yourself, dammit'.

'Nice.' Nicky nodded her approval.

'Secondly… I had dinner with Jonah on Thursday night.'

After a few seconds where I genuinely worried one of her eyeballs might pop out, she managed to pull her jaw back up to say, 'I knew that haircut must be more than an excuse to grill Hazel.'

'It was meant to be with Ellis, too. A friendly catch-up. But… oh, I don't know. I've been feeling flutters I haven't felt since… another lifetime.'

Since the last time I hung out with Jonah, was the truth. I'd never felt I-can't-breathe-eat-sleep-stop-thinking-about-you love for Brayden.

'Show me that list again.'

I handed her my phone.

'"Stop pretending I'm busy to avoid Nicky's smugly superior friends"?'

'Ah. I'd forgotten about that one. Sorry.'

She laughed. 'No, some of them can be a bit smug.' Her face softened. 'But if you're not feeling up to going out, please don't pretend.'

'What, so you can keep bullying me until I cave?'

'Precisely.' She narrowed her eyes in thought. 'How about this? I'll come up with some Libby-friendly things to do if you promise not to make up excuses not to do them.'

'Sounds good.'

'And I'll only bring along people who are actually nice. Like Theo, or Shanice.'

'Deal.'

She scanned the rest of the list. 'Okay, so the house stuff is moving forwards. You've, what, had a bath? Since when is that an achievement?'

'It was no ordinary bath.'

'Fair enough. But the rest of these: only watch TV if it's something you genuinely like; declutter; learn how to love Libby Donahue, or at least start acting like it. I love this list. You'll be back to old Libby in no time. No. You'll be a *new* Libby. One shaped by ten years of work and motherhood.'

'That's the plan.'

She got up to keep walking.

'Do you think I can do it?'

'Declutter the cottage? I'll help if you like.'

She turned back when I didn't reply, quickly assessing my anxious expression.

'Change your life, one small yet significant choice at a time? Become more like the woman and mum you want to be?' She reached out a hand to pull me up, rolling her eyes. 'If those Bloomers can do it, you certainly can.'

I hesitated.

'Don't suggest for one second that you think our Bloomers can't make it. I've not wasted all that time, money and tears on one of Libby's over-optimistic delusions.'

'Well, given that the woman Josie wants to be is Beyoncé, I don't think it's quite the same.'

We laughed so hard it sent echoes vibrating through the leaves above our heads.

26

The next few days jostled and lurched along like a fawn taking her first few steps.

Sunday, Toby spent on college work while the kids and I tackled the mounds of junk in the hallway – that way, if Mum turned up and I decided to shut the door in her face, she'd only get to see a pristine hallway. Finn and Isla started enthusiastically, waned about three minutes in, and spent the rest of the afternoon being distracted by random things they found – 'My old wellies! A dinosaur with no head!' – then refocussed with the promise of ice creams once we'd finished.

I should have prepared myself for the dismal walls and battered flooring that emerged from underneath all the mess, but Toby promised me that a coat of paint, a polish and a new lampshade would make all the difference.

Sunday evening was batch cooking and organising for the week ahead, and on Monday various Bloomers had a go at soothing a crotchety baby Hazel while Toby kept his promise about the hallway.

Dad was momentarily stunned when he brought the kids

home from school, until he wandered into the kitchen and realised the transformation was merely hallway deep.

'You can reassure Janet that we now have a working oven, landing light and shower,' I said, offering him iced coffee, because it was far too warm for a hot cup of tea today.

Dad looked confused. 'I'm not sure Janet would be interested. Just because we've started spending time together, I don't tell her every little thing about my daughters' lives. Is that the kind of thing your friends talk about?'

'What friends?'

His bushy eyebrows bounced up and down. 'Well, apart from Toby and Shanice... I heard you had dinner at the Ruddy Duck with a friend last week. Or is the mysterious stranger something more?'

'Oh, for goodness' sake. Who told you that?' I knew the Bigley grapevine was good, but that was ridiculous.

'Janet's cleaner's daughter works behind the bar there.'

'So you do talk about me?'

Dad smiled. 'Millie was wondering if your friend had moved to the village and, if so, was he single.'

Oof. Millie was one of Nicky's wild-swimming friends. She was working at the Ruddy Duck while studying for her PhD in something to do with the economics of sustainable farming. A few years younger than me, but light-years more interesting. She designed her own clothes from recycled fabrics, had a side business making chutney from her allotment and was totally the kind of woman to assertively pursue a man she found attractive, given the limited supply in Bigley Bottom.

The jolt of jealousy I felt at the thought of Millie and Jonah rendered me speechless.

'Ah. More than a friend, then.'

'Not even a friend, at this point,' I managed to reply after a slow sip of coffee. I was nowhere near ready to tell Dad it was Jonah. 'Someone whose sister's joined the Bloomers and he's her birth partner. He wanted my advice on a few things, that's all.'

'So can Janet pass on the good news that he's available?' Dad blinked nonchalantly over the rim of his glass.

'If she wants. He doesn't live in Bigley, though.' Ugh. I sounded like a sulky teenager.

He shrugged. 'On second thoughts, it's probably wiser to leave it be. If word gets out that I'm playing matchmaker, half the village will be knocking on my door. And knowing this village, not only the single half, either.'

'So why did you ask, then?'

He smiled into his drink, eyes carefully avoiding mine. 'Because I'm guessing this friend possibly wants to be more than a friend, but you might need a little prompting in finding out whether you want that, too.'

'What? Is Millie even interested?'

He laughed. 'Millie is very interested. But shall we both agree she's not the only one?'

* * *

I was very interested in Jonah. I was fascinated to discover what had happened to him since our goodbye broke my heart. How the angry, withdrawn teenager had become someone who caught the eye of people like Millie. I still didn't know anything about his job, what he liked to do, whether he still loved fantasy books or liked to cook.

I was interested in whether he'd got the tattoo he'd planned, a jackal pacing across his pec.

And if so, I wanted to see that tattoo. Not to mention how

disconcertingly interested I was in what it would feel like to trace my fingers over what was once smooth, olive skin.

After the conversation with Dad, by the time Jonah knocked on my door on Tuesday evening, I was maddeningly interested in whether he'd been thinking this much about me.

'Hey.' He stepped inside, glancing around with admiration at the deep aqua hallway, the gleaming floor and artfully arranged items on the newly polished cabinet containing all our shoes. 'Nice place.'

'Don't get your hopes up. I'm working on one room at a time, and so far this room is it.'

I led him into the kitchen, which, while both clean and reasonably tidy, thanks to an hour racing up and down the stairs hiding boxes of random clutter, followed by another one scrubbing, was still a dingy disgrace rather than the stunning space it could be. The only thing going for it was that it wasn't as bad as the living room. It was also a slightly more businesslike environment to be carrying out a private antenatal class with a distractingly attractive man.

'How's Ellis?' I asked as I made us both a drink. It was still sweltering, but I needed the familiarity of a warm mug to wrap my hands around.

'Still getting a bit dizzy, but the iron tablets should hopefully help. If she remembers to take them.'

'Okay.' I brought our drinks over and positioned myself around the corner of the table from where he was sitting. 'How is she really?'

Jonah had dropped her off a few minutes late for the Bloomers session yesterday, but after the first couple of hours she'd claimed a midwife appointment and left on the back of a moped, arms wrapped around someone who hadn't bothered with a helmet, let alone offered his pregnant girlfriend one.

None of the local community midwives would schedule a Monday morning appointment for a Baby Bloomer. The clinic nearest to Hatherstone, where Ellis lived, was Thursdays.

I suspected her ghostly pallor and stringy hair were due to more than iron deficiency. The way her sunken eyes darted across the cabin as she chewed on the scrappy remains of yellow fingernails sent a coil of fear slithering through my guts.

Jonah hunched over his tea, face a blank mask. I'd forgotten how he did this – went completely still, like a small animal playing dead to avoid a predator.

'She's...' He tailed off, as if realising the futility of trying to lie, despite having spent most of his childhood pretending things were fine when the reality was appalling. I shifted my chair a little closer to the table and leant forwards, keeping my voice gentle.

'I saw her yesterday. She reeked of weed. Nicky sat her by an open window to prevent the other mums from getting high off the fumes.'

'No.' He glanced up, and there was fear warring with denial in his eyes. 'Damon must have been smoking around her. Or someone else in his house. She stayed there Sunday night.'

'She came in your car, so you must have smelled it. Jonah, you've been around enough weed to know this was not second-hand smoke.'

He shifted back, arms folding as his jaw clenched and unclenched while he fought with the truth.

'It's not your fault,' I said, softly.

'Then whose is it?' he asked, eyes burning into mine. 'I'm her brother. The only adult left in our family. It's my job to take care of her. To protect her from scum like Damon.'

'She's also an adult. You can't control her. If you need to blame someone, blame your mum. Or the broken social care system that let her down over the past nineteen years. If you really want to go down that road, blame me.' I had to stop, my voice cracking. 'I'm the reason my parents couldn't adopt her. If she'd stayed with you and Billy, everything would have been different.'

He dropped his gaze. 'In that case, we're back to blaming me. We both know that was my fault.'

'No.' I shook my head, adamant. 'You were a vulnerable child, going through the worst experience of your life. You had no idea how these things worked. I knew full well what would happen if we got caught, and I did it anyway.'

'You were more of a child than me.' One corner of his full mouth twisted up. 'And you're wrong. Those were the best months of my life.' He looked up again, amber eyes gleaming.

For a long moment I couldn't breathe, couldn't think. It was simply me, and Jonah, and the all-consuming passion that had once burned between us, and had always remained an ember, nestled deep inside me, never once going fully out.

'Either way, whatever happened...' I had to stop and clear my embarrassingly raw throat '...Ellis is making her own choices now. All you can do is try to support her in making the right ones.'

'Which she's clearly not.' He slumped against the back of the chair. 'So what do I do?'

'Be there for her. Provide decent meals when she's home, a place to rest and space to think. Keep dragging her along to the classes and other appointments – something might get through to her at some point. Listen. Try not to judge. Or nag. Learn a whole heap of useful information this evening that you can pass on when the time comes.'

'In your experience, what are the chances of her keeping this baby?'

I took another drink of tea while I considered how to answer that.

'It depends upon how she reacts to being a mum. Some women completely turn things around once they've held their baby for the first time.'

'Some don't.'

'Some don't.'

'What happens then? Will they take the baby into care?'

'Again, every situation is different. There's a whole load of help for parents who are struggling. They won't remove a child simply because their mum smokes a few spliffs. You know that. But if mum can't or won't care for baby safely, they'll try to identify a family member who can look after baby instead. Foster care or adoption is the last resort.'

Jonah's expression was grim as he drained his mug. 'We'd better get started, then.'

27

Around an hour later I could tell that Jonah's brain was getting full. Other than the subject matter, it felt disconcertingly – intoxicatingly – as if we were back in one of our GCSE study sessions. The thrum of electricity, like a storm brewing. When I could focus on potential childbirth scenarios rather than how Jonah's slender fingers still gripped his pen in the same way, or how the two furrows that appeared between his eyebrows when he was concentrating were that bit deeper, I noted how little Jonah knew about the topic of babies.

'I'm deducing from all these questions and note-taking that you aren't a dad.'

He quirked one eyebrow in response. 'I told you, I'm single.'

'So am I. I also have two kids.'

He nodded. 'I always swore that if I ever became a father, I'd do whatever it took to be there, make it work with their mother. But I guess that's another thing we can't ultimately control.'

'You can increase the odds, though. For example, by not marrying the first man who asks, because you're scared of a future alone and think you don't deserve anyone better.'

'You didn't love Brayden?'

Did I detect a glimmer of hope in his voice?

'No, I did. Just not that much. And neither of us gave it time to see if that would be enough.'

'You don't think love's enough?' The forehead furrows were back.

'Not when it's about a momentary feeling rather than a conscious choice, day in, day out, whether we feel like it or not.' I sat back, cradling my mug for moral support even though it went cold ages ago. 'I was so mad about it, after Brayden cheated on me.'

'He cheated?'

I rolled my eyes. 'For over a year. He missed Isla's birth because he was with his other woman.'

'Idiot,' Jonah muttered under his breath. Despite the toned-down language, the scowl on his face was so reminiscent of the boy I'd fallen in love with, it knocked me off guard.

'Yeah, well,' I went on, once I'd steadied myself, 'I was just as bad. I grew up witnessing real love every day. My parents loved their foster kids with a devotion that was tough enough to withstand pretty much anything. I refused to question whether Brayden and I could share that kind of love. If he was even capable of it, let alone wanted it with me. Probably because deep down I already knew the answer.' I paused to take a deep breath. 'I loved you more than I loved Brayden, and it wasn't enough. It was stupid to make promises about forever without knowing if we could keep them or not.'

Jonah was staring at me again.

'Sorry, this is completely inappropriate. You're here for an antenatal class and I'm rambling on about my failed marriage. I don't know what I was thinking...'

He remained completely still.

'I have no idea what you're thinking now, either...' I gabbled, starting to gather up the paperwork.

He gave a small shake of his head, mouth twisting ruefully. 'It's hard to think anything when I'm with you.'

What?

My hand fumbled the pen it was clutching, sending it rolling off the table and clattering onto the floor.

'I stopped thinking completely at "I loved you".'

The air had grown so heavy, hauling it into my lungs felt like a huge effort. Jonah waited, watching me, his face the bland expression that I knew hid a kaleidoscope of emotions.

'You knew I loved you,' I said, hunching into my shoulders, brain scrambling to catch up with my pounding heart.

'I *hoped* you loved me,' Jonah replied, his voice a deep rumble. 'Being with you was the first time I felt remotely lovable.'

'Are we really going to talk about this?' I said, so quietly it was almost a whisper.

Jonah's mouth twitched. 'About how we felt then, or how we feel now?'

I hadn't noticed it happen, but we'd ended up right at the corner of the table, so close that, as we angled towards each other, I could feel his controlled exhale, catch the tang of leather that lingered even without his jacket.

I knew that if I stretched out my hand to touch the soft hairs on his forearm, it would feel exactly the same.

'Although, to be honest,' he went on, probably because he could tell I was beyond speech, 'for me, there's no difference.'

Before I could do anything, there was a sudden noise from behind us.

'Mum!'

I jumped back about two feet, my chair almost toppling onto the manky linoleum.

'Finn!' I wheezed. 'What are you doing up?'

'Isla was crying. Didn't you hear her?'

I mentally shook myself back into the present day, Isla's wails clear now that Finn had opened the kitchen door. They grew louder as she shuffled down the stairs, appearing in the doorway at the same moment I gathered my wits about me enough to stand up.

'Mu-u-u-u-u-ummy!' She threw herself against my bare legs, clutching at my dungaree shorts, and I quickly scooped her up into a hug.

'Did you have a nightmare, darling?'

'Yes!' she said, little chest hitching as she mumbled about a mean prince taking her away to his castle, her snotty, tear-stained face buried in my neck.

'Have you had an accident?' I whispered, quietly enough for Finn, taking in the scene with narrowed eyes, and Jonah, quietly slipping a stack of handouts into his rucksack, to pretend they hadn't heard.

'The prince wouldn't let me go to the toilet!' she sobbed, clearly not at all bothered about who might hear. 'My bed's all wet, too.'

'Who is this man?' Finn demanded in a growl.

'This is Jonah. His sister's having a baby but she's not very well, so he's having a class by himself.'

'Since when did brothers do antenatal classes?' Finn folded his arms across his Nottingham Forest pyjamas.

'Since the sister lives with her brother, so he wants to learn about how to take care of a baby, too. So he can help her.'

'I don't believe you!' Finn shouted. 'You do classes in the cabin not in the kitchen and you were about to kiss that man. I saw you.'

'Kissing?' Isla squealed. 'Mummy, I think he's the bad prince. He looks mean and scary!'

I turned to Jonah, Isla clinging to me like an overheated baby koala as she whimpered, her nightie damp under my hand. Finn had rummaged through a random drawer and was now brandishing a potato masher.

'I'll leave you to it.' Jonah managed a polite smile. 'Thanks for the class, it's been extremely informative.'

'Hang on!' He was almost at the front door when I hurried after him, Isla bouncing against my midriff. 'I have to ask you something.'

Jonah turned, one hand on the doorknob, which seemed like a sensible move given that I was angling my hip to prevent Finn, now holding a ladle in his other hand, from pushing past me.

'What job do you do?' I asked, feeling as ridiculous as I must have sounded.

'Um. I teach at Charis House.'

'You're a *teacher*?'

Charis House was another one of those rare, magical places, like the Green House, that welcomed young people who'd otherwise run out of options. It was infamous for helping lost, angry teenagers to uncover their passion, decide on a purpose and then develop the skills, training and self-belief to have a go at it. A good few of my foster siblings had spent time there, studying textiles, catering or construction.

'How?'

Jonah nodded at the limpet clinging to my neck. 'You want to talk about this now?'

'No! Not now. Not ever!' Finn yelled, stretching up on tiptoes to glare over my shoulder.

'No. I'm sorry...' I risked holding Isla with one arm so I could reach back and put the other one around Finn. *I'll message you*, I mouthed. *Sorry*.

Jonah's eyes met mine for one heart-faltering moment, he gave the smallest of nods, and was gone.

* * *

It was too late to message Jonah by the time I'd put the weapons back in the utensil drawer, changed both Isla and her bed and settled the children back to sleep, only managing to ease their anxiety by explaining that Jonah had once been my foster brother 'Auntie Nicky used to call him Bronah!' I laughed, ignoring the boulder of guilt as I presented a highly filtered account of why this strange man was in my house in what to them was the middle of the night.

'Is he going to start sleeping here, like Toby?' Isla asked, causing all sorts of images to tumble through my head.

'No! Why would you ask that?' I tucked the clean duvet up around her shoulders.

'Well, if his sister can't look after her baby then maybe he could live here, too. Like Toby and Hazel.'

'Jonah has his own house to live in. He'll take care of his sister and her baby, if she's not better by then.'

'That's nice.' She nuzzled down even deeper. 'I think he might be a good prince. In disguise as a bad one. A bit like the Beast.' It took me a second to realise she was talking about the Disney animation.

'Well, actually he's a teacher.' A teacher! I still couldn't believe it. 'But otherwise, you might be right.'

28

THEN

For the couple of weeks after I'd been in Jonah's bedroom, I barely saw him. Every few days I left another note with a silly reason to stay alive in his bag, but Mum had stopped driving us to school, deciding the exercise would do us good, so I'd no idea if he'd added any new songs to the playlist. The countdown to exams was like a timebomb ticking in the background as I struggled with practice test papers and daydreamed through revision lessons, from which he was noticeably absent.

Then, one lunchtime, I was walking down the busy school corridor to meet my friends when, out of nowhere, a boy called Davis Hammond appeared right in front of me. I tried to keep moving, but he reached out and put his hand against the wall, blocking my path.

'Libby.'

'What?' I tried to sound bored and impatient. Davis was a genuine creep, and not in a hot way. After being paired up with him on a science project in the autumn, I'd occasionally caught him staring at me in lessons but had tried to convince myself he did that to everyone. Even when Katie and Alicia assured me otherwise.

'Come to prom with me.'

I pulled back in shock. I'd done nothing to give the impression that I'd be interested in going anywhere with him, let alone prom.

'Um... no, thanks.'

'Why not?' he asked, shaking his head in confusion. 'Has someone else already asked you? Because I put the word out that you were off-limits.'

'I'm going with my friends.'

He leant closer, reeking of cheap aftershave and sour sweat.

'Alicia's going with Luke Hughes. He already told me. What, are you and Katie a couple now?'

I tried again to step past, but he angled me further into the wall. He was tall and heavyset, and I was starting to panic.

'None of your business.'

'Of course it's my business when you're blowing me off after flirting with me all year. Messing around with lads only leads to trouble. It hurts their feelings.'

'I haven't flirted with you!' I stammered. 'I've barely spoken to you in months.'

'Maybe not.' His smirk sent chills across my skin. 'But I've seen you looking.'

'Back off,' I said, hating that I sounded so weak. 'I said I'm not interested.'

His eyes narrowed. 'Yeah, I think I can probably come up with something that'll interest you.'

He stepped even closer, close enough to have grabbed me if it hadn't been for the missile that suddenly knocked him to one side.

After I'd caught my breath, I turned to find Davis writhing around on the floor with Jonah.

Davis was spluttering, his eyes almost popping out of his head.

Jonah was like a wild animal. A jackal.

I vaguely registered the gathering crowd, but no one dared step in to save Davis. They probably thought he had it coming.

'Mr Barnes!' the crowd hissed, parting to allow our assistant head teacher through, where he wasted no time in yanking Jonah off Davis, a millisecond after Jonah's elbow crunched into his opponent's face.

'My office, now,' Mr Barnes yelled, loud enough for the corridor to instantly grow silent. 'Everybody else, get the hell out of here.'

I would probably have remained standing there if it hadn't been for Katie taking one arm, Alicia the other as they dragged me outside.

'What the hell was that?' Katie squealed, once we were safely in the corner of the field where we ate lunch on warm days.

'Jonah King launched himself down the corridor, knocking half of Year 10 out the way, and tried to kill Davis,' Alicia breathed, a little more discreetly. 'I think he literally might have murdered him if Barnes hadn't showed up.'

'I... I don't know what happened,' I said, my teeth chattering as the adrenaline subsided.

'Yeah, not true.' Katie squinted at me. 'We saw you. We were on our way to rescue you when the vampire got there first.'

'That was totally *Twilight*,' Alicia agreed.

'Only Jonah King isn't a vampire. Or obsessed with me.' I rested my head on my knees, trying to steady my vision.

'Oh, really? Can you come up with a better explanation,

then?' Katie said. 'Because we've seen you giving him that longing look like you're dying for the chance to save him,' she replied. 'It's like when you got obsessed with Carlos in Year 9.'

I lifted my head, now seeming to weigh about twice as much as the rest of my body.

'He's my new brother.'

I think they'd have been less surprised if I'd told them he was a vampire.

* * *

They arrived at my front door later that afternoon in a flurry of excitement and pastel revision folders.

'Hi!' my friends called to Mum, jostling into the kitchen where she was plating up slices of home-made flapjack for Ellis and Billy, who were currently playing Pop Up Pirate with their brother in the living room.

'Ooh. That looks good,' Katie said, leaning over the tray. 'Tests have shown that oats are great for memory.'

'I hope you girls are here to revise, not to create another one of your videos.'

'Ugh, Mum!' I screwed up my face in embarrassment.

'We shut down ALK Music at the start of Year 10,' Alicia said, not the least bit ashamed of the shockingly awful lip-sync performances we used to film in the garden.

'We wondered if Jonah might want to revise with us?' Katie asked, her face a picture of innocence despite the black eyeliner and fake nose-ring she'd added for reasons that I could only assume revolved around my foster brother's hotness.

'Oh, well, that's very kind of you.' Mum picked up a tray containing the snacks and three glasses of juice. 'I'll see if he wants to join you once he's free. Oh, and make sure you leave a piece of flapjack for Nicky. She needs as much help with her memory as you lot.'

We set ourselves up in the dining room. I'd have preferred the privacy of the attic, but it was too cramped for three people when the weather was this warm.

'Did you see him playing that little kids' board game when we walked past?' Alicia giggled. 'It was really weird seeing him smile. Like, he has teeth. Who knew?'

'Well, clearly Libby did,' Katie said, flipping open her ring-binder. 'I have So. Many. Questions.'

'If you're going to be taking notes, then I don't have any answers,' I shot back.

'Notes will not be needed. I shall be memorising everything.' Katie gave a wicked smile that sparked a lurch of possessiveness in my stomach. My friends weren't cool, but Katie's confidence made her far cooler than me. More importantly, she wasn't completely, utterly out of bounds to Jonah.

'Does he talk, ever?' Alicia asked, hunching over her notebook.

'Ever?' Well, that was an easy answer. 'Yes.'

'Like, making conversation or just minimal answers to direct questions? Is he moody, or does he get all polite with your parents? Ooh, does he talk to *you*?' She went on and on until I had to give her something. I was paranoid they'd grow suspicious otherwise, and despite me having told them about every crush I'd ever had – the grand total of three boys, including Year 9 Carlos who, I admit, I did grow slightly fanatical about for a few months – this was far too dangerous to even hint at.

'He's quiet, but not rude. Unless he's triggered about stuff to do with his mum, and anyone would get angry about that. We revised together a couple of times, so talked a bit then. Apart from that, I barely see him.'

'Does he ever smile apart from when he's with his brother and sister?' Alicia asked.

'Not really.'

Yes. But only at me.

'Does he have loads of grey jumpers, or is it the same one?'

'Okay, that's enough. I know you're my best friends, but he's my...'

'Temporary brother,' Katie suggested.

'Well, Mum and Dad have asked if he can stay with us. So it won't be temporary.'

'Don't you have to wait for court?' My friends had seen enough foster children come and go to have grasped the basics.

'Jonah's seventeen, so the judge won't make him live with his family if he doesn't want to.'

'Libby.' Mum appeared in the doorway, glowering. 'You know that kind of information is private. Especially when Jonah goes to your school.'

'Well, it's kind of a done deal, isn't it? We know Jonah can stay.'

She shifted uncomfortably. 'We've told Jonah that we'd love him to stay. He hasn't decided if that's what he wants yet.'

'What?' There was no way he was considering going back to his mum. So if Jonah didn't want to stay here, that meant he'd be looking at a semi-independent residential unit. I couldn't imagine a single reason why he would choose that over living with my parents, who were known throughout children's services for their phenomenal skills with troubled teens. Unless the problem wasn't my parents, of course.

Like I told my friends, I'd barely seen Jonah since I brought him a coffee. He'd been in his room, or in the pupil support unit at school, or just wherever I wasn't. He seemed to be timing his kitchen snack-raids for when I was out, or asleep. He'd said his door was always open, but when he ignored me all the time, it was hard to believe that.

A ripple of dread crept from my toes all the way up my body until it settled as a tight band of tension around my head.

I waited another fifteen minutes before telling Katie and Alicia I had a migraine, rudely shooing them out before Jonah's sibling contact finished so I wouldn't have to face him in the hallway. The second they left I sprinted upstairs and pulled out my journal.

I'm such an idiot. If Davis thought I was flirting, then what must Jonah think, when I probably actually was? I took Wagon Wheels to his room. Could I have been more lame or obvious? I sat on his bed and held his hand. That's probably classed as sexual harassment. He'd be too scared to say anything because it's my word against his, and if I kicked off he'd think no one would believe the damaged foster kid over me...

And now he's hiding from me, and wants to leave a lovely home because I'm a loser with a crush on her foster BROTHER.

After pacing up and down in a panic for a few minutes, I added a list of potential options to undo the mess I'd caused.

- *Die of humiliation*
- *Convince him that I hate him (which doesn't explain the Wagon Wheels, and honestly, enough people dislike him without me pretending to be another one)*
- *Be totally clear that it was just a sisterly hand-hold*

Option three was a no-brainer. I decided the best way to convince Jonah that I didn't have a crush on him was to pretend I liked someone else.

I put the plan into action at dinner that evening.

'So, I was stood behind Carlos in the queue for lunch today, and he said, "Libby, do you think that curry is chicken or pork?" And I was like, "Um, well, the sign says it's chicken korma, so I guess it must be chicken?"' I burst into a peal of laughter that was irritating enough to me, so it only showed how patient my parents were that they merely smiled and nodded encouragingly.

'Um, what?' Nicky screwed her nose up in confused disgust. 'Um, please tell me that's not the end of the, um, story?'

'Well, my guess is that it turned out to be pork,' Dad said, with an expectant grin.

'Or...' Mum pretended to think. 'Was it neither? That's it – Quorn, and they'd fooled the lot of you!' she said, pointing a triumphant fork in the air.

'Er...' The part of me that hated myself glanced over at Jonah, who was calmly eating his lasagne, absorbed in a book. I reminded myself that it was worth it, if it meant he chose to stay, and pressed on with acting like a simpering airhead. 'No. It was chicken.'

Mum and Dad both sagged melodramatically into their seats.

'Sometimes I genuinely think I must be adopted,' Nicky muttered. 'Either that or I *should* be.'

'At least you didn't embarrass yourself in front of Carlos!' Mum crowed. 'It's a while since we've heard that name. I thought he had left Bigley Academy?'

He had, in what I hoped was a coincidentally short time after I confessed my undying love for him in front of our whole tutor group. I'd wept into my pillow about it for weeks. Jonah wasn't at school anywhere near often enough to figure out there was no Carlos any more.

'So, yeah. Once I'd reassured him it was chicken, he had the curry. With chips, though, not rice.'

'And what did you have, Libby?' Dad asked.

'Let me guess,' Nicky said, taking a strand of her now jet-black hair and twining it around a finger. 'You had curry too, with chips, not rice! Because, like, um, you and Carlos have so-o-o-o-o much in common.' She trailed off with a bat of her eyelashes.

I didn't have to fake my flaming cheeks. It was harder to force my pasta into a stomach clenched at my own patheticness.

'I'm done.' Jonah closed his book and stood up, disappearing before Mum had finished asking him to put his plate in the dishwasher.

* * *

'Carlos Romero?'

'What?' I nearly dropped my glass of water. It was almost midnight, and after yet another night of contemplating whether I was going to implement option one in my journal after all, I'd tiptoed downstairs and snuck outside.

Was I hoping Jonah might be there, smoking his last cigarette of the day?

I added that to my abandoned list of Reasons for Jonah to Keep Living: *savouring the last cigarette of the day*.

Well. Maybe not *hoping*. Aware of the possibility? I'd put a cardigan on over my T-shirt, just in case.

After all, it would be another opportunity to convince him that my heart belonged to Carlos.

He was sitting in the garden chair again, the glow of a

cigarette moving towards his face for a mesmerising second as he took a long drag.

Stalling for time, I made a show of pulling out another chair from under the table – quietly, so as not to alert my parents sleeping above us – and spent far more time than was necessary getting comfortable in the wooden seat.

'That... *story* at dinner was about Carlos Romero.'

'Er, yes.'

He leant towards the table, his face all shadows and angles in the moonlight as he stubbed out the cigarette.

'Funny. A Carlos Romero transferred to my old school from Bigley two years ago.' He paused, glancing at me with a gleam in his eye. 'I'm wondering what's most implausible. That there'd be someone else with the same unusual name at the same school. Or that you would invent such a bizarrely boring story.'

I swallowed so hard he must have heard me.

'What did you conclude?' I asked, unable to resist darting a little closer to danger.

Jonah clenched his hands in a double fist and rested them on his knees, still leaning forwards. His hood was down for once, and hair hung over his face as he tipped his head towards his hands.

'When I was fifteen, my mum came home early from the pub while I was smoking a spliff in my bedroom. I ran downstairs, grabbed a beer from the fridge and sat on the sofa, pretending to look shocked when she stumbled in. She went mad at me for stealing a can, but didn't bother going in my room. Alcohol was one thing, but she'd sworn that if she ever caught me with drugs, she'd smash my phone up.'

'I admit it's a better story than the curry one. But is there a point to it?'

He angled his head slightly upwards to look at me, his face mostly obscured by unkempt fringe.

'I guess if your parents think you're flirting with Carlos in the dinner queue, it's better than them wondering what you're doing out here with me.'

29

NOW

I collapsed into bed around eleven, determined to keep up with the new system and get some sleep, despite the evening's events swirling around my head like overexcited butterflies.

Had I imagined it? Or misinterpreted what he said? Because, if my recollection was at all correct, Jonah King had not only told me that he found it hard to think around me, but he had also said that he still felt the same now as he did then. And back then, he had loved me.

Or, at least, he'd thought he did. A broken, mixed-up seventeen-year-old's version of love, anyway.

But while I'd had no idea where Jonah was after he'd moved out of our house, and no way to find out, he'd known my address and had my number.

I had messaged him a few times, but he hadn't replied, and I hadn't had the courage to keep trying, so I'd concluded that I was a convenient distraction while his life was flipped upside down. Back then, I had hoped this revelation would make the situation easier to bear, but it had only made me feel worse about being reckless enough to have messed everything up for something that wasn't even real.

So what did that mean now?

Was Jonah playing around, flirting with me for fun? Did he blame me for what had happened and was looking to reel me in to break my heart again?

Was he any more capable of true love now than he had been then?

The more time I spent with Jonah King, the more I realised that, whoever he'd become, he still had the power to decimate my heart, if he chose to.

My phone buzzed.

Hey

Jonah.

My heart instantly shot into the back of my mouth.

I hope it's not too late to message

I held my breath and did what I'd always done when it came to him – said exactly what I was thinking, before I had a chance to really think it.

Ooh, only by about thirteen years

He replied instantly.

Ouch

But, as you will have by now deduced, I'm still awake

I hope the kids aren't still up?

Just me. Kind of hard to sleep when your first love confesses that he can't think when he's with you

Which is ironic. Considering that when I'm not with you, you're all I can think about

My fingers froze on the keypad.

After about half a minute, Jonah messaged again.

Sorry. That was too much. I sound like a total sleaze.

You're still one of the only people I can be completely open with. I've missed it.

I've missed you

I reminded myself that I had children now, responsibilities. I couldn't slip back into an ancient, doomed romance without thinking it through. The first time I'd lost my heart to Jonah had hurt enough people. I couldn't risk doing that to Finn and Isla.

I counted to ten, decided that was enough thinking, and replied.

I've missed you too

Two seconds later my phone rang.

'Really?' The last time I'd heard Jonah sound breathless, I'd been in his bed.

'So, we *are* going to talk about this?' I asked, feeling giddy.

'I never stopped loving you, Libby.'

I buried myself further under my duvet. The night air wafting through my open window was fresh and clean from an earlier rainstorm. An owl hooted in the distance.

'I'm not that girl any more. You don't even know me now.'

'I've spent two evenings with you. Seen you at work, and with your children. It might not be enough for my head to determine how much you've changed and who you are now. But my heart inconveniently refuses to care about that.'

'Sometimes I wonder if I ever knew the real you before. Let alone now.'

'Libby, you were the only person on this planet who knew the real me.'

There was a brief silence.

'I would give anything to have the chance for us to get to know each other properly again.'

'I have so many questions,' I said, my voice trembling, because I was terrified and elated all at the same time. I still couldn't quite believe that I was talking to Jonah, let alone talking about this. 'But this all feels so much, so fast. It's overwhelming.'

I couldn't afford to get swept up in my attraction for Jonah again. I needed space and time to allow my head to stop spinning before things went too far.

'I want to give you all the answers.' I could hear him smiling back. 'But however much I'm compelled to, we don't need to rush. I have to persuade a group of school-phobic kids to try Shakespeare tomorrow, and I've met those Bloomers. You can't face them after barely any sleep.'

I couldn't help a small laugh. 'I can't recall the last time I had a good night's sleep.'

That wasn't true. The memory hit me with a sudden, vivid intensity that sparked a wave of longing so powerful I had to close my eyes.

'Really? I remember you sleeping through two alarms and panicked pounding on my bedroom door.'

Of course he remembered, too.

'Like I said, I've changed.'

'How about just one question each tonight? You go first.'

'Did you hate me, for being yet another person who'd ruined things for you?' Once again, my words slipped out before I could consider them.

'I told you, I never stopped loving you.'

'I caught my husband cheating on me. I know how possible it is to love and hate someone at the same time.'

'Then no. I was the one who ruined things. Not you. And what you gave me – that tiny shred of hope that I wasn't the pointless freak I'd convinced myself I was. That someone like you could see something worth loving in me? Libby, you were the first person who made me want to survive, not for Ellis or Billy, but for me. You saved me.'

I suddenly felt as though I had more room to breathe, as something that had been lurking deep down inside me, a tight coil of guilt and sorrow, unfurled and slipped away.

'Okay. My turn.' Jonah took in a deep breath. 'I mean, I was going to ask something like what's your favourite film, or when did you set up the Baby Bloomers. But seeing as you set the tone... Did your parents ever forgive me?'

He might as well have reached down the phone line and punched me in the chest.

'Honestly? They never spoke about it.' I gripped the phone tighter. 'But I'm not sure my mum ever got over you having to leave. Or that Ellis and Billy didn't get to live with us, either. But if she blamed anyone, it was me.'

'That doesn't make sense. They made it clear they blamed the older bad-boy for leading their innocent daughter astray.'

'That was in the heat of the moment. You know it's not how foster carers really think. You were a vulnerable young person. I knew the rules and I definitely should have known better.'

'Wow. So they decided you took advantage of me?'

'Like I said, we never spoke about it.'

'I really did screw everything up, didn't I?'

'Some might say the only way we screwed up was by getting caught.'

Another heavy silence.

'I wasn't ready for you. For us. I'd have destroyed things eventually, one way or another. All I've been able to hope in the years since is that getting caught up in my determination to destroy myself didn't end up damaging you.'

I thought about my parents living separate lives. The postcards. My rushed marriage and inevitable divorce.

Two precious children. A charity that changed lives, helped families stay together against the odds, unlike my own.

A woman, lost and lonely, trapped under the weight of a List of a Billion Things to Do.

But then, a new list, new hope. A new haircut and a repaired shower curtain.

'The ramifications were tough. I won't lie. Although much tougher for you. But knowing that someone once considered me worth risking everything for? If I saved you, then you saved me, too. Maybe not then, but countless times since.'

I felt rather than heard him take a deep breath in, readying his reply. I knew him well enough to speak before he had the chance.

'Don't say it.'

I squeezed my eyelids shut, holding back the tears.

If Jonah told me he loved me again, I'd find it impossible not to believe him. I still had so many questions. Far too many fears.

'Don't say goodnight?'

I smiled, shaking my head even though he couldn't see.

'A couple of hours ago my son was brandishing a ladle at the bad prince. Even if your heart thinks I haven't changed that much, my life has. If we're going anywhere with this, we have to take it slowly and keep it light.'

'If?'

'When.'

'Another question tomorrow night?'

'Maybe a bit earlier. I have a private class that finishes at nine-thirty.'

'I'll call you at ten.'

'Okay.'

'Sleep well, Libby.'

It was almost midnight. My alarm was set for six-thirty.

It was the best night's sleep I'd had since the last time Jonah King had wished me goodnight.

30

The rest of the week passed in a haze of work, doing my best to implement organised, stress-free parenting and live out my new list while bouncing a fractious, teething baby on my hip so Toby could smooth out yet more of those minor annoyances that had been like rust on the already wonky, ill-fitting wheels of my life.

On Wednesday and Friday, at ten o'clock, when the only sound in the house was the thumping of my giddy heart, Jonah called. We limited ourselves to an hour, and Jonah respected my request to take things slow. We talked about my children and his siblings, as well as the young people we worked with. I shared how I'd built up my business, and Jonah described starting out as the world's worst, angriest youth worker before growing into someone who loved teaching. Looking forward to that one hour carried me through each day.

Conversation with Jonah had always felt so natural, and it was becoming clearer that what had happened all those years ago hadn't been some silly, teenage infatuation. It had been real. What was happening now was real.

I was amazed and flummoxed and brimming over with secret wonder.

The only thing nagging at the back of my befuddled mind was what on earth I was going to do about it. So, of course, I decided to keep on keeping on, Libby-style, and worry about that some other time.

Then, on Saturday morning, as I was getting the kids ready for a cinema trip with Brayden and mentally prepared for an eight-mile hike in the Peak District with Nicky, another postcard plopped through the letterbox.

Guernsey.

See you soon!

I slumped onto the hall floor, quickly pretending to be tying the lace of my walking boot when Toby shuffled in from the kitchen, having entered the house through the patio doors. I'd babysat Hazel while he'd celebrated finishing college the night before, relocating the travel cot to my bedroom. Despite me having been up three times in the night soothing her back to sleep, he looked in far worse shape than me.

'Good night?' I asked.

'What?' He appeared confused for a second. 'Oh. Yeah. All right.'

'Your daughter is watching *Bluey* with the kids.' I was about to add a snarky joke about him sauntering in at ten-thirty, but then I noticed his face twisted up in distress.

'Courtney messaged,' he blurted.

'Ah.'

'She agreed to see us. To, like, talk. I mean.' He yanked at his curls in agitation. 'Later today, at the Ruddy Duck. She wanted to meet without Hazel, but I told her that's not happening. She's not seen her daughter for weeks.'

'What are you hoping to talk about?'

'I dunno. Everything. Why she left. Whether she's coming back. If it can work if we have a place to ourselves. What she's doing with the Child Benefit, for starters.'

'That sounds quite ambitious for a first conversation. Maybe go with one question each, to start? It works really well.'

'Nah. This might be my only chance. I've got to get it all out there. I even made a list, see?'

He was scrolling through the extensive bullet points on his phone when Isla skipped out of the living room.

'Mummy, how long now until 28 July when my baby sister is born? I made her this drawing and I can't wait to give it to her!'

'Um...' I did a swift calculation in my head. 'About four weeks. But babies can come sooner, or later, it's hard to predict exactly when.'

'Well, she's got to be borned on the right day because I wrote it on her drawing, see?'

Isla shoved the piece of paper in my face, and, once I'd pulled back to get a proper look, it was enough to momentarily displace all thought of the postcard thanks to her startlingly detailed picture of Silva, silver hair sticking up in every direction, splayed on a birth ball with a giant baby half out of where babies come from, the biggest smile on its face and brandishing a rattle. Brayden was standing in the corner, a speech bubble coming out of his mouth displaying the word 'push'.

'What's this?' I asked, pointing to a pink scribble across the bottom of the picture.

'The bloody show,' Isla replied, with the gravitas of an antenatal educator's daughter.

She launched into a torrent of inane chatter about all the

things she was going to do with her sister once she was born. I nodded, smiled and suggested she might have to wait a while before they could bake cookies, trying to ignore the words on the postcard clanging inside my head like a fire alarm.

The twenty minutes between the kids clambering into Brayden's car and Nicky's Tesla whipping into the drive felt like forever.

'Postcard?' my sister asked, the second she saw my face.

'This morning.' I shut the front door behind me and walked around to her passenger seat. 'You?'

'Yesterday. I was at the surgery all day, so didn't find it until the evening. Didn't want to spoil your Friday night, in case you had plans.' She nodded to the card on her dashboard, identical to the one I'd received.

'That was your cue to stun me with the revelation that you didn't spend the evening alone drinking and watching reality TV about other people's love lives.'

'I was not alone. I babysat Hazel, so spent most of it walking up and down the garden, singing nursery rhymes.'

'Well, I suppose a change is as good as a break.' She accelerated out of the driveway and headed into the countryside.

'How long until she gets here?'

My confidence in Nicky's parental intuition was absolute.

'A couple of days?' She grimaced. 'Put it this way, my angel of a husband is currently cleaning the house. I've stocked up on decent wine and Waitrose snacks because, while I'm still not sure whether to host her or roast her, I have this unhealthy need to prove that I'm a thriving, successful woman despite her abandonment. And there's no way we're letting her talk Dad into inviting her back.'

'But are we agreed she's visiting you, not me? One step

beyond my hallway and she'll know I'm barely surviving, let alone thriving. Plus, if it comes to it, you have a spare room.'

'There's no way it's coming to that.' Nicky glanced at me, eyes wide with horror. 'I'm thinking polite drink then a not-so-polite point towards the nearest B & B.'

'What if she's run out of money? I can't think of many other credible reasons why she'd suddenly come home.'

'No.' Nicky screeched to a stop in the middle of the road. 'She can't stay in my house. No. That's not our problem. She didn't think twice about whether we'd need any help while she was off finding herself.'

'What if she's ill?' I asked, my voice barely a whisper, because that was the only other reason I could come up with.

Nicky swiped at a furious tear. 'What if we'd been ill, Libby? Or were having a baby, or the anguish of not being able to have babies, or a hideous divorce from a dropout. Never mind job stresses or social and emotional stagnation.'

'Social and emotional what?' I asked, somewhat affronted because I knew she wasn't referring to herself.

'I didn't know what else to call it.' She was openly sobbing now. I could count on one hand the number of times I'd seen my sister cry since Mum left, and two of those were happy tears when Finn and Isla were born. 'Dammit, Libby. I don't think I can do this. I shouldn't blummin' well *have* to do this!' She dropped her head onto the steering wheel, so I reached over and pulled her up against my shoulder instead.

'At the risk of sounding like a misogynistic oaf, did you get your period?'

She nodded, pressing her face into my neck like Isla always did when upset. 'I know there was no chance of being pregnant, but it still hurts so much. We saw the private consultant last week about that trial treatment, and they rejected me. Apparently, I'm too "inadequately equipped for pregnancy" to even try. Inadequate!'

I squeezed her tighter. 'It sounds as though he's too inadequately equipped for practising medicine.'

'It was a woman,' Nicky cried. 'She has a giant photo of her five children on the wall behind her desk.'

'I'm so sorry.'

Nicky took a shuddering breath. 'I assessed a fifteen-year-old for pre-eclampsia yesterday.'

While my sister would never breach patient confidentiality, I suspected it might be Petra, from the Green House. I'd mentioned to Maria, when she'd picked her up after Thursday evening's class, that Petra's hands and feet looked a bit puffy and it might be worth getting them checked out.

'She asked if the baby could die, and for a second I swear she half hoped I'd say yes.'

There was nothing I could do but rub her back and gesture to the annoyed driver stuck behind us to go around.

'I wanted to shake her. Then pin her down with my Pinard stethoscope until she signed that baby over to me. Instead, I had to smile reassuringly, listen to the heartbeat of the new life she never wanted and send her off to hospital.'

'You've never mentioned adoption before,' I said, once she'd dried her eyes, blown her nose and restarted driving.

'I never dare consider it, normally. How can I, when I spend two days a week with young women, some of whom are genuinely weighing up their options, and others who will have that choice taken away from them?' She shook her head. 'It's only in my most utterly wretched moments that the thoughts squirm in uninvited.'

'Why not invite those thoughts in?' I asked. I'd always wondered why this wasn't an obvious option for Nicky and Theo, given our childhood. 'Share them with Theo and see what he thinks.'

'I don't know how I'd do it,' she said, one final rogue tear trickling down her cheek. 'How I could look our Bloomers in the face, knowing some of them are going to have their babies taken into care, if I've got one of them at home. We know adoption is rarely a straightforward happy ending.'

'We also know first-hand how desperately those children need a safe, forever family.'

She clenched her jaw. 'Yes. But not with me. Now, can we please talk more about when you're going to start dating Bronah?'

31

Despite the tearful start, we had a fabulous day. Nicky was well used to the exhilaration of scaling peaks to admire the glorious vistas, the air so clean it was like breathing in mountain mouthwash, the sky so vast it couldn't help but put my petty problems in their place.

We talked more about our parents, work, Theo's huge family and my ex-husband's expanding one. Toby and Hazel, and how my house was on its way to becoming a functional home. Jonah, who Nicky declared she always knew was a decent guy underneath the hoodie, and had now proved it by working for Charis House, a school where we'd seen plenty of young women find a safe place to flourish.

I asked if she needed to skip Bloomers this week, but she was adamant.

'Libby, if I missed work every time I faced another non-baby knock-back, you'd need to boot me off the board because I'd hardly ever be there.'

'How did I not know this was still such a struggle for you?' I asked, somewhat breathlessly as we were tramping up a steep section of hillside, hurrying past a herd of cows staring at us menacingly.

'Because I do a good job of hiding it,' she said, slowing her pace so that I could keep up.

'I thought that, with Mum gone, we were always there for each other.'

'Oh, Libby.' She slung a slender arm over my shoulders. 'You haven't even been there for yourself.'

'I'm sorry.' Lately this seemed like all I had to say.

'I know. Don't be. I have a freakishly-in-touch-with-his-feelings husband, remember? Plus a couple of friends going through the same thing. I'm just happy you're showing up now, for both of us.'

'Just in time for Mum to insert herself back into our family like a hand grenade.'

Nicky cringed. 'I was wondering whether I should invite the in-laws along when she shows up. Rub it in her face a bit.'

'Potentially. Although, the flip side to that is she won't have to feel bad for not being there, seeing as you have a whole new, nauseatingly lovely mother. Plus, that's still you needing to prove something to her. I thought we'd decided not to care what she thinks.'

'Do you remember Flemming?' Nicky asked after we'd mercifully reached the end of the cow field and climbed over the stile.

'Of course.'

Flemming had been ten when she'd lived with us for a few months. She had a vicious mother who she'd not seen for years for her own safety. On Mother's Day, Flemming spent hours making a card for the 'best mum in the world'.

'Our mum didn't stab anyone,' Nicky went on.

'Well, if she had, then it might explain her leaving the country so quickly with no contact details.'

'Either way, if Flemming couldn't stop caring, how can we?'

* * *

After a whirlwind day, Brayden dropped the kids off an hour early, with the excuse that they were tired and Isla was starting to get teary.

One look at Brayden, once Finn and Isla had rushed past me to start building the new Lego sets he'd bought them, and it was clear who'd been too tired to keep going.

'Fun day?' I asked, trying not to sound smug. I'd tried to explain to Brayden that these big days out weren't sustainable, especially once the baby was born, but why would he take the advice of the woman who'd raised them single-handedly for years?

'Fantastic.'

His pinched face and slumped shoulders begged to differ.

'You know they'd be equally happy playing Lego at your house?'

'Yeah, well, I think they deserve some treats after years of the park and that nasty chicken place,' he said, with the hint of a sneer that I decided to presume was aimed at Café Fried Chicken, not me.

'You chose the venue, and you were the one who could only spare two hours away from your business,' I replied, focussing on smiling sweetly rather than poking him in his patronising eye.

'Nevertheless,' he said, flicking that off as an elephant does a fly, 'Silva and I have spent six years cultivating an adventurous lifestyle, and she's determined children won't change that.'

'You were living with me six years ago,' I said, louder than I'd intended.

'You know what I mean.' He looked at me, quickly deduced that, no, I did not, and did a classic Brayden backtrack. 'Sorry. I meant five. Obviously. It's been a long day. I mean...'

I shrugged. Somehow, the recent events in my life made it so much easier to not let Brayden get to me. 'Apology accepted. I'm very much over you adventuring with Silva while I was painting the nursery single-handed with a toddler ramming cars into my ankles and a bucket on standby for the regular barfing up of my anti-sickness tablets.'

And in that moment, standing in the doorway to my delightful new hallway, my muscles aching from the eight-mile hike, I realised that it was finally true.

'But you didn't go off adventuring with another woman for nothing. Remember how hard you found it? The endless cycle of nappies, sleepless nights, baby crying, mum crying, house a mess, no time to do anything even if you managed to summon the energy. I've been working with new parents for longer than you've been cultivating adventure, Brayden. There's no way a new baby isn't going to change things. In my experience, it's far more helpful to be realistic about that now.'

'It doesn't have to be like that,' he said, face turning grey. 'Silva's not you.'

'No. She's not trained or experienced in caring for babies. I'm not saying she can't do a fantastic job. I'm sure together you'll be great. But she's got no idea what it's really like. You do.'

I looked at Brayden, inwardly wrestling with what he wanted versus what he knew to be true, and, for the first time, I felt genuinely sorry for the man I had once sworn to love and cherish 'til death did us part. He'd missed out on huge chunks of his children's lives, chasing intangible Insta dreams over the responsibility of fatherhood. He'd no idea what it was to be an honourable human being. The kind who did things like making space in his life and his home to care for his troubled sister and her baby. Or who stayed up all night finishing his college project so he didn't have to put his daughter into a strange nursery because, after begging a woman he hardly knew for a place to stay, he'd committed to working every spare minute to pay her back for it.

I hadn't wanted, or particularly liked, my ex-husband for a long time. But now I chose to forgive him. He couldn't help being him. It had been my mistake marrying him in the first place, and he certainly wasn't worth any more of my wrath or frustration. I could only hope that he found a way to do things differently this time around.

* * *

I was sitting in the garden that evening when Toby came and found me, Hazel strapped in a sling on his chest.

'How did it go?'

He'd appeared in the kitchen and announced that he was cooking dinner a few minutes after Brayden had left, turning up his dance playlist and bouncing around pretending he was having a great time. Isla, never one to sit playing Lego if there was a party in the next room, had immediately joined us, and I hadn't had a chance to ask how his meet-up with Courtney had gone until now.

He sank onto the other half of the bench.

'Not great.'

I waited for him to go on.

'She said she needs to think about what's best. For all of us. Had this spiel about how Hazel would be better off without a miserable mum who wasn't ready. Where she's living isn't a good place for a baby, which is probably true.'

'Does she want to keep her relationship going with Hazel, to see her for a few hours at the weekends, if she can't cope with the thought of having joint custody?'

'I don't know. I think she might think it's easier just to cut off all contact, put it behind her.'

'She can't believe that's best for Hazel.'

'When I tried to argue, she threatened to put her up for adoption, called me controlling and manipulative.'

'I really don't think she can do that. You're proving you can make it work.'

'Thanks to you.' He gave me a weak smile.

'Thanks to you. You've handled this whole thing amazingly well. Hazel is blessed to have you.'

He wrinkled his nose. 'I guess you don't hear me crying myself to sleep all the way over in the cabin.'

'You've lost your girlfriend, your home and things are still rough with your mum, at the same time as becoming a single dad. I'd be worried if you hadn't cried about it.'

He swiped at his eyes, then bent to kiss his daughter's head. 'Yeah. It's been a lot.'

'And it's only been a couple of weeks. Courtney might just need more time to work stuff through. She said she's not decided yet.'

He nodded, jaw clenched to stop it wobbling.

'Have you arranged another meet-up?'

'Nah. Said she's got a lot on at the moment.'

He tried to laugh, no doubt comparing her schedule to his, but it ended up in a sob.

I shuffled up on the bench and stretched my arms around Toby and his daughter while we sat there and watched the sun go down. I'd learned in my many stints as a birth partner that sometimes there are no words, nothing you can do to take someone's pain away. But you can sit beside them, and often that's the best thing you can do.

32

I felt about a stone lighter over the next few days. Letting go of the dregs of my bitterness towards Brayden, flipping my perspective onto what I'd gained, and he'd lost, as a result of his selfish choices, made everything seem different. It was hard to believe that only a few weeks ago I was treading water, clinging onto Dad for dear life and in everyone else's business so I could ignore how defeated and lonely I was.

'Have you been secretly meeting Jonah without telling me?' Nicky asked through narrowed eyes during our Wednesday lunchbreak. I was relieved to see that she was cradling Bolt, Daisy's baby, without appearing as if she wanted to run away with him or start sobbing. 'You look strangely well.'

'Nope,' I said, which was the truth. Phone calls didn't count, did they? 'Look at me, Nicky. And you should see my house. Isla didn't cry once today. I went along to the quiz night at the pub with Dad and Janet last night, and a mum from school insisted I join her team instead of hanging with a load of old codgers – that's not an insult, it's Dad's team name. I spent the evening having fun – *fun!* – with people my own age who aren't even pregnant, and then came home and slept for six hours straight. I have a list of meals for the week stuck on my fridge, and none of them include processed nasties. I think I might actually be starting to remember what happy feels like.'

'Okay, that's all great and I'm thrilled for you and everything, but can we get back to why the heck you haven't seen Jonah?'

On Friday, I picked up a dismantled shelving unit that someone in the village had been giving away for free. While Toby sanded, stained and straightened it out, I spent the weekend sorting through the mess in the living room, ruthlessly whittling it down to what could be neatly tidied away, the kids helping me because Brayden and Silva were busy at a wedding. I spent half a minute flicking through their posts on Instagram, made a mental note that Silva's baby bump had definitely dropped since Tuesday's class, winced at how hard Brayden was trying to look as though he was enjoying himself despite the panic behind his eyes, and then blocked their account.

* * *

One reason I hadn't seen Jonah was because Ellis still hadn't come back to Bloomers. We'd spoken a couple more times on the phone, and it was clear that the stress of watching his sister slide back into self-implosion was wearing him down.

'You need to do something fun,' I said on Saturday evening, keen to share the benefits of my newfound wisdom.

'I am. I'm talking to you. And after that, I've got the new Brandon Sanderson, plus a giant box of Maltesers to eat while I'm reading it.'

'While glancing at the clock every ten seconds, anxiously waiting to see if Ellis comes home?' I leant back against the new cushion on my restored garden bench. It was a perfect summer evening, still light at nine-thirty and the air sweet and gentle. 'Swap the book for a film and throw in a tub of Pringles and you've just described my Saturday nights for the past five years. Minus the phone call. I'm not judging, but it's not what you need right now. You should go out, somewhere you can forget about everything for a couple of hours.'

'Libby Franklin, are you asking me out on a date?' He replied using my maiden name, as if without thinking, but the words hung between us with the weight of a whole potential future.

'Um...' Was I? Did I mean with me? I stared up at the cerulean sky and tried to remind myself of all the reasons why now was not the time to get entangled in a heady romance. All I heard was an imaginary Nicky sarcastically pointing out that according to me there was never a good time, so I might as well choose a bad one.

'I mean, I suppose I could find someone else to have fun with, if you think it would help...'

'We agreed to keep it light. We can do a light date, can't we? A walk or a drink somewhere wouldn't be a big deal.'

What a fib. Any time with Jonah was a humongous deal. Let alone one classed as an official date.

Before I could wait for his reply, someone knocked on the front door.

Given how late it was, for a panicked couple of seconds I wondered if it was another Toby looking for a place to stay. Maybe word had got around that the antenatal teacher took in stray parents.

For another horrible moment I wondered if it was Mum. Then I heard an all-too-familiar voice calling out.

'Liz? Libby? Lizbeth?'

Please, no.

'Keep your voice down,' I shout-whispered, rushing around the side of the cottage. 'Finn and Isla are in bed.'

'Liz. Oh, thank goodness. I really need to see you,' Brayden whined, even louder.

I opened the front door then jostled Brayden into the living room. He was wearing a white shirt, unbuttoned halfway down his waxed chest, and a pair of red and yellow checked trousers that reminded me of Rupert the Bear. He'd clearly come straight from the wedding.

'What the hell do you think you're doing, turning up at my house completely bladdered?'

'Sorry. Sorry. I'm sorry,' he slurred, slumping onto the sofa, gripping his bowed head with both hands.

Closing the door into the hallway, I took a slow, practised breath. 'Sorry about what?'

'I don't think I can do it.'

I was too irritated to start grilling him on something I had no interest in talking about, but he drivelled on anyway.

'You were right, last week, about when the kids were born. I flaked. It was so much pressure, you know? Like, my youth was over. Boom! I suddenly had no freedom. I was trapped. And no man can stand being trapped, Liz. It's fundamental human nature. We instinctively fight to escape.'

'Right. Despite all the dads who stay, and see their children as a joy and a blessing, rather than a prison,' I said, with a hint of a growl.

'Exactly!' He waved a flaccid finger at me. 'That's it. All those other dads stay. But I couldn't hack it. We were at this wedding, and it was all "I'll love you forever and ever" and I started thinking about how I meant that, when I said it to you, but then as soon as Finn was born, I panicked. I know I was only a kid.'

'You were older than me!'

'But what if that wasn't it? What if I just don't like being a full-time dad? If Silva and me can't have all the fun stuff, the parties and everything, then what if there's nothing good left?'

'Apart from a baby, you mean?'

'Yeah. Apart from a baby I might not even like.'

'And your two other children.'

'Yeah.'

'I'm going to ask you again, Brayden. Why the hell are you here, talking to me about this?'

He looked up, face drooping like a bloodhound. The pity I'd felt for him earlier had just about evaporated along with my patience.

'Well, I can't talk to Silva, can I?'

'She's your partner! She's the first person you should be talking to. How do you think she'll feel about you absconding from a wedding to cry on your ex-wife?'

'I had to ask you! You saw how I handled it the first time and you're not just my ex-wife, you're my antenatal teacher. You know about this stuff, so you can tell me how to do it differently.'

'You want me to tell you how not to be a total waster of a dad like you were to our children? How to man-up, and do a half-decent job this time, rather than running off with a woman you met at the gym?'

He nodded, eagerly. 'Yes. Please tell me. I'll pay you as an extra class, if you like.'

I opened the door to the living room again. 'Go home, Brayden.'

'You aren't going to give me any advice?' He looked like a puppy I'd kicked in the face. 'You said now the course has finished we can call you if we've any more questions.'

'That's the best advice I can give you. And I said call, not turn up at my house, drunk.'

I shooed him out and stood there for a moment, one hand pressed against my forehead.

'Wow.'

The sound of Jonah's voice startled me, and then I remembered I'd slipped my phone into my dungarees top pocket as I'd run around the side of the house.

'You heard that?'

Of course he had; I'd forgotten to hang up, and he'd been on speakerphone.

'Sorry. I thought it best to stick around in case things got nasty.'

'Right. Thank you.'

'Are you okay?'

I slid onto the now spotlessly tidy floor, resting my back against an armchair. 'Yes. I have a lot of opinions about Brayden, but I've decided not to give him the power to determine if I'm okay or not.'

'I can't help wondering how on earth you ended up marrying him. You were smarter than that at sixteen.'

'Maybe. But then my world imploded, and I was not smart for a long time.'

He was silent for a few heartbeats. 'I can't tell you how sorry I am for putting you through that.'

'I think we've already clarified that, due to me being a functioning human being capable of making her own decisions, you were not to blame for what I chose to do. Crediting yourself for my crappy marriage really is taking your newfound ego a bit far.'

'Are you ready to tell me about it yet? What happened after I left?'

I switched off the speaker and pressed the phone to my cheek. 'Maybe that's something we should do face to face, not over the phone.'

'Perfect. I'll cook you dinner.'

As much as that offer made me smile, I forced myself to take a moment. My stomach was still twisted in knots from the conversation with Brayden, and I wasn't about to ruin my recent progress by making a rash decision I could regret later.

'Talking through our painful past is a very weird premise for a first date.'

'It's not a date, then. Just the curry I promised you thirteen years ago. We can save our light date for next time.'

Jonah had been waiting thirteen years for me. There was nothing remotely light about any of this.

33

THEN

I'd been speechless, that night in the garden, after Jonah had called me out on my fake crush.

I guess if your parents think you're flirting with Carlos in the dinner queue, it's better than them wondering what you're doing out here with me.

'Wh-what?' I finally managed to stammer, after what felt like a lifetime of Jonah's eyes lasering into mine.

'It's not allowed, is it?'

'Me being in the garden with you?' Feigning confusion was my only defence.

He simply raised one eyebrow, before eventually pushing back his chair and standing up.

'At least this time you're wearing a jumper,' he muttered, before disappearing into the shadow of the house.

The night chill had turned the skin on my legs to ice before I trusted them to stop trembling enough to follow him.

It was excruciating, trying to work out if Jonah reciprocated my feelings or not. The songs, the lingering stares and secretive smiles, the comment about me wearing a jumper all implied he did. But it was so far-fetched that even an optimist like me couldn't dare to hope it was true – despite arguing with myself that an optimist would be hoping it *wasn't* true, as that was far better for everyone.

Then, after walking home from an English exam a few days later, things got even more complicated.

'Another family conference,' Nicky announced, skipping down the stairs as I was trudging up them. I made no attempt to hurry as I dumped my bag, changed out of my uniform into denim shorts and a T-shirt and retied my ponytail.

'Libby, glad you could join us,' Dad said as I slouched into a seat at the kitchen table.

'Are we waiting for Bronah?' Nicky asked, grabbing a home-made cookie from a plate that forewarned my parents meant business.

'Not this time, no,' Mum said. 'He's out with his social worker and doesn't know we're talking about this, so please don't mention it.'

'Sounds ominous.' Nicky waggled her eyebrows at me.

I was in no state to reply. The fear that this could be about me and Jonah sent a surge of panic through my bloodstream. I raced through the possibilities – they'd learned that Carlos left Bigley ages ago, or had figured out the playlist – *oh, my goodness, had they read my journal*?

'Not at all. But it is serious, and we didn't want to get his hopes up,' Mum answered.

'You both know that we've told social services we'll happily continue caring for Jonah, moving from short-term fostering to a permanent placement, but he's not been sure whether this is what he wants,' Dad said. 'Well, he's finally explained why.'

I was going to throw up any second.

'He doesn't want to give up hope of living with Ellis and Billy,' Mum continued.

'But the chances of there being a family with space to take three kids, including a teenager, are virtually non-existent,' Nicky said, through a mouthful of cookie.

'Virtually. But not completely,' Dad said. 'Social services are wondering whether they've already found one.'

'Who?' I couldn't help blurting.

'Ta-da.' Mum waved at us from across the table.

'You're going to foster Ellis and Billy, too?' Nicky asked. 'I thought they were being put up for adoption.'

'They are.'

My parents allowed the aftershock of that bombshell to reverberate across the kitchen.

'You're going to adopt Ellis and Billy?' Nicky asked, sounding stunned.

'We're thinking about applying to adopt all three of them,' Dad said, his eyes suddenly brimming with tears.

'You know how we feel about them,' Mum went on. 'Thirty-nine children and we've always known we were just a rest-stop on their journeys. They weren't meant to be ours. But this time, right from the start, it felt different. It would be incredible to see the siblings back together, and there's no way that will happen unless we step up.'

Dad reached to take her hand. 'But, of course, that also depends on you two. It's a huge ask, a massive change for all of us, and we won't go ahead unless everyone is certain.'

'Like we're going to be the selfish birth-kids who say no to keeping siblings together?' Nicky said. 'You can't put that on us.'

'More like, you're going to be the honest, informed, realistic birth-kids who help us to work out the best decision for all of us.

Just because you two aren't vulnerable or traumatised, it doesn't mean your wishes or your lives matter any less.'

'Could have fooled me,' Nicky muttered.

'This will change things forever. We need to know what you honestly think about it.'

'Where will they sleep?' Nicky asked, first. 'Will I still have a bedroom when I come home for the holidays?'

So started a three-way conversation that went on for over an hour. Occasionally someone would ask what I thought about a practical or emotional issue, but the only way I could answer was to focus on Ellis and Billy, who I loved enough to happily become a forever-big-sister to, rather than allow myself to contemplate what it would mean for me and Jonah. Or Bronah, as he really would be then.

I spluttered a couple of sentences about how it would be nice to have permanent siblings, rather than the endless merry-go-round of new children moving in and out.

We concluded the family meeting by agreeing to think about it for a few more days, then talk again, but it was a meaningless delay. It was clear that three of the Franklins had already decided, and the fourth one wasn't going to be honest with them.

That left me with only one option. I had to get over Jonah King, and quickly.

I also had to burn my journal.

My biggest regret was not burning it right then and there.

34

NOW

With the antenatal course including Brayden and Silva having finished a week ago, I now had a precious Tuesday off before the new group started. I felt relieved that it was over, as well as proud that I'd remained mostly professional. The classes had also provided some reassurance that the new baby could be a good thing for my family, rather than presenting more problems.

Dad was picking up the children, leaving me time to catch up on other tasks, including a visit to the Green House to see Petra and her new baby, who had come home from hospital a couple of days earlier.

It was now mid July, and the farm was always glorious during the height of summer. The fields surrounding the Green House hollow were an uplifting patchwork of yellow rapeseed, green polka-dotted with sheep, and the silvery brown of barley. The trees lining the lane leading up to the house were heavy with new fruit, and the gardens bustled with colour and life.

Maria walked me around to the terrace behind the house where Petra was cuddling her tiny daughter.

'Hey, how are you?' I sat down in the chair beside her.

'I'm okay.' Petra gave a rueful smile.

'Really?' I squinted at her. 'After what you've been through, I'd expect you to be completely knackered and maybe still recovering from the shock.'

I'd been right about Petra having pre-eclampsia. Things had escalated in hospital to the point where the safest option had been to medically induce labour a month early.

Petra sagged in her chair. 'I'm sore and I'm tired, and there are some very weird things going on with my body right now. But, I don't know. After all those weeks scared about not being ready, as soon as I saw her that changed. It's like, I can't even remember how I existed without her.'

'Are you going to introduce us?' I said, reaching over to waggle her baby's bare foot.

'This is Emily.'

'What a beautiful name for a beautiful baby. Mary told me that she's doing really well, despite the stressful start.'

Petra bent to kiss her on the forehead, before handing her over to me, her face glowing with pride.

'She was five pounds eleven but has already put on two ounces.'

We chatted for another half-hour or so, Petra happy to let me hold Emily as she described her time in hospital and I answered some of her questions.

We agreed that she'd come along the following day to the postnatal Bloomers session, and I stood to pass Emily back to her, but Petra was distracted by two figures coming through the garden gate.

'There's Bob,' Petra said as they started walking towards us. 'He promised to take me shopping for more preemie baby clothes.' She squinted at the man beside him. 'That's not Benny, though. He's got hair.'

The other man was definitely not Benny. It was Jonah. I'd not seen him in two weeks, and it was discomfiting how being in the same garden as him made my stomach flip inside out.

'Ah, Petra. Nice to see you up and about, enjoying the lovely morning.' Bob beamed as he reached the patio.

Petra shrugged. 'Emily isn't really into lie-ins.'

'Have you been keeping her in the shade?'

'Yes, and she's got her sunhat on.'

'Very good.' Bob nodded enthusiastically, before placing a hand on Jonah's shoulder.

'Ladies, this is Joe. Joe, meet Petra and her daughter, Emily. Oh, and this is Libby.'

Jonah had briefly taken his eyes off mine to smile hello to Petra, but he aimed them straight back at me. 'Yes, I've known Libby for a long time.'

'Really? Since your Green House days? She used to come here with her parents back when she was a lass, but she must have made an impression if you remember her from way back then.' He leant closer to Petra as if sharing a tasty crumb of gossip, which from my perspective it certainly was. 'Joe lived at the Green House when he was younger, too. How long were you with us, Joe?'

'Um.' Jonah dropped his gaze, a bloom of pink spreading up from his neck across his cheeks. 'About five years.'

'Five years! Long enough that when he changed his surname, he picked ours. Joe Green. Our son from another mum.'

I was very grateful for the distraction of the baby in my arms. Focussing on the solid warmth of her tiny body against my shoulder, I did my best to suck in enough oxygen to prevent my head spinning.

The Green House was a forty-five-minute walk from where I'd grown up. As Petra and Bob chattered about nothing much, I skimmed through my memories to find when I'd stopped visiting the Green House for their bonfire nights and barbecues. Probably that same summer Jonah had left.

Had I stopped going because I'd been too miserable, hiding away and burying myself in GCSE resits until Katie had dragged me along to her youth group and I'd met Brayden?

Or... had my parents stopped inviting me?

I remembered with a flash that I had gone a couple of times with Brayden – to a Christmas party, and the following Easter Egg hunt. Then I'd started at the University of Derby, and that had been that until Bloomers began.

'So, Libby, did you keep in contact with Joe while he was on his travels, or only since he returned to Sherwood Forest?'

'Oh, um, he came along with Ellis to a couple of the Bloomer sessions.'

'Of course! Of course. Lovely young woman. We were very disappointed she turned down a place here. I think she'd have got on well with Verity and Victor.'

Petra burst out laughing. Verity and Victor were miniature goats, famous for their terrible tempers.

'Well, it was lovely to see you, and of course to meet this gorgeous girl, but I'm going to head off now.' I carefully handed Emily back to her mother, reiterated how much I was looking forward to seeing her the next day, and practically fled into the house.

I was six steps down the tiled hallway when Jonah caught up with me.

'Hey.'

'Hi.' I couldn't look at him. I didn't know what to think, let alone what to say.

'I guess we need that dinner,' he said, his voice uncharacteristically nervous.

'I don't know, Jonah. *Joe*. Is it really a good idea, raking up the past? It's bound to hurt one of us.'

'It sounds like you're already hurt,' he said, quietly. 'And there's nothing you could tell me that will hurt more than if you don't even give us a chance.'

'Finding out from Bob that you were living so close to my house is not pleasant. Hearing you explain why you chose to never contact me, despite that, despite the promises... everything you said... That would crush me.' I was whispering now, my throat tight with the tears I was battling to keep at bay. 'Please don't ask me to do that.'

'Okay.' He took a deep breath, and to my surprise his words were fierce, with no trace of apology or regret. 'You can come up with your own theory about what happened, use that as an excuse to avoid any chance of finding out whether what we have is real. Is worth risking our hearts for. Or you can come to dinner with me on Friday, and I can explain how I have loved you and missed you every single day – every night,' he groaned, 'since they dragged me away.'

The tears I swiped off my cheeks were answer enough, but I managed a weak nod, just in case he wasn't sure.

'Now please let me go before someone finds me blubbering in the hallway.'

He turned to go, but then changed his mind, stepping forwards to cup my face in his hands and press his lips gently against a stray tear still on my cheek. 'I'm not going to hurt you.'

The first time Jonah King kissed me, it had felt like the answer to every stray longing in my heart.

This time was even better.

35

On Wednesday, it happened.

The only good thing I can say about it is that Nicky and I were together, and the kids were still on their way home from school.

It had already been an unsettling day. Toby had found me when the Bloomers were having lunch, vibrating with excitement as he explained that Courtney had decided to give things another try, and he was catching the bus up to Sheffield with Hazel that afternoon. I wished him well, made him promise to let me know how it went, and arranged to drop all their things off on Friday if he wanted to stay.

At three-thirty, a taxi pulled into the driveway, which wasn't unusual on Bloomer days, but it was when Nicky had already helped the last mum load her pram into her carer's car and waved them off.

'There's definitely no one still hanging around?' Nicky asked, peering out of the cabin window, her hands full of dirty mugs.

'No. Toby and Hazel should have left about an hour ago.'

'Who's this, then?'

Before I could hazard a guess at all the people I hoped it wasn't, Nicky clutched my arm, her intuition flaring.

'It's her.'

We both blurted the same swear word.

The back door of the taxi opened, and out stepped the woman we'd been hoping and dreading to see for five years.

'What the hell do we do now?' I murmured, not that there was any chance of her hearing me as she wandered over to the cottage's front door.

'Improvise?' Nicky replied. 'Stay true to ourselves? And no matter what, we damn well stick together.'

We slipped out of the cabin door, which faced the side of my house, scurried across the garden and entered the kitchen via the patio.

'Here.' Nicky grabbed my shoulders, then fluffed up my hair before tucking one side behind my ear, untucking it, and then brushing it back again. All her crop needed was a quick smooth over.

'Everything else presentable?' she asked, breathless with tension as she bared her teeth for inspection.

'All good.'

'You, too.'

'I guess we're ready as we'll ever be.'

'Which is totally not ready.' She laughed, a little manically.

'Did you think she looked old?' I whispered.

'I don't know,' she whispered back. 'I was freaking out too much to—'

Mum knocked on the door with a jaunty rhythm that reflected the tone of the twenty-one postcards stuffed into the back of my understairs cupboard.

'Did I tidy the hallway this morning?' I gabbled. 'I don't think I've vacuumed it since the weekend.'

'Who cares?' Nicky hissed back. 'We don't give a crap what she thinks, remember?'

Only we did. We gave more craps about this than our hearts could bear to admit. Even so, shoulders back, hair in place, I strode down my only slightly messy hallway and opened the door as deliberately casual, couldn't-care-less as I could manage.

'Mum.' The shock was still like a mallet slamming into my midriff.

'Libby! Oh my! Oh, look at you, darling! I've been looking forward to this moment for 3,872 miles!' Mum stepped forwards, arms automatically reaching out to hug me. I hurriedly stepped back, leaving them grasping at empty air, which was how she'd left me five years ago.

'Before you come in,' Nicky barked, springing in front of me, 'we need to say something.'

Mum's jaw dropped open. She blinked at us a couple of times. She wore a yellow T-shirt displaying the Invisible Women support group logo with cotton shorts and well-worn trainers. Mum's hair, dark like mine with a few strands of grey when she'd left, was now mostly silver. She looked physically older, naturally. But her posture, the light dancing in her eyes and bounce in her step were completely new.

'Of course,' she said, with an apprehensive smile. 'Go ahead.'

'Right. Firstly, while you were off finding fancy-free Helen, I turned thirty-one. I've been "going ahead" without your permission for a very long time. Secondly, Libby's kids will be home in half an hour. You will be gone by the time they get here.' She didn't mention that Dad would be with them. 'Thirdly, none of this is okay. If you thought this would be some joyous reunion, then you're even more selfish than this whole farce has proven already.'

Mum's smile vanished. 'I did wonder if it might be like this.'

'Fourthly,' Nicky said, her entire face covered in angry blotches, 'you'd better find a seat in the garden because you have five years and two months of explaining to do, and Libby doesn't want you in her house yet.'

Five horrendously awkward minutes later, we were perched on two benches like emissaries from rival armies trying to broker a peace deal. I was so grateful in that moment for Toby and the time he'd taken to cut the grass and tidy up the borders. I'd hastily filled a jug with iced water because if I'd put the kettle on, Nicky would have yelled at me, and we were all in need of cooling down.

'You did get the last few postcards?' Mum asked, with horribly fake brightness. 'I wanted to keep you updated.'

'Yes. Did you get ours?' Nicky asked, her tone even jollier.

There was a moment of confusion before Mum cottoned on to the sarcasm. 'I loved seeing all the Facebook updates. That was a very thoughtful gesture.'

'In 2020, you went four months without any contact,' I said, the first time I'd properly spoken. 'The world had turned upside down, and after you finished the cruise we had no idea what was going on.'

'You knew I was in Spain,' Mum said. 'Literally nothing was going on. I had no news to tell.'

'And you didn't think to phone, or message? You didn't wonder whether we had any news?'

'We thought you might have died of Covid in some backwater hospital,' Nicky said, her flat tone the biggest clue that she was hiding a tornado of emotions. 'We sort of hoped you had. It felt easier than you simply not giving a crap.'

Mum jerked back in astonishment. 'How could you think I didn't care? I'm your mother. I thought about you all the time. And you knew why I had to go...'

'Why didn't you ever comment on our posts?' I said, my voice cracking. 'You never phoned on Isla's or Finn's birthdays, let alone sent a present. You barely acknowledged that they even existed.'

'Plenty of parents move abroad when their children are adults.' Mum was starting to bristle. 'I spent twenty-seven years pouring out every last ounce of strength, love and energy into fifty-three children—'

'But not *your* children!' Nicky cried in exasperation, her blank façade disintegrating. 'Then you abandoned us. And Dad. You didn't even have the guts to properly separate, just left him dangling. What did he do to deserve that?'

'I hardly abandoned you.' Mum looked askance. 'You were settled and sorted with jobs, your own families... Adults with your own lives. You surely can't begrudge me some time to recover mine. I had a breakdown. I needed to recover. And I'm not going to discuss your father, who I'm sure has more than made up for me spending some time away.'

'When you left, we might have been sorted,' I snapped, incredulous that she was arguing about this rather than expressing how sorry she was. 'What about two months later when Brayden walked out on me and our two tiny children to shack up with another woman? You don't think I could have done with my mum at least sending me a sympathetic text then?'

'Oh, darling! Brayden left you? You never posted about that.' Mum pressed a hand against her cheek in shock.

'On a public Facebook page? Of course she didn't!' Nicky sprang up and started striding up and down the patch of lawn, waving her arms about. 'We also didn't post about my cancer scare, or the four miscarriages, the last one of which has left me with zero hope of ever becoming pregnant. We didn't share that I'm a partner in a GP practice, or that Libby is living with an eighteen-year-old lad and his daughter. That Isla has anxiety attacks, and her brother likes smacking people over the head with random objects. Or how Libby has been lost – *lost* – hiding away in this decrepit cottage for years now, and I've been too busy hiding from my own problems to help her. We needed you! Not to look after us or even babysit your grandkids if you've really had enough of children, but, I don't know, just to share some of your amazing advice, or listen to our problems, say you're proud of us or… give us a damn hug!'

All three of us were crying now. There was only one time in Franklin history when that had happened before, which inevitably prompted my next statement.

'Don't pretend we're being mardy about you needing some time away. Five years without being able to call you is beyond bonkers. It's downright cruel. And the only explanation is that you'd been waiting since I was sixteen to punish me for sabotaging the future you really wanted. A five-year sentence. Which is fine. If you had the decency to admit it. But what's totally not fine is that you punished Dad and Nicky, too.'

There was a stunned silence. Nicky came and sat beside me again.

'That's not what this was,' Mum said, her words stiff as though her lips had gone numb. 'I was very ill. I simply couldn't carry the weight of anyone else any more. The only way to do that was to make a complete break. But it wasn't a punishment.'

'You weren't still angry with her?' Nicky asked, slumping back like a deflating balloon. 'You can swear what happened with Jonah had nothing to do with you rarely phoning, no videocalls, no invites to join you on the high seas?'

'Oh, you know I can't handle that type of new-fangled technology.' Mum huffed. 'Most of the time I had no phone signal.'

'Stop it,' I said, causing Mum to jerk her head towards me in surprise. I'd been an unassuming twenty-four-year-old when she'd left. I wasn't that woman any more. Even if the transformation had only happened in the past few weeks. 'It's time to cut the crap. If you want to see either of your daughters again after you leave in—' I checked my watch '—eight minutes, then start being honest. Because if the last few years have taught us anything, it's that we really don't need you. So, if you'd like to have any sort of relationship with us at all, you'd better find a way to make us want you in our lives again.'

Mum looked at the grass for a long moment, before nodding to herself, the decision made.

'Yes, I was deeply upset by what happened with Jonah, Libby. I tried not to blame you, but we were unable to fully forgive each other, and that caused too much anguish and guilt on top of being so ill. And when the problems between us started impacting your dad, it felt like my bitterness was poisoning everything, and I didn't know how else to fix it. The Invisible Women showed me that a break would enable us to draw a line under it and start again.'

Nicky was pale with anger. 'Your ridiculous support group didn't suggest counselling, or us simply talking it out together? Anything that didn't coincidentally involve you taking an around-the-world holiday?'

Mum tipped up her chin. She looked just like Isla. 'It was torture, thinking about you girls, my grandchildren, getting on with your lives and me not being a part of it. If you're wondering whether I felt awful, then the answer is of course. Then, as time passed, the idea of coming back grew worse and worse, knowing how upset you'd be, sure that the distance between us would be near impossible to bridge.'

'Five years.' I had heard her explanation, but it was like oil spilling on water.

'It was only meant to be one year, and then lockdowns everywhere... I ran out of money so needed to work for a few months. Then another lockdown started...'

Nicky rolled her eyes. 'You could have bought a cheap disposable phone and given us your number. Arranged a time when we could speak properly.'

'I was afraid you'd never call.' Mum started crying again. 'I'm so sorry to hear about Brayden, and the other things you've been through. I can never make up the lost years to Finn and Isla. But please trust me when I say that I had to do this. I wouldn't have left if I had any choice.'

'You need to go now,' Nicky said, sounding as unsympathetic as I felt. 'But I have one thing for you to consider. We spent our whole childhoods doing our best to love all those children. Being jealous. Even scared of a few. In our house. All the time. We shared birthdays and Christmases and every other normal piece of growing up. And we aren't complaining. In so many ways we are stronger and better people for it. But knowing what it was like, how hard it was sometimes, you should have at least checked in on us, even if you needed to leave us.'

As Nicky paused for breath, Finn's excited chatter drifted over the side fence. I got up and hurried into the house, shooing the kids into the living room as soon as they stepped through the front door.

'Mummy, I haven't taken my shoes off yet!' Isla protested. 'What about the mud on the rug?'

'Whoops. Take them off here, and I'll fetch you a snack. I need you to wait two minutes while I talk to Grandad.'

'What's happened?' Dad asked, following me back to the kitchen.

'Mum's here.' I nodded through the window to where Mum was struggling to swing her enormous rucksack onto her back.

He froze, eyes fixed on the window. 'How is she?'

'She cried a lot.' I shrugged.

'What are her plans now?'

'We didn't get that far.' As Mum started trudging around the house, I hurried down the hallway so I could intercept her on the front drive.

'Nicky says I can stay at hers,' Mum said, when I caught up with her. 'She's driving me over.'

'One night.' My sister looked as though every muscle from her furrowed forehead to her toes were clenched. 'And we still need to talk about Dad.'

'It's been really good to see you.' Mum was crying again. 'I know we have a lot more to discuss, and you're still very upset, but I can't tell you how much it meant that you allowed me to—'

'Did you know Jonah lived at the Green House?' I interrupted, unable to bear any more platitudes.

Mum stopped, her eyes flicking to Nicky, as if she were going to help her out.

'Did Dad know, or was this something else you kept from all of us?'

I refused to accept her trying to imply that Dad and I somehow ganged up against her. Mum had been the one to step away from our family, a long time before she actually left.

'I knew.' Mum dropped her head in what I hoped was shame. 'I didn't think it would be helpful to tell your dad.'

I shook my head. 'You say you didn't want to punish me, but you banished the man I loved and then never even gave me the chance to see him, let alone to say goodbye.'

36

THEN

I had one exam left, and was down to counting the hours until this month would be over and we could have the extended summer break before starting sixth form. I'd ricocheted between exam rooms and last-minute cramming, trying to make up for all the revision sessions where I'd sat and daydreamed about the boy who was definitely avoiding me. My stress about whether I remembered the stages of cell reproduction or random quotes from *Romeo and Juliet* was nothing compared to the churning torrent of anxiety caused by the situation with Jonah.

As a family, we'd had two more discussions about what we wanted to do, and it was officially unanimous – although, unofficially, I didn't know whether to feel more terrified that Jonah would end up staying here with his siblings, or for some reason go. I tensed up every time I saw one of my parents, paranoid that they would bring up how I'd made Jonah feel uncomfortable, or that they were wondering whether I needed to talk about something, because they'd seen the way I looked at him...

Thankfully, Nicky was buried in her much more important exams, spending most evenings either in her room or studying at a friend's house. She barely even ate with us, so I didn't have to face her sidelong glances every time Jonah spoke. Which was also rare. He'd taken to eating meals at weird times of day due to sleeping in and then staying up half the night. The snack synchronisation was a thing of the past. Mum and Dad let him get on with it, putting his disrupted schedule down to exam stress. I knew differently.

My parents had wanted to wait until exams were finished before talking to Jonah about adoption, but, with the court hearing approaching, there wasn't time. They ended up taking him out for a burger one evening, leaving me and Nicky waiting at home. Unable to think about revising while such an important conversation was going on, we ended up in the living room with a film and a mountain of junk food.

'What do you think he's going to say?' I asked, as Katherine Heigl tried on yet another of her twenty-seven bridesmaid's dresses.

'I don't know.' Nicky kept her eyes on the television. 'It seems like a no-brainer, getting to live with his brother and sister, but it's a big thing, choosing to become part of a whole new family. I could see him asking us to adopt Ellis and Billy, then opting to move into supported accommodation next year.'

'Yeah. That would make sense.' I tried to sound casual, even as part of me gripped onto this as a potentially perfect solution.

'You know him better than I do,' Nicky went on, grabbing another handful of popcorn. 'What do you think?'

'I mean—' I rolled my eyes '—does anyone really know Jonah King?'

'Well, I guess we're about to find out,' she said, pausing to listen as a car pulled into the driveway.

We both sat back, ultra chill, but no one came into the living room. Nicky stopped the film at the same second I stood up, fake chillness abandoned.

'What happened?' Nicky asked, finding Mum and Dad in the kitchen making a drink.

'He was very appreciative,' Dad said. 'He told us he really loves living with us and knows Billy and Ellis would have a good home here, too.'

'But?'

My heart was scrabbling up the back of my throat.

'He wants us to apply to adopt the younger two, no matter what. But he's still thinking about what he wants.'

'Totally called it!' Nicky crowed.

'Really?' Mum asked, sounding defeated. 'Perhaps, then, you could shed some light on why he's so torn?'

'It's the middle of exams,' I stuttered. 'He probably doesn't want to make a massive decision like that right now. If you'd been through the kind of stuff he has, you'd want to be sure the next family you were part of were okay.'

'Oh, we have raised a pair of wise young women.' Dad sighed. 'Of course he needs more time to build a bit of trust. The problem is, we don't have more time.'

'Talk to him again, after Thursday,' I said.

'Well, obviously not on Thursday.' Mum plastered on her 'fun foster mum' face. 'We've got the post-exams cake and karaoke! Aren't Katie and Alicia coming?'

'Oh, my friend Theo's coming, too,' Nicky said, with a casual flick of her hair that betrayed how much it really meant to her. 'As a *friend*, before you start being weird about it.'

'Are you going to sing him "You're the One That I Want"?' I asked, unable to resist.

'I don't know, maybe you should invite Carlos and we could do a duet?' she snarked back before disappearing.

'I know Jonah sometimes talks to you. If he says anything, will you let us know?' Mum asked, handing me a coffee. 'I don't mean betraying his secrets. But if he thinks something that isn't true, or is worried about something we can explain better?'

I shrugged. 'He doesn't really talk to me about anything like that. But yeah, I guess so.'

She handed me another coffee. 'Here, why don't you take this up? I think he's seen enough of us for one evening. You could suggest a last-minute study session together?'

* * *

'You took your time,' Jonah said, raising one eyebrow after opening his door to find me standing there with two mugs.

'Mum made these literally one minute ago.'

'I made the invitation six weeks ago.' I caught the flash of a smile, and my breath froze in my chest.

'Oh.'

He stood back, inviting me in. I glanced down the stairs, but my parents had taken a bottle of wine into the garden. We were safe, for now.

'I wasn't sure that offer was still open.'

He took his preferred navy-blue mug, correctly assuming that was the one with four sugars in, and we took up our previous position of me sitting awkwardly on the bed, him leaning up against the desk, as poised as a panther.

'Why not?'

'I thought you might be avoiding me.'

My inability to lie to this boy made being in his room potentially disastrous. I equally couldn't resist taking the risk.

He took a slow sip of coffee. 'I am.'

'Well, I'm hardly going to come knocking on the door of

someone who'd rather go hungry than be in the kitchen at the same time as me.'

'I know. That's why I'm avoiding you.'

'You're not making any sense.'

'None of this makes any sense!' He shook his head. 'I finally get the chance to have a safe place to live. A proper home, with a good family. Who want to adopt me. *Me!*' He did that thing where he looked over at me up through his fringe, despite his eyes being a good couple of feet above mine. 'And all I can think about is how badly I want to screw it up.'

'Is that why you've not said yes? Because you think you might screw it up?'

'Libby...'

Oh boy. He could have made a whole extended CD of his voice repeating that one word and I'd have listened to it on a loop until the disc melted.

He came to sit next to me on the bed. I hoped he didn't notice the tiny ripples across my coffee due to trembling hands.

'Me wanting to screw it up is enough of a problem.'

'Because you don't think you deserve it?' I asked, desperately hoping that wasn't what he meant. 'We've had plenty of kids who've tried to sabotage their place here because they couldn't cope with a safe home.'

'Oh, I know I don't deserve it. But Ellis and Billy do, so I'd say yes and make it work just for them. I'm talking about you.'

'Don't say it,' I whispered.

Say it, my heart begged.

'Doesn't change it.' He turned his gaze back out towards the room, drank more coffee.

'But it changes what we have to do about it.'

'So, your plan is to ignore how we feel, keep living as brother and sister?'

'You don't know how I feel.'

My heart, pummelling against my T-shirt, was probably a clue.

He smiled, and inside something cracked open and all the feelings I'd been squashing down for three months spilled out.

'I don't think I can keep pretending. I don't want to pretend. Not with you.'

'Then you'll have to say no,' I breathed, amazed I had any breath left.

'Or... we spend the next two years being utterly, excruciatingly honest with each other, and do a very good job of keeping it a secret from everyone else.'

'I can't feel like this about my adopted brother.'

His smile grew. 'I don't know how you feel.'

I ducked my head. How I felt was terrified. Embarrassed. As vulnerable as if I'd brought him the coffee dressed in my underwear.

'Tell me.'

'I can't.'

He gently rested his fingers against the side of my cheek and turned my face towards his. We were so close I could have counted the flecks of dark brown in his eyes, if my brain had been functioning.

'Tell me.' His murmur sent shivers across my skin.

I slowly, unsteadily, moved the stupidest, most brazen few inches forwards of my life, and leant until my lips were about to touch his.

'Jonah?'

A knock on the door sent me jerking back so quickly the dregs of my drink splashed onto the duvet.

Jonah hadn't moved.

'Yeah?' he called, eyes not leaving mine.

'I'm about to put a load of laundry on. Do you still want your jumper washed?'

Sighing, he pulled off his sweatshirt, revealing about eight inches of smooth skin as his T-shirt rode up, then opened the door just wide enough to shove the sweatshirt into Mum's hand, mumbled something about getting an early night, and closed the door before she could reply.

'I should go.'

He leant against the door. 'You don't sound very sure.'

I shook my head, gripping my curls with both hands. 'I'm very not sure!'

He moved away. 'Then you should go.'

I watched out of the window until Mum, having loaded up the washing machine, rejoined Dad in the garden.

'Just so you know,' Jonah said as I carefully opened his door again, listening out for Nicky chatting on the phone in her bedroom. 'I am completely sure.'

'That I need to go?'

'That I want you to come back. Once you're sure, too.'

'I don't want to screw things up for you.'

He reached forwards and tucked a stray curl back behind my ear. 'I was screwed the first time I heard you sing "Wuthering Heights".'

Nicky's bedroom door flew open, her voice suddenly far clearer.

I did the last sensible thing I'd do before everything exploded, and fled.

37

I managed about three hours of anxiety dreams before hauling myself out of bed around ten the next morning. I didn't need to be in school until the maths exam the day afterwards, and my parents had taken Nicky prom dress shopping, so the house was quiet when I tiptoed down to find breakfast.

'Hey.'

I swivelled around from where I was rummaging in the fridge to see Jonah dressed in a crumpled white T-shirt and dark jeans. For reasons that were possibly as twisted as the rest of this situation, I couldn't stop looking at his bare feet.

I glanced down at my own feet, which looked perfectly normal. I'd put on a sundress covered in pastel flowers with a swirly skirt that reached halfway down my thigh. It was deliciously daring enough to make me feel almost, sort of beautiful.

'I was thinking about pancakes,' I said, trying to sound as if yesterday hadn't happened but probably failing due to my nerves having gone haywire.

'Perfect. I'm an excellent tosser.'

I twisted my head to the side, raising my eyebrows in an 'excuse me?' gesture.

'Okay. Delete that. I need caffeine before I say anything else.'

He padded over to the kettle and switched it on, leaning back against the worktop and unashamedly watching as I measured flour into a bowl, then whisked in milk and eggs.

'Didn't sleep well?' I asked, eventually, my scrambled brain unable to come up with anything more inspiring.

'What do you think?' He twisted up his mouth in wry amusement. 'I was in the garden at midnight.'

'Oh. If I'd known…'

'No, you wouldn't.' He poured the now boiling water on top of the instant granules and sugar, and walked over to where the milk sat on the countertop in front of me.

'I probably wouldn't.'

'But you were awake, too?'

'Only until about five.' I shrugged, with an exaggerated blasé smile.

'What's the plan for today, then?'

I checked the oil in the frying pan was hot and ladled in a scoop of batter.

'Revising? Trying not to panic about all the revision I should have done earlier?' I darted my eyes at him before focussing back on the pancake. 'Thinking about you every ten seconds and freaking out about what I'm going to do.'

'Only every ten seconds?' He stepped close enough for his bare arm to brush against mine. 'I'm hurt.'

'What are *your* plans, then?'

'Oh, I don't know now. Yours sound better. I think I'll switch.'

So we spent the rest of the morning, a picnic lunch that I insisted Jonah ate with me in the garden on a blanket, and half the afternoon talking, flirting, gazing bashfully at each other and valiantly not mentioning anything to do with where this was heading while occasionally flipping open a maths study guide and scanning a question we were too distracted to try to answer.

I'd thought endlessly about what it would feel like to spend time like this with Jonah. Alone, with no threat of being discovered or making a fool of myself.

I'd never imagined it would be like this. Easy, peaceful and fun all at the same time. It was *light*. As if us being together dispelled all the darkness tormenting his soul.

'So, those notes in my pocket?' He laughed, after I'd been teasing him about his hair, which had grown almost to his shoulders, and he'd shown me where he planned to get a jackal tattooed across one side of his chest. 'Did you get those ideas off the Samaritans website or what?' We were lying next to each other on the blanket, and he elbowed me in the ribs, making me squirm.

'So, those songs in the car? Did you specifically search iTunes in order to send me secret messages, or what?'

I poked him back, but he grabbed my wrist, pulling me up against him so that I ended up half lying on his chest.

Oh boy.

'I did. Yes.' He moved his hand to entwine his fingers around mine. 'You could have given me a sign that you'd noticed, instead of torturing me with your silence.'

'I wrote more notes, didn't I?'

'Because you don't want me to die,' he said, his voice dropping.

'It's safe to say that I don't, no. That would be pretty horrible for everyone.'

'But you *really* want me to stay alive. Not just because it would be a horrible thing to happen to a foster kid.'

'What, you mean because I'd miss you?' I asked, trying to

sound playful as I wrinkled my nose, because Jonah talking about this so calmly chilled me to the bone.

He wasn't joking around, though.

'Tell me that you'd miss me.'

I took in a deep breath. My ribcage pushed against his chest, warm and solid beneath me. As I let it go, I could feel his heart thumping.

'I already miss you,' I said. 'I miss you when you hide in your bedroom for days on end. When you turn in the opposite direction to avoid me in the corridor at school. When I creep down to the garden at night and you're not here. Or I hang about for a pathetically long time in the kitchen, but you don't show up. The thought of you moving somewhere else, where I can't accidentally bump into you on the stairs, makes me miss you so hard I can somehow pretend I'm happy for you to stay as my foster brother. As Bronah. The thought of you never being here? Jonah, if you died, half my heart would die with you.'

I tried to sit up, but he tugged me back down again, his eyes scanning my face.

'I know it's crazy, I've only known you a few months, and I'm sixteen and never had a boyfriend and we've not even kissed or anything yet. But I can't help it. I feel... I like you even more than Carlos Romero, and he had to move schools because of me.'

'Shut up.' Jonah smiled, reaching his head up and pressing his lips against mine.

It was my first kiss.

From the way his mouth progressed the gentle peck into something deeper, his hand cradling the back of my head as he pulled me even closer, I guessed it wasn't his.

After a while he expertly nudged me onto my back, bracing himself on his elbow as he paused to stroke the hair off my forehead before smiling at me, waiting for me to smile then bending to kiss me again.

A sound from another garden caused me to freeze, pulling back as panic pulsed through my veins.

'It's someone closing a car door. Not here.'

I glanced to the side. It was nearly three o'clock. Who knew what time everyone would be home?

'Let's go inside,' he said, pressing a kiss against the side of my neck that sent more shivers across my skin.

Not wanting to break the spell, we gathered up our things and scurried up to his bedroom, where we carried on as before until the unmistakable chug of Dad's car sounded the alarm.

'How are you feeling about tomorrow?' Mum asked after Nicky had shown me her gorgeous dark red dress and we'd sat down for reheated chicken casserole because no one could be bothered to cook after a long day.

'Okay.' I shrugged. 'Could be better.'

'Could be worse?' Dad asked, hopefully. 'How about you, Jonah? Did you have a productive final revision day?'

'I did, thanks.' Jonah nodded. 'I learned a lot more than I expected.'

'Excellent!' Mum beamed. 'You might get that pass after all.'

'Way to sound encouraging, Mum.' Nicky snorted. 'You might, Bronah, if every question happens to be precisely what you studied, and there's a full moon and the invigilator doesn't spot the list of equations smuggled in your sock, you might, just, possibly, sort of pass!' She ended brightly, with a perfect imitation of our mother.

'I didn't mean that!' Mum laughed, always happy to be the

butt of our jokes because she'd seen far too many tears around this table. 'I was trying not to up the pressure and stress Bronah out.'

'Ew, Mum!' Nicky groaned. 'You can't call him that.'

'Why not?' Mum asked, flummoxed. 'It's his nickname, isn't it? Libby calls him that.'

Not after today, I didn't.

I could feel myself blushing even thinking about it. I dared the tiniest of glances at Jonah, sitting opposite Nicky as usual, and he winked, almost causing me to choke on a chunk of pepper.

'Are you all right, Libby?' Dad asked, frowning.

'Yes.' I stopped, coughed, took a drink of water and coughed again.

'You're not coming down with something? It's quite common during exams, everyone's so run-down.'

'Actually, I am feeling a bit... peaky. I might head up, if that's okay.'

'Why don't you try a nice, steamy bath?' Mum suggested. 'See if you can clear your airways, relax before you try to sleep.'

'Right.'

Keeping my eyes firmly downwards – because talking about steamy baths in front of Jonah would have been embarrassing even if I hadn't spent the past few hours smooching him on his bed – I made a clumsy exit.

I didn't have a bath, instead opting for a quick shower once my parents had finished clearing up dinner.

Jonah's door silently swung open as I padded past. By the time I'd run downstairs to tell Mum that I was exhausted and going to sleep, and tiptoed back to peek inside, Jonah was on his bed, leaning back against the wall with his legs crossed. His smile was like an invisible force, pulling me inside.

'Mmmm.' He wrapped his arms around me the second I climbed onto his bed. 'You're all… steamy.'

'I had a shower, actually.' I giggled. I'd dressed in leggings and a T-shirt before leaving the bathroom, still adhering to at least one fostering rule, but it was true that my skin was pink and soft from the hot water.

'Still steamy.' Jonah pressed his face into my neck, nuzzling beneath my damp curls. 'You smell like… warm Libby.'

'It's coconut,' I said, backing off. I was a little unnerved by his reaction.

To my relief, he let me go, reaching out after a few seconds to wrap his little finger around mine. 'You're beautiful.'

'Thanks.' As if I weren't warm enough. I gave an embarrassed shrug. 'You're not so bad, yourself.'

'You look a bit… are you scared? Libby, I'm not going anywhere with this.'

'I already told you.' I feigned a huff. 'I'm not scared of you.'

He flicked his fringe back off his eyes, giving me the full force of his amber gaze. 'Okay… nervous?'

'Of course I'm nervous!' My eyes darted to the bedroom door. 'I don't even have a hot drink as an excuse this time.'

He picked up a notebook from his bedside table. 'Picking up revision cards.'

'I don't have to come in, close the door and sit on your bed to pick up revision cards.'

'If they adopt me, will the rules change?'

I thought about that. 'There won't be any social worker rules any more. But Mum and Dad have been living by these rules for a long time; I can't see them throwing them all out the window.'

'You're allowed in Nicky's room. What's the difference?'

I shook my head. 'I don't want to kiss Nicky?'

'You want to kiss me?'

'Well, duh. I think this afternoon was a bit of a clue.'

'Why aren't you, then?' He leant forwards, coming to a stop tantalisingly close to my mouth, leaving it up to me to span the last few millimetres, which I did, brushing my lips against his.

'When you're adopted, the rules won't matter. We have to stop,' I said, once I'd pulled away long enough for my head to unscramble. 'Even in secret. And it's forever, so we can't ever start again.'

He looked away, clenching his jaw before giving a sharp nod. 'I know.'

'But this was still the best day of my life. I know it's wrong, but I can't regret it.'

'Well, that only confirms I've made the right decision. I don't want just one day of this.'

His hair had flopped back over his face, and he glanced at me through the light-brown strands, waiting for my reaction.

'No.'

'Yes.'

'No, Jonah.' I paused, made an effort to keep my voice quiet. 'You can't turn down this chance. Not because of me.'

'Even if you walked out that door and decided you hated my guts, touching me made your skin crawl and you ignored me until one of us moves out, it won't change how I feel. Even if we never kiss again, I will still love you. And not in a brotherly way. At all.'

I closed my eyes. It was the best and the hardest thing I'd ever heard.

'I love you, too,' I whispered.

'Then I can't do it. I won't do it.'

'Maybe you just need some time,' I gabbled. 'If we try to stay away from each other, work really hard at being friends. I don't know – you could get a girlfriend easily. My friend Katie thinks you're hot, she'd go on a date with you...'

'So, let's say I start going out with Katie.' He grimaced at the very thought, which sent a ripple of pleasure through me. 'Will it change how you feel about me?'

I waited before answering, wanting so hard to do the right thing and lie. 'No. But I can live with it. If it means you, Billy and Ellis get the family you need.'

He leant forwards again, looking right into my eyes. I saw a smile dancing behind the gold, and I knew then that I wouldn't change his mind. 'The only way I'm becoming part of your family is if you marry me.'

'Woah. That's a big statement.'

'So is I love you.'

'Have you changed your plan, then?' I asked, aware that for the first time Jonah was talking about a long-term future. 'Were my notes successful?'

He laughed. 'What, trying to persuade me that elephants were a reason to stay alive? They were not.'

He pressed a gentle finger against my mouth, shutting off my protest.

'But knowing that I get the chance to spend another day, and another, and another, with someone like you... knowing that someone like you... No, not someone like you – just *you* – cared enough about me to write all those stupid notes. Yes. My plan has changed.'

'But your new plan is to say no to the adoption.'

'My plan is to move into one of those supported accommodation units as soon as possible. The kind where they don't have rules about girlfriends staying over.'

'My parents will be heartbroken.'

'They'll get over it. I'll be here all the time to see Ellis and Billy.' He took hold of my hand. 'And my girlfriend.'

'What will you tell them when they ask why?'

He squinted. 'That I'm head over heels in love with their daughter?'

I tugged on his hand.

'That I'm very grateful, but I've spent years taking care of my brother and sister, and I don't trust myself to stop if I'm living with them again. They deserve a proper mum and dad, not a screwed-up seventeen-year-old. And I deserve a chance to be seventeen, without worrying about them all the time. I don't think I can do that if we're in the same house.'

'Is that true?'

'Would it make you feel better if it was?'

'Yes.'

'Sorry.'

'Well, if it convinces Mum and Dad, then that's the main thing.' I nestled up against his chest. 'I still can't believe you love me.'

He was quiet for a few moments. I closed my eyes, revelling in the feel of his arm around my shoulders, his chin resting on the top of my head.

When he spoke, the words were soft.

'I didn't think it could be like this.'

'Like what?'

Another silence.

'I can't remember the last time I didn't have to hide myself from someone.'

I held him tighter, tears burning behind my eyes.

'I know you won't hurt me. It's just not in you to do that. And I know your parents and Nicky wouldn't try to hurt me either. But I could disappoint them. They look at me with this… eagerness. Like, if only I had the chance, there's this amazing person lurking behind the million screw-ups. You, on the other hand.' He sighed. 'When you look at me, I feel like I'm already amazing. Like I could save the damn world, because you believe in me. It's not pressure. It's freedom.'

We carried on talking, and kissing, and talking more for hours, only pausing while we heard my parents climb the stairs and go to bed. Somewhere around 1 a.m., after I snuck down to the kitchen for drinks and chocolate biscuits, we moved underneath the duvet. There was touching, yes, but Jonah didn't try to remove any of my clothes, and I wasn't brave enough to ask him, even if I'd been brave enough for him to do that.

At some point, our words faded away and, without even realising it, we fell asleep.

38

NOW

The kids, sensing that their mum was back to feeling anxious and overwhelmed, bickered and whined from their exile in the living room while Dad and I talked in the kitchen.

He listened and nodded and asked a couple of questions, and I wilfully ignored the tiny corner of my brain still rational enough to notice that, rather than seeming shocked, or even upset, he appeared fidgety and distracted. I'd started cooking enough burritos for four people, still chuntering away, when his phone rang.

'No. Not yet. I'm still here, yes.'

A pause. Dad kept his eyes on the floor as he wandered into the garden, sliding the door behind him. What he failed to notice was the open window, allowing his words to drift in anyway.

'Libby's had a big shock. She needed to talk about it.'

'I know I promised, but something has come up. It's serious, this time.'

'I'm sorry, Janet, but I'm going to have to rethink... No. I meant what I said. She's an adult and I can't plan my life around her, but this is different... No. I don't know. This isn't just about her...

Look, can we please talk later? I don't know when. I'll call you. I'm sorry. Bye.'

Dad slipped back inside, looking as if he'd been told off by the head teacher.

'Janet?'

He cringed. 'Yes. She, er. Well.'

'The window's open. I heard everything.'

He jerked his head up. 'Not her side?'

'No.'

His sag of relief wasn't reassuring.

'I've had enough farting about for one day, Dad. What's going on?'

'I've promised Janet that I'll take a few months off looking after the kids, starting at the end of term.'

I leant back against the countertop. It wasn't a surprise, but still hit me like a hammer.

'Janet has decided to retire, and, well, the school governors are fuming because it's all a bit quick, but we're not getting any younger. Her sister died recently, and the family were asking if anyone wanted her campervan. So. Well.'

'You're going travelling?' I asked, a semi-hysterical laugh bubbling up.

'Don't panic, Libby. We've planned a fortnight in Scotland, maybe a few days here and there touring Wales. And I would have spoken to you and my grandchildren as often as you'd let me. I wouldn't have left you and Nicky; it would just have a been a lot simpler if I wasn't tied here three days a week.'

I sank onto the nearest kitchen chair, my frazzled brain trying to process what he'd said.

'You said you *wouldn't* have left me.'

Dad reached across and took hold of my hand. 'You know I would never do that.'

'Not that you won't leave.' I gripped his hand in return. 'Why did you speak as if you aren't going any more?'

Dad frowned, as if it were obvious. 'Your mum.'

'My mum, or your wife?'

He paused before replying. 'I don't know.'

'What about Janet?'

Dad shook his head. 'Janet is a lovely friend. But I've been avoiding facing what happened with your mother for far too long. If me and Janet are meant to be, she'll understand that I need to sort this out first. At the very least, I need to be here for my girls. I don't care if you're adults; this is my mess as much as anyone's – I'm not running off to Scotland and leaving you to deal with it. If we've learned anything the past few years, it's that disappearing doesn't solve anything.'

'You don't even know if she wants to speak to you.'

'Well, for the first time in five years, she won't have a choice.'

Dad stood up and came around the table to kiss me on the head. 'We've both got a lot to think about, so I'll head off now. No doubt your sister will be phoning you the second she can shake off your mum.'

'Dad?' I followed him to the front door, where he waited for me to continue.

'I'm so sorry. For all of it. Everything. For causing all of this in the first place...'

He wrapped his arms around me, burying my head in his chest as I started to weep.

'You lost your wife.'

'My wife chose to leave,' he said, firmly. 'There are more reasons for that than I can bear to go into today, but none of them started with you and Jonah.'

Dad pulled back to look at me. 'Would you blame Finn's

terrible twos or your difficult pregnancy with Isla for Brayden leaving? Was that their fault?'

'Of course not! They're children.'

He smiled. 'As were you, Elizabeth. And even in the years that followed, you were still our child.'

I nodded, wiping my eyes on the handkerchief he offered.

'Go on that holiday, Dad. I can find someone else to look after the kids for a couple of weeks. Even if you don't go with Janet, you should still go. I mean, after all these years, isn't it time you found the "real Tony"?'

Before he could answer, there was a knock on the front door, followed by the familiar sound of Hazel crying.

'I'll leave you to it,' Dad said, opening the door to let Toby in before heading to his car.

'Everything okay?' Toby asked, bouncing a screaming baby on his hip as we walked to the kitchen.

'Nope. Everything okay with you?'

His grin instantly collapsed.

'Reunion's off, then?' I asked, patting his back a few agonising sobs later, Hazel cocooned between us, still sniffling.

'I was looking at your loft,' Toby said, abruptly changing the subject as he surreptitiously wiped his face on the shoulder of my top. 'There used to be an outside staircase, round the back. The door is still there. Nice-sized windows. It must have been an annexe once. There's probably electrics and decent flooring, although they'd need updating. It'd be easy to convert into a granny flat, only for an idiot teenager.'

'An idiot teenager? Not you, then?'

'Could get someone over to have a look at it, see what they think. Are you cooking Mexican? It smells awesome.'

'By wonderful coincidence I have a burrito going spare.'

'Want a salad making?'

I handed him a tissue, and a pack of tomatoes.

When Finn and Isla came in to help their honorary big brother set the table, for a few blissful minutes it felt as though I was the kind of woman who could survive anything. Mum turning up, Dad not being around so much, Toby turning my loft into a bachelor pad, Brayden's second not-even-close-to-midlife crisis... an actual date for the first time in ten years.

After all, I'd survived worse.

39

THEN

I woke to the sound of thumping on a door. Brutally loud and accompanied by shouting that it took my startled brain a few seconds to process.

'Jonah? Open the door, please, or we're coming in.'

Why was Mum banging on my door asking for Jonah?

Oh no. Oh crap.

I opened my eyes and saw, not the green of my attic bedroom, but Jonah's dark-blue walls. He stirred beside me, shaking his head and squinting his eyes.

'Jonah?' Dad.

Eyes widening, Jonah froze, mouthing a string of swear words. Before I could decide whether to dive under the covers or bolt for his wardrobe, the bedroom door opened.

For three seconds it was as though the world stopped turning.

Mum and Dad stood in the doorway in stunned silence.

Then all hell broke loose.

Shouting, crying, Dad ripping the duvet off us – thank goodness I was still dressed, and Jonah had his shorts on. Small consolation in the grand scheme of things, but I preserved that tiny iota of dignity, at least.

Jonah tried to physically shield me from the torrent of anger, but that only enraged Dad even more. Abandoning any hint of professionalism, he wrenched Jonah to the side, grabbing my wrist to yank me off the bed.

'Dad, stop!' I was too stunned at that point to cry or resist. 'Nothing happened! Please, stop!'

'You being in this boy's bed happened,' Mum screeched. I'd occasionally seen my parents grow irate at social services, ignorant teachers or having to stand by helpless as one of their foster children suffered, but nothing like this. They'd borne physical blows, verbal abuse – one girl ripped up Dad's late parents' wedding photo – and never once lost their temper.

I huddled in the corner as Mum grabbed a sports bag and started stuffing Jonah's things into it, sobbing.

Jonah, on the other hand, had been confronted with his worst trigger – screaming, out-of-control adults. He'd instinctively switched to survival mode, posture aggressive as he swore and shouted, trying to get up in Dad's face.

After a seemingly endless couple of minutes, Nicky appeared.

'What's going on?' She pushed her way in between Dad and Jonah, bracing them apart with held-up palms.

'Dad?' Her voice was loud but it quavered. 'Mum, stop! What are you doing?'

'Jonah's leaving,' Mum said, shoving a pair of jeans into the bag.

Nicky spotted me then, eyes going round as she started to process the cause of all the drama.

'They found you, then,' she said, head shaking in dismayed disbelief. 'Best get out of here before you make things even worse. Both of you.'

She grabbed the T-shirt now in Mum's hand and shoved it at Jonah.

'They aren't going anywhere,' Dad spluttered, but Nicky was having none of it.

'They're going downstairs, where they're safe, while you two fricking well pull yourselves together before you do something that'll get you both struck off.'

'Irrelevant,' Mum snapped, her voice thick. 'I'm done. This is too much. I can't do it. I shouldn't bloody well *have to do it*!'

'Go with them, Nicola,' Dad barked. 'They aren't to be alone together.'

'What, you think we're going to start getting it on in the living room while you're up here ransacking my stuff?' Jonah scoffed.

If possible, Dad's face turned even more purple, his fists clenching. Nicky pulled a furiously impatient face at me, and I slipped past her out of the door. To my relief, Jonah followed me. I went straight to the kitchen, expecting him to come too, but instead the front door crashed shut, echoing through the sudden silence.

* * *

My parents' social worker, Robin, arrived an hour later. Clare, social worker for Jonah, was not far behind. I'd hidden in my bedroom the second Jonah disappeared down the road, and remained there until Robin knocked on my door and asked if I would be kind enough to come down and have a chat about what had happened.

I'd had an hour to try to come up with an explanation, a justifiable excuse for being in Jonah's bed at ten-thirty in the morning. With Jonah.

The best I could do was present an edited version of the facts.

We were chatting, both feeling stressed about exams, got cold so we went under the duvet. We clearly hadn't had sex, nothing like that had happened before, there was no relationship. Blah, blah, blah.

I pushed back my shoulders, tried to look innocent, and sauntered into the kitchen, coming to a dead stop at the journal sitting in the middle of the table.

'You read my diary?' I cried. 'You went into my bedside drawer, took out my diary and read it. That's... why would you do that?'

'You were missing!' Mum said, sounding as distraught as I felt. 'You have a maths exam this afternoon and you were nowhere. Your phone was in your bedroom, bed clearly hadn't been slept in. We waited an hour, called Katie and Alicia, and they didn't know where you were either. None of your shoes were missing. The front door was locked from the inside. We were frantic with worry.'

'So you know, then,' I said, all the fight seeping out of me. 'Is there any point talking about it?'

Robin cleared his throat before either of my parents could answer.

'We know that you clearly had some feelings for Jonah.'

'And you also know that they were only feelings. Up until yesterday.'

'What happened yesterday?' Robin asked, stroking his beard. I liked Robin. He'd been a social worker forever and had seen pretty much everything. He used to take me and Nicky out for milkshakes sometimes, and had become a something of a replacement for the grandad we hardly ever saw because he lived in a care home miles away.

'We spent the day hanging out and revising together. In the garden. Later on we were both feeling stressed about the exam, so

I went into Jonah's room and we talked for a bit. It got really late, and we ended up falling asleep.'

'You talked in his bed?' Clare asked.

'On his bed. You've seen the state of his room. There wasn't anywhere else to sit.'

'Your parents found you under the covers.'

'It got chilly!' I knew, rationally, that there was no way to salvage this. Not now they'd read the obsessed ramblings in my journal. But I could try to make sure Jonah didn't get into too much trouble. At least, little enough trouble that we could keep on having contact once he moved out.

'They also found me fully dressed.'

'Well, it's easy enough to slip a T-shirt and leggings back on,' Mum snapped. 'We were banging on the door for a good minute before we came in.'

'Why don't you just say it?' I said, the words choking in my throat. 'Ask me if we had sex.'

'Well, I think that's pretty obvious.'

Mum couldn't look at me. Her knuckles were white where she gripped the cold mug of tea in her hands.

'Is it? Because we didn't. We did nothing like that. Yes, I like Jonah. But if you read my journal, you know that I was never going to do anything about it. I wouldn't let a stupid crush ruin his chances of being adopted.'

'But you did, when you spent the night in his room,' Dad said, the disappointment on his face even worse than the anger earlier.

'It was one night! We were chatting and we fell asleep! It was extreme circumstances and we won't do it again. Obviously!'

'Libby,' Robin said, gently. 'You know Jonah can't stay.'

At that moment the front door opened, and the unmistakable sound of Jonah's boots clomped down the hallway. Before Clare could intercept him, he was standing in the kitchen doorway, his face a mask.

'Jonah,' Clare said. 'Libby was just telling us that last night was the first time anything had happened between you.'

'Nothing happened!' I cried, trying to send Jonah desperate messages with my eyes, which he refused to acknowledge.

'Oh, for goodness' sake, Libby. Please stop this charade,' Mum said.

'You want to know the truth?' Jonah asked, sounding as if he couldn't have cared less.

'That would be very helpful, thank you,' Robin said.

Jonah leant against the doorframe. 'We kissed. It was the first time it happened, but it wasn't the first time I wanted it to. And I'm not going to pretend I don't want it to happen again.'

'What the—?' Mum jumped up so fast that Robin reached out and steadied her with one hand on her arm.

'I'm sorry you found out like this, and that we didn't wait until I'd moved out. We didn't plan for it to happen. But I love Libby. I'm not some deadbeat loser taking advantage of your daughter.'

'That's exactly what you are!'

I bit the inside of my cheek so hard I tasted the tang of blood. It was the first time I'd seen Dad cry. Mum, however, was simply furious.

'We take you in, offer a home to your brother and sister – to be your *family*. And this is how you repay us? You not only took brazen advantage of my daughter, you took advantage of me, Tony, Nicola… everyone you hoodwinked with your good-guy, tough-life persona. You've made damn fools out of all of us.'

I was too stricken to protest as Robin herded me and Jonah off to our bedrooms. An age later, Jonah messaged me.

I'm sorry. I'm an idiot for thinking that speech could win them over. I know better than anyone that life isn't a soppy film. I guess you gave me a reason to start hoping for a happy ending. I'm sorry for dragging you into my screwed-up crapheap of a life. No matter what happens, I love you x

I replied straight away.

I loved that speech. They're mad now, but when they've calmed down I can talk to them, make them see. Don't give up on a happy ending just yet. I love you too xxx

A few minutes later, the shouting and crashing started. It wasn't hard to grasp what was going on.

Jonah was leaving. To ensure our family had no further contact with him, Ellis and Billy would be staying with their current foster carer. Placing their brother far enough away to safeguard me meant he'd be hundreds of miles from his siblings, too.

I ventured out of my room, sure that I stood as good a chance as anyone of helping Jonah to calm down, but Robin firmly sent me back, failing to appease me with his offer to bring up a drink or some lunch.

'My exam starts soon.'

'He'll be gone well before then.'

'Then I need to say goodbye!'

He shook his head, sadly. 'That's not going to happen.'

I tried phoning, three times. Sent more texts. There was no reply, but I reasoned he wouldn't be looking at his phone.

When there was the unmistakable sound of people lugging suitcases down the stairs – despite Jonah yelling that he didn't want any of it, they could burn the lot – I half ran, half stumbled down two flights of stairs to catch up with him.

'Libby, get back inside,' Mum ordered from where she stood rigid in the hallway as Dad heaved a bag into the boot of Clare's car. I ignored her, hurrying onto the drive in my bare feet just as Jonah was about to get into the passenger seat.

'Jonah!'

He quickly lifted his head to find me, eyes wild, hair a matted mess and an angry red mark across one cheek. 'I'm sorry.'

'I know. I'm sorry too.'

'I love you!'

Before I could say anything else, Dad had grabbed hold of my arm and steered me back in the house. By the time I slipped free, the car had gone.

'Where's he going?' I asked, fraught with desperation, following Robin and my parents into the living room.

'They found a residential unit,' Robin said. 'Quite lucky at such short notice.'

'Where?'

'I can't tell you that.'

'Fine, I'll ask him myself.' I started to flounce off, as if I were the one wronged, rather than the person who'd chucked a petrol bomb into the middle of our family.

'How about you get ready for your exam, and we can stop off for a KFC on the way there?' Robin said, although it clearly wasn't a suggestion.

I looked at my parents, two shell-shocked statues clasping hands on the sofa.

Now probably wasn't the time to say that I hated KFC. I changed into my uniform, collected my bag and went to stare at an exam paper, tears dripping onto my paltry effort at solving a quadratic equation and plotting points on a graph.

40

NOW

Nicky called me just after ten.

'She's gone to bed. Still on French time.'

'How was it?'

She sighed. 'I hid in the kitchen sorting dinner while Theo made polite conversation. We had about an hour around the dinner table, her asking tentative questions about my job, Theo's family. You and the kids. Me replying as neutrally as possible. I'm trying to pretend she doesn't have the power to upset me, but at the same time I still want her buried in guilt.'

'What are her plans for tomorrow?'

'I'm pretty sure she's hoping to see her grandchildren. No mention of Dad.'

'Ugh. Isla could really do without more randomers dropping into her life. Toby, Silva and Baby Brayden are enough for one summer.'

There was a brief pause. 'Maybe it wouldn't be terrible for the kids to meet her properly. Mum is great with children.'

'Yeah. Especially seeing as Dad might not be around so much.'

'What?'

We talked until the necessary processing had deteriorated into gratuitous grumbling. I was determined not to allow Mum's disruption to negatively impact my new sensible bedtime routine, but there wasn't a lot I could do about the thoughts careening about my head for most of the night, making sleep seem like a cruel joke.

Thursday morning, I stuck on my best calm-capable-mum persona, aware that I sounded like an actor in a cheesy advert as I bundled the kids off to school. I smiled robotically through three post-birth video calls with previous private clients, and had time to set up the online bookings for my autumn classes and update the website. All while ignoring the four calls and even more messages buzzing through from a new, unknown number, having glimpsed one message as starting, 'Darling daughter, I am devastated…' before turning my phone screen down.

Nicky called while I was waiting to pick Isla and Finn up from their after-school football club.

'Your turn,' she said, with all the authority of an older sister. 'Stop dodging her calls.'

'You're working today. It's no one's turn.'

'She came to the surgery and introduced herself to Martha!'

'Yuck.' Martha was one of the receptionists.

'Precisely. She obviously knew nothing, so made Mum a cup of tea and invited her into the staffroom. She's been hanging around for nearly three hours waiting for me to take a break. I had to ask Nadia to bring my matcha tea into my room. My step count is fifty-seven, and half of those were scuttling to the patient toilets so she didn't spot me in the corridor.'

'Why didn't she just come here?'

'She's waiting for after school, banking on you not making a scene in front of the kids.'

'I really can't be doing with this today.'

'Libby, my last patient projectile-vomited in my hair. It's your turn. Call her.'

I didn't call, but I did read the messages and reply that we'd be home at five. She'd grind me down at some point, so might as well get it over with.

* * *

'Hey, I have some exciting news,' I said, once the three of us were walking home along the footpath.

'Did you kiss that man again?' Isla asked.

'Ew!' Finn scowled as I reminded her that there'd been no kissing.

'Is our new baby sister born? Oh, did Toby fix the scary hole in the ceiling where the monsters hide?'

'What hole? And no, none of those things. Your Grandma Helen is coming to see you.'

'The one who sends me pictures on my birthday sometimes?' Isla asked, dark eyebrows shooting up her little forehead. 'Did she come in a boat?'

'How is she going to sail a boat to Bigley?' Finn scoffed. 'Down the ditch?'

'She could have put it on the back of a lorry.' Isla pouted. 'Or had one of those boats with wheels like in your book.'

'She doesn't work on the boat any more, so she came on a train and in a taxi,' I said, before Finn could pour further scorn on his sister's suggestions.

'Did she bring us presents?' he asked instead.

'I don't know. But it would be rude to ask, wouldn't it?'

'Zak and Bert's grandparents give them presents all the time.

A postcard doesn't count, so she might have all my birthday presents saved up.'

'I'm not sure. There wasn't a lot of room on the boat to store presents.'

'Well, I think she owes me at least a small one.'

I corrected his rather rude attitude, even as my heart believed that Mum owed my children far more than a few presents.

When we walked up the drive, our visitor was already waiting at the front door, fiddling with the hem of her patterned shirt.

'Did you bring our birthday presents?' Isla asked, stopping a metre or so in front of her grandma, arms folded across her muddy football top.

'Um...' Mum flashed a panicked glance at me. 'Your birthday is in February.'

'Yes. February the tenth. But you didn't give me a present yet.'

'Isla.' I took her hand and moved forwards, key ready to open the door. 'We talked about that. We didn't send Grandma a present, either.'

'Did we send her a card?' she asked as Mum stepped back so we could go inside without having to squeeze past.

She'd been back for twenty-four hours, and I still hadn't touched her.

'No. We didn't know where the boat would be that day.'

'Post people can't deliver a letter to a boat.' Finn bumped against Isla as they took their shoes off in the pristine hallway. 'What are they going to do – swim out to find it?'

'They could drive a postman boat!' Isla retorted. 'Why do you think everything I say is wrong? And stop bumping me. That hurt from where I fell on the grass!'

Oh dear. The tension was already rising. Isla's cheeks had flushed, and her fluttering eyelids were sending out SOS in Morse code. Having welcomed potential disaster into my home, the only way I could defuse it was to behave as if everything were perfectly lovely and I couldn't be happier.

'Why don't you show Grandma your Lego while I fetch drinks and a snack?' I said, purposefully directing them to the recently tidied living room, rather than the still shambolic kitchen.

'I'll help,' Mum offered.

'No. Thank you.' If I smiled any harder, my face would crack.

For the next hour I sat simmering in an armchair while Mum worked her magic with my children. Alongside the games and genuine interest in Finn and Isla's lives, she told vibrant stories about fascinating faraway places and interesting encounters with all sorts of people and strange animals.

It was captivating and infuriating at the same time. Seeing what my children had missed out on, while unable to resist enjoying at least something of their delight at experiencing it now.

'We need to get on with dinner,' I said, eventually. 'School tomorrow and we have a schedule to stick to.'

'Mu-u-u-um,' Finn whined. 'Surely we can forget about the chart for one night?'

'Remember what happened last time you tried that?' I asked. 'The Roman picnic?'

'Are you staying for dinner?' Isla asked Mum.

'I'm sure she's very busy. Maybe another time.' I stood up, making it clear that this wasn't up for debate.

'Oh.' Mum was fiddling with her shirt again. 'I thought... well. Nicola said I could only stay at hers for one night.'

'Haven't you found anywhere else?' Bigley was a small village, but there were a few B & Bs in the area, and, failing that, Sherwood Forest had caravan parks. Hardly any worse than a sailing boat.

'I just assumed... I mean...'

I turned to Finn and Isla. 'Toby's working in the garden. Can you go and ask him if he wants any dinner, please?'

'Isla's turn,' Finn said automatically.

'I asked both of you to go. Now, please.'

I waited until they'd grumbled their way down the hallway, then turned back to Mum.

'You seriously assumed you were staying here?'

Mum fiddled with a strand of hair, a gesture Nicky always did on the rare occasion she felt nervous. 'Well… I hoped you wouldn't mind.'

'For how long? Are you going to ping-pong between me and Nicky until you decide to run off again?'

'It's hardly outlandish, staying with your children when you come to visit.'

'Not for people who actually have a relationship with their children, no.'

'Darling, I have apologised and explained. I'm here now, please don't make either of us suffer any more than we have to.' Mum had switched to her 'placating an angry child' face. I wanted to slap it off.

'Where did you intend to sleep?'

'I'm sure you can squeeze me in somewhere. I'm not fussy.'

I thought about it, genuinely. I couldn't let my own mother sleep on my knackered sofa. That would mean sacrificing my bed, while I decamped to here, or on cushions on Isla's floor. I imagined her making the kids breakfast while I took my time in the shower. Even walking them to school so I could go for a run or start work on the kitchen.

And then I pictured how every one of those moments would be tainted with my anger, hurt and confusion. I'd spent so long feeling mad at Brayden, frustrated and ashamed of myself. Fretting about Isla. Rushing about trying to look after people who, with a bit of help, were far better off taking care of themselves.

I was getting my life together, at last.

My house was finally becoming a sanctuary, a place where I felt at peace.

For my and the children's sake I *would* try to find some measure of healing with my mum. I would work towards forgiving her, and give her the opportunity to finally forgive me.

But I would do this at my pace, not hers.

'I'm sorry,' I said. And I meant it. 'I'm not ready for that. You're welcome to visit for Sunday lunch, if you like.'

'Thank you,' she said, after a stiff silence. 'I appreciate the invitation.'

'I'll ask Nicky and Theo. See if his family want to come, too.'

'Can I bring anything?' Mum said as I walked them to the door.

I shrugged. 'Isla wasn't joking about the birthday present.'

41

I spent Friday sifting through the kitchen cupboards, Toby following after me with a paintbrush, in between both of us keeping Hazel amused. He'd offered to babysit while I had dinner with Jonah that evening, but I'd already asked Dad.

'He could look after this one, too, if he fancied it,' Toby said, feeding Hazel her bottle. 'Some of my mates are heading to the pub and I think it would be good to take my mind off things, blow off a bit of steam.'

'Leave her with me another time,' I said, unceremoniously dumping a pile of old toddler scribbles into a bin bag. 'Dad's got a lot going on at the moment, and it's a long time since he's had any experience with teething babies.' I deliberated over an indecipherable cardboard sculpture that had been gathering grime on the windowsill for years. 'You could try asking your mum?'

Toby looked up at me, sharply. 'What? Have you spoken to her?'

'No. But it's been a month. She's Hazel's grandma. Seeing my mum with Isla and Finn yesterday reminded me how deep that bond can be. I know things were bad, but I don't think she intended to end her role in Hazel's life completely.'

'Yeah, but asking her to babysit at the last minute will just make her feel used again.'

'Not asking might make her feel forgotten.'

He finished feeding Hazel, then sent a tentative message asking how his mum was, and whether she'd thought about seeing Hazel at some point.

Five minutes later he found me putting on my shoes, ready for the school run, and showed me the reply.

Did your babysitter cancel last minute?

He sent a quick message back.

No! If you don't want to see her, just say

Of course I want to see her!

Another message soon followed.

I was cutting your tutor's hair and she told me you were third highest on your course. You should go out and celebrate. Get Hazel's travel cot ready and she can stop the night here, give you a lie-in.

Aren't you working tomorrow?

Don't worry about that

I'd reached the school gates when he forwarded me one more message from his mum:

I'm proud of you, son

I had to turn away when Janet appeared in the playground so she didn't see my tears and start worrying about me again.

Jonah was expecting me at seven. Dad was babysitting while I had dinner with an 'old friend', on the agreement that I was home by nine-thirty. He was going with Janet to a late showing at the Bigley Country Park outdoor cinema.

However, Mum was loitering at Nicky's house when she arrived home from the surgery, so she turned up on my doorstep just after six.

'Has she said any more about her plans?' I asked, letting her in.

'She managed to book a caravan at the Peace and Pigs campsite for the next couple of weeks, so I guess at least that long.' Suppressed agitation propelled her into the kitchen. 'Hey, this is looking fantastic!'

'Maybe that'll be long enough to determine whether she's staying.'

'I think that depends on us.' Nicky stopped admiring my freshly painted cupboards and looked at me. 'Let's change the subject. You have a date. Please tell me that's not what you're wearing?'

Due to the fact that it wasn't a date, but an evening spent discussing my first heartbreak with the man who did the breaking, I'd opted for my nicest pair of jeans and a simple teal T-shirt that brought out the blue in my eyes.

Nicky was having none of it, chuntering on about it being a Friday night as she ransacked my wardrobe, yanking out a cream playsuit covered in tiny daisies, which I'd forgotten existed.

'That's years old,' I protested. 'I was nearly a stone lighter when I bought it.'

'It's a timeless classic. And you were too skinny when you bought it.'

It turned out that it did skim my curves far better than it used to hang off my hipbones, and I didn't hate the hint of cleavage at the square neckline. My legs had a faint tan from the hours I'd spent in the garden recently, and once Nicky had added a knotted headband and a swipe of mascara and lip gloss, I was pleasantly surprised by what I saw in the mirror.

'It isn't too much? Jonah's only seen me in dungarees and jeans.'

'That's Work Libby. This is Fun Libby, who happens to rock playsuits and summer dresses.'

'I don't own any decent dresses.'

'Not a problem. You can have some of mine. Now, I'd better go. Theo's away and I'm scared to leave Mum alone too long in case she decides to move herself in. Message me first thing in the morning to tell me how it went.'

My fears about giving the impression I was on a mission of seduction weren't helped when Isla and Finn both burst into giggles when I walked into the living room, earning a nudge of rebuke from Dad, busy helping them set up a board game.

'She looks weird, though!' Isla squealed.

'Like Georgie's mum.' Finn gasped.

'Yes!'

I was making an about-turn, already undoing the belt on the playsuit when Finn said, 'I didn't know Mum could look so pretty.'

When your eight-year-old son says you look pretty, you listen.

I slipped on my white trainers, kissed all three of them goodbye and left.

* * *

Jonah lived in a compact, new-build brick house on the edge of Hatherstone, the nearest village to Charis House, the school where he worked. I stopped by the small patch of front lawn and took a couple of steadying breaths. I didn't bother visualising my happy place to calm down because I was hoping this might become one of them.

A flowerpot stood by the black front door. That the boy I'd known as Jonah King would plant sweet peas made my heart ache. The difference our paths had taken in our twenties was disconcerting, to say the least.

'Hey.' He opened the door the second I knocked on it. 'I was looking out for you,' he admitted, seeing me flinch in surprise.

'I can't pretend I wouldn't be doing the same if it was the other way around.'

'Is it okay if I say how lovely you look?' he said as we walked down a short hallway to a spotless, functional kitchen.

'As nice as Georgie's mum, apparently.'

He whistled. 'Whew. A compliment indeed.'

I shook my head, grinning. 'Georgie's mum had a botched facelift a couple of months ago. She tries to deflect attention from it with tiny, too-tight dresses and no underwear.'

Jonah kept his gaze firmly on my non-botched face as he offered me a drink. He looked pretty lovely himself, in a navy shirt and faded jeans, hair slightly mussed. I made a mental note to ask when he started wearing colour.

We swapped updates on Mum turning up and how Ellis was doing – in summary: not great – while Jonah added prawns to a wok of fragrant vegetables and noodles and dished up what I realised with a tingle of pleasure was a sticky chilli prawn dish, my teenage favourite.

'I can't believe you remembered.'

Jonah put the plates on the square table, and we sat down opposite each other. 'I can't believe you'd think I'd forget.'

I grimaced. 'Well, you seemed to instantly forget about *me*...'

'I already told you, I never stopped thinking about you. Not once. The paltry number of crappy relationships I've had since all fizzled out after a few months – weeks, usually – because dating other women only made me miss you harder.'

'You disappearing the day you left kind of makes that hard to believe.' I took a slow sip of my drink. I was driving home but had permitted myself one low-alcohol beer.

Jonah took a moment while we both started eating, then he began to speak. 'That day, I was driven hours to a residential unit in Shropshire. I wasn't allowed anywhere on my own for the rest of the summer because I was considered a flight risk. I might have dabbled in teenage delinquency, but I didn't have the skills to sneak out of there and back to Sherwood Forest without getting caught.' He paused for a moment. 'Were you expecting me to show up?'

'Well, maybe. I was sixteen and madly in love. I liked to think I'd have found a way to get to you if I'd known where you were. Said goodbye properly, at least.'

He stabbed at a chunk of pepper. 'If I had, what then? They'd have only dragged me back and made things even worse.'

'Okay. I get that you couldn't come back. But why didn't you reply to my messages or call me? Were you mad at me?' It was ridiculous, but I had to force the words past the ache clogging up my throat. I'd been married since then. How could I possibly still be so upset?

There was a horrible silence.

'You messaged?'

I sucked in a painful breath. 'Of course I messaged! I was

frantic with worry. Drowning in guilt at being yet another person who'd ruined your life. I was desperate to know if you hated me or not.'

'I tried to call you in the car, but my phone was dead. By the time we got to the new place it was late, and they wouldn't allow phones in the bedrooms past curfew. When I asked for it back the next morning they said there'd been no calls or messages, you didn't want to speak to me and I wasn't allowed to contact you. When I kicked off about them deleting your number, they confiscated it. After I complained to my social worker, she got me a new one, but it was a crappy pay-as-you-go with no Internet.'

'Oh, Jonah. I'm so sorry.'

Phones weren't such a lifeline back then as they were now, but for a teenager in a strange part of the country, with no family, friends or anything familiar, having a few numbers in your phone, access to the Internet and social media was one of the ways to survive.

'Things were savage at that place. I don't want to go into it, but some of the other kids... getting through each day was bad enough. They wouldn't let me have contact with Ellis and Billy unless I kept the rules.' He rubbed his hand over his face. 'I'd like to tell you that if I'd known you were waiting, I'd have done anything to get to you. But surviving took everything I'd got.'

'I had to wonder if Mum was right.' Jonah had set the table with paper napkins, and I grabbed one, pressing it against each eye before I could keep going. 'I was simply a momentary distraction from everything else that was going on.'

'I hate that you thought that about me.' He winced. 'That you might still think that.'

'I didn't. I couldn't. When I remembered what it was really like, I knew it was real. But you ghosted me, Jonah. The only logical conclusion was that either you'd played me or you blamed me for getting sent miles away from your brother and sister. Maybe both?'

He leant forwards across the small table, his meal forgotten. 'Now you know it was neither. But you don't seem very relieved.'

'I might be. If I didn't know that for five years you were living at the Green House.' My voice disintegrated. 'You were an adult by then. No having to listen to social workers any more. If you really loved me, why didn't you contact me?'

That hung between us for a long moment. 'I was going to.' He slid his beer bottle closer and started picking at the label. 'I moved there a year after being in the other place. A space came up in one of the annexes for eighteen-year-olds, and because Ellis and Billy were still local, they offered it to me. It was like getting dropped off in paradise. Only after so long living in hell, I'd grown to resemble a demon.' He rolled his shoulders. 'I couldn't bear for you to see me like that. But you know the Green House. It's impossible to be there long and not start to hope. I was going to give it a bit of time, get enrolled in college, wait until I could get through the day without smashing something. Then they had this Christmas party.'

It felt as if every drop of air suddenly vanished from the room.

'It seemed like a miracle. Like maybe Ellis was right, and God did care after all. Because suddenly, standing underneath that massive, ridiculously over-the-top Christmas tree they'd had me help set up on the back terrace, there you were.'

'Oh, no.' I closed my eyes, in an attempt to soften the blow I knew was coming.

'Holding hands,' Jonah went on, slowly, the anguish he must have felt in every syllable, 'with some perfect-looking, smiling, Christmas-chuffing-angel.' He sighed. 'Which is just as it should have been. I'd have been pleased for you if I hadn't been too busy wrestling the urge to rip his arm off.'

'It was our first date,' I rasped. 'If I'd known you were there, I'd have ditched him in a heartbeat.'

'Yeah. Like I'd offer you a mess like me over someone like him.'

'I was seventeen. The chances were it wouldn't have lasted. What about when things started to get better for you?'

'I saw you again. Two years later. It was Christmas again, and I'd been thinking about you more than usual, so I had to catch myself when you walked into the Charis House Christmas Spectacular.'

The school where Jonah now worked held an infamous talent show every Boxing Day. A few children living with us had performed there over the years, so we all went to cheer them on. I guessed Jonah had been doing the same for children from the Green House. If he'd been on stage, I'd have noticed. I couldn't believe I hadn't noticed him anyway.

'You were with him again. Showing off your ring. Talking about your midwifery course. I made sure you didn't see me.'

I wanted to say that it still wouldn't have been too late. I'd have picked Jonah over Brayden on the morning of my wedding. But who knew what I'd have done back then, when for a brief chapter I'd felt as if I'd finally started to atone for the mess I'd made?

'I was happy for you, honestly.'

'You could have come and said hi anyway. We might have ended up friends.'

He looked up from the bottle. 'I couldn't ever be friends with you, Libby. I told you how I feel.'

'So what's this, then?'

'This is me trying to convince you to give me another shot.'

He waited for me to look at him.

'This is me telling you that you were right. It was real. I

wouldn't have believed it was possible to love you more than I did back then.' He shook his head in amazement. 'I love you more every time we speak. You are the most incredible person I've ever met.'

'I'm really not,' I said, laughing through my tears. 'Honestly, I've been mostly a total flop since Brayden left. A neurotic mum, lousy sister. My dad is my only real friend.'

'An amazing antenatal teacher, businesswoman and creator of a successful charity? Unofficial big sister to dozens of Bloomers, auntie to their babies and not to mention stand-in mum to one very lucky young man and his daughter? Who still has time to renovate her house and go on eight-mile hikes on her days off. I heard you won your team the tiebreaker at the pub quiz.'

I pressed my fingers into my hair, knocking the headband sideways, befuddled by this turn in conversation. 'Yeah, well. Things have been improving since... well, now that I think about it, since you showed up again.'

'Does that mean you're ready to go on a proper date with me?'

If he kept smiling at me like that, I'd be ready to do pretty much anything.

'Didn't you have some questions for me before we talk about that?'

He nodded. 'I also have an eye-wateringly expensive chocolate tart I picked up from Hatherstone Hall Farm Shop.'

'The one with a pistachio crumb?'

'Or there's a tub of their home-made ice cream.'

'Okay. I thought you hadn't changed that much, but now you're asking me to choose between chocolate tart and ice cream and I don't know who you are any more.'

'Chocolate tart *and* ice cream coming right up.'

'Throw in a decaf coffee and I'll answer anything.'

42

It was hard, describing to Jonah how Mum had freaked out after he'd left. How she'd insisted she and Dad take five months off fostering, cancelling our summer holiday on the pretext of the loss of income, when really she didn't want to spend two weeks pretending not to be furious with me.

It didn't help that the menopause knocked Mum totally off-kilter for a long while, causing unnerving anxiety and insomnia. When Nicky left for Cardiff, the three of us skulked around the house like shadows. I continued hiding in my room, or at friends' houses, while Mum used the excuse of making the most of their 'sabbatical' to spend more and more time out of the house.

While caring for a toddler in November, things improved slightly, and when Nicky came home for Christmas we put on a good show of being a functional family. Dad and I started talking again, about practical matters mostly, but I knew he held nothing against me for what happened with Jonah. Mum was another matter, blaming her health for why she was withdrawn and often irritable. But I was used to being a footnote in the Franklin family, and once we started welcoming larger sibling groups on emergency placements, Nicky sharing my bedroom if ever they coincided with university holidays, I retook my place in the background.

By then I was with Brayden, who treated me as if I was the most important person in the universe. I followed him to the University of Derby, which was just far enough away for me to move into student accommodation, and it was easy enough for us to keep up the pretence of all being well when I visited home. It wasn't deliberate, after all, that Mum had booked a mini cruise with a friend on my birthday. And when Brayden invited me to spend Christmas with him in my first year, I jumped at the chance after hearing that Nicky would be in the Alps with Theo's parents. It was far more fun celebrating with Brayden's family, where I could be merry and bright while almost forgetting that it was my fault our family was so fragmented.

When Brayden proposed to me on Christmas Eve, I didn't have to think about it. We got married that summer, when I was twenty and he was twenty-one. We had a momentary stumble after finding out I was pregnant a few months later, especially when horrendous sickness meant I had to drop out in my second year. But we picked it back up again. I retrained as an antenatal teacher and started teaching at local community centres. We had a beautiful, healthy baby boy, and once Brayden's cycling app suddenly took off, we could afford a treat every now and then.

When Mum and Dad retired, I assumed it would be an opportunity for them to work on their increasingly strained marriage, and maybe even help her to breach the distance with me. Instead, she ended up spending months in bed, refusing to see either of her daughters, burrowing herself deeper into the online groups that seemed to offer some hope.

We were all so relieved when Mum grew well enough to get up and about again that we overlooked most of her comments about needing time for herself. Then she dropped the bombshell about the world cruise. A week later, she'd packed her bags and gone.

It was about the same time I realised she had no intention of properly keeping in touch, and eight years of paranoia wasn't so irrational after all, that I came home early from a parenting class and found my husband in bed with another woman.

'It's still hard to comprehend why it was so difficult for her to forgive you,' Jonah said, once we'd taken our coffee into his small living room and settled on a brown leather sofa. 'She'd shown grace to plenty of teenagers who'd done far worse.'

'Yeah, but those kids had good reasons for acting the way they did. Mum always related the kids' behaviour to their backgrounds, their parents. She'd based her life's work on having superhuman parenting skills. Discovering her child could make such a monumental muck-up was like a personal affront.'

'So, to avoid feeling responsible, which would mean upending her whole identity, she deflected the blame onto you.'

'Yes. Which was fair enough, because it was me. I didn't end up falling asleep in your bed because I felt neglected. And she never believed we didn't have sex. But she also got angry at Dad, because he forgave me, and I guess that made her feel both guilty and betrayed.'

As we'd talked, we'd shifted position so that we leant against opposite arms of the sofa, facing each other, my legs stretched out, feet tucked to one side of his hip. It was how we'd spent hours on that one beautiful day thirteen years ago. Jonah reached down and rested his hand on my ankle, so casually I wasn't sure he even realised.

'She loved you, Billy and Ellis. As far as Mum was concerned, I'd ripped away her future children, her dream to see you reunited, your chance of a safe, happy family, for the sake of a silly infatuation. She had to stand by helpless while her own daughter shattered three lives who'd already suffered more than enough, when she'd been so desperate to save them.' I sighed. 'Something broke inside her. She never allowed herself to care so wholeheartedly for any kids again.'

'Well.' He gently squeezed my foot, and I realised that he knew exactly where his hand was. 'You can tell her you didn't ruin my life. Ending up at the Green House was one of the best things that ever happened to me. And like I said, if anything, meeting you saved me. I don't know how I'd have got through that year in Shropshire if I hadn't held out hope of one day seeing you again.'

'Can you say the same for Ellis?' I asked, my throat aching.

'We know as well as anyone that just because she's lost now, it doesn't mean it's hopeless.'

We talked a little more about our lives over the past ten years, how Jonah became a teacher. After leaving the Green House he'd rented places around Mansfield, our nearest town, ensuring he was close enough to see Billy and try to keep track of Ellis. He'd finally settled in Hatherstone to be near his new job at Charis House.

Oh, and he'd started wearing colours at the Green House.

'My grey sweatshirt was falling apart, and Mary bought me a bright red one. The first time I wore it a girl tried to give me her number, so I figured it was the way to go.'

'I don't suppose I'm allowed to be jealous that you changed your whole look because of another girl.'

He grinned. The sun coming out from behind a cloud. 'You can be as jealous as you like. Though this might help.'

Then he sat up, lifted his shirt and showed me the jackal running across his ribcage.

I moved closer, stunned to see entwined around it was a letter L.

'L for...'

He nodded, still smiling. Unable to resist, I reached out and stroked the ink with my fingers. Then our eyes met. I rested my hand against his bare skin, and we both leant forwards, anticipating the kiss.

The second our lips met, the front door crashed open, and Ellis tumbled into the living room.

'What the—?' She stopped dead, face screwing up at the sight of us together on the sofa.

'Hey.' Jonah scrambled to his feet, but Ellis was already backing away.

'I can't believe you let that tramp into our house,' she snarled, holding one arm up to prevent him from getting too close.

Ellis looked even worse than the last time I'd seen her. Her hair was bleached a patchy, green-tinged blonde, hacked into a mullet style that accentuated her drawn face. A vest top revealed a near-skeletal frame, running shorts hung beneath a protruding bump and her sallow complexion was flecked with patches of raw, dry skin.

'It's bad enough you dragging me to her snotty classes. Now, what, you're shagging her again?'

'Woah.' I felt a flood of warmth at the tenderness in Jonah's tone. 'We're not sleeping together. Libby came over for dinner, that's it.'

'A thank you dinner for ripping our family apart?' Ellis jabbed at the air, punctuating the words. Her whole body twitched in a way that made me ache for the baby growing inside it.

I stood up, scanning the room for my bag.

'Screw the pair of you. I only came back to get my stuff.'

'Ellis, please, let's talk about this.' Jonah moved to put his arm around her, but she stumbled away.

'Nah. My man's waiting in the car. He's going to take care of me. I've finally got someone who puts me first.'

'Will Damon take care of your baby?' It was probably foolish for me to get involved, but I couldn't let Ellis leave without trying.

'What did you say?' she spat, spinning to sneer at me.

'Is his place safe for your baby? Will he put them first, too? Make sure you have nappies, clothes and sterile bottles? What about when your baby won't stop crying all night? Will Damon take better care of your baby than your brother can?'

For a second she faltered, revealing the scared, damaged teenager hiding behind the anger. Then she held up both middle fingers, told us both in no uncertain terms where we could shove her stuff, and left.

We were still standing there, frozen in shock, when my phone rang. Worried it might be Dad, by the time I'd found my bag still hanging off a kitchen chair I answered it without bothering to check the screen first.

'Libby?'

'Yes?' It wasn't Dad, but I was rattled enough that it took a couple of beats to identify the voice.

'I'm sorry to bother you so late on a Friday night, but my contractions are six minutes apart. They're hurting quite a bit and I was wondering if you would come and hold my hand?'

43

'Um, what about Brayden?' I asked. I mean, women in labour aren't always thinking clearly, but this had to be a joke.

I waited while Silva huffed and puffed her way through a contraction, unable to resist counting how long it lasted. Around twenty seconds, so still a way to go.

'I don't know where he is,' she said, in a tiny voice.

My stomach sank like a stone.

'I've tried calling, social media, everything. He's not answering. I would be worried something's happened to him except that...'

'It's okay, you can tell me. I was married to him, remember.'

'He's taken his overnight bag. And his Future Cycling award.'

Oh dear. This wasn't good. I recalled the drunken mess staggering into my living room a week earlier.

'When did you last see him?'

There was another pause where I worried that Silva might be having her next contraction – in which case I'd be hanging up and calling for an ambulance – but she answered soon enough, meek with shame.

'Wednesday morning.'

'Has he been online since then?'

'Not since yesterday. I've messaged him every different way I can think of to say the baby's coming. I've tried his parents, his closest friends. I know I've no right to ask, but it's going to take Mum hours to get here from Cornwall.'

I squeezed my eyes shut, my antenatal teacher's instinct fighting the resentment that she had the audacity to do this to me. 'Haven't you got a friend you can ask?'

'If I did, would I be calling you?' Silva broke off to let out a sharp hiss before carrying on. 'I'll pay you if you like, whatever the going rate is plus extra for a Friday night.'

I thought about the sorry state of my own address book and held off judgement.

'I need to speak to my dad – he's babysitting. If he's okay with it, I can come and wait until your mum gets here. But you need to phone the midwife and let them know if you're still aiming for a home birth.'

'Thank you!'

She hung up, meaning I had to call her straight back to ask for her address.

Dad, however, wasn't budging. 'I have plans. I made that clear. Your responsibility is to your children, not Brayden's partner.'

'I know, but if it was any other of my clients then I'd help.'

'Not if you had no childcare, you wouldn't.'

'Are you refusing to stay longer because you don't want me to do this?'

'I'm refusing to stay longer because I promised Janet that we would have time to get a good spot at the cinema. She thought it unwise that I took care of the children at all this evening, in case something like this happened.'

'What do you mean, something like this? I don't usually have random women phoning me begging me to be their stand-in birth partner because their partner has gone AWOL.'

'Can't your friend come and help?'

I glanced towards the kitchen, where Jonah had started tidying up, and decided now was as good a time as any.

'My old friend is Jonah.'

There was a brief silence.

'I thought it was the friend you met at the pub.' Dad was straining to keep his voice calm.

'That was him. It's a long story, and I promise I'll explain when I can, but, for completely unrelated reasons, he can't look after the kids this evening.'

Another pause.

'I need to leave at nine-thirty. I'm trusting you not to let me down, Libby.'

I daren't reply to that loaded statement, reminding myself that Dad had enough going on. I reassured him I would find someone else, and hung up.

I called Toby, who answered with a photo of him holding a pint of beer in one hand and a shot in the other, surrounded by leering lads and empty glasses.

Next Nicky, who mercifully answered.

'Please let this be an emergency that can get me out of here. A nice one, like a woman in labour by the side of the road and no available ambulances.'

'How about a woman in labour with a home birth planned and a missing partner?'

'Ooh, perfect. Tell me more.'

As soon as I mentioned who it was, and that she'd asked to hold my hand, Nicky interrupted.

'No.'

'But...'

'Not happening. You are not getting dragged any further into that drama. Hasn't she got any friends she can ask?'

After a brief back and forth, my big sister refused to debate with me any more.

'I'll go. You get home to your kids.'

'You've never met Silva.'

'The chances are whichever community midwives are on call on a Friday night have never met her either. If I take over from Dad, Mum will come too. We can't spring that on him.'

'Ugh. Fair enough. I'll message you her address.'

The second I hung up, my phone rang. Dad again.

'Are you on your way?'

'About to be.' I checked the clock. Nine-fifteen. The cottage was a twenty-minute drive. He could wait an extra five minutes.

'Only... Finn overheard our previous conversation and woke up your sister to tell her the baby was coming, without me realising. They crept downstairs while I was explaining the situation to Janet.'

I didn't think it was possible to feel more flustered than I had a couple of minutes ago, but my anxiety took great pleasure in proving me wrong.

'Filling her in on what?'

'Um. On Brayden being missing.'

'Please, no. Are they upset?'

Dad didn't need to reply, as the all-too-familiar sound of Isla crying grew louder in the background.

'She wants to talk to you,' Dad said, and a couple of seconds later the wails died down to gulping sobs.

'Mummy?'

'Hello, darling. You sound quite upset.'

'Grandad said that Daddy is lost and no one can find him!'

'He's gone away for a few days, that's all. Like a holiday.'

'That's not what Grandad said!' she shrieked. 'He's run away or got hurt or is dead! And now the baby is coming and I don't want a new baby, I want my daddy!'

'Darling, please try to listen—'

'You have to find Daddy!'

'I really don't think that—'

'*You have to find my daddy!* I need my daddy!'

And in my crappy parenting panic, knowing that Silva and her baby needed him, too, accepting that I probably had as good a chance of finding my ex-husband as anyone, I made the kind of stupid promise that I regretted the moment it slipped out of my mouth.

'Okay. Okay, I'll find him.'

'And you won't come back until he's stopped being lost!'

'Don't worry. It will be okay. You know how good Mummy is at finding things.'

Before I'd finished speaking, Dad was back on the line.

'Janet is picking me up in ten minutes.'

'Yes. It's fine. I promise you can leave in ten minutes.'

'What can I do?' Jonah asked, appearing in the kitchen doorway as Isla still rang in my ears.

I tried to think. There was no way I was sending the man who Isla thought was stealing her mummy to the house when she was semi-hysterical. I would go to Silva and ask Nicky to look after the kids. Except that Nicky would already be well on her way to Brayden and Silva's home, which was the opposite direction to mine. There was no way either of us could be there in time. I ran for my car, anyway.

Then Dad called me back.

'Panic over. Your mum has turned up.'

I was too busy driving like a maniac back to Bigley to discuss that any further, and when I called Dad while waiting at a red light, he didn't answer.

The only thing that got me home in one mental piece was the lingering warmth of Jonah's kiss, pressed against the top of my head as he hugged me goodbye. For a woman who'd been trying to make it on her own for so long, the tenderness in that gesture meant so much more than if he'd kissed me on the lips or asked when he could see me again.

This man made me feel like long-lost treasure.

I didn't know what would happen next, but I was praying I didn't mess it up again.

* * *

I skidded into the drive and tumbled out of the car, half falling through the front door. I was greeted by the sound of Isla still squealing. I hurtled into the living room, my heart coming to a dead stop about halfway up my throat.

'Hey, Mum!' Finn said, curled up under a blanket on the sofa, a book resting between him and my dad.

Isla looked up from where Mum had been hiding under another blanket, using teddies as puppets. Her face crinkled with joy as she tried to explain whatever had made her laugh.

No doubt about it, my mother was a genius when it came to everyone's children but her own.

'Libby!' Mum exclaimed. 'We thought you were *busy*.'

She mouthed the word busy, but my kids sprang to attention.

'Did you find him already?' Isla asked, eyes round with hope.

'Not yet. I wanted to check that you guys were okay first.'

I looked at Dad, eyebrows raised in question.

'I thought you were going out?'

He glanced at Mum, then back to me, shifting position on the sofa. 'Um. Yes. Well. This seemed more important.'

'Right.' More important than keeping his word to Janet. I gave him another pointed look. It was none of my business, but we both knew what had changed his mind.

'We're as okay as we can be while our dad is missing,' Finn chipped in, sounding about as old as Dad.

'Okay. That's good to know. I hope you're going to bed soon, then.'

'We're going to bed once we've settled down and had another story each,' Isla said, rolling her eyes. 'Grandma and Grandad do know how to take care of children, you know. They looked after about fifty thousand million children before Grandma went sailing.'

'Right. Yes. I do know that.' I darted forwards to kiss each of my children goodnight yet again before turning to Mum, my head still spinning. 'Thank you. I'm not sure how long I'll be, but there's plenty of food and Dad knows where the teabags are. Just... don't go in the dining room.'

I was irrationally thankful for my spruced-up kitchen, given the circumstances, but enough of the house was still a junkyard.

'It's the least we can do.' Mum nodded.

The truth of that made me want to kiss her then give her a hefty boot back out of the door.

44

I jumped back in my car, turned on the engine, then decided it was probably worth taking a minute to think about where Brayden might be. After driving out of sight from the cottage, I pulled back over and tried calling and sending a couple of messages, just in case it was only his partner he was ignoring, then searched his social media for non-existent clues. I didn't want to believe he'd found another woman to escape to, but Brayden had never been good at keeping in touch with his friends, and I felt sure his parents wouldn't lie to Silva, given the situation.

Think, Libby.

Who else had Brayden confided in, back when we were married?

I started with his sister in Wales, whose number I still had in my phone. She was initially wary, then disgusted when I told her why I was calling.

'If he'd shown up here, I'd have dragged him back to the reality of his poor choices myself.'

Woah!

'Libby, I thought it was a rash move getting married so young, but for that wastrel to walk out on you and those gorgeous children was inexcusable. I hope you're now happily dating some prince who treats you like his princess.'

'Um...'

'Ah, sorry, the dog's just barfed on my bed. Can I call you back? Even better, let's hang out next time I'm back in Notts. I've missed having a sister.'

After that revelation, I tried a couple of old friends, all who claimed with sincerity that they'd not seen or spoken to Brayden in years. It seemed I wasn't the only one he'd ditched once his app started making money.

I scrolled through my contact list, then a thought struck me. Brayden had freaked out while at a wedding last week. He hadn't posted any photos – a clue in itself that things weren't great – but Silva had. In a couple of them, Silva was posing up close, but in the background I could see a blurry image of Brayden, sitting with a man who I recognised as his long-time personal trainer, Clint. I'd never had Clint's details, but a quick search via Brayden's old gym revealed his website, with a contact number and email address.

'Yo.'

I briefly explained that I was looking for a client, Brayden.

'Sorry, I've not seen him in yonks.'

'How about last Saturday?'

'What?'

'At the wedding.'

'Oh, yeah. Yes. Now that you mention it, he was there. Yep. Not seen him since, though.'

'What about his sessions this week?'

'What about 'em?'

'Did he attend his sessions?'

'Nope. He stopped training with me, ooh, a while ago now.'

Clint might have been able to bench-press a rhinoceros and transform feckless men into competent cyclists, but acting was not one of his talents.

'So, he isn't staying with you for a few days?'

'What?' His attempt at full-on flabbergasted erased any lingering doubt. 'Why would he be staying with me? That's mad.'

'Can you please tell him that his partner is in labour?'

'Huh?'

'I mean, if you happen to see or hear from him. Silva is having the baby. Now.'

'Silva's having the baby?' This was genuine incredulity, this time. Clint lowered his voice to a whisper. 'Honestly, I don't think that will help. He's sort of flipping out about becoming a dad, you know what I mean?'

'He's already a dad!' I shot back. 'And two children are worried sick their daddy is dead in a ditch somewhere. Your website says you harness men's inner beast so they can become their best. Putting aside that I can't believe anyone would buy into that nonsense, a "real man", as you describe it, wouldn't abandon his partner when she's giving birth. Use your transformational gibberish to get him to grow up. Now.'

'Yeah... to be honest I've been trying. Him moping about, whingeing on about how tough things are, is killing my vibe, know what I mean? I've been trying to talk him into going back for the past couple of days. No joy. I don't suppose you could have a go? I mean, you've sold it to me.'

I took a couple of deep, calming breaths and realised that action, not breathing, was the only solution. 'Let me speak to him.'

'Oh, no. He'll just hang up. I'll drop you a pin.'

Clint ended the call, and a few seconds later a notification buzzed showing me his address. My maps app reckoned it would take forty minutes. I rang Nicky.

'I've found him, but he's not going to come out of hiding without some incentive. I'm toying between threatening to key his car and setting his award on fire.'

'At the risk of going over old ground, Libby, what were you thinking when you said yes to that man?'

Ignoring her, I asked how things were going with Silva.

'So far, so sweaty. The midwives are finishing up another birth, aiming to be here before the head crowns. Which by my calculations should be a good couple of hours away.'

'That soon? Shouldn't they be sending someone else out, then?'

'Yes, they should. But it's a full moon, babies are showing up all over the place, and this one has a qualified GP with her. The only other option is hospital, and Silva says the lighting there will ruin her complexion in the photos.'

'For goodness' sake. Shall we go home and leave them to it?'

'Like we'd walk away from a baby in need.'

'Okay.' I braced myself. 'He's in a village on the other side of Newark. I'm going to fetch him.'

'Rather you than me.'

'I'd rather *you* than me, and that's saying something considering the alternative is mopping the brow of my ex-husband's baby-mamma.'

'I'm loving this kick-ass Libby. I have every faith I'll be seeing you and the dropout before I see this little girl's head.'

* * *

I spent the forty-minute drive composing kick-ass, no-nonsense speeches in my head that would have Brayden charging back to the four-bedroom riverside town house in Newark that he shared with Silva. Most of these rapidly descended into verbal whiplashings, furiously detailing failings spanning the past ten years, which I knew would only further convince him he was a failure as a father, and his baby was better off without him.

It took everything I'd got, after parking in front of Clint's artificial lawn, hustling past his row of garden gnomes and knocking on the doorbell that played 'I'm Coming Out', to keep things encouraging.

I channelled Clint's 'wimp into warrior' vibe as he led me through a chintzy living room containing more soft furnishings than a Dunelm superstore and into a back office, where Brayden sat on a sofa-bed playing *Call of Duty*.

'What the hell?' I barked, forgetting all my good intentions of staying positive as I twisted around to hiss at Clint. 'You might be an expert at bringing out inner beasts, but this is way too far.'

Brayden was wearing grimy jogging bottoms and a vest top. His hair was frightening. There were piles of empty crisp packets, takeaway cartons and beer cans scattered around, and it smelled like the boys' changing room back at Bigley Academy.

I held my breath, leant into the room and turned the Xbox off at the wall.

'What?' he asked, as if coming out of a trance. 'Is there a power cut?'

'If you're referring to the power supply to your brain, then quite possibly, yes.' I marched in front of the monitor, arms folded, ready for war.

'Libby.' He shrank back, a mix of shame and defiance. It wasn't only the stench that resembled a teenage boy.

'Get your stuff. Time's up for regressing to a man-child. Your girlfriend needs you.'

'I can't,' he stammered. 'I'm not cut out for all this.'

'What, life? The child you created? Being a grown adult?'

His eyes darted to one side. 'Maybe.'

'Silva's about an hour away from giving birth. If you stop farting about then you might just make it in time for her to agree to take you back.'

'What? She's not due for another two weeks.'

'Are you deliberately acting clueless so I give up and let you go back to your pretend-hero games?' I snapped. 'Or are you going to buck up and have a go at being an actual hero for once?'

'I can't do it, Libby,' he whined. 'I don't know what to do.'

'Then how about you start by asking Silva what she needs from you?' I grabbed a handful of clothes and started stuffing them into a bag, before the whiff put me off and I decided he could fetch his things later. 'I can guarantee it won't be you staying here twiddling with your joystick. Even an inept, stressed-out birth partner is better than nothing. All she wants is someone who loves her to hold her hand.'

It took another five minutes of verbal harassment and downright bullying, but eventually Brayden slouched off the sofa-bed and agreed to go home.

'Nope,' I said, when he started heading for his own car. 'I'm not risking that. Get in my passenger seat.'

He started to protest, but one look from me across the bonnet and he was hastily sliding into the seat, not even bothering to brush off the biscuit crumbs.

'Call your partner,' I ordered, half wondering what our marriage would have been like if I'd been this assertive.

'I don't know what to—'

'Tell her you're sorry and you'll be there as soon as you can.'

There were a few moments of silence.

'I've sent her a message.'

'She's in advanced labour! She'll not be checking for—'

'She replied with okay. Followed by angry face, knife and aubergine emojis. Are you sure this is a good idea?'

By the time I'd found a parking spot and herded Brayden up the steps to his front door, it was eleven-thirty. Nicky yanked her ex-brother-in-law into the living room and stepped outside before I could go in, closing the door behind her.

'She's eight centimetres dilated and practically ripped the gas and air out of the midwife's hand the second they arrived. Our work here is done.'

'All okay?'

'With regards to the birth, it's perfect. The descriptions of how she's going to exact revenge on Brayden were enough to curdle her colostrum.'

'That's the first time you've not called him the dropout.'

'Yeah, well.' We paused as she reached her car. 'It's the first time I've felt a tiny bit sorry for him. Almost.'

She wouldn't have said that if she'd seen him in Clint's back room.

'Will they let you know when baby's arrived?' Nicky asked.

'They won't need to.' I rolled my eyes, moving on to my car, several metres down the road. 'It'll be all over Instagram before they've cut the cord.'

45

I arrived home to a cottage in semi-darkness. Dad was sweeping the kitchen floor and Mum was upstairs, scrubbing the bathroom.

A nice gesture, but it was going to take more than cleaning my toilet to win me around.

Stepping in when I needed her, no fuss, no questions? That had produced a definite crack in the concrete wall I'd spent years constructing around my heart.

'The kids went to bed about ten minutes after you left,' Mum whispered, once she'd tiptoed downstairs and pulled off her rubber gloves. I didn't even own a pair of rubber gloves. She must have brought them with her. 'They were both utterly convinced that you'd be able to find Brayden, so fell asleep with smiles on their faces. I know things have been hard, Libby, but you've done a fabulous job with those two. I'm presuming it was mostly you, given tonight's antics.'

'Thank you.' I had to swallow back the lump in my throat. Coming from my mother, that meant far more than I wanted it to.

It seemed that beneath the hurt and anger was a daughter desperate for her mum's approval.

'We liked Brayden, back when you married him,' Dad said, asking if I wanted a cup of tea with a twitch of his eyebrows towards the kettle. 'He seemed good for you. A solid foundation. We honestly thought he'd turn out to be a decent, family man.'

'Just goes to show. You aren't always the experts on sussing out a situation.' I sighed, sinking into a kitchen chair. 'There's decaf tea in the blue tin.'

'Tea, are you serious?' Nicky asked, suddenly appearing in the doorway with a bottle of wine. She must have let herself in with my spare key. 'I was on my way home, and then I remembered Theo's away, I'm full of adrenaline and I have a load more slagging-off-the-dropout to be doing before I can sleep.'

One-and-a-half bottles later, we'd finished discussing Brayden and Silva and peered at photos of Platinum Precious on their Instagram that included no hint of the evening's drama – naturalbirth, proudmama, birthwithoutfear, empowered. They had tagged my business account, prompting me to switch off the notifications a few minutes later. Mum decided to change the subject.

'I'm sorry, girls.'

'Excuse me?' Nicky asked, twisting around to where I sat next to her on the sofa and muttering, 'Small talk was going so well – why does she have to ruin it?'

'I'm sorry for not being there for nights like this. For not realising that there'd be times you'd need my practical help as well as a mother's shoulder to cry on while I reminded you how ruddy outstanding you are. Libby...' She paused, blinking a few times before she could continue. 'I'm sorry for blaming you for what happened with Jonah. It was unforgivable to let things deteriorate the way they did. I could shift the blame onto my breakdown. A mid-life crisis or the menopause. It's irrelevant. I spent the best part of my life helping children who had been let down by their birth parents, and then I... then I... I don't know how I could have been so foolish!'

Nicky frowned. 'The problem is, saying sorry doesn't undo any of it.'

Mum rubbed a hand across her eyes. 'No. But it does mean that I'd undo those awful years before I left, if I could. I've been an appalling mother and I don't know what to do about it apart from scrub your grouting and promise that I'm staying for as long as it takes to make it up to you.'

'What about Dad?' I couldn't fail to notice how naturally my parents had been acting towards each other. Almost how things had been before Mum became ill.

'We've talked,' Dad said, his tone giving nothing away.

'And? What happens now?' Nicky asked.

'Well, I don't know about you, but I'm ready for bed.' Dad got up. 'Shall I call us a taxi?'

* * *

It was only once the cottage had settled back into the near silence of those early-morning hours that I remembered to turn my notifications back on. About a dozen thank-you messages from Silva, which I ignored for now, a few comments and queries from people interested in antenatal classes, and a message that made my insides flutter.

How did it go? Did you find him?

I tapped out a couple of sentences about how I'd found

Brayden at his personal trainer's and he'd made it in time for the birth. Despite it being two in the morning, a reply came back almost instantly.

I'm so sorry about Ellis

Don't be. I understand why she feels like that. I'm sorry she's gone to live with Damon. You must be worried sick.

Yeah.

There was a brief pause. I could almost hear what Jonah was thinking, so I said it for him.

Maybe not the best time to start dating someone she blames for ruining her life

Another pause before he replied.

I've tried to figure out how we could do it. Keep things quiet, meet places she won't know about. But if I'm starting something with you I have no intention of finishing it, and when she eventually finds out she'll be even more upset that I hid you from her.

While I was still digesting that, another message arrived.

But it kills me. I love you and I can't contemplate letting you go again. The teenage voice in my head keeps shouting that Ellis is with Damon – she won't even know if we're together or not. Me and you are the least of her problems, why should her six-year-old memories get to keep us apart?

I knew why. Because there was a baby about to be born. A

baby born into generations of trauma. A baby who deserved every chance it could possibly get to be safe, and loved and cared for well, by people who were well. A baby who needed Jonah.

To be honest, there's a lot going on here, too.

I tapped the message out, holding the phone up to prevent my tears dripping onto the screen.

Isla and Finn have enough to deal with right now, and I'll need to be a steady anchor while Brayden tries to get his act together. Mum is sticking around, and she's finally ready to talk about things. You being there isn't going to make that easier. Maybe the sensible decision is to postpone our date for a while.

Since when were you and me sensible?

Since I had two kids, a business and a charity to run

Three dots appeared, disappeared, appeared again.

Do you mean postpone for a while. Or indefinitely?

I don't know

Indefinitely, then

And because he deserved to know this, even as we broke each other's hearts, I said the words I'd been holding back for weeks. Thirteen years.

I love you

I know. You were worth it. Both times. I will always love you too

Did it help, knowing Jonah thought I was worth it? That he was as miserable as me? If I really loved him, should I be hoping he was happy?

Oh, it helped. Absolutely.

46

A week later Bigley Primary school broke up for the summer. There was a hastily organised leaving party for Janet, who had been there so long she'd taught two of the other teachers. I stood under the shade of an oak tree at the edge of the school field with some mums from the pub quiz, who invited me to become a regular team member. As we chatted and laughed, I kept one eye on Isla picking daisies and the other on Finn kicking a football with some friends.

I felt sort-of normal.

Apart from my wounded heart, of course.

It was a constant ache, all too often accompanied by tears, but it would heal. I knew this, because I wasn't allowing myself any debate on the matter. Kick-ass Libby was kicking her ass back into the real world. After a few days to wallow in losing Jonah again, I had got back on the list of small but significant choices. The dining room was nearly sorted, I was eating, exercising and sleeping infinitely better, and we'd planted lettuce and carrot seeds in the new raised beds that Toby had built.

We spent Saturday picnicking with Theo's family, after a very brief introduction to Platinum Precious – Isla declaring her the most beautifullest baby in the whole world, ever, while Finn announced that she looked like a cabbage. Both my parents came, and I took only minimal pleasure from observing Mum grasping quite how big a part of Nicky's life her in-laws were.

I had even, in a flash of inspiration, stopped sulking about everyone else's travels, and booked an adventure of our own.

Well, a week camping for me, the kids, Toby and Hazel in Devon at the end of August, but it was a start.

* * *

The first few weeks of the summer holidays passed in a blur. Dad had asked Janet if they could slow things down for the time being, but she'd been thoroughly put off by what she called his 'family entanglements', so he continued to look after the children while I worked. More often than not, Mum joined him, and they seemed to settle into a companionable partnership, although they were being very tight-lipped about whether at any point it might develop into anything more. I did note that no one had mentioned divorce, and one morning when Mum popped into the surgery, Nicky spotted her sneaking a leaflet about relationship counselling into her bag.

Hearing about the different activities Isla and Finn got up to with their grandparents, added to the thrill of a new sister to cuddle, I started to worry that a week camping would be boring in comparison. I didn't protest, though. It was the least these grandchildren deserved.

When a terraced house went up for rent in the village, it seemed the obvious answer, and Mum signed a six-month lease.

She also started volunteering to look after the babies at the Bloomers Wednesday sessions while the single parents enjoyed their 'fun time'. The new mums called her 'Nana Helen' and revelled in her stories about me and Nicky as little girls, some of which were even true. That led to a part-time job helping out at the Green House to top up her pension and the savings that Dad had set up for her when he'd sold the house. On a good day, I could appreciate that her relationship with our family was healing. On a bad day, I felt jealous and angry and wanted to yell at her for keeping it a secret when Jonah lived there. But as the weeks passed, the bad days were fewer, and the good days felt better.

When a man on one of the rival pub-quiz teams asked me out, for a stuttering, shocked second or two I almost thought about saying yes.

Instead, I settled on 'not yet', which he very graciously accepted.

We started clearing out the attic, and to my surprise found robust floorboards underneath the clutter, piles of dust and dead bugs. Toby's uncle, who was a building contractor, sorted out the paperwork and admin – which was less than we feared due to it already being classed as a living space – and taught Toby how to install an outside staircase, while someone else completed the rewiring and made sure everything met current building regs.

Dad offered his DIY services, but Toby's uncle had no patience for the kind of man who mistook a pair of pliers for an adjustable wrench, so Dad quietly got on with babysitting Hazel instead.

Overall, it became a summer of new starts alongside wrangling with old issues. Challenging, yes. Tiring, absolutely. But I felt – mostly – on top of it all. I was coping.

'No, you are not!' Nicky barked, on one of our now regular Saturday no-parents-allowed hikes, when I expressed this out loud. 'Libby, look at you.'

I instinctively looked down at my new leggings and sporty top. I thought I was starting to look okay.

'You're *thriving*.' My sister laughed.

I basked in that thought for a few more strides.

'I'm thinking I might get a dog.'

She grabbed my arm. 'Do it. Theo and I have been talking about the same thing.'

We walked for a while in silence, but my sister's mood gradually dropped to pensive, her face reflecting the shadows beneath the pine trees.

'We've been having therapy.'

'What?' I stopped dead on the path. 'You and Theo have a great marriage. Don't you?'

She nodded, pausing beside me. 'We do. But we needed to figure out whether we have a complete marriage. Or if we want to find another way to grow our family.'

The air in the forest was completely still as I waited for her to go on.

'We aren't going to try any more pointless fertility treatments, or adopt. Maybe one day we'll think about fostering older kids. But right now we've decided that focussing on what we have will be enough.'

'What you have is incredible.'

'It is. I don't know why I'm crying about it. I'm married to the best man ever. My closest friend.' She squinted at me. 'No offence, sis.'

'None taken.'

'We love our work, our hobbies. Our amazing family. We're healthy, apart from this one thing.'

She shrugged, appearing painfully vulnerable. I reached out and brushed away her tears with my thumb.

'It's enough,' she said, with a watery smile. 'More than

enough.'

'Now all you need to believe is that *you* are enough,' I said, slipping my arm through hers, appreciating this rare role-reversal, even as I ached for her. 'With or without being a mother.'

She nodded. 'I know. Hence the therapy. And weirdly, Mum being back helps.'

'Who'd have guessed that our mother turning up would be the answer to so many problems.'

We started walking towards a clearing lit up with August sunshine.

'Not me.'

'Hence the therapy!' we exclaimed together, jostling against each other like little girls.

'Maybe you should try it.' Nicky raised her eyebrows, back in big-sister mode. 'See if it can help mend that broken heart. It seems to be working for Mum and Dad, too.'

'Yeah. I think I'll try a dog first.'

We'd just turned around and were heading back to the cottage when Toby phoned. Our holiday was in a couple of days' time, so I presumed he was going to ask about sleeping bags or a camping stove.

'Yeah, so there's someone here, looking for you.'

'Did you ask who?' For a second, my heart jumped at the thought it might be Jonah.

'Hang on, she's waiting at the front door. Let me ask what she wants.'

There was a brief pause while I heard Toby clomp down the hallway, before he suddenly swore.

'Um. You'd better get back here, soon,' he gabbled. 'I think her water just broke on the doormat. Oh,' he added, sounding more than a little strained. 'Her name's Ellis. And she says her contractions are seven minutes apart.'

47

I felt grateful for weeks of working on my fitness as Nicky and I sprinted back through the trees. Most women had hours, sometimes days, to wait after their waters had broken before labour got into full swing – Daisy being an exception when she'd had Bolt on my kitchen floor – so we didn't bother calling anyone just yet. However, I was anxious to find out what had brought Ellis to my door.

Twenty minutes later, I staggered into the house to find Ellis sitting at the kitchen table, Toby hovering around her like a nervous chicken.

'Ellis, hi.' I crouched down beside her, scanning her skinny frame while still catching my breath. 'Tell me what's happening.'

'I made a mess on your floor.' She half laughed, half grimaced.

Her posture and tone of voice were my best clue as to whether things were progressing. When Nicky arrived a few seconds later, having fetched her GP bag from the car, she caught my eye with a nod of relief. There wasn't about to be a baby born on my floor this morning.

'Welcome to the club. I think that makes about a dozen of you so far. Did Toby clean it up?'

'He did,' she said, straggly eyebrows shooting up. 'Only gagged once, too.'

'Do you want a drink?'

'More water would be good.'

I stepped back to allow Nicky to ask Ellis the necessary questions while using her eyes and ears to also assess the situation. As I made tea for Nicky and me, water and a plate of toast for Ellis and shooed Toby off to check on Hazel, I glanced over, making a non-medical professional assessment of my own. Ellis looked exactly as she had when I'd last seen her. Only, if possible, even more vulnerable. Far more scared. She wore an old robe that Toby must have found in the bathroom, and her complexion was stark against the peach terry towelling.

'Ooh, is that one now?' I heard Nicky ask, in the doctor's voice she used that always made me think of hot chocolate and soft blankets.

Ellis nodded vigorously, eyes shut, jaw clenched tight. I counted fifteen seconds until she sagged against the back of the chair again. Still plenty of time.

'When did you last see the midwife?' Nicky continued.

'I dunno. A few weeks ago.'

'Right. I think that, given the situation, it would be a good idea to get you and baby looked over properly in the hospital.'

Ellis jerked her head up. 'No.'

'No?'

'I'm not going to the hospital. He's waiting for me there.'

'Who is?' Nicky asked.

Ellis turned her face away with a scowl.

'Damon?' I asked, bringing her water and the toast over.

A sharp nod.

'We can go to a different hospital,' Nicky said. 'I can call the Nottingham labour suites, see who has room.'

'No.'

'Ellis, it would be a really good idea to get your baby checked out.'

'Then do it here!' she cried. 'You're a doctor, aren't you? If I could go to the hospital then I wouldn't be here, would I?'

I sat on the chair next to hers, shuffling it close enough to gently cradle her hand. 'Have you taken something?' I asked, softly.

A few furious blinks, then Ellis crumpled onto my shoulder. 'I didn't want to. He made me. I told him it wasn't safe for the baby, I wasn't doing it any more, but he said it wasn't my choice. I'm his woman and he's paying for everything, so I show him respect. Then he did this.'

She gestured feebly with her chin. After asking permission, Nicky opened the front of the dressing gown, and I was thankful for her doctor's detachment as she carefully inspected the bruise across Ellis's chest.

'If I go to hospital, they'll take my baby.' She gasped.

Nicky began to protest, but Ellis wasn't listening.

'I'm high on only Damon knows what. Beaten up. Homeless, because there's no way I'm going back there. I can't take care of myself, let alone a baby.'

'Ellis, there's plenty of support—'

'Yeah? Like the support they offered my mum? They snatched her kids in the middle of the night and dumped them with strangers. I know how social services work. I will have this baby by myself in a back alley before I let them get hold of me. Once you're in the system, they do what they like with you. Let alone your baby. They don't listen to people like me!'

Nicky and I had no reply to that. We knew that, for young

women like Ellis, we could make no promises that her voice would be heard, her views and wishes respected. The chances that the system would indeed shunt her onto an overloaded, broken conveyor belt of box-ticking and back-covering was higher than we'd care to admit.

'What would you like to do?' I asked, after waiting for another contraction to pass.

'I want you to work your Bloomers magic and get this baby out safe. I'll figure out what happens next, next.'

'How about we call the community midwife, and she can help with a home birth?'

'How about I just leave?'

Nicky and I stood up, exchanging glances over the top of Ellis's head. It wasn't against the law for her to give birth unassisted, but there was a big difference between women like Astrid, who came to Brayden and Silva's class and planned a 'freebirth' with no midwife or doctor present, and a teenager who'd admitted she was under the influence of drugs.

Sensing our reluctance, Ellis got up and started lumbering towards the doorway. 'I thought you of all people would understand. You're a doctor. It's not like I've gone to some nutter who wants to make placenta pâté. Besides, after everything, this is the least you can do.'

'After everything?' Nicky looked at me. I'd not told her that Ellis still blamed me for Jonah leaving.

'Wait.' I followed Ellis into the hallway. 'How about this? Nicky will monitor you carefully, and if you show any signs of baby being in distress, or something going wrong that she can't handle safely here, we transfer you to one of the Nottingham hospitals, where there'll be no risk of Damon.'

Ellis stopped walking, so I pressed on.

'And I call Jonah.'

Her face disintegrated as she crumpled against the wall. I called for Nicky as I rushed to help her.

'He won't come,' she wailed as we led her into the living room and onto the sofa. 'He hates me.'

'You know that's not true,' I said, smoothing the hair off her brow as Jonah used to do when she was a little girl. 'He loves you, and he's been desperately worried.'

She clenched her jaw. 'He chose you, didn't he? A girl he'd not seen in years. Over his own sister. Just like last time.'

'No. He didn't choose me. He chose you. I haven't seen Jonah since the night you left.'

'What?' Ellis looked at me, baffled. 'Why would he do that?'

'Because he loves you.'

'But he loves you!'

'He loves you more.'

She shook her head. 'I didn't even really mean it. I was looking for an excuse to be mad at him so I felt less guilty about ditching him for Damon. He made me feel bad, because I knew he was right and Damon would be a disaster. But, I dunno. I guess piece-of-crap-men is just one more toxin I'm addicted to.'

While Nicky helped Ellis to get comfortable I went back into the kitchen and called Jonah. Before he'd picked up, the front door banged open.

'Mum! Platinum Precious smiled at me! Mu-u-u-um!'

I raced out of the kitchen just as Finn and Isla disappeared into the living room. Before I could catch up with them, they both quickly backed out again.

'Not another one!' Finn groaned. 'Does that mean we can't watch telly?'

'Can I watch the baby being born instead?' Isla asked, eyes lighting up as I started herding them in the direction of snacks. 'I know all about babies now. Silva says I'm a nature-all.'

Fully aware that they'd be stuffed with treats – Silva's all-natural, organic-only diet had lapsed somewhat since becoming enslaved to the demands of a crying poop factory – I decided that extreme times called for extreme measures, and opened the emergency box of Maltesers.

Once safely portioned out, I took a seat opposite them.

'The woman in the living room is having a baby, and for lots of reasons she's decided to have it here. Auntie Nicky's with her, so that's okay, but she also would like someone she knows really well to be with her, like Silva wanted Daddy when Platinum Precious was born.'

'Like the baby's daddy.' Isla nodded sagely.

'Yes. But she doesn't see the baby's daddy any more, so he can't come.'

'Then what about her mum and dad?'

'Her parents have both died.'

'Aw, that's sad!'

'So, she'd really like her big brother to be there.'

'Ew!' Finn screwed up his face. 'You'd better not want me there when you have a baby, Isla.'

'*Anyway*, Ellis does want her brother there. But you need to know that her brother is Jonah, who you met once before. He came here for an antenatal class for Ellis, actually,' I went on as Finn and Isla wrinkled their foreheads in confusion. 'And you saw me with him and thought he might be my boyfriend.'

'Him!' Isla stood up, hands on hips, as though she'd just unmasked a murderer.

'Okay.' Finn shrugged. 'Can I go and play football?'

'Can I play too?'

'You're in goal,' Finn instructed as they slipped out of the patio doors.

Shaking my head, I picked up my phone. After eight years, the unpredictability of my children could still catch me out.

* * *

'Libby?' Jonah sounded breathless. I felt a rush of warmth that he'd not blocked or deleted my number.

'Ellis is here.'

'What?' He instantly sharpened. 'At your house?'

'She's in labour and is refusing to go to hospital. Nicky's with her,' I added quickly, sensing his spurt of panic. 'Everything's fine so far, and we've agreed that if anything starts to look different then we'll take her to City Hospital.'

'She's booked in at King's Mill.'

'Which is why she thinks Damon's waiting for her there.'

There was a brief silence where I felt him trying to hold himself together. I knew he'd succeed. This man had been through far worse.

'How is she?' he asked after a while, his voice sounding strained.

'She's really hoping you'll come.'

'I'm already in the car. How is she really?'

'She's... here, not with Damon. Which is something.'

'It's everything.' He sighed. 'There is literally nowhere I'd rather she be than with you and Nicky right now.'

I didn't tell him that she was still high from only Damon knew what. Better to let him discover that when he wasn't hurtling along country lanes trying to reach his baby sister.

48

My rational head didn't mind at all when I opened the front door and Jonah hurried straight past me to the living room, where his sister was squatting on one of our birth balls watching a Netflix dating show.

My heart swooned when, a few seconds later, he darted back to where I hovered in the doorway and grabbed hold of my hand, looking me straight in the eye. 'Thank you.'

I could only nod in response.

'Ah, hello, birth partner.' Nicky poked her head out of the kitchen door. 'Glad you could make it.'

He followed her into the kitchen, only to find Isla, Finn and Toby set up with a Boggle game.

'Is there somewhere we can talk?'

I led him into the dining room.

'How is she?'

Nicky met his anxious gaze with honesty. 'She's coping well so far. I'm not sure what might be floating around in her system, but at the moment all the vital signs are good and baby's doing fine.'

We quickly filled him in on what we knew.

'Is it safe, her being here?'

Nicky grimaced. 'It's not my first choice, but it's as safe a second choice as we're going to get right now.'

Jonah gripped the back of a chair with both hands.

'It's a lot safer than being with Damon,' I said, wishing I dared put a reassuring arm around him. 'We won't take any chances.'

Nicky had no such reservations, placing both hands on his shoulders as she looked Jonah right in the eye. 'Time to pretend everything is calm and under control and go and be a birth partner.'

For the next few hours things were as fine as we could have hoped. Ellis did a few laps of the garden, watched television while we rubbed her back or feet, and dozed on her brother for a while.

I busied myself creating the kind of birth environment I dreamed all my clients could have. Soft lighting, gentle music, a cool breeze from the open window and everything a mum could possibly need on hand, ranging from heat pads to ice chips.

Before the kids went to bed, Ellis had a bath under Nicky's professional eye. After spending longer than I'd intended chatting to Toby in the cabin while fetching some aromatherapy oils, I found Isla and Finn under the kitchen table in a pile of cushions and both their duvets, reading in the light of a new camping lamp.

To my utter astonishment, Jonah was hunched under there with them.

I stood, transfixed, listening to him reading *The Lion, the Witch and the Wardrobe*. They were facing away from me, completely engrossed in his brilliant voices, and I watched as Isla, exhausted after a busy day and dramatic evening, nestled her head against his arm.

Whenever I thought I couldn't possibly love this man any more...

'Hey, this looks cosy,' I whispered, when Jonah reached the end of the first chapter.

'Oh, hi.' He ducked his head around to face me. 'They wanted to get comfy, and we thought it best to avoid the living room,' he explained.

'Keep reading!' Isla said, jabbing the page.

'Ahem,' I said, pointedly.

'Keep reading, *please*.'

'Just until Ellis has finished her bath,' I said. 'Then it's straight to bed.'

A short while later, when I was tucking her in, Isla said to me, 'I don't know why you didn't make Jonah your boyfriend, Mummy. He's really lovely and not a bad prince at all.'

'Well, I have been a bit too busy to think about a boyfriend.'

'Yes, but it's the summer holidays now so you aren't that busy any more. And anyway.' She rolled over, snuggling under the covers. 'Jonah could help you with all the busy, like Toby does. I think he'd be good at it.'

I pictured him again, back curled over the book, head scraping the underside of the table, his voice deep and tender, and I couldn't disagree.

* * *

'Time to get something to eat.' Nicky woke a half-asleep Jonah with a nudge just after one in the morning. 'Things are about to get interesting.'

'How can you tell?' he asked, struggling upright on the sofa before glancing at Ellis.

She was kneeling on the floor, leaning over the birthing ball, eyes closed and clearly somewhere deep inside herself as she rocked forwards and back.

I stayed with Ellis while Jonah and Nicky refuelled. It was so very bittersweet, him being here. The way he cared for Ellis, holding her hand and gently murmuring to her, reminded me of how they'd been when he'd lived with us. The way she responded with utter trust reminded me of how much they'd lost when he'd had to go.

I settled on the floor next to Ellis, reaching over to rub her back when she let out a long moan, face tightening with another contraction.

'Can I have a drink?' she asked when she could speak again. 'It's so hot.'

I was on the other side of the room searching for her water bottle when Nicky wandered back in, picking her stethoscope off the table. When I turned back to bring Ellis a drink, the second I spotted my sister's face my heart plummeted.

She pulled me to one side.

'What's wrong?'

'Baby's heart rate is not happy. It could be nothing.'

'But it could be something.'

She gave a tight nod.

'Car or ambulance?'

Nicky held her stethoscope to Ellis's bump for another endless minute before nodding to my phone, ready and waiting in my clasped hand.

* * *

Waiting for the ambulance was like one of those nightmares where you're desperate to get somewhere but can't seem to make any progress. A frightened mum wouldn't be helpful for baby, so we had to straddle the line between 'this is potentially nothing' and making it enough of a something to persuade Ellis that she needed checking out at the hospital. There were tears, protests, clinging to her brother as she teetered on the brink of hyperventilating. In the end, he looked her right in the eye and told her straight.

'I will not let that man near you or your baby. I haven't forgotten how to handle monsters who fight dirty.'

Ellis closed her eyes, shaking her head.

'Didn't I always keep you safe?' Jonah's voice had dropped to a low rumble. 'You know when I say I'm ready to die to protect you, I mean it.'

She gripped his hand through another contraction, leaning her head against his shoulder when it had finished, her weak nod enough for us to grab her flip-flops and slip a loose shawl around her shoulders as, with a wave of relief, we saw the beam of headlights swoop across the living-room window.

Once the paramedics were on the scene, I retreated out of the way. This was a place for family and Nicky's medical expertise only. But as they carried her out to the ambulance, Jonah dashed back inside the house.

'Will you come with me?'

'To the hospital? Nicky would be better...'

'Nicky isn't who I need right now.'

'Are you sure?'

He didn't bother answering; the desperation in his eyes spoke for him.

Once, this was all I'd wanted. To somehow, in some petty way, be able to offer him some help, some comfort.

Never did I imagine he'd straight out ask for it.

And it was standing in my sweaty old T-shirt and joggers, the candlelight from the living room flickering across his face, that I realised this was still something I wanted, despite all the potential complications and unanswered questions. Not more than anything else in the world – I was a mother now, after all – but enough to say yes. Yes to tonight, and yes to being there tomorrow, to see what it would bring.

I took hold of his hand – rougher than it was before but still fitting perfectly around mine – and followed him out into the night.

49

A couple of hours after we arrived at the maternity unit, a midwife came to let Jonah know that his nephew had been born via caesarean section. He was tiny, and they would need to keep a close watch on him, but his vital signs were good and it looked as though he would be okay.

'Can I see my sister?'

'It's fathers only at this time of night. We might make an exception for your mother, given Ellis's age, but we have the other mums to think about. Their sleep is precious.'

'Please. I just need to see her.'

The midwife took in his dishevelled clothes, grey complexion and distraught face and deduced that this was no ordinary brother-sister relationship.

'Let me check with Matron once she's settled on the ward. It'll be a while, though. I'd suggest you get some rest then come back in visiting hours.'

Jonah adjusted his position on the plastic waiting-room chair, as if to confirm that he'd not be going anywhere except for upstairs to the postnatal ward.

'You don't have to stay,' he said, once we were alone in the waiting room again.

I answered that by taking hold of his hand.

'She told me that she didn't mean it,' Jonah said softly, just as my eyes were drifting shut a while later. 'About you and me. She knows it was as much my fault as yours.' He stopped, bumping my leg with our clasped hands before I could argue.

'Saying it was someone's fault makes it sound like it was wrong. Something we should regret.'

'Don't you regret it? How we hurt your family?'

I sighed. 'If we'd never had that time, we'd be brother and sister now. If we'd not been caught, you'd have ended up in a horrible hovel with no Green House to save you. So, I guess any regrets I might have will depend on what we end up deciding to do now.'

He released a slow sigh, keeping his gaze on the door straight in front of us, leading to the postnatal ward stairs.

'Libby, I hope it's obvious that I've already decided what I want. I really, really tried to regret acting on my feelings for you, but those two days are still the best of my life. I can't tell you how it made me feel, loving you and knowing that you loved me, too. I'd do anything to have that back.'

I turned to him, my throat swelling with sympathy. 'You've spent the last few hours thinking your sister and her baby might die. Now isn't the time to decide anything.'

He shook his head, frowning. 'I decided the moment you walked into that antenatal class. I already told you my feelings have only grown stronger since then.'

'But you said you wanted to postpone our date indefinitely.'

'No, Libby. You said that.' His face softened. 'You were clear, you have children now. You're finally beginning to repair your relationship with your mum. I've already ruined things once. I'll not do anything that you think could risk jeopardising your family again.'

'I didn't want to jeopardise anything with you and Ellis after *I* ruined things!'

'But now we've agreed, once and for all, that we've no regrets about what happened. Nothing got so broken it can't be mended. We have no reason to let the past control what happens next.'

He looked at me, and I felt sixteen again.

At the same time, I felt every one of the years that had passed since. Thirteen years of lessons learned, wisdom earned, tears and smiles, victories and tragedies. I was a woman now, beginning to know who she was, how much she was worth, what she wanted and what it would take to get it.

The truth was I had decided that thirteen years ago, too.

I would have told him in the quiet of an empty waiting room at 3 a.m. except that the midwife came back and ushered us upstairs.

Of course, seeing him perched on a hospital bed, cradling his newborn nephew with utter rapture on his face, too overcome to speak as he kissed his sister on her forehead, I only wanted him more.

I did have the grace and good sense to wait until we were on our way back to the cottage before I told him.

'I've been thinking,' I said as we sped along the empty road past fields and farm buildings draped in the shadows of approaching dawn.

'Oh?' The car did a little wobble into the centre of the road.

'If I've learned anything in life, families are complicated. As long as people are involved, there's going to be a mess at some point. My family is crammed with issues and overdue conversations and randomers inviting themselves to live with us. I am also, to put it mildly, a work in progress. I didn't think I was ready for a relationship. I couldn't dare to believe I was ready for *you*.'

Jonah said nothing, just kept on listening, so I carried on talking.

'But we are starting to create something beautiful and strong. I'm absolutely convinced that you'd fit right in. Not that I'm asking you to be a part of our family...' I added, hastily.

Jonah cleared his throat. 'For the record, when you're ready to do that then the answer will be yes.'

'Right. Okay.' I fought very hard to resist the urge to go ahead and propose right then and there. 'But we could maybe, I don't know, have a pizza and a movie with the kids sometime? I think they'd really love to hear you read the rest of *The Lion, the Witch and the Wardrobe*.'

'Are you finally asking me out on that date?'

I shuffled in my seat. 'Well. Technically you asked me, so I'm just getting around to saying yes.'

'About damn time.' Jonah laughed, and with the sun rising over the treetops of Sherwood Forest, bathing the world in the red-gold exuberance of a brand-new day, knowing that, for now, all was well and, whatever came next, there was every chance it would end up okay, I had to join him.

'I might need a few hours of sleep, first.'

* * *

There was, however, one thing I didn't want to wait for. I'd messaged Nicky to let her know when I'd be back, and she not so tactfully slipped away as soon as she saw us standing on the doorstep, waving off my offer of a cup of tea with a grin and a promise that she'd catch up with me soon, a big emphasis on *soon*.

'Saying thank you doesn't really seem like enough.' Jonah shook his head, his forehead furrowing.

'I'm just so grateful Ellis came here.'

He nodded. Now wasn't the time to contemplate the alternative.

'There is one way you could thank me,' I added, ducking my head because my sleep-deprived mouth was running faster than my exhausted brain could stop it.

'Oh?'

I slowly, deliberately stretched my arms up and wrapped them around his neck. My heart pounding, not with fear but with hope and thirteen years of pent-up longing.

'Oh.' Jonah's eyebrows flicked up. Then he grinned.

And then he kissed me.

A long, slow, deep kiss that held the sweetness of past memories and the promise of a whole future full of challenges, chaos and a heap of craziness, but most of all a lifetime's worth of love.

50

It was early spring. The forest beyond the freshly painted cottage fence was trimmed with baby leaves and hawthorn blossom. After a busy week appearing on a panel at a midwifery conference, losing out on the pub-quiz crown by one point and smashing a personal best in a 5K run through the trees, I headed downstairs for another big first.

I was having a party. A thirtieth birthday party, in fact.

We would be resurrecting some old family traditions. Isla couldn't wait to blast out Taylor Swift on the karaoke. Mum had insisted on baking a cake, with a big '30' candle, using the new oven in the two-bedroom cottage she'd recently moved into with Dad. Nicky had asked whether both those bedrooms were being used, but was told that, even if we were a much closer family these days, some questions were still off-limits.

This evening, however, I had extended my celebrations beyond my immediate family. I found Brayden and Silva already in the kitchen, taking photos of the tray of canapés they'd brought along while Finn pulled faces at Platinum Precious – or Patty, as she'd gradually become known –

chortling in the sling on her daddy's back. I heard Toby thundering down the outside stairs, the lighter footsteps of his new girlfriend stepping more carefully behind him. They appeared at the kitchen doors with Hazel, whose face lit up as she started determinedly crawling towards the nana she was named after.

Nicky and Theo were in the garden, where assorted members of Theo's family – *my* family, as they insisted I call them – kissed me on the cheek or threatened to crack a rib with a suffocating hug. Dad was at the barbecue, chatting to the women from my pub-quiz team, their children chasing each other around the vegetable patch along with Isla and her new best friend, a scruffy rescue dog she'd called Barbie.

Ellis was sitting quietly in the living room, holding her son, Leo, as a shield against the hustle and bustle, while Billy and my mum kept her company. Mum being able to reconnect with Jonah, Ellis and Billy, and taking on the role of stand-in auntie, if not quite the mother she'd once longed to be, had been one of the keys that enabled us all to finally move on. Coming here today was still a big deal for Ellis. A crowd, alcohol, the party atmosphere, the potential of people asking her questions that she wasn't ready to answer, but we'd promised to look after her, and Dad would drive her back home to Hatherstone as soon as she'd had enough.

It took longer to find the one person I was really looking for. Every time I spotted him someone else would stop to wish me a happy birthday, or compliment the garden, the party, or me in my shimmering party dress. The times my heart perked up as I anticipated him crossing the garden towards me, he'd get intercepted by someone saying hello.

As the sun began to sink below the horizon, we gathered around the fire pit, pulling up various chairs as we handed around drinks, blankets and slices of birthday cake. I finally got a chance to say a proper hello to Jonah.

'Have I said how beautiful you look?' he asked, squeezing in beside me on a comfy garden seat in the shadows, wrapping his arms around my waist to pull me closer.

'Ooh, only about six times. I reckon you could manage a few more. How beautiful is that?'

He laughed against the back of my head. 'As beautiful as a newborn baby.'

'What?' I twisted around, feigning horror. 'Red-faced and wrinkly? Not a great look for the first day of my thirties.'

'I was thinking more perfect, soft skin.' He leant forwards and kissed the side of my neck. 'Clear, innocent eyes... Yeah. The comparison kind of runs out there.' He smirked. 'Your eyes aren't that innocent, either.'

He thought for a moment as we listened to Shanice from the hair salon smashing her version of Lizzo's 'Good as Hell'.

'How about as beautiful as the sunset?' he tried.

'Better. Not that original when it's right in front of us.'

There was another long silence, then Jonah turned serious.

'As a diamond?'

'I like that one,' I started to reply, until I noticed that one of the hands previously around my waist was now holding an open velvet box. 'Oh. *Oh.*'

He nestled up against my back. 'I have loved you for so long, I can't fathom a second of my life without you in it. Libby, I love your kids, your ugly, smelly dog. Your parents and random lodger. I am undone by how you love my brother and sister, and my nephew. A while ago I told you that if you asked me to be a part of your family, I'd say yes. I've given up waiting to be asked; I'm inviting myself in. If you'll have me? Us? I know that coming as a gang means it won't always be easy. But, Libby Franklin, will you marry me?'

'Pah, who wants easy?' I spun around, my whole body alight with happiness. 'Clearly not me.'

'Please answer, before I pass out from stress in front of your whole family.'

'You mean *our* family?' I leant forwards and kissed him, relishing the moment a few seconds longer. 'Yes, Jonah King. Joe Green. I would love nothing more than to marry you.'

We leant forwards to kiss again, but the second our lips met a shout came from across the lawn.

'Mu-u-u-um! Isla's been sick on the tomato plants and now she won't stop crying! Ugh – and Barbie's trying to eat it!'

'Are you absolutely sure?' I said, resting my forehead against Jonah's as Isla's wails drifted across the garden.

'I've never been surer of anything.'

And then he slipped on the ring, gave me that kiss and went to clear up the mess.

ACKNOWLEDGEMENTS

This book needed less research than usual, because I wrote about things that have been as much a part of me as telling stories. So, a huge thank you to the 500-ish women and their birth partners who for ten years trusted me with helping prepare them for the great adventure that is parenting. I must also thank Julia Childerhouse and my sister-in-law, Reiko Robbins, for allowing me to hold their hands during the home births of Katie and Kasumi. Without a doubt, two of the most incredible nights of my life. Thanks also to Nick and Paul for not minding me being there!

I have had the privilege of fostering ten children over the past four years, but felt it was worth clarifying that the characters in my books, their backgrounds and the situations they find themselves in are entirely fictional. I would like to thank the social workers and other professionals who have worked so hard to support me, my husband and these precious children, especially our supervising social workers, Nicola Clegg and Lynne Cummins. Your dedication has ensured we never felt alone, which makes all the difference.

Enormous thanks as always to the Boldwood Books team, who continue to make being an author far more wonderful than it is difficult. Special mention to my fabulous editor, Sarah Ritherdon, and Sue Smith and Helen Woodhouse, who caught many a mistake in the editing stages. I remain delighted to be represented by Kiran Kataria, who, on top of everything else, has enabled my books to be translated into nine languages in the past couple of years.

To all those who continue to read, buy, borrow or blog about my books – you have meant that this year I can celebrate ten years of being a published author. Please keep sending me your lovely messages and emails – it genuinely keeps me going on those days when I wonder if I'm writing the most boring book in the world.

Asher and Bella – I can't say how thankful I am that you are part of our family. Ciara, Joe and Dom – I was young and clueless when I started, but raising you will forever be the best thing I've done. George, I'm so pleased that my books have made your dream come true. I hope you enjoy it!

ABOUT THE AUTHOR

Beth Moran is the award winning author of ten contemporary fiction novels, including the number one bestselling *Let It Snow*. Her books are set in and around Sherwood Forest, where she can be found most mornings walking with her spaniel Murphy.

Sign up to Beth Moran's mailing list for news, competitions and updates on future books.

Visit Beth's website: https://bethmoranauthor.com/

Follow Beth on social media here:

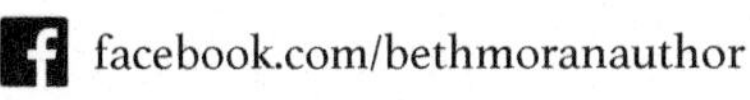

facebook.com/bethmoranauthor

x.com/bethcmoran

instagram.com/bethmoranauthor

bookbub.com/authors/beth-moran

ALSO BY BETH MORAN

Christmas Every Day

A Day That Changed Everything

Take a Chance on Me

We Belong Together

Just The Way You Are

Let It Snow

Because You Loved Me

Always On My Mind

We Are Family

Take Me Home

Lean On Me

It Had to Be You

Printed in Great Britain
by Amazon